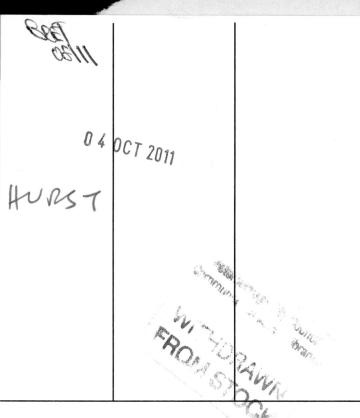

DRIVER: NEMESIS
A Story from the DRIVER®
Game World

Alex Sharp

CORGI BOOKS

TRANSWORLD PUBLISHERS
61–63 Uxbridge Road, London W5 5SA
A Random House Group Company
www.transworldbooks.co.uk

DRIVER: NEMESIS
A CORGI BOOK: 9780552163965

First publication in Great Britain
Corgi edition published 2011

A CIP catalogue record for this book
is available from the British Library.

Addresses for Random House Group Ltd companies outside the UK
can be found at: www.randomhouse.co.uk
The Random House Group Ltd Reg. No. 954009

The Random House Group Limited supports The Forest Stewardship
Council® (FSC®), the leading international forest certification organisation.
All our titles that are printed on Greenpeace approved FSC® certified
paper carry the FSC® logo. Our paper procurement policy can be found at
www.randomhouse.co.uk/environment

Typeset in 11/14pt Palatino by Falcon Oast Graphic Art Ltd.
Printed in the UK by CPI Cox & Wyman, Reading, RG1 8EX.

2 4 6 8 10 9 7 5 3 1

Acknowledgements

My thanks for all his help and support during the writing of this book to Gavin Williams.

New Orleans,
pre Hurricane Katrina

Chapter One

Midnight on Canal Street and the hot tarmac was smoking like a factory stack. Steam rolled off it in fat fluffy sheets, ghostly plumes that shredded away into the treacly night air over New Orleans. Fleeting fingers of lightning flickered along the dark line of the horizon, promising that, even though one storm had passed by, there was always more to come.

Overlooking the street, wet iron balconies gleamed. Flags and party streamers bearing ads for Jell-o shots whipped back and forth in a fresh Gulf breeze that chased its own tail down the narrow side alleys. Moisture made the apricot-coloured stucco on café walls shine as if they were varnished. Rainwater chuckled in the storm drains, while the cheery hubbub of voices spilled through window cracks and airing grates to make the neon night sing.

It wouldn't be long before the bar-goers who'd been driven indoors to seek shelter from the squall would be back out on to the pavements. Soon they'd go parading along the boulevard again, bright-coloured

9

'drinks-to-go' lolling in their hands, laughing and joking and dipping their heads into random doors and yelling to friends across the street. But not yet.

Right now the avenues were empty. There was a sense of stillness, of anticipation. Of a moment, waiting . . .

Indoors the air was so clammy it was like a sheet of wet muslin pressed to your face. *Exactly as a burial shroud might feel*, thought John Tanner as he stared down the barrel of a 9-mm semi-automatic handgun.

He was standing in a stuffy little lock-up off an ivy-choked courtyard somewhere so deep in the French Quarter that you couldn't find it on any map, and the pistol yawning in his face was 'Saturday night special', a fifty-dollar junk popgun, which – like a lot of cheap Eastern Bloc surplus weapons – was just as likely to blow back and perforate the kid wielding it as it was to kill Tanner. So, as well as having no impulse control, Quentin had no class. All the money the kid was saving on his budget firearm he was most likely putting aside to trick out his pick-up truck, loading it down with so much redneck bling that, if he survived long enough, eventually you wouldn't be able to see the vehicle under all the gun racks, light bars, grille guards, CB antennas and 16-inch chrome-plated Monster Truck Nuts.

Tanner snorted at the kid, shaking his head in amusement. This only prompted Quentin to shove in closer, his eyes bulging as he tried to intimidate the larger man, the handgun weaving dangerously in the 20-watt illumination, its barrel glinting like a guttering pilot light. It was clear that the kid felt he was entitled to Tanner's abject terror right now, and the fact that the broad-shouldered wheelman eyed him coolly rather than grovelling in the dirt only made him angrier.

'Ask me that again! Go on!' the kid screamed. 'Say what you just said one more time, ya ignorant dickhead! You were told! You were told!'

Tanner blinked, but real slow, as a tiger might if it were menaced by a mouse. He didn't say a word, yet neither did he step down. Quentin was close to exploding now, shoulders jerking, his whole body vibrating with electric fury.

Quentin was a skinny, ginger, raggedy-assed exclamation mark of a man, like rope that's been beaten against a rock. For a Louisiana swamp redneck he was almost fluorescently pale, though perhaps that was more a testament to how much time he'd spent in jail during his short life, a theory that the blurry, lopsided tattoos wreathing his biceps seemed to support.

Tanner, by contrast, was a buff 195-pound advertisement for good ol' American cowboy genes and hard living: dark-eyed, rough-faced, with cheekbones like knife cuts and the weathered good looks of the Marlboro man's younger, fitter brother. His hair was a jagged wind-blasted swipe and he wore his blue jeans and lucky Halvarssons Thunder Classic motorcycle jacket so perfectly he might as well have been born with them on. Tanner's gaze was a relentless black laser, his grin something to be photographed for a fashion magazine – or feared.

Tanner grinned at Quentin.

'Say it!' yelled Quentin. 'Say something, anything! Or I swear to God, freaking Allah and all of the Big Easy Rollergirls that I will drill you where you stand.'

Tanner took his time before replying. When he did so he languidly tossed his words over the shoulder to the second driver, Bowman, rather than deigning to speak to Quentin himself.

'Do I really have to put up with this?' he drawled. 'I've been driving for your crew for three months now. I've been shot at, I've been cut up, I've run missions in hailstorms, gales and nigh-on hurricanes and not complained once – but now I can't even ask a simple question? Does that seem right to you, Wayne?'

Being ignored caused Quentin to jig about in apoplectic rage, but he didn't dare butt in when Bowman was about to speak. The hulking, impeccably suited Creole shifted his weight against the side of his gleaming plum-red Cadillac CTS-V, and showed a sinister smile that revealed the silver teeth grill he wore, studded with the design of an inverted ankh. His nest of serpentine dreads audibly rustled as he shook his head.

'You know,' he rumbled at Tanner, 'there's a grand ole Creole saying . . . which I just made up. It says, "Guns don't kill people, questions do." Sometimes, cousin, you ask the wrong questions.'

Tanner shrugged, regretful rather than offended, but not in the slightest bit panicked by Bowman's ominous reply.

'That's a shame, because all I asked your mentally

challenged associate here was, "So, when do I get to meet this Indian guy I've been working for all these weeks?" Doesn't a man even get to see his employer? I know this is a sketchy line of business, but doesn't that smack of disrespect to you? Or are all of his soldiers so terrified of the woo-woo voodoo boss man that it's turned you into hair-braiding, panty-wearing, scaredy little girls?'

This calculated act of disrespect was the last straw for Quentin. He roared and shoved his gun barrel up against Tanner's jaw, grinding the flaky grey metal into his flesh. Even the laconic Bowman looked a trifle concerned by the prospect of what might happen next.

Tanner waited for moment, eyes averted, a faint smile playing over his lips, then he said to Bowman: 'You should tell your monkey that to maximize his threat level in future he might want to think about flicking his pistol's safety to the off position . . .'

Doubt crimped Quentin's forehead and his wild dancing gaze left Tanner's face for a fraction of a second, just long enough to sight along his thumb and check whether he had actually forgotten to unclick the 9 mill's safety—

He hadn't. But by then it was already too late. Tanner's right palm slapped the gun to one side with enough force to drive Quentin off balance, while his driving boot flashed out and swept the younger man's feet from under him. Yelping in surprise the kid plummeted and his torso struck the ground with a surprisingly meaty slap for someone so scrawny.

Tanner still held Quentin's wrist in a combat grip, and now exerted a savage swivelling pressure to make him release the pistol. The redneck's deafening screech masked the clatter of the gun.

Tanner briskly kicked the weapon far out of the boy's reach, before twisting his arm into an L-shaped lock behind his back. This jammed Quentin's cheek into the dust and made sure he had no chance to free himself. Quentin spun a painful doughnut on the filthy brick floor, staining his denim jacket with motor oil, screaming strangled obscenities and kicking impotently. Bowman's laughter was as deep as a tropical thunderstorm.

'Tanner, I like you,' he boomed. 'As villains go, you're a stand-up guy. I trust you as much as I trust any crook. You ain't from Nawlins, and you ain't from Louisiana, but you're the best damn driver I've ever worked with. Friend, you can twirl that dipshit there into any pretzel shapes you like—'

'No! No he can't!' shrieked Quentin from the ground, his shoulder flexing in unnatural agony. Bowman ignored him.

'You can make balloon animals outta his skinny limbs all night long, but I'm afraid, to answer your earlier enquiry, "When am I gonna meet the Indian?" the answer is: No one meets the Indian if he doesn't ask you first. Ever, period.'

Tanner sighed, then, as an afterthought, he booted Quentin hard as he could. This whole situation was beginning to get on his nerves.

The kid squealed like a stuck hog.

Chapter Two

'So, just who the hell is this Indian anyway?' Detective John Tanner of the San Francisco PD had asked three months earlier as he sat on a ruby patent-leather sofa in Police Superintendent Anton Powell's gloriously appointed office.

Framed letters of commendation dotted the walls beside ostentatious photos of Powell grinning as he shook hands with senators, civic leaders, bishops, foreign dignitaries and even a couple of presidents. Tanner had been in many police HQs over the years, but he'd never yet seen a room decorated in velvet flock wallpaper or sporting antique oak bureaux with genuine gold handles. Until today. Apparently the New Orleans Police Department's aggressive strategy of withholding money seized at crime scenes and re-investing them directly into 'operational services' had a very broad definition.

Powell cut the end from a cigar, threw a snakeskin-booted ankle over one knee and relaxed back into his opulent Levenger Huntington Executive Chair, puffing contemplatively at the ceiling fan. He directed pungent jets of smoke at the blades, which sliced them apart with a satisfying soft *whoompf*. Powell was plump and blond, with a sandy complexion. If you took only a cursory glance you could discount the Superintendent as baby-faced and cheery, but on a deeper look you might notice how watchful his lidded gaze could be, how rarely he blinked, and how careful he was never to crease his clothes. The buttons on his uniform gleamed with a starry lustre, but Tanner instinctively knew he'd never polished them himself in his life.

The seconds stretched like taffy and Tanner's question remained unanswered. Powell was clearly someone who felt powerful when he made other people wait unnecessarily. Tanner had met the type before, many times, mainly as bosses, and he wasn't about to give Powell the satisfaction. He waited patiently for the reply, until finally . . .

'The Indian is the genuine devil himself in human form.' Powell swung his gaze down from the ceiling and smiled like a friendly lizard, winking. 'That's not the official New Orleans Police Department line, of course.'

Before he could continue, someone knocked at the door and barged directly into the room without waiting for permission. Powell favoured the new arrival with a slightly frosty smile.

'Ah, Al, right on time. Detective Tanner, this is Albert Cochrane, my Deputy Chief from the Bureau of Investigations. Say good day to our guest, Al.'

Tanner offered his palm to Cochrane, a hefty fiftyish troll in straining uniform shirtsleeves, sweaty half-moons rising beneath his armpits. Cochrane's glare was pugnacious, punching out from beneath a pair of beetle brows, and he was clearly a man whose complexion bore the brunt of his temper; blotches of high pink were already creeping up his cheeks, invading his sloppy, receding hairline. Cochrane ignored Tanner's hand and disdained the space on the sofa next to him as well. He stomped across to Powell's shoulder and hovered there, ramrod stiff, as if he was the Superintendent's butler rather than his second-in-command. He pointedly wouldn't even glance in Tanner's direction. *Shit*, thought Tanner, *here's trouble*.

Powell made a tiny moue of displeasure at his subordinate's attitude and then brushed it to one side with a politician's breezy fluency.

'André "the Indian" Sepion,' he continued, and tossed a slim manila folder into Tanner's lap. 'Don't bother reading it. Just look at the pictures.'

Ghoulishly intrigued, Tanner flicked open the file and immediately clicked his tongue against his teeth in revulsion. As an undercover cop Tanner was used to seeing death in all its many colours, but this was an atrocity archive of stunning savagery. He'd never seen quite so many shades of *red* all splashed together like that before.

'Are those bite marks?' he asked, grim-faced. 'Did an *animal* do that?'

17

'Dogs,' Cochrane spat, communicating directly rather than via petulant body language for the first time. 'Bull mastiff hounds, evil black fuckers, head full of fangs and a raging boner for tearing your throat out. Sepion traps his victims in cages with those monsters after he's lovingly trained his demons to kill. He bloods them on rabbits and stray cats first, before weaning 'em on to smaller rescue dogs. Regular animal lover, the Indian, probably cuz he's not far removed from one himself.'

'Of course, we've nothing actually to connect Sepion to these killings,' Powell smoothly cut off Cochrane's torrent. 'All the victims were dealers from a rival crew, and the bodies were scrubbed of any forensic taint before they were dumped. Most of our intel is second-, third- or even fourth-hand. What's more, the man is a virtual ghost. Doesn't have a social security number, never opened a bank account, doesn't use credit cards or possess any fixed or temporary abode we can locate.

'We're pretty sure he hails from Mound Bayou, Mississippi, originally, out of Cajun stock, though there's Creole and Native American in him too – that last is where he got his street name from and that's the legend he plays up. After that, maybe his folk died, maybe they didn't? Maybe he went to live in a swamp cabin with twenty inbred half-cousins – maybe he didn't? Who knows? Maybe he went all *Jungle Book* and was raised by a clan of 'gators? Yeah, that has a certain ring to it, but the truth is we simply don't know. The next event we can date for sure is that he ended up in the Big Easy running with a gang called the Holy Fives, who had some weird fetish for blood-drinking. Five years later, Sepion's got his own crew. He's calling himself the Indian and he's become, almost overnight, the most notorious drug baron in Nawlins and every punk and his mommy is telling boogieman stories about him. Flip to the back of the stack.'

Tanner did as he was instructed; then regretted it. 'More dogs?'

'Ah, no, I'm afraid, appalling as it seems, the victim did that to himself.'

Tanner did a revolted double-take at the new photos, before frowning his scepticism back at Powell, who shrugged uncomfortably.

'Sepion has a penchant for feeding his enemies industrial-strength hallucinogens, then subjecting them to a barrage of psychological torture techniques, *Clockwork Orange* style – you know, constant loops from horror films, sleep deprivation, isolation, that sort of thing. The fella in the photos did that to his own face after he'd become convinced that bugs were crawling out of his ears and nostrils. He survived, by the way. He's in a mental institute down Baton Rouge way and screams if the lights go off for a second, ever, even by accident.'

Tanner shivered a little at this revelation, but Powell wasn't done yet.

'We've heard rumours that he likes to bury people

and keep them alive underground for days, even weeks, via an air-tube. Then again, perhaps that's just another part of the legend. This is Sepion's power, you see, the ability to generate fear and superstition. He's managed to cultivate a near-mythical reputation on the streets. Even the criminals are scared enough that they claim he has voodoo powers.'

'There's a fine line between ruthless and psychotic and the Indian prances over it like he thinks he's in the fucking Bolshoi,' growled Cochrane.

'This is why it's so important we take him down, Detective Tanner, and why I invited your Commissioner to send you here today. We all know your peerless record in undercover operations—'

'Look, Super, I'm not having this!' Cochrane blustered in. 'We're on the verge of catching him. Just give me another forty-eight hours—'

'Sorry, Al,' said Powell. His tone was soft, but everyone in the room knew Cochrane's plea had been guillotined away like rotten wood. The Deputy Chief made a noise at the back of his throat like a vacuum cleaner in distress. Tanner wondered if steam was going to start jetting out of his ears, but Cochrane managed to control himself with an enormous effort.

'The Indian is infamous in every quarter of the city,' Powell continued as if there had never been an interruption. 'Ordinary people fear him as much as the criminals, and they've begun to hate us for not catching him. Without the support of the populace, no police force can operate effectively. The Indian is a symbol of our failure and that has to change.

'Even with Al and his team's sterling efforts, however' – Cochrane stiffened – 'all we have to show for our work to date are four costly and time-consuming covert operations that have failed to get close to Sepion or infiltrate his organization. We don't even have an up-to-date mug shot. Now, your Commissioner has said he's happy to loan you to us if we can thrash out the arrangements today. You'll be our cleanskin. You don't have the stink of NOPD about you. You can drive like a felon, smell like a crook and think like a villain. Tanner, we need you.'

Tanner was conflicted. He'd only come to the Big Easy as a courtesy to his boss, who owed Powell for a murky favour from way back when. Powell seemed just the type to bank all his good deeds, hoarding them for decades until the right opportunity for payback arose. He probably had them all indexed on spreadsheets somewhere. When Tanner had come into this office he'd fully intended to turn down Powell's offer flat, then go off on a steamboat tour for the rest of the day. That, however, was before he'd seen the photos.

'I come with my own team,' he said after a slight pause. Did he really want to get tangled up in this rat's nest of department politics? The photos, though . . . The blood; those bites like yawning sliced watermelons . . .

'We can't babysit a full support squad, detective, you'll have to make do with our local resources—'

'It's just one officer. Detective Tobias Jones is my

man on the outside, or we don't do this,' Tanner said, surprising himself. Was he actually going to say yes, after all the fucked-up missions he'd been dumped into down the years? 'Also, I'll need to be able to run this operation exactly the way I see fit, no oversight, no interference,' he hastily rolled on. 'If I have to commit multiple crimes to take down the Indian, then so be it. If that's not acceptable, well, I'll just go persuade my boss that he can't do without me after all and you fellas can stay here chasing your shadows.'

That's their out, Tanner decided. *It's my way or the highway.* Most bosses would rather hike to Alaska in flip-flops than surrender that level of control. Powell considered Tanner's ultimatum for all of about three seconds before nodding.

'Super, no! I gotta protest!' Cochrane exploded.

Powell didn't even look at the Chief as he jerked the leash. 'Chief, be quiet. The adults are talking.'

Cochrane's mouth opened. Nothing came out. His cheeks blossomed wine stains and he stalked over to the window. He stared out at the waving palms and fig trees flanking the driveway. Perhaps his therapist had prescribed this as a strategy to control his temper tantrums? Powell might be a long-game greasy-palms political creep, but Cochrane was just a blowhard with a badge.

'Very well,' said Powell. 'We can make that work. You and Jones will be seconded to New Orleans PD for the duration. We'll get your resources sorted out and work up a legend for your cover. You'll have full latitude to commit felonies – within reason, detective – to expedite the successful completion of your mission. Log all the other crime you witness – theft, trafficking, whatever – to keep the paperwork tidy, but don't let that draw you away from your primary focus: bring . . . down . . . the Indian.'

In a showy demonstration of manners Powell stood and escorted Tanner to the door, where he pumped the undercover cop's hand as if they were on the campaign trail.

'So, you sure you can take our Nawlins heat, Detective Tanner?' Powell enquired with an insinuating smile, dialling up his accent for effect.

'We get hot enough in San Fran sometimes. I'll cope,' Tanner countered, not rising to the bait.

'Well, I'm sure you'll do fine,' the Superintendent replied with just the tiniest sneer. 'I'm counting on you, Detective Tanner. We all are.'

Tanner returned Powell's handshake without cringing and even managed to suppress the urge to check he was still wearing his wristwatch afterwards.

Out in the corridor Cochrane suddenly turned on Tanner, stabbing him into the wall with a fat forefinger.

'We don't need you, boy. I don't care what your so-called car "skills" are or how sweetly you kiss-ass perps to make them think you're part of their big happy scum clan. That ain't real police work. Pounding the streets is real policing, boy. Collecting evidence, taking witness statements. Good, honest work. That's what solves crimes, not your grubby grandstanding. You ain't an officer of the law, you're a circus stunt driver. I'll not have some Bay Area glory hound wreck my investigation: I'm watching you every step of the way, boy. You so much as drop a crap that looks a bit crooked then I'll come down on you like a ton of hammers. *Comprende?'*

'I understand, sir. You'll be getting your fingers good, brown and dirty in my shit,' Tanner told the Deputy Chief – and new enemy – with a perfectly straight face.

If you know you're going to hell anyway you might as well enjoy the ride, and the look on Cochrane's face almost made up for the massive headache he was obviously going to cause.

Chapter Three

Bowman had a silver pocket watch, an exquisite antique timepiece, which he occasionally twirled as if he was performing yoyo tricks when a conversation flagged.

Presently, he was standing poised under the grainy cone of light from the lock-up's single bulb, holding that watch out at full extension, singing quietly to himself. Tanner leaned against the crumbling brickwork by the roll-down garage door, still as a statue. Quentin perched on a nearby workbench playing nervous finger drums against his knees, thighs, the bench, the wall, his skull – anything within reach, basically. The anticipation was like an airtight seal around the room.

Half an hour earlier, Tanner had stood in an alley behind a boisterous sports bar off Lower Decatur Street whispering into his collar. Nearby karaoke was bellowed wildly out of tune and frat boys roared. Tanner's eyes strayed to the old US Mint, which was visible through the narrow slot between avenues, a towering Greek Revival pile, all sweeping classical lines and roseate walls. A titbit of tourist trivia bubbled up in his mind. The building had been employed as both a US and Confederate Mint, but it had also been used as a Federal prison. That seemed very fitting tonight.

'It's on,' he told Jones, who was sitting inside the blacked-out GMC Savana, parked in a quiet spot beside Woldenberg Park adjacent to the Riverfront.

'It's a pretty sweet heist, if you think about it.' Tobias Jones chuckled amiably in Tanner's ear. His voice was the embodiment of the man: steady, relaxed, smooth.

Tanner always joked that Jones was too handsome to be a cop, which was why he made him stay in the van. Not that Jones being handsome was a joke. His partner really did have the glossy good looks of a movie star. His hair was an impeccably coiffed Lenny Kravitz-style short 'fro, while his skin was a perfect mix of buttery dark tones like burnished tigerwood. He didn't smile often, but when he did you knew it meant something. Jones prided himself on being the very acme of the styled-out, image-conscious soul-man: silk shirts, tailored jackets, chinos and designer Italian leather boots. His apartment back home in 'Frisco was like a *Style* magazine photoshoot come to life. Every piece of furniture was angled just so, each individual component of the decor chosen to smoothly jigsaw with every other piece: blond wood, cream Irish linen, brushed aluminium, African art.

Tobias Jones was a careful, not to say meticulous man. He certainly enjoyed life, and the finer things it had to offer – art, international cuisine, the occasional trip to the theatre, regular yoga – but always remained in control. He never drank, always ensured he got the regulation eight hours a night sleep, ate an organic, balanced diet and exercised at precisely the same time every day.

It was this undeviating progress through life which made Jones the consummate undercover handler. He couldn't guarantee to keep Tanner safe, but he could guarantee to have all the exit strategies covered in case anything did go wrong.

Jones and Tanner had worked together for so long that there was an automatic shorthand between them. Tanner knew Jones was always there for him, on the wire, dedicated to the mission and focused on keeping him alive. That was why Tanner sometimes let Jones ramble on if he was in the mood.

'So there's these sheriffs' offices all over the Greater New Orleans area, Metairie and Harvey and Elmwood, and further afield too – spots like Lafourche and Laplace – hey, don't the names round here just roll off your tongue? Say what you like about the French, they sure know how to make a place sound musical. Anyway, Powell's had all these offices seizing money from stop-and-searches and drug busts for months now. All that seized cash gets funnelled back to him to be ploughed directly into department coffers . . . or his office renovation fund, ha ha. What does the Indian decide to do? He hits the armoured truck that's hoovering up all that money from the four corners of the district while it's on its way back to NOPD HQ. He lets Powell do the collection work for him. Plus, it's all snaky money in the first place, poorly logged bills of dubious origin. Any of that goes missing, it's an admin apocalypse trying to trace it. You gotta admire the *cojones* on our villain, is all I'm saying.'

Something was still niggling at Tanner, though. In spite of having Jones running support for him he just couldn't relax into this op. He kept worrying at the fiddly details as if he was probing a mouth ulcer.

'Cochrane's been briefed, yes?' he demanded. 'He knows to tell his men to just give up the safety boxes? No one plays the hero. Everyone rolls over and shows their bellies, yes?'

'He knows. He doesn't like it, but he knows,' Jones replied. Somehow this assertion didn't reassure Tanner as much as it should.

Even now, three months in, Tanner still had mis-givings about the case. He certainly wasn't a man who believed in signs or portents – John Tanner made his own luck, and was the driver of his own future – but he could definitely sense the prickly electricity of an approaching storm.

'Showtime,' Bowman suddenly announced with his sparkling tombstone grin.

Tanner nodded tersely; time to go to work – for both his masters.

Quentin bounced off his roost, fizzing with barely contained energy. He whooped at the ceiling and actually slapped his thigh.

'I'll bring my BMW M3 round the front!' he exclaimed. 'I parked her out on the street, just in case I dinged her coming in. I don't EVER normally let another man touch my baby, let alone drive her, but for all you're a shit-sucking son of whore, Tanner, I know you're an ice-cold wheelman and, damn, it'll be sweet to finally hear my baby roar on a real job.'

Tanner was just staring at Quentin. It wasn't clear that he'd heard anything after 'M3'.

'We take my car,' he finally grated, pivoting at the hip to flick the dirt cover off the sleek angular shape waiting behind him.

Tanner's beautiful 1970 Dodge Challenger RT gleamed in the meagre light, its low-slung yellow chassis seeming to shimmer like gold. Everything about the vehicle spoke of classic design, its lines, its no-nonsense angles functional and timeless. The black stripes emblazoned along the bonnet made it look like a bright, proud flag. Bowman whistled in appreciation. 'Never git tired of that,' he murmured.

Quentin, however, seemed to be trying to sneer with his entire body. 'Shit, that ole tin can?' he scoffed. 'No way, José. That broken-assed seventies trash bucket is older than my pa. I could pedal a pushbike faster than that!'

Without a word Tanner slid into the driver's seat and turned the key. The Challenger exploded into life on the first twist. The engine's throaty thrum set the air a-tingling and they all felt it through their skin.

'Oh,' said Quentin, very quietly.

Seconds later they were roaring out into the chaotic swirl of downtown New Orleans. Heads turned. Drinkers pointed at the Challenger, yelling approval.

As they passed by Quentin's BMW Tanner allowed himself a tiny smile.

Heading out towards the city limits, Tanner casually palmed on the sound system and a rolling twang of chords filled up the car's interior.

Once more Quentin reacted with hooting disapproval. The kid simply couldn't sit still. He had the jazzy, pointless energy of a five-year-old hyped up on sugar.

'What's this? C'mon, chief, yer killing me with this shit! You not got any Kid Rock?'

Quentin reached for the CD deck but Tanner's hand lashed out like a rattler and snagged his wrist in a painful grip. Quentin hissed.

'This is Motown,' Tanner told the redneck gravely. 'Like it, or leave by the side exit.' He indicated the passenger door ominously. Quentin shut up.

Tanner swung the Challenger deftly round a pothole scarring the tarmac. Dubbed the Crescent City, New Orleans is coiled along the banks of the Mississippi. All through the territory the water table is so close to the surface it simply isn't practical to repave the roads every time a pavement cracks, so a skill at slaloming between the various humps, holes and perilous imperfections is a must for any driver in New Orleans.

Tanner, of course, made these navigations seem like second nature.

New Orleans is a city thick with history, reaching down into its very foundations. The tangled French, Creole, Irish, German and African heritage is evident in its cuisine, its music, the languorous tropical attitude, and especially the architecture: French Colonial-style plantation houses, puffed up with fancy columns and side-gabled roofs, rub shoulders against iconic Creole townhouses with their arcades, arches and wrought-iron balconies. Right now Tanner and Quentin were roaring past rows of distinctive shotgun houses, named after the observation that since the rooms are all lined up you could fire a gun through the house and not hit anything. The predominant style for the region, they were thin rectangular houses laid out like orange-juice cartons raised on brick piers, end-capped by pretty porches under roof aprons supported by struts and lacy Victorian jigsaw brackets. Tanner felt faintly out of place, as if he was driving through the pictures of a kid's history book.

In many ways New Orleans has more in common with the ragged haphazard sprawl of old European cities, rather than the sane flat grids that characterize most modern American metropolises. Its eighteenth-century roots still peep through. Many of the Crescent City's streets were originally intended for horses and buggies, so the roads tend to be narrow, bumpy and weirdly arranged. These idiosyncrasies would actually work in their favour tonight. The plan was to ambush the armoured van as it returned through the sleepy Boho suburbs. These neighbourhoods offered them a wealth of pinch points to box the vehicle in – leafy residential streets, businesses, parks – and subsequently there would be a host of wide straight avenues perfect to facilitate their quick getaway.

Tanner noted with satisfaction how easily the Challenger's motor was running. He had pretty much taken this car apart and rebuilt it from scratch so many times down the years that he could instantly tell from the tiniest vibration if something was off. Not tonight, though. Whatever else was scratching at Tanner's composure at least his ride wouldn't let him down.

Tanner thumbed the headset the gang had provided. He wasn't much of a techie guy, but a hands-free approach made sense for any potential tight situations on the job.

'OK, care to tell me who the mystery third driver is going to be?'

'Sure, cousin,' Bowman's bass tones drawled into Tanner's ear. 'OK, so you won't be meeting the Indian any time soon, that we've established, but your skills *have* been noticed. You're going to be partnered with Sepion's right-hand man. He's meeting us for tonight's job. The Indian wants you two to work together in the future, so this is an audition for that, to see if you can both play nice together.'

Better than nothing, thought Tanner. At this rate he might even get close to the Indian before he retired.

'OK,' he shot back. 'So who exactly is this super-duper hotshot we're going to be gunning with?'

And that was when the entire mission took an alarming swerve across the central reservation, as the Creole answered: 'Cat with the handle Jericho, my friend. They say he's as good a wheelman as you, so I reckon it'll be a match made in heaven – or hell, depending if the angels and demons on your shoulders get along.'

Jericho.

Tanner's palms gripped the steering wheel a little tighter as recognition pierced him. A flash of Rio de Janeiro sunlight; Jericho grating the words 'I'll find you' as they both stood together beside the ocean, the flames of the helicopter they'd just shot down flickering over his shoulder. They'd been working as a team then, too. Tanner was posing as a gangsta with a grudge. Jericho had been the number-two man for the kingpin Solomon Caine, but that mission had required Tanner to double-cross the stone-cold hitman and stick a gun in his face. It was likely that would have left a lasting impression on Jericho.

I'll find you.

Jericho. Here, now. Shit. Two options: abort, or pedal to the metal?

Tanner pawed over the pros and cons in his mind, batting them back and forth like a cat with a mouse between its claws. It was true Jericho had never found out that he was a cop when they'd tussled in Rio, but there was also a good chance that (a) he bore a grudge, and (b) he'd like to rip that payback straight out of Tanner's hide.

Tanner knew what Jones would say: 'Throttle back, make sure you live to fight another day.'

Working in deep cover was like extreme driving in many respects. You were constantly living off the surface of your skin, making split-second decisions that could clinch the prize or kill you in an instant. It was intense, raw, exhilarating. You didn't have time to check back with the committee, you trusted your gut and played by instinct. If you had the time to breathe, then you weren't doing it right. You were fearless or you went home, probably in a box.

That's what Tanner lived for.

He stamped on the gas and the car sprang forward like a puma pouncing. Quentin yelped with indignation as the vehicle bucked and he slammed his crown against the roof. Tanner ignored his griefing.

The cop flicked his wheel and hung on to it through the lock, caressing the throttle as the Challenger drifted round a snake-loop corner, moving so smoothly the car might as well have been running on oiled castors.

'Shit,' Quentin whispered in awe. 'How'd you learn to do that fancy crap? Were you really into slot car racers when you were a little un? Me and my brother lifted this track outta next door's trash once. We duct-taped it back together, then stole my ma's staple gun . . .'

Tanner ignored him. A speeding dark shadow

suddenly filled the rear-view mirror. Tanner squared his shoulders and nodded to himself, checking his grip on the steering wheel was secure. Showtime.

The blunt black bull-nose of Jericho's Dodge Ram SRT10 pulled level with them like a shark breaking the surface of the water. They matched speeds, and Tanner threw a glance left. Jericho dead-eyed him from his ride's inky interior. There was the promise of violence in that look. His eyes were chips of ice studded in a face like storm-beaten rock decorated with a satanic black goatee with a slicked back widow's peak above his cliff-face brow. Jericho was a burly tower of muscles and coiled power. He might move slowly but he could strike like lightning when he wanted; and if you knew that beforehand, then you might survive meeting him.

Jericho put two fingers to his temple in an ironic salute. He transformed the gesture into an imaginary pistol, which he used to blow Tanner away. 'I . . . see . . . you,' Jericho mouthed.

'So then, motherfucker, let's tango,' Tanner muttered under his breath. He was about to ram on the gas and slide into battle mode when his headset crackled to life.

'Got the van sighted,' murmured Bowman in his coffee-with-a-dash-of-cream tones. 'Everything's following the script, smooth as silk.'

'Check that, Bowman. On you in five,' grumbled Jericho over the common channel.

Whoa, thought Tanner. *We're still going ahead with the*

heist? Was Jericho really going to complete the raid exactly as planned – with Tanner's help – and *then* try to clip him? It sure showed some audacious balls, he'd give the hitman that. Was he daring Tanner to break formation and confront him now? Were they playing chicken?

Tanner reached out and surreptitiously patted the butt of the Hi-Point .45 ACP he'd taped up underneath the dash. Bring it on.

'Once we get into the back of the van how long will it take you to do your juju?' Tanner demanded of Quentin.

Quentin hefted the bag of safe-cracking tools in his lap and pulled a face. 'If it's a classic Nawlins PD set-up, 'bout ten minutes, give or take. If they've gone and upgraded any security, then half an hour to never. At that point we might as well slink back home to watch Springer reruns instead . . . Just saying.'

'OK then, let's roll.'

Chapter Four

The raid went down like a dream.

The bulky armoured vehicle nosed its way down an avenue overhung by blazing red maples. At regular intervals the street was cross-hatched by back lanes, and these proved perfect ambush points, screened from the main drag by the flaming scarlet trees and shadowed by the houses.

First, Jericho's Dodge jerked out in front of the van, causing the vehicle to screech to a halt. The driver's frightened eyes met Jericho's flat cold glare through reinforced glass, and he must have known right then how much trouble they were in. Or at least his performance appeared authentic, and Tanner hoped to hell that Cochrane had briefed his men thoroughly enough.

In panic, the van reversed swiftly, only to find Bowman's Cadillac barring his exit. Alarm mounting, the driver desperately tried to negotiate a three-point turn, while his colleague drew his sidearm to defend them. However, before the manoeuvre was even half complete – and with the van skewed at a drunken angle, obstructing the whole street – the side door was wrenched open and they found themselves staring down the twin barrels of Jericho's dual custom sawn-offs.

Tanner pulled up at right angles to Bowman, his engine ticking over, and he watched through the windshield as Jericho ripped the drivers out of the truck and kicked them to the kerb. He had their wrists smartly secured with their own cuffs in a matter of moments. Tanner turned to Quentin, who was positively vibrating with adrenalin in the passenger seat.

'Go on, Little Safe Cracker that Could, shoo!'

Quentin flew out of the side door as if the elastic holding him down had been sliced. He bounded towards the van as eager as a new-born foal, his bag of tools flapping against his slender shoulders. He vanished into the back of the armoured vehicle, where he presumably set about whatever locks, latches or other obstacles the NOPD had installed with the excitement of a kid in a candy store. *Let's hope they haven't upgraded*, thought Tanner with a wry smile.

Less than three minutes had elapsed since the take-down had begun – textbook teamwork – but the clock was really ticking now. This was a residential area, and already civic-minded householders could be peering through their blinds as they feverishly dialled the authorities. Off in the distance, Tanner could hear a commercial helicopter *thwup-thwupping* its way in a shallow arc over the far shore of the Mississippi, probably ferrying some tycoon from one very important meeting here to an equally important meeting over there. Jericho prowled up and down outside the van, shotguns hooked over his shoulders.

His gaze snagged on Tanner, who was watching him. They shared a moment of mutual hostility. Seconds simmered. Without giving away the slightest telltale on his face, Tanner slid the Hi-Point .45 out of its duct-taped holster. . . before Jericho abruptly cut his gaze away and continued stalking. Tanner relaxed his grip.

Moments later Quentin proved his reputation wasn't all bluster. He emerged from the van's interior wearing a shit-eating grin and with his scrawny arms overflowing with fat sacks of bank notes.

The raw-boned uncoordinated redneck sprinted towards the Challenger, whooping and yelling, but Tanner flailed a palm back at him, baffled that the kid was savvy enough to outfox a safe-deposit box in minutes, but couldn't follow a simple three-step plan that they'd gone over ten times in the lock-up.

'No, you idiot!' he yelled at the redneck. 'Put the money in the SUV! It's a truck, goddamnit. Trunk space!'

Quentin made an exaggerated 'oh' as he understood and twisted back in the opposite direction. But before he could move any further, a dazzling searchlight transfixed them from above and a familiar voice distorted by a loudhailer boomed: 'TURN OFF YOUR

ENGINES, PUT DOWN YOUR WEAPONS AND COME OUT OF THE VEHICLES WITH YOUR HANDS IN THE AIR . . .'

Tanner spat a curse. Cochrane!

So it hadn't been a commercial 'copter after all. The street was instantly swamped with noise and motion. NOPD officers fanned out from their concealed hidey-holes, patrol cars roaring out of back streets and yards . . .

Except, crucially, they were all stationed on the other side of the van. This meant that an armoured vehicle was shielding Jericho, Quentin, Bowman's Cadillac and the Challenger from their ambush. It was a tactical blunder of jaw-dropping proportions. Only Jericho's Dodge was exposed to police firepower.

A grim smile stitched across Jericho's face. He kicked the van door wide to provide more cover and opened up with both shotguns across the hood. The police assault teams immediately returned fire and within seconds the sleepy street had been transformed into a pitched war zone. Bullets pranged off bodywork, ricocheted off lampposts; fragments of flying metal filled the air, deafening muzzle cracks, yells of pain. Bowman joined in, too, squeezing off rounds from a huge sleek Glock carefully aimed through his side window.

Quentin screamed and threw himself lengthways into Tanner's passenger seat.

'Go! Go! Why aren't you GOING?' he screamed as he scrambled to get his ass folded up inside the car.

Tanner simply tuned the kid's shrieks out, along with the other white noise raging around them. His situational awareness froze the scene into its most crucial tactical components: the cover, sight lines, kill zones, possible escape routes, and flanking points. The gang might have a slight geographical advantage, but they were outgunned to the nth degree and horribly exposed. Damn Cochrane and his petty grudges; he'd tossed their whole operation up into a hurricane without a second's thought.

Movement caught Tanner's eye: a lone patrol car had snuck up along one of the side lanes and was now poised, revving, directly opposite Jericho. Tanner could see the cop's gaze locked on the hitman, his entire focus sucked down to that one point in space and time; Jericho was completely unaware of his peril. The black and white leapt forward as a blur—

Time slowed to a slideshow in Tanner's mind. He knew, instantly, from the angle and speed of the attack, that the cop would ram the van door with up to twelve tons of force. Jericho would be crushed into the metal, killing him instantly. A lethal thorn in Tanner's side would be swept aside, and he wouldn't have to worry about the Rio vendetta derailing his mission any more.

But the police driver hadn't issued a warning. He hadn't provided Jericho with any chance to surrender or to put down his arms. He'd gone out of his way to attack by stealth, striking directly at a man's back. In the crudest sense he really was acting as judge, jury and executioner. Even if Jericho was a monster, did that mean any means used to stop him were justified?

Tanner's boot jolted on the gas and time flowed back into motion. The Challenger struck the speeding police car in a teeth-shattering impact, deflecting the other vehicle away from Jericho and into a pair of adjacent family hatchbacks instead. The cop lolled in his seat, his head bumping on the wheel, unconscious. A stunned silence descended across the street, embalming it in a moment of utter stillness. The other cops stopped shooting. Glass tinkled to the asphalt. Tanner exhaled.

Jericho was staring at the wrecked squad car steaming mere feet away from him. He looked up at Tanner and realized what had happened. His expression was unreadable, but he bobbed a brusque nod at the wheelman before diving into the driver's side of the armoured van. The engine caught first time. A beat later the police on the far side of the vehicle realized what Jericho was planning, but by then it was already too late.

The van became a speeding metal fist as it punched through Jericho's Dodge, the patrol cars and the blockade barriers. Officers scattered in all directions as they leapt for safety. Jericho roared off into the distance, fiery fragments of red maple branches, glass shrapnel, plastic and shorn metal spinning in his wake. Half of the police cars that were still roadworthy immediately followed. Now the gang's accidental road block was speeding away in the other direction the remainder of the pursuit vehicles were free to live up to their name.

But Tanner was already half a block away, hammering along one of the back lanes. Sirens swiftly gave chase. Tanner grinned. Now he was having fun. The Challenger fishtailed out of the alley mouth, Tanner's hands moving like lightning as he finessed the gears; a plume of boxes and trash bags was launched across the road. One sly stroke of the wheel corrected their course, and the Challenger roared away down the new boulevard.

The white shaft of the 'copter's searchlight tilted and swung in Tanner's rear-view before veering away sharply as Cochrane and his sky cops gave chase after Bowman's Cadillac. *Good luck with that, asshole*, thought Tanner. He'd shared enough late-night drinks with the Creole to know that he had any number of boltholes burrowed away in the tangled snarl of the French Quarter's back streets. Once he reached the heart of downtown – pfft! – the Creole was vapour.

Things weren't looking so optimistic for the Challenger, however. They barrelled over four or five crossroads, not even thinking about bothering to slow. The scene of the ambush was miles behind them now, but it felt as if every mobile police officer in the entire greater New Orleans conurbation was pursuing them; a stream of red/blue sparks howled after them through the night-lit streets.

There were some skilled, dogged drivers leading the police pack and the Challenger was definitely suffering from its recent close encounters. Tanner could feel a pull to the right and heard half a dozen wince-inducing discordances grinding amidst the sweet thunder of the engine. It was at moments like these Tanner considered how much easier his job would be if he could just tell people he was a cop. Maybe he should tug Quentin's T-shirt over his face and stick his police badge out of the window?

Yeah, let's call that the back-up plan.

Tanner over-steered gracefully round a narrow junction, skating woozily across the gleaming tarmac while remaining beautifully in control. His skills were second to none, but the police pack was still gaining. They were out of the suburbs now, speeding through a business park, grey blocks on either side, windows flashing back momentary blades of reflected light. Out on the periphery of his vision Tanner noted a tangle of roads that flowed towards the expressway and the sloping corkscrew route out of the city. An idea had begun to form in his mind. He changed his route mid-manoeuvre, turning too sharply. His control slipped for a scattering of seconds.

The Challenger's tyres sketched out an impressive zigzag of burnt rubber behind them before Tanner regained his steering and powered off in the opposite direction. The pursuing convoy was strung out behind them like a necklace of glinting rubies and sapphires.

Tanner flashed towards the spiralling overpass, following its pasta swirl of ramps as they rose towards its apex and the final section of road leading to the interstate. There were no red or blue lights in his rear-view – for now. Tanner calculated that he had a thirty- to forty-second lead. The Challenger screeched to a halt. Quentin almost lost his mind.

'What are you doing? They'll be here any second. What you waiting for? You're a driver, DRIVE!'

'They'll have road blocks outside the city, and the Challenger's not in any fit state to run them. They'd just hem us in, or take out the tyres with sharp-shooters. We need a better exit strategy. I'm proposing a short cut . . . down there.'

He indicated the highway running at right angles *below* the overpass, and then gunned his engine. The car was aimed at the weakest point of the outer barrier. Quentin sucked in a horrified breath as he realized what the wheelman was proposing.

'You can't make it. Man, man, man, MAN! You can't, you can't. You can't make it, chief. NO!' the kid cried incoherently. 'You can't make it.'

Tanner floored it. Time crystallized around them.

'I can,' he said.

They hit the jump.

Then: black sky, stars, a serene sense of floating and suddenly the road below was zooming up to meet them, filling the widescreen, and—

SLAM!

The Challenger whirled and spun and skidded seemingly all at once. Tanner fought the steering wheel as if it was a wild boar bucking in his grip. Round and round they went as Tanner gradually tore back control, inch by inch, until finally, jarringly, they came to a shuddering halt. The bodywork groaned like a submarine under deep-sea pressure.

Tanner put out a palm to the dash as his inner ear slowly caught up and eventually agreed that they weren't still being hurled around like ball bearings in a centrifuge. Next to him Quentin was ripping out yells of laughter and relief.

The convoy of cop cars curved away across the overpass above them in entirely the wrong direction. Tanner leisurely bumped the hard-used Challenger into gear, and they cruised off for home with several thousand dollars' worth of cash bags rolling around in the wheel wells.

Tanner dropped Quentin and the money off, then he took a drive out to the dark and silent docks. He pulled up on stretch of wasteland in the shadow of a brace of disused warehouses. He slid out of the car and straightened with a hiss. *Ow.* He'd be black and blue tomorrow, that was for sure. It felt as if he'd been in the saddle for days. He blew air raggedly between his lips and leant against the car to enjoy the faint cool thread of river breeze playing across his face. He started to chuckle.

Jericho came out of nowhere.

He was moving too fast for Tanner to counter or react. Tanner was caught in the open, unarmed and unprepared, slumped against the side door of the Challenger. His mind flashed to the concealed .45

under the dashboard. It was less than two feet away, but it might as well be on the far side of the moon for all the opportunity he'd have to grab it before Jericho reacted.

The hitman had the cold drop on him, his trademark sawn-offs already unholstered, jutting like steel snake heads from hip height. Tanner braced himself for the scalding storm which would surely blast him out of this world. His focus snapped on to Jericho's trigger fingers. If he could somehow anticipate the shot he might be able to leap aside at the very last second—

But, to Tanner's amazement, Jericho slid his guns back into their holsters, took a step forward, raised his right palm and shook Tanner's hand.

Chapter Five

Tobias Jones was not a happy handler. He couldn't stop shaking his head, or growling.

'As a cop you make a great bank robber,' he told Tanner.

'It wasn't a bank, Jones, it was a security van. Who the hell's been feeding you your intel?' Tanner drawled sarcastically, amusing himself.

As good a friend as Jones was, Tanner simply couldn't help winding him up. Even though they were basically the same age, the fact that it was Jones's job to look out for him, combined with his constant attempts to get Tanner to improve his lifestyle (eat better, try sushi, work out), made it feel as if Jones was his older brother.

Laughing with his mouth full, Tanner proffered the greaseproof paper bag but Jones just flashed him a pitying look. Tanner chuckled again, before gazing off into the green distance.

They were leaning against a bald cypress tree, sitting on the grass in Audubon Zoo not far from the famous white tiger enclosure. The tigers weren't much in evidence today, but the constant flow of visitors streaming past didn't seem to mind. The sun was a beating throb overhead, but the shade was cool. Tanner twisted off the cap on a fresh beer, threw back a refreshing swig.

Jones regarded him with exasperation. 'Come on. These cracker-ass tigers aren't gonna show,' he muttered. 'Let's see if we get any more luck at the reptile house.'

'Because I don't spend enough time with reptiles?' Tanner quipped.

Jones glanced around, a trifle uneasily. 'I'd just feel better if we got indoors. Too many prying eyes out here.'

In the dim stuffy warren of the reptile exhibit tropical forest ambience was being piped out from hidden speakers: hooting calls, hisses, pops and drips. Tanner and Jones hung out in a quiet spot next to a row of glass-fronted cabinets whose occupants were either extremely shy, or no longer resident.

Tanner tapped on the glass, peering into the dense foliage within. Green bars recessed along the ceiling bathed the interior in environmentally authentic lighting, but the 'famous' Boyd's Rainforest Dragon, Puff, advertised on the brass information plaque, was conspicuous by his absence.

'First tigers, now reptiles,' he snorted. 'Reckon we should see if there's an empty cage with "The Indian" on a sign outside?' He blew out a world-weary sigh before enquiring darkly, 'So, what did Powell say about Cochrane?' Jade illumination painted in the hollows of his cheeks. 'At least tell me he's getting shit-canned for the stunt he pulled?'

A cloud crossed Jones's face. 'Cochrane's claiming he had rock-solid intelligence the Indian was actually with you, and he wanted to catch him in the act. He says he couldn't raise either of us on our cell phones to confirm it.'

'Jesus! That man has pure bullshit for blood. Powell just buys that crap then? I trust him even less than Cochrane, but at least he's been four-square behind our op. He's got his whole reputation riding on catching Sepion.'

'He knows Cochrane went off the reservation, for sure, but that's all department politics, man. Cochrane's well respected by the rank and file, so Powell's stuck with him unless he actually catches the man with his hand in the cookie jar and forensics confirm the crumbs on his mouth are choc chip. That debacle last night wasn't even close.'

Tanner cursed. Guilt lanced across Jones's handsome features.

'I feel just terrible 'bout this, John,' he muttered. 'It's totally my fail. I should have talked to the van's security detail myself, done my due diligence and got wind of what Cochrane was planning. I – I don't know what to say, man. I let you down.'

Tanner shrugged. 'Don't beat yourself up. Cochrane

was determined to ream this operation from the get-go, and things didn't turn out too badly in the end. Plus I gave Cochrane's wheel boys a good workout, running them around all over town . . . What?'

Jones had begun to stare at him, his eyes pinching suspiciously. 'You enjoyed it, didn't you? That was your Christmas, you reckless motherfucker!'

The wheelman held Jones's gaze for a few beats but couldn't sustain it and dissolved into mirth. He shrugged with a sheepish grin.

'Goddamn!' his handler exclaimed. 'A mission goes totally shit sandwich but *you* were loving every minute of it!'

'What can I say, Jones? Adrenalin is my drug of choice.'

'And I'm the one who has to bail you out when you overdose! Christ . . . Look, how long we been doing this? I know how much you care, but sometimes you don't take this stuff seriously enough. We shouldn't be at the goddamn zoo today! We should be debriefing in a safe house.'

'Hell, Jones. Let's just relax, eh? It's all good. Live a little.'

'This isn't living a little, this is living dangerously. Anyone could explode your cover in a second, man. What if someone spots us together?'

'They'll think we're dating?'

'Can you not even pretend to treat this with the gravity it deserves?' Jones retorted hotly.

'No one's gonna know me here,' Tanner explained

soothingly. 'Look around you, it's wall-to-wall families and tourists. This is a nice place; I'm a bad man. I'm running with bad men. The likes of Jericho and Bowman do not pop down to Audubon Zoo to see the koala bears of an afternoon, trust me! You worry too damn much.'

'Worrying is my job, motherfucker.'

'Look, Jones, sometimes I go out and get hammered after a mission, right?'

'Yeah, and I have to come and haul your flat white ass outta the gutter every time.'

'And we have a butch little wrestle in the street, that's cool; but, see, that's my pressure valve. All of this is: the drink, the adrenalin, the kicks, even the fucking zoo! Coming here today and being around normal families doing normal things gives me a kick. It reminds me of what we're really fighting for. I get to see who I'm protecting from the slimeballs I have to be around every other day of the week. This is something you can't properly understand because at the end of the day, you stay safe back in the van. I'm the one in the thick of it. I'm the one running with the wolves.

'I knew that was what the job was when I signed up – and I wouldn't have anyone else but you backing up my play– but you have to let me unwind my way. It's *my* neck that's on the line.'

Once Tanner had finished his speech Jones looked as if he'd been gut punched. 'Look, ah, man, shit—'

Tanner held up a palm and his partner fell silent. They both stood side by side, staring into the empty green glowing box. Moments dawdled past in uncomfortable silence.

Tanner felt bad for off-loading so heavily on Jones. The handler-uncover cop dynamic was tough. It was all about trust, but that had to flow both ways. Tanner might think of Jones as the big brother to be annoyed, but in turn Jones thought of Tanner as the little brother he had to protect. He needed to know that wasn't the case.

Keen to improve the mood, Tanner tried to cheer up his partner in the only way he knew how. 'You still rolling around in that Chevy Camaro P.O.S.?' Tanner asked with a smirk. 'Want me to get one of my new buddies to steal you something better?'

Jones snorted. 'You know what, man, I don't care. It gets me from point A to point B, and looks fine doing it.'

They laughed together warmly, cracking the tension down the middle. Afterwards, Jones became business-like again. 'So, let's focus. Where we at? The Indian?'

'Still in the shadows, but this Jericho business is an unlooked-for win. If we play this right, it might lead us straight to the top. It means I have to work on the Jericho angle full-time, though.'

'So then. Jericho? You two got over the beef you had in Rio?'

'Yeah.' Tanner paused and stared at his hands, as if he couldn't quite believe what he'd done with them. 'I never thought in a million years I'd be saving the skin of a snake like Jericho. I dunno, sometimes it kinda makes you wonder whether the long game is really worth it. Now Jericho and me are partners? What a freaking world.'

Abruptly, Tanner's cell phone chimed from his jacket pocket. He fished the device out, checked the text message and frowned. There was a pause.

'Who that?' Jones asked, sensing the worm of tension now wriggling back between them. Tanner sucked his lip thoughtfully.

'My new partner wants to meet up in half an hour.'

Chapter Six

Jericho insisted they hook up, alone, at an isolated street of partially demolished industrial units not far from the docks. Tanner got out of the Dodge Challenger SRT8 he'd borrowed from Bowman, which he was driving while his own Challenger was in the shop, and leant against the hood listening to James Brown through the window. The whole arcade was deserted; dry brown vines drooped from municipal plant containers on a sun-bleached concrete apron. Jericho's unexpected loyalty was too good an opportunity to pass up, but even so Tanner still brought along a snubnosed .38 special loaded with jacketed hollow-points in his ankle holster.

Jericho arrived in a Dodge Ram SRT10 virtually identical to the one he'd lost during the heist. Did he have a fleet of the things just sitting gathering dust in a warehouse somewhere? Tanner ambled warily over to the driver's side. The window whirred down as he approached. Jericho looked as much like an assembly of boulders in the shape of a person as ever, but there was a fresh gash along his left eyebrow and a trail of raw scabs running from jaw to ear. The cut on his brow was bronzed with disinfectant wash, but hadn't been stitched. Clearly that would leave a scar, which was exactly what Jericho wanted.

'Get in. We're taking my car,' the hitman rumbled.

Tanner cocked his head. 'I do all my own driving. Control freak, y'know.'

Jericho's gaze was like a cold dark tunnel, but his smile appeared genuine. 'Can't a fellow soldier offer to chauffeur you around? We're comrades, Tanner. It's all about the trust.'

Tanner thought this over for a beat. He flicked a glance back at Bowman's Taurus, then dismissed that concern. Bowman had surely stolen it himself in the first place, so if it got jacked here, well, what goes around comes around, right? Tanner shifted slightly and felt the comforting weight of the .38 lashed to his leg.

No one ever won the race by staying at home, he reflected. He shrugged and jumped into the passenger's side of the Dodge. Jericho floored the pedal and they roared off towards destinations unknown.

'The money Quentin managed to grab was trash,' Jericho told Tanner as they rolled into the housing projects where concrete and cracked asphalt shimmered in the midday sun. Black and Latin teens hung out underneath 'No Loitering' signs outside 7-11s, saluting raucously as Jericho breezed by. 'Had to burn it all, bills were marked,' Jericho continued. 'Question is: who tipped off the heat?'

So soon, thought Tanner? *Already I'm being asked to second guess my moves and we're barely half an hour into this new 'partnership'*. Was Jericho asking because he now considered Tanner a genuine confidant, or did he actually suspect the wheelman of being the mole? Was this just an elaborate ploy to smoke him out?

'You think there's a snitch in the crew?' Tanner replied slowly, choosing his words with care, adding just a hint of worried confusion. Unlike an actor, Tanner didn't have the luxury of a warm-up before he went on stage. He had to bring his 'A' game at the drop of a hat.

'Isn't that the logical conclusion?'

'Maybe, but didn't you vet all your guys yourself? Isn't it more likely it was the guy in the department who sold us the information in the first place?'

Jericho chewed this over for a few moments, his face an unreadable mask.

'You might be right,' he eventually conceded. 'I trust all my soldiers. At the end of the day, it's not for me to decide. That's above my pay grade. I'll let the Indian know. If he wants to let the dogs off the chain and hold an inquisition, that's his call.'

Tanner relaxed a little. Jericho had clearly bought his patter.

The Dodge was prowling through Central City New Orleans now. It cruised past the notorious Magnolia

Projects, their blocky housing units oversized and awkward, marooned on a checkerboard of sandy scrub grass and parched pavement; this was the dark sticky heart of the metropolis, murder capital of the USA. It was a forbidding testament to the savage infections a combination of crippling poverty and violent crime could inflict on a community.

Tanner shifted in his seat and scanned the busy street like a machine-gun turret scoping for targets. Gangs of young men roamed here although it was the middle of the day, resplendent in gang colours and fierce fashions: seventies-style collared leather jackets, garish tees and jerseys, waterfalls of gold chain dripping off their necks and wrists, designer shades, Argyle beanie hats.

No one went to work, or school. They patrolled the baking streets, or primped and posed on corners, gun butts peeking discreetly out of their waistbands, all affecting the cocksure swagger of the secretly armed. The humid air rolled like molasses down these concrete canyons, making the skin of the boys and girls shine as they strutted. Boarded-up businesses sat next to empty trash-filled lots on a never-ending loop outside the car window, the colours all drained tans or washed-out greys. Here and there, the elegant green branches of live oaks or vibrant splashes of street art broke up the monotony, but Tanner knew this was a feral, lawless place.

'So what we at today?' he drawled airily.

'We got to do the rounds of all the uptown dealers.

It's even more important since the van raid went south. We have to keep the money flowing, but also we need to stamp down our authority. Normally I'd just send one of my lieutenants, but after last night's fiasco we gotta walk round the lion cages and flick our whips some. Discipline's gotten slack and nobody deals in the projects without offering up his tariff to the Indian.' He paused to look over at Tanner, expressionless: 'Plus, you and me get to talk.'

''Bout what?'

'Just talk.'

Uh oh, thought Tanner.

They spent the afternoon shuttling between the infamous Magnolia, Calliope and Melpomene Projects, where they met with low-level dealers, a selection of jittery youths and strung-out middle-aged meth freaks in gloomy airless rooms laced with the stench of weed, cheap cologne and burritos. Muscle waited at the doors, badly maintained Uzis in their sweaty fists; neat brown and white packets sat on tables next to precision scales; ragged blocks of mismatched bills were placed into Jericho's gaping sports bag. On they went, from drug den to drug den, for the whole of the afternoon. Just the extent of the Indian's network was troubling.

In the car in between, they talked, though it felt more like jousting to Tanner.

'You saved my skin, sure,' Jericho told him. 'But

we've got something else to discuss, you and me, haven't we? What went down between us in Rio.'

'The past is the past as far as I'm concerned,' Tanner replied. 'You want to make something of it?' he asked casually.

'The past?' Jericho said, ignoring the real barb of the question. 'Yeah, let's talk about the past. Let's hear your back story, Tanner. Maybe there's something in your history that'll allow me to excuse your behaviour in Rio.'

Tanner's legend – his undercover character's biography – was actually based on his own wild past. It made it easier that way, more authentic to talk about, and he was less likely to forget the details in the heat of the moment or under pressure of, say, having a gun pressed into his temple. That said, as he had told and retold some version of this story it had gradually begun to feel ... distant. It was almost as if he was talking about someone else, as if the undercover Tanner was the one who owned his past and the real Tanner was simply a faceless shadow.

'My past?' he mused. 'Nothing much to say. Broken home. Got a sister. Don't see her that much. She went off with Mom and there's bad blood between us now for other reasons. I stayed with my deadbeat dad. He slapped me about some, the drunken fuck, until I got big enough and tossed him down the back stairs and broke half his teeth. Didn't get to school much. Hung out round the local chop shop instead, after falling in with some local villains. Found out about illegal street racing there, which is where I cut my driving teeth. Sharpened those skills pulling Touge races and cannonball runs, me and my buddy Slater. Things didn't work out so well for him, though.'

Tanner paused, and chewed his lip. This emotion was real but he choked that shit off and barrelled onward with a terse shrug.

'We made pin money betting on our own races, but after Slater wiped out, I realized that game was for chumps. Decided to reinvest those skills in a sector with real payback potential. Joined a gang as a get-away wheelman and the rest is history.'

Jericho chewed his tale over in silence.

'I can feel that,' he eventually responded. 'Pretty similar to how I got into the life. We've got that in common. I was the son of first-generation Moroccan immigrants, so that's what I was kicking against ... Going after the American dream by any means possible—'

Suddenly, Jericho shut up like a letterbox snapping closed and they drove on in stony silence for a short distance. When he spoke again Jericho's voice was as toneless and blunt as ever, but his meaning was conciliatory.

'We're good about Rio. The past is the past. Who gives a shit, eh?'

Feeling as if he'd passed some sort of test, and even though he didn't really enjoy what that might say about him in this context, Tanner relaxed a fraction.

Was he bonding with Jericho? That was a chilling thought.

It was interesting to observe how his 'partner' dealt with his crew. Some of the dealers he stonewalled with barely contained disgust, others he coldly raged at, some he greeted as old friends, a few he even joked with in a sinister way. If there was a hidden pattern to this seemingly random strategy, though, then Tanner wasn't able to fathom it. He decided it was worth a risk at the direct approach.

'Interesting leadership style you've got going on,' he asked idly when they were next back in the Dodge. 'Keep them all guessing, is that it? They never know which Jericho is going to walk through the door and so have to keep their noses clean and stay on their toes?'

Jericho didn't respond for some time. He drove with a mechanical, passionless efficiency, jaw jutting ahead as if it were attached to the road by invisible wires.

'It's about control,' he finally admitted. 'Doesn't matter how you win it. It can be money, fear, violence, guile. I simply work out which levers to press for each scumbag. Control is the only important thing. It doesn't even matter whether other people know you have it. Fame and notoriety are just drugs for weak minds.' He broke off as he negotiated a dogleg round a hillock of cracked asphalt. 'Think of the ten most powerful men you know about; there's another ten behind them, ten times more powerful, whose faces you'll never know. Don't focus on the figureheads, look to the shadows. That's what the Indian worked out a long time ago.'

This unexpected mention of Sepion – the real target of the whole operation – encouraged Tanner to chance his luck and fish some more.

'So, you're the Indian's right-hand man? I've been hearing all these legends about him since I've been in the city, but what's he really like?'

Jericho appeared to think for a moment.

'He's really private.'

Which was as far as that particular dialogue went.

Pausing under the sagging communal porch of an ostensibly vacant housing unit, Jericho suddenly turned to Tanner and said, 'This one's a little different. Tycho's a dealer, but he's been stealing from his stash and selling it on the side for a massive profit. The Indian wants all that money back. We recover it by any means.'

'You couldn't have told me this earlier?'

'This is still part of your interview process. Want to see how you improvise and think on your feet. By the way, you're going in first . . . Oh, and my sources tell me his brother tipped him off that we were coming.'

'Great,' Tanner muttered under his breath. 'Tycho!' he called amiably into the house. 'I know what you must be thinking, but we're just here to talk! See if we can't sort this out between ourselves, without having to involve the Indian or his dogs. We're coming in now . . .'

Reassuring, reasonable, measured.

The instant he went through into the hallway Tanner felt a breath of displaced air gust across his face, and instinctively dived aside. The tip of a Louisville Slugger swung through the space his skull had just occupied a heartbeat ago. Tycho followed up with another attack, a crushing overhead blow. On the floor, Tanner rolled nimbly to one side and the bat smashed the filthy floor tiles where he'd lain with a gunshot crack. The wheelman kicked out at the dealer's ankle, but Tycho leapt back to evade Tanner's boot, then he danced a junkie's jig of rage, fear and frustration. He was a strung-out leathery strip of skin in a droopy grey singlet and ill-fitting combat pants. A face that looked like a scrunched-up fist of fuzz, acne and bad teeth made it impossible to tell whether he was fifteen or fifty. He wore a sodden stars and stripes bandanna to keep the fever sweat out of his bugging-out eyes.

'I know you! You ain't the boss of me! I'll fuck you up, man!' he screamed.

The moment this hysterical warning was delivered the dealer bolted out of sight through a nearby doorway, disappearing into the depths of the building.

'Great,' Tanner muttered again.

Jericho helped him to his feet and motioned for silence. Using short, curt gestures they hatched a plan to split off and outflank Tycho. The building had been condemned. There were luminous yellow scraps of the Housing Authority tape vainly forbidding entry to the upper floors on grounds of public safety. Vandals had gone to work on many of the plasterboard walls, transforming this whole lower floor into a dismal maze of shadows and potential hidey-holes with the occasional unexpectedly beautiful shafts of sunlight poking through shattered partitions. Corridors had been reduced to ladders of crumbling stumps, while sodden mildewed tongues of wallpaper lolled off the few walls that remained.

Tycho was used to the muddled geography of this place, but Tanner and Jericho were methodical and disciplined. They communicated so well that Tanner was unwillingly reminded of his work with Jones, of how they were so in synch as partners that they could almost anticipate each other's thoughts. It was like that now. A slow, tension-filled game of cat and mouse evolved over the next few minutes, with the two intruders gradually choking off the dealer's escape routes. At first Tycho managed to keep still, to wait in hidden corners, move with stealthy design, but as he ran out of places to hide he started to panic and make mistakes.

Finally, Tanner caught a flash of movement out of the corner of his eye. Tycho was making a desperate dash for the front door. The wheelman spun and lunged, crashing into the wiry man as he sped by. He tackled Tycho to the ground where he swiftly pinned him to the warped floorboards. The dealer thrashed and moaned, but he wasn't going anywhere. Jericho came to stand over them, radiating grim satisfaction.

Tanner understood that this was a situation where he wasn't going to be able to get away with just harsh language. He threatened and bellowed at the top of his lungs into Tycho's sneering face as long as he could, and after that he hit him. Tanner had spent hundreds of hours in unarmed combat training, and had emerged with a thorough technical knowledge of human anatomy, as well as how to damage it. He knew where to strike Tycho and with precisely how much force so as to limit any real damage, but also, crucially, how to put on a good show.

Jericho circled the defiant dealer, crooning in a voice like gravel churning in a washing machine, playing a sympathetic role as only a psycho could.

'Look, just tell us where you stashed the cash, Tycho, and we'll let you off with a warning. No one need know. You're a good earner, loyal. I don't want to hurt you . . . but Tanner here, he's a maniac. They say he ate off a man's face once for stealing his parking space.'

Tycho spat blood in Jericho's general direction from an impressive but superficial cut on his lip. 'I'm not telling you anything!' he screamed hoarsely. 'Cut me if you like! Go on, I dare you!'

Tycho was as stubborn as he was stupid. It was clear he was going to take his dogged insolence to the grave if necessary. Jericho's expression went flat. He shrugged off any pretence of empathy and chambered shells into his sawn-off.

'I'll take that dare.'

Tanner's mind raced. He placed a restraining hand across the shotgun and Jericho's chest. The hitman's eyes flashed with irritation, glinting like dull pewter in the grainy light. But Tanner grinned at him.

'I've got a better idea,' he hissed with a quick glance over the shoulder at the still defiant Tycho. 'You'll like this . . .'

Tanner explained to Jericho what he had planned, and the icy roughneck began to grin properly for the first time since Tanner had met him: a leering toothy gash; it made Tanner feel decidedly queasy to have been the cause of it.

Tycho was screaming. Jericho was laughing. Tanner was just trying to concentrate: it was hard to see where you were driving when there was a flailing drug dealer lashed your car's hood.

Tycho's howls and the meaty revs of the Dodge echoed off the concrete walls of the underground car park as Tanner swung the heavy vehicle through its paces. It was a serious test of the ace wheelman's skills to negotiate the cluttered space – slaloming in and out of the pillars, weaving around parked cars – yet still keeping Tycho safe, while at the same time making him believe he was about to be crushed to death at any second.

Tanner drove to the extreme end of the low-ceiling space and turned around. He gunned the engine. Tycho had collapsed, but now abject terror roused him as he realized what new horror Tanner had planned.

'No! No!'

Tanner kicked the gas and the truck accelerated from nought to sixty in five seconds straight at the concrete wall at the far end of the garage. Tycho let rip to a barely human shriek – before Tanner flicked the Dodge into a tyre-shredding one-eighty spin the instant before they hit.

'I give in! You insane fuckers! Stop! Stop! I'll get you the money!'

Jericho guffawed. Tanner smiled at him coldly.

'Do you believe him? I'm not sure I believe him.' He rolled down the driver's side window, and called out conversationally to his victim, 'I'm not sure I believe you, Tycho.'

Tanner set off again, looping around and round the central block of parking bays, faster and faster, taking each corner tighter and tighter so that Tycho was nearer and nearer to being crushed with every circuit.

'It's hidden in one of the upstairs bedrooms. I'll take you. I'LL TAKE YOU!'

'OK then, I'll stop . . .'

Tycho shrieked again: 'Don't brake. Don't BRAKE!' he wailed pitifully.

Every time the car jerked to a halt, Tycho was

wrenched forward, tearing painfully at his shoulder muscles. Tanner tapped on the brake once, just a touch. Tycho bawled. *That's for swinging a bat at me, you little prick*, Tanner thought.

The money was in a grubby refuse sack beside a nest of desiccated dead rats under rotten floorboards in a dilapidated upstairs bedroom. Tycho was on his knees weeping quietly as Tanner gingerly retrieved the sack. He checked the contents and then nodded to Jericho. 'It's all here.'

Which was when Tycho decided to bust out yet another ill-advised tirade.

'It's all your fault, Jericho,' he blubbed furiously. 'I was a stand-up guy before you recruited me! I might have been a dealer, but I was going to stay clean. "There's enough for everyone," you said. You're the one who kept giving me the spare gear and now I'm crawling the walls and stealing the Indian's money. I'll fucking eat out your eyes in hell for what you've done to me!' he screamed, his eyes bulging like over-fried eggs.

Goddamnit, Tycho, thought Tanner desperately, *I've spent the last two hours trying to keep your damned hide intact. What is it with this death wish?*

Jericho stiffened. Moving with terrible deliberation, he stalked towards Tycho and hunkered down beside him. Tycho quailed, but Jericho just watched the broken man for a while with his head on one side, like a curious wolf fascinated as to why its meal was still whimpering.

Tanner tensed. *Shit, this is it*, he thought. Jericho was going to kill Tycho right in front of him. Could he really be witness to a cold-blooded murder and not step in? He'd already tried everything, short of shooting Jericho. He'd intervened once already. Again, and Jericho would know something was amiss. He couldn't risk his cover and Tycho was basically pond scum. He was a dealer. He sold crack to fifteen-year-olds. He'd have slaughtered Tanner without compunction if he'd had the chance rather than face up to his own mistakes.

But none of that was the point. A life was a life. The law didn't make any distinctions between who was worthy and who wasn't, who deserved its protection and who didn't. It was easy to be nice to nice people. Tanner had sworn to uphold the law and, in the deepest parts of his soul, he believed in those truths.

His fingertips drummed against his thigh. He was sure he would be able to crouch and draw the snubnose before Jericho could react. Put three or four rounds into him and easily argue to the review board it was a justified homicide. Of course, he'd also be pumping lead into any chance they ever had of breaking the Indian's reign of terror.

Jericho drew out a 9-inch carbon-steel bowie knife from a concealed scabbard and brandished it in front of Tycho's face. Tycho's eyes bulged with terror and darkness spread out from the khaki crotch of his combat pants as his bladder released.

Jericho's blade dipped – Tanner's hand twitched—

Jericho slashed the twine binding Tycho's hands together and set him free.

Both Tanner and Tycho stared in utter disbelief. Tycho staggered unsteadily to his feet, his trouser hems dripping, and threw his palms out to Jericho in gratitude or supplication.

'If you breathe a word of what happened in this room, I will kill you in your sleep. Then I will go to the houses of anyone you have ever cared for and kill them too,' rumbled Jericho. 'Here is a reminder so you will never forget this day and my warning.'

He stepped in quick as a flash and, before Tanner could stop him, he slashed at Tycho with the tip of his blade. A slender red line appeared on the dealer's cheek. It began to weep just as Tycho's hand darted up to stem the tide. Within seconds his knuckles were covered in gore and he had to press his shirtsleeve over the gash. Despite the disfiguring cut, however, the dealer was still pathetically grateful for his reprieve.

'Th-th-thank you, J-Jericho. Y-you won't regret this, I-I swear!' he babbled, wincing and weaving, dripping scarlet spats in the dust. 'You can rely on Tycho. I'll be your eyes and ears, I-I'll be your eye in the sky, your ear on the street, I'll—'

'Go,' Jericho grated.

Tycho didn't wait to be told twice. He half ran, half flailed out of the room in his piss-stained combats, whooping with hysterical relief. They heard him bouncing unsteadily all the way down the stairwell and out on to the scrub land beyond.

'I don't get it,' Tanner commented into the booming silence that followed Tycho's exit. He really didn't. Jericho began to clean his knife with precise strokes of a soft swatch of cloth. He was utterly absorbed by the task and the fiery lustre of the blade.

'Mercy is a tool,' he rumbled without looking up. 'It's not a cudgel, like violence. Mercy you use like a scalpel. You slice a single precise incision to get exactly what you want. In movies the gang boss always claims he has to kill those who fuck up because otherwise he'll lose the respect – but do you think Tycho will ever tell another living soul about this afternoon? About how he begged for his life, grovelling in the shit and dirt, about how he pissed his pants like a little girl when I just looked at him?

'No. This was his moment of total humiliation. He'll never mention it again as long as he lives, if he can get away with it. But he'll always remember how I saved him . . . by putting my knife away. Tycho is mine now. He'd snitch on his own grandmomma if I told him to.' Jericho slid his blade back into its scabbard with a smooth *snick*. 'Come.'

Jericho left the dingy room, but Tanner remained for some moments, alone with his troubled thoughts.

Jericho dropped Tanner back off at the abandoned arcade just as the sun was setting. The Dodge Challenger was still there, glinting in the molten bronze light. As Tanner unlocked the car, Jericho's shadow fell over him from behind. The wheelman's shoulders tensed. He still got the adrenalin jags whenever the hitman was close. Couldn't help but imagine that his 'partner' was imagining cross-hairs on the back of his neck.

'We're recruiting new drivers tomorrow, trying out some wannabes,' the hitman said. 'The Indian wants us to crew up for a renewed push against the Red Blades. Going to run hopefuls through their paces out on the real streets, see their skills in action. Come along. It'll be like being back in your street-racing days and your input might be useful. Also . . .' He hesitated for a beat, as if weighing something up, then: 'You did good today.'

Jericho's approval made Tanner flinch inside, but his demeanour remained flinty.

'We work well together. I think this partnership is going to pan out.'

Jericho stretched out his palm to Tanner, who noticed there was a bright smear of blood on his thumb. Tycho's blood. Jericho wasn't smiling. The hitman's hand – and the moment – hung in the air, waiting.

Jericho's patronage and his 'friendship' – whatever that actually meant for a sociopath – would be invaluable for Tanner in his pursuit of the Indian. Finally, he'd gain access to that inner circle and could work at sabotaging the even greater monster. For the sake of the greater good, sometimes one had to do a little evil; that was the undercover cop's deal with the devil. Tanner had known that from the first day of his very first mission.

Tycho's blood glinted brightly in the afternoon sun.

Tanner took Jericho's hand and shook it firmly, not showing a hint of the churning uncertainty he felt inside. Far away beyond the horizon, distant thunder rolled.

Chapter Seven

The last time he'd seen her was fifteen years ago, and she'd been a snot-nosed kid at the time, but Tanner recognized her immediately. She had a new heart cross pendant around her neck and a star-shaped scar over her temple.

Julia Navarro definitely wasn't a kid any more.

She leaned against her car – a scrappy supercharged little Honda S2000 – in the line-up of wannabe drivers. Her hair was a punky tomboyish hood, black spikes in her eyes, ragged tails flicking out back. She was petite – five-one, five-two – and trim, with the sleek fit body of a sprinter, high shoulders, great posture. As a kid she'd been kind of cute and eager, over-excitable and slightly annoying, but the intervening years had transformed her into this slim wary beauty; a girl gearhead in designer leather and shrinkwrap jeans with smooth caramel skin, lips full as petals, and fiery dark eyes that missed nothing.

Until a few minutes ago a squall had been lashing the docks with waves of silver needles. Now the bodies of the waiting cars looked as if they'd been pebble-dashed with diamonds. The blacktop beneath their feet shone in the gauzy moonlight. Gusts still blew along the lanes between the stacks of shipping crates, which towered like canyon walls on either side. The red, yellow and orange steel containers resembled a gigantic child's Lego set left out in the rain. The cars of the candidates rocked on their suspension as they were buffeted by the wind, but the air the breeze carried was sweet and fresh, charged with the scent of the ocean. The dark sky overhead remained turbulent, a vortex of violence.

To the left loomed the stark bulk of the colossal cargo shed. Its size was matched by the sheer industrial brawn of the docks to their right: a profusion of cranes, berths, piers, moorings for tankers and ocean liners, along with the monumental black silhouettes of the ships themselves. It was all spread along two miles of the shore, the longest wharf in the world. The Port of New Orleans handled over six thousand vessels a year, with 84 million tons of cargo, and threaded unseen through that hurly-burly many of Sepion's illegal interests passed. The Indian was the invisible king of this place.

Even at this hour there was enough activity to mask the racket of their driver try-outs, while donations to 'financially sympathetic' officers of the harbour police service further guaranteed that their impromptu race track wouldn't be disturbed. A starting line had been sprayed out in soluble paint at the head of the highway between cargo crates with the intention that the paint would wash away by morning. However, the rains had spoiled that plan. The starting line had seeped and run until it ominously resembled an oily pool of blood.

One of the other wannabes – a lumpy blond jock wearing an oil-stained NFL Saints jacket and ridiculous aviator shades – had been leering at Navarro ever since she'd stepped on to the dock. Now, he nudged the driver next to him and oafishly whistled at her.

'Hey-hey, chiquita! Wanna double-declutch my gear stick?' he sniggered, grabbing his crotch. The other drivers guffawed.

Navarro didn't react straight away. She was languidly tapping away at her cell phone. Once she was done, she closed the clamshell phone with a sigh.

'If you're talking about that Muscle Mary piece of shit you're driving, then the stick'd probably come off in my hands. If you meant your dick, then the stick'd probably come off in my hands. But at least then I'd have a treat to throw to the Indian's dogs when he welcomes me on to the team. Not that something so tiny would make much of a snack . . .'

She didn't look in the jock's direction as she delivered this verbal smack-down. The other drivers – all young, all male – hooted like hyenas.

'Arrrw, kitten!' cackled the driver the jock had tried to enlist in his boorishness. 'She scratched you good, brother!'

'Uppity little bitch,' the jock hissed, bristling with aggressive embarrassment, and took an enraged step towards Navarro. Tanner had crossed the gap in a handful of heartbeats and shoved him back so hard that he bounced off the side of his tacky Ford Mustang Shelby GT500. He skidded on the wet champagne-yellow bodywork, and had to catch himself before the frictionless surface pitched him on to the wet tarmac. His aviators didn't fare so well, however, and plummeted to the ground with a pathetic crack.

'Show a little respect to your fellow candidates, dough boy, or I'll take it as a personal insult. Think you really want to insult me . . . personally?'

The jock had no stomach for a fight and folded like a bad poker hand. He just shook his head and ducked his gaze, a beta male surrendering to the king silver-back. Tanner held his gaze for a few moments longer just to burn the submission into him. Then he turned a fond smile towards Navarro.

She punched him in the chest.

The blow hurt. She wasn't messing around and clearly knew how to make a punch count.

'Step off, asshole! I fight my own battles,' she spat. Then her eyes widened as she recognized her unlooked-for guardian for the first time.

'Tanner? Christ, is that really you? What the hell are you doing here? This is amazing!'

Before any cascade of revelations about their history together came spilling out, Tanner had seized Navarro by the elbow and towed her behind one of the shipping containers. He hoped the other drivers would merely dismiss his intentions as dishonourable. Nothing could be further from the truth.

'You can't be here,' Tanner told her bluntly before she could squeeze out another word. Up until that point Navarro's face had been lit up with affection, but these words curdled her expression into a scowl.

'Don't come that attitude with me!' she blustered. 'What, just because I'm a woman you automatically assume I can't leave those bottom-feeding jackasses over there choking on my fumes? I just about worshipped you as a kid, but here you are spouting exactly the same kind of Neanderthal horseshit I've been kicking against my whole life—'

'I meant', said Tanner with enormous self-control, 'what are you doing mixed up with gangs like this? I thought you'd be smarter than that.'

'Who the hell do you think you are? You haven't seen me since I was ten years old, Tanner. What makes you think you've got the right to dictate anything to me now.'

'I just don't understand how you could actively choose to place yourself into this dangerous life – especially after what happened to your brother. You're auditioning to be a wheelgirl for the most vicious gang lord in all of New Orleans!'

'Firstly, he's my half-brother and, secondly, you're the very last person in the world who should be lecturing me about what we can learn from his accident. If you hadn't noticed, you're already a wheelman for the most vicious gang lord in New Orleans, so what does that make you? How dare you judge me seconds after barging back into my life? You don't know a damn thing about me now!'

A wash of emotion rinsed through Tanner like ice water. He realized with a shock how he'd let the past overwhelm him. Navarro wasn't the kid, Julia Jaybird, whom he'd once known. She was a grown woman with her own adult obsessions, desires, loves and probably a whole chain of fucked-up decisions dragging behind her, any one of which might have brought her to these docks tonight. He couldn't get involved. If he tried to protect her – openly at least – then he would be the one putting both of their lives at risk, and potentially endangering the entire operation.

Tanner clenched off his feelings and tried to slip smoothly back into his role.

'Fuck. I'm sorry, Julia,' he whispered huskily. 'I didn't mean to rant, it was just a surprise you being here . . . and to be reminded of Jason, tonight. Look, it would help a lot if I just knew *why* you want to join Sepion's crew.'

Navarro toyed with the silver heart cross pendant in her right hand, stroking it with the ball of her thumb. Her eyes were black pearls in the low light. 'We all got duties and promises we have to keep, Tanner. We do what we have to do to honour them. Look, I'm not a little girl now and I don't need you to look out for me. I really *do* know what I'm doing.' As they talked a fine mist of rain swept its curtains across them. Navarro shivered. 'Right now, I've got to get my head in the game. These conditions are no joke.'

A part of Tanner wanted to hug her but he restricted himself to a terse head bob, before heading back towards Jericho, who was sitting nearby in the parked Dodge, as inscrutable and heavy-browed as an Easter Island head. It was like watching a statue come to life as the hitman checked his watch. Tanner almost expected to hear stone grinding and watch a puff of chalk jet out of his elbow joint.

'Let's get this started,' he announced.

Tanner chewed his lip. He still hadn't quite recovered from the shock of seeing Navarro. His mind whirred. The image of an excited ten-year-old girl cheering beside another rain-slick road kept niggling him.

'The conditions are getting pretty treacherous now,' he mused with cautiously pitched scepticism. 'Wouldn't it be safer to come back tomorrow night? See what they can do when they aren't worrying about flying off into the river?'

Tanner was wondering if he could just talk to Navarro in a more relaxed context; whether he mightn't be able to chip away at her stubborn resolve. Jericho cut that dead.

'They'll have to drive in far worse conditions than this if they make the Indian's team. We go now.'

Tanner pursed his lips, a fresh objection percolating on his tongue. Should he press it?

No.

The whole operation was already teetering over a precipice, what with Cochrane and Powell's machinations. Stick to the plan.

'OK,' he muttered and started making his way back towards the improvised starting line. The drivers had already slotted their cars into a grid and the air was thick with fumes and the din of their eager engines.

I'm just not sure about this rain, Tanner thought to himself.

Chapter Eight

'I'm just not sure about this rain, bro,' Jason Slater had murmured, fifteen years earlier, his palms playing a nervous drum solo against his steering wheel.

'Dude, this is the biggest race of our lives!' Tanner shot back at him through his driver's side window. 'You can't pussy out.'

Tanner's olive Ford Mustang Cobra sat side by side with Slater's brick-red Mitsubishi Eclipse in a pack of revving, growling street racers spread out along a street in the Nob Hill district of downtown San Francisco. The racers and their party-happy crowd of spectators had materialized out of the night like a flash mob and cordoned off the whole block with trucks and SUVs in a matter of minutes. The whole enterprize unfolded like a military operation. This race had been planned for months and was organized by a meticulous committee. This was the big one. The Bullitt run.

There was an almost carnival-like atmosphere. Clubbers in fly fashions dashed back and forth like urban birds of paradise showing off their finery. Drag queens organised Mexican waves; people cheered and performed clumsy off-the-cuff dance routines. Hip-hop shook out of car speakers. Brake lights glowed like embers among ashes; headlights dazzled like suns. Tricked-out custom rides hovered on neon clouds, glowing emerald and fluorescent jade. Lowriders bounced their chassis up and down, hydraulics hissing like a circus ride. Every tribe was represented: oil-stained gearheads, jacket-wearing poseurs, preppies, motor geeks, hardcore metallers; the whole cast list of trendsetters and trend-followers.

Race co-ordinators strode about communicating via squawking walkie-talkies and there was a comms truck constantly monitoring local police chatter. People were surprisingly tolerant of the rain, which twirled like a constantly shifting veil across proceedings, flattening primped-up hair-dos and making pimped-out bodywork gleam.

'This is huger than huge!' Tanner ran on, shouting to be heard, hyped with adrenalin. 'Do you know how many losers here are going to be walking home because they pink-slipped their rides just to buy into the race in the first place?'

'Uh-huh,' Slater replied tightly. His gaze was glued to the rear bumper of the car in front. Tanner caught the subtext instantly and groaned with dismay.

'No! Why? I thought you had the wedge?'

Slater grimaced uncomfortably, squirmed in his seat. 'I threw all my money into an import engine swap and the sweetest new supercharger I could find.

But look, it'll more than pay back the investment when I cruise over the finish line and collect my winnings! There's no way I'm going to lose this car.'

Tanner's face showed his disbelief. Before he could scoff out loud, however, a loud thump on his hood caused both men to jump. Slater's half-sister was leaning into the windshield, grinning and giggling like a mad thing, delighted to have taken them by surprise. Her chunky mouth braces glinted across her teeth, while her frayed ponytail bounced unselfconsciously back and forth as she did a silly laughing jig.

'You gonna smoke my brother, Tanner?' Julia Jaybird sniggered. 'You gonna beat his ass into the dirt? Are ya?'

'Hell no!' Slater craned over to shout. 'And you should be back home! If your dad finds out I let you come to the race, we'll both be dead! Go on, skedaddle!'

Julia ran round the front of Slater's car, shined her ass cheekily off his bodywork, and ran off giggling towards the line of spectators bracketing the street. Slater shouted PG-rated abuse after her retreating signature blue windcheater but Tanner just chuckled.

'Cut her some slack, man. She's a good kid. Maybe all of this excitement will turn her into a car designer when she grows up?'

'Ha, no fear!' Slater snorted. 'That one's a total nerd. Loves school, wants to be a freaking science teacher! Ten years old and already she's plotting her way towards middle age with a houseful of cats.' His brow creased abruptly as his mood veered in a new direction. 'Look, dude, I didn't mean for you to find out about the pink slip, but you're not going to beat me. You might have edged ahead these last few races, but up 'til then we were going punch for punch. In overall wins, we're still equal. I don't want you going soft on me just 'cause I've put my car on the line.'

'Whoa, I'm not throttling back just 'cause you're a tool who bet his car on a race he can't win! I'm in it to win it.'

'Well, bring it!' Slater replied, laughing.

The whole event felt light-hearted and impulsive. A hubbub of speed freaks and excitement junkies all gathered together in a mob, fizzing with anticipation. Underneath Tanner and Slater's jesting, though, there was a real steel edge. They might be best friends, might have sweated over each other's vehicles and helped to build and rebuild them endless times, but they'd been fiercely competitive ever since their first meeting in shop class a decade ago.

They were close as brothers – and brothers always compete. That was what drove them both on. It was what made them strive to be better. To be the best.

As Slater and Tanner smack-talked, an Asian guy in scarlet designer leathers and wraparound specs leapt up on the roof of an SUV. The crowd let out a collective 'ooooooh', which dissolved into good-natured laughter. Red Leather Guy grinned, and struck some spontaneous Schwarzenegger-style *Pumping Iron* poses to play up to the crowd. Cheers went up, more laughter.

Someone passed the red leather guy a streaming flag. The spectators fell silent. Music systems were killed, dance moves abandoned. All you could hear was the growl of the racers' engines like a swarm of gigantic bees. Red Leather Guy conferred with his comms team through his walkie, then he nodded. He turned to address the crowd, palms out like a rock star:

'The police have all their resources tied up with a warehouse fire in western SoMa,' he announced. 'So let's do this thing!'

The flag whipped up and hung there, trembling. All eyes were pinned to that billowing scarlet banner, transfixed by spears of rain.

The flag swept downwards.

Air horns boomed. The crowd roared.

And twenty cars screamed out over the spray-painted blue starting line and plunged down into the sloping chaos of night-time San Francisco below.

Navarro was streaking ahead, her windows and wheel trims flicking back reflections as if they were fireflies. The other cars were relegated to playing catch-up, the jock's yellow Ford Mustang Shelby GT500, a black Dodge Viper, two virtually identical scarlet Honda NSXs and a surprisingly sluggish Chevrolet Chevelle SS in dirty gold driven by a Haitian with cornrow dreads. Their trailing cars jerked clumsily in and out of hairpin corners which Navarro flew through with deft Scandinavian flicks and high-gear handbrake turns.

Tyres screeched and skidded alarmingly in the

driving rain, which was now hammering down like the wrath of God itself. Droplets exploded, rebounded, hissed like fat on a hotplate. Visibility plunged alarmingly. Navarro, however, seemed to be driving by radar as she never slowed or faltered. In spite of the weather, she manoeuvred with a fearlessness born out of either supreme confidence, or an utter recklessness that bordered on a death wish. It was as bravura a performance of advanced driving as you were ever likely to see. Beneath his professional appreciation for her abilities Tanner's unease for the Julia Jaybird he once knew was growing steadily.

Jericho had outlined a merciless obstacle course for the candidates. Initially, all the cars flashed along parallel metal ravines, before swerving out into the designated 'track' itself. The course snaked all around the maze of cargo containers and silent hulks of loading machinery that dotted the darkened dock. Jericho had even press ganged Bowman and Quentin into manning a couple of forklifts – the former with casual, lollipop-chewing efficiency, the latter with over-excitable mania – to rearrange various crates to construct an even more challenging jumble of blockades and blind spots. The wharf had been transformed into a treacherous puzzle designed to push the drivers' skills – and their reaction times – to their limits. It was the automotive equivalent of trying to thread a needle on a rollercoaster: you needed absolute concentration, a rock-steady grip, and a strong stomach.

Tanner, Jericho, Bowman and Quentin sheltered under the overhanging cowl of a security shed to observe the race, ragged sheets of rainwater spilling around them in a fine mist.

'Your girl there's gonna toast this fer sure,' Bowman observed. He was leaning against one of the peeling yellow bars that surrounded the security hut. The railings made it feel as if they were in a judge's enclosure, and Tanner had a momentary flash that they should have brought score cards to hold up.

'What's her name again, cousin Tanner?' Bowman drawled.

'Navarro. Julia Navarro,' Tanner murmured, his gaze locked on to the distant turmoil of whirling wheels and speeding chassis.

'So you knew her back in the day?' Jericho asked simply. He stood with his arms crossed, feet apart, unconcerned by the downpour or its backsplash.

Tanner hesitated for half a beat: Jericho seemed relaxed and conversational, but this was a topic as slippery as the wet wharf. He needed to tread very carefully, and not get drawn into any dangerous improvisations. Stick to the established legend.

'Yeah, a bit. Knew her brother better – half-brother really. He was my buddy. We pulled street races together in SF. She moved to New Orleans with her pa when she was still a kid. Don't know what happened to my bro in the end. We . . . lost touch.'

Jericho nodded without looking back at Tanner. He wasn't radiating any increased suspicion.

'She's good. Real good,' Jericho observed drily of Navarro's crisp gear control. As they watched she pulled a textbook 180-degree J-turn, stunt driver-style. It allowed her to escape a dead end before being blocked in by the crush of her straggling competitors.

'Yep. She really is.' In spite of all his misgivings Tanner couldn't keep the affectionate admiration out of his voice. Julia Navarro had turned into one helluva a driver.

The low friction surface the rain had caused was actually a gift for many of the gnarlier manoeuvres the drivers were attempting – it made it easier for a car's back end to slide when handbraking, for instance – but it was also what caused the first casualty. The jock was bringing up the rear and desperate to catch the leaders. He attempted to coax the Shelby into a hasty drift round one of the shallower maze corners, but he just didn't have enough torque going into the turn to keep the rear wheels spinning once he'd started the oversteering. The Shelby's rear swung out and slammed into one of the larger steel containers, crumpling his wing and bringing the car to a shrieking halt. The jock gamely tried to restart the Shelby and the engine caught first time, but when he tried to pull away the wheels just spun on air. A quick look over his shoulder showed him that his bumper had been partially ripped away and become hooked up on the dented crate. He wasn't going anywhere without getting out in the rain and physically freeing the Shelby, probably with a tyre iron. The jock was done.

The black Dodge, the Chevrolet and the Hondas roared on through the remainder of the container course, still trying to catch Navarro. Tanner was torn. Did he really want her to win? It would undoubtedly complicate this already vexed operation even more.

The first stage of the race saw the competitors zigzag their way out towards the far limits of the dock, beyond easy sighting range of the security hut. Tanner strained to hear their engines over the rush of the storm. Soon the pack reappeared, though: the return leg was more or less a straight run all the way along the water's edge.

Navarro's lead was intact, but the two red Hondas were harrying her closely. Suddenly they began manoeuvring in concert, working together to box her in. Navarro fought valiantly, but one Honda pulled up beside her and kept fishtailing, which drove her to inch inexorably towards the edge of the dock, while the Honda behind constantly rode her bumper, knocking and clipping and shoving. Neither driver seemed to care if they damaged their bodywork, just as long as they spun her out of contention.

'That's not part of the game plan, Jericho,' Tanner told the hitman, trying to keep his unease in check. 'They aren't supposed to co-ordinate and they certainly aren't meant to work together to fuck the others over.'

But Jericho merely shrugged, indifferent. 'When

they go out on assignments they'll have to synchronize and work as a team, anyway. They're showing initiative and it's not like we're hiring boy scouts to run Meals on Wheels.'

Tanner snapped his gaze away from Jericho and stared back into the swirling rain, strumming with impotent concern. His cheeks gleamed with water, but his mouth was dry. Navarro was being driven off the wharf, and while Tanner's face only showed mild professional interest, his hands gripped the yellow railing so hard his knuckles were white.

Tanner's knuckles were white on the steering wheel, his breathing a tight fast semaphore. The olive Cobra boomed over a hump, neck and neck with Slater's Eclipse as they barrelled at 60 miles an hour down the perilously steep Taylor Street. This was the most famous stretch of the Bullitt run, a recreation of the teeth-rattling chase from the eponymous sixties thriller.

Tanner was leading the pack with Slater. The others were lost way back in the matrix of streets behind them, having fallen prey to capricious traffic, question-able engine maintenance, or each other's sabotaging plays. Now it had become as much a battle of wills for Tanner and Slater as it was a contest over who had the better-maintained machine or possessed the faster reflexes: each driver was determined he would not be beaten. For the two young men, this race had the intensity of a family feud.

The Taylor Street incline was sharp, but not a uniform slope. This meant that every time cars hit an intersection they would level off, momentarily, then be launched up into the air as they cleared the cross street. Both cars struck such a jump at sixty-five then soared through a 20-foot arc of faith – Tanner's stomach felt as if it had dropped straight through his ass and out of the bottom of the car – before landing on the street again with suspension-wrecking force. The cars bounced like spacehoppers tossed out of a helicopter. Neither man was worried his vehicle wouldn't survive the drop. Even at nineteen they knew more about the capabilities of these machines than all the subjects they'd taken at school. The real concern was that if you didn't land just right the wheels might dig in and the car could flip. If it flipped once on a gradient like this then it'd keep on tumbling all the way down to the bottom and your chances of surviving that were close to zero.

This meant that Tanner and Slater's fanatical rivalry could turn deadly given even the tiniest error. Neither of them were willing to throttle back, though. They dived on down the hill, barely in control of the head-long plunge or their fiery emotions. Tanner stole a glance through his side window and saw Slater hunched over the wheel like a twisted demon, his hands like inhuman claws on the wheel. It was a shock. Sure, Tanner felt an overpowering adrenalin rush and the burning desire to win, but it wasn't turning him into someone who looked like that . . . was it?

Somewhere behind them the wail of police sirens pealed out. Given how well prepared the race had been, it was a shame that the cops had swung into action so quickly. Already, pursuit cars would be trying to run down the swarm of slower competitors, while many of the drivers would choose to simply abandon the race instead and melt away into the night. Sure, this might mean they'd forfeit their cars to the pink-slip trade, but at least they'd stay out of jail and enjoy a few days driving around before the organizers came to collect – though collect they certainly would. The organizers were a very serious, dangerous criminal syndicate. They were people you definitely honoured your debts to if you wanted to retain all your soft extremities. Perversely, this was the same reason these illegal races were so attractive to ambitious drivers: serious gang involvement guaranteed an equally serious purse for the winner. Many thousands of dollars could be made in just one thrilling night.

The Cobra and the Eclipse swerved into Filbert Street going west, and powered away still in lock-step, neither driver prepared to give even an inch to the other. Both drivers were matched in skill and speed, weaving in between the sparse traffic, running straight through traffic lights as if they were nothing more than Christmas lights strung up by the road, drifting, flicking, oversteering and feathering the throttle for all they were worth. At this speed they ate up the city streets. They flashed past bars, hotels, churches, Safeway supermarkets, parks; all in a neon smear of graffiti and night-blued colours.

Of course, it was only possible to approximate the famous Steve McQueen chase in the real world. The march of time had altered pertinent street geography and the film-makers themselves had cut and pasted reality to fit their own narrative, teleporting from Russian Hill to Larkin to Daly City willy-nilly whenever they pleased. To compensate the race organizers had conjured up a hair-raising route that stitched together enough of the iconic set pieces from the original to honour its spirit. However, it was one of those jigsaw stitchings that finally gave Tanner the edge. Both cars veered down an alley leading towards the next movie-star hill. Slater's acceleration faltered for a second, though, as he reacted to a road he'd only seen in the daytime, but which was now clogged with parked cars.

Tanner seized his moment and surged in front of his friend, effectively blocking Slater out. The alley was so narrow that with all the parked cars there was simply no room for Slater to pass him. Tanner knew his friend would lose thousands and forfeit his beloved Eclipse but the sensation he experienced when he passed Slater was still one of the sweetest he'd had in his entire life.

Afterwards, Tanner relaxed. He was confident that with this lead, his superior knowledge of the route and the performance limits on both cars that he could keep ahead of Slater and cruise all the way to the finish line without breaking a sweat. He drifted gracefully out of the mouth of the alley heading on to the next swooping hill.

He glanced towards his side mirror and his eyes widened in alarm: Slater was trying to undertake on the corner!

'You insane fucking moron! No! You haven't got room!' Tanner hissed.

His eyes met Slater's in the rear-view's cold surface: Slater's face was a twisted mask of concentration. A look of inflexible, frantic obsession. His friend had pushed beyond all his own performance limits. Like a car stress-tested to destruction he'd lost the ability to put on the emotional brakes. All Tanner could do was accelerate and keep on trying to win, whatever the cost.

An instant away from being barged into the Mississippi, Navarro went on the offensive. Taking a leaf out of her attackers' playbook, she played ruthless with her ride and twitched momentarily on the brake to startle her pursuer. The Honda driver following her also instinctively stamped on his brake and jerked back, which allowed Navarro the stolen second she needed to get behind the car that had been shoving her from the side.

She intentionally clipped the second Honda.

The rival car spun out of control, its hood whipping wildly around. Momentum pulled its wheels against the lip of the wharf's edge and tipped the car on one side. A plume of sparks launched out as it ground along its wing for the fraction of an instant. Then the car nosed over the brink – dipped – and plummeted.

The river cratered and threw back an explosion of water on to the dock as it greedily swallowed the Honda. The vehicle wallowed for agonizing moments before sliding beneath the glassy surface.

But Navarro's wheels had also locked. While the Honda was dragged underneath the water, Navarro's car spun like a top.

Time slowed into snapshot frames for Tanner, as it always did when action bloomed around him. He was aware of raindrops crystallizing in the air, the rough edge of his leather collar cutting across the back of his neck, the cold dumb bar of the railing clenched between his palms. The amber glow of sodium light flared like a camera flash. Normally, when action exploded near Tanner he was the one causing it, and he could at least intervene directly. Here, he was marooned in frozen desperate time, powerless to help.

For a heart-stopping moment, he thought there was no way Navarro could tame her rotation, and must surely follow the Honda's trajectory over the side—

The second Honda flashed past Navarro's whirling car.

The dirty gold Chevrolet zoomed past and struck the spinning S2000 a glancing blow.

The driver of the first Honda bobbed to the surface with a screaming gasp.

The impact from the Chevrolet turned out to be a tiny miracle. It checked Navarro's spiralling momentum by just enough for her to wrest back control of the S2000 and coax it to a shuddering standstill, mere inches from the lip of the wharf. After that . . . nothing. Tanner watched intently, eyes narrowed. The car just sat there. Was Navarro injured?

As Tanner stared at the S2000, the second Honda roared past him over the finish line, but it didn't break his concentration. It was followed a moment later by the slightly limping Chevrolet. The less fortunate Mustang driver hauled himself out of the water on to a slimy metal ladder set into the wall of the wharf. Once back on land he trudged towards the security cabin, sopping wet and miserable. He paused to shoot a look of furious, impotent frustration at the silent S2000.

The S2000's engine coughed, revved, turned over, once, twice before finally catching. The headlights burst into life and the vehicle started to chug its wounded way towards the finish line, moving like a marathon runner who's hit the Wall and is now tottering along on sheer ragged willpower alone. Gradually, however, the car picked up speed until it was tearing towards them at a fantastic lick.

Whoosh, Julia Navarro blazed over the finish line. But she didn't brake there, she carried on going back into the maze of shipping containers and proceeded to run through an entire lap of the whole track.

Quentin cackled and punched the air.

'That was some full-on *Wacky Races* shit right there!' he exclaimed with squeaky excitement.

* * *

As they screamed round the corner Slater lost control.

In the mirror Tanner saw the frenzy of his hands blurring on the steering wheel. The Eclipse fishtailed, slewing wildly across both lanes. A yellow cab was speeding up the slope in the other direction, and swerved desperately on to the sidewalk to avoid Slater. The combined screech of tyres, screaming of engines and outraged bawl of the taxi's horn was what Tanner thought the end of the world might sound like. Acting on sheer impulse, he kicked his accelerator to keep ahead of the catastrophe unfolding behind him.

Rubber was left in scorched stretches on the black-top and the Eclipse scraped along the line of parked cars like a wood-planing tool, but miraculously Slater managed to control the skid. Something still wasn't quite right, though – buckled wheels, or wrecked suspension – and this threw shudders all through the vehicle. Velocity threw them straight into the next intersection, launching both cars up into the night air again. Tanner's Cobra seemed to float in space for an endless beat, before returning to earth with a bone-jangling jolt. Slater landed a second later, but something wasn't right.

The Eclipse flipped.

Tanner watched the vehicle pirouette over and over in the letterbox of his rear-view mirror, looking more like a toy than a ton of high-performance precision racing car. He held his breath as the car struck—

Slater had shot into the leap at a slight angle, which meant that, mercifully, the Eclipse didn't roll all the way down to the bottom of hill. Instead, it barrelled end over end four or five times diagonally before slamming into a stationary white camper van.

Tanner screeched to halt, panting like a frightened dog.

He craned over his shoulder to look back along the trail of devastation the Eclipse had left, a path of twisted metal, pulverized glass and shredded rubber. Motor oil was splashed around like a Jackson Pollock abstract. Sirens were already screaming up the block, racing towards the corner of the nearest intersection, an ambulance and two or three police cars. They'd be here in seconds. The air flared with their strobes, painting Tanner's cheek alternately with ice and flame.

The centre of the camper van had been crushed like a cardboard box someone had stood on. The Eclipse occupied that concertinaed divot, upended on its roof, steaming, ticking, leaking dark fluids, which had begun to trickle down the incline towards Tanner's Mustang Cobra. Tanner couldn't stop himself from staring at those ominous rivulets as they slowly approached him.

Tanner was nineteen, high on excitement and fear, trembling with the after-burn of an adrenalin over-dose. Every fibre of his being screamed at him to reverse back up the hill to try to help his friend; however, he knew if he did so he'd be immediately arrested and almost certain to face jail time. What's more, genuine trained medical support was mere moments away, so what could he realistically to do to aid Slater?

Yet there was a darker truth at play in Tanner's reluctance: he simply couldn't face what he might find inside that pounded metal shell. He already blamed himself for this tragedy. If he'd only throttled back when he realized how unbalanced Slater had become then this might never have happened. This was guilt that Tanner simply wasn't equipped to deal with right now.

Tanner kicked his accelerator and streaked away down the hill.

It was the hardest decision he'd ever had to make, and it still haunted him fifteen years on. How different his life might have been if he'd made a different decision that night.

Julia Jaybird's brother didn't die, but he was gravely injured. Slater spent the next four months in intensive care as a pre-trial detainee, followed by an extensive course of physical therapy as an in-patient at a secure rehab unit. After that he stood trial on multiple counts of reckless endangerment in the first degree, of which he was convicted, and attempted vehicular man-slaughter, of which, thankfully, he wasn't. The next time Tanner saw his friend was across a chipped plastic-topped table in a state correctional facility. Slater hadn't mentioned Tanner at any time during his trial, so the young wheelman had escaped any legal penalties for his involvement in the race.

At first Slater had refused to see Tanner. When he finally consented to the meeting he was surly and uncommunicative. The facial scars he'd been left with, and the prosthesis he wore to replace the leg that had been amputated beneath the knee, had made his time in jail even more difficult. He'd become withdrawn, depressed, and regularly got into fights. This meant he ended up bonding with a clan of tough career criminals. Slater coldly made it clear that he didn't want anything more to do with his friend. He was cutting all the ties with his old life. There was no way he could have the future he'd once planned. Instead, he just had to take whatever other opportunities were offered to him, however violent and unpalatable. He intended to quarantine himself, so that the disaster he'd made of his life wouldn't infect those who had been closest to him. He was telling Tanner to his face, but he'd already decided that he wouldn't see Julia, her father Ernesto or his mother again, precisely because they meant so much to him. After he'd delivered this message he briskly asked the guards to return him to his cell and Tanner was left with no option but to leave, struck numb with remorse.

This outcome turned out to be just the wake-up call young John Tanner needed. It was a bucket of ice water thrown over his life at exactly the right moment, just when he was poised, teetering, over two potential futures. The day after he visited Jason in jail Tanner applied to join the police force.

From that point onwards it seemed as if Tanner and Slater's lives described parallel-universe trajectories, following two possible arcs originating in one single shattering event. They'd been as close as brothers once, and similar in so many ways, but now they peeled off in diametrically opposed directions: one became the poster child for how discipline and direction could turn your life around; while the other was a cautionary tale illustrating how violence only breeds more violence, and that impatience, anger and resentment were no substitute for a vocation. As a cop Tanner tried to keep an eye on Slater's progress, but the reports he got back were never pretty. They described a succession of increasingly serious run-ins with law enforcement, lengthier and lengthier prison sentences, and the gradual transformation of a once-promising young man into an unrepentant felon. For his own part, Tanner's career with the SFPD streaked ahead like a perfectly maintained race car. He felt he was really helping people. He had a route to follow and a map showing him how to get there.

The last time Tanner saw his former best friend, Slater was dressed in an orange jumpsuit and was chained to a gang of ferocious, sullen tattooed thugs as they all shuffled their way on to a prison bus heading for a full life sentence at San Quentin.

It was the same day Tanner won his promotion from patrol officer to police detective. As he held the gleaming badge in the palm of his hand he thought how different his life could have been.

Chapter Nine

The gang was deep in conference outside the security hut. It was some time later and the storm had finally eased. The sky above was cloudless and creamy with a hint of moonlight. In the distance Tanner could hear the yelp of hounds, possibly guard dogs at the gatehouse alerted by early morning revellers weaving their way back home.

Navarro, the squat Haitian and the black Dodge Viper driver – a thin, soft-spoken Canadian with the eyes of a serial murderer – waited quietly in a semicircle beside their cooling rides. The surly jock had managed to get his Shelby unhitched and clattered off into the night, probably to get slaughtered in some all-night truck stop where he'd bore a gum-chewing waitress with bitter stories of his high school sports glories and how he 'coulda been a contender'. The red Honda drivers – a couple of Japanese-American twins – went to see if they could find some lifting gear to drag the submerged car out of the drink. All the failed contenders were too terrified of the Indian – and humiliated by their performance in the race – ever to breathe a word of the evening's events to anyone outside of the gang.

'Navarro's the best,' Jericho stated flatly.

'But she didn't come in first. She was last of the losers,' Bowman rumbled. 'She's a hothead behind the wheel, reckless. Plus, you saw how she riles the troops. Is it really a good idea to have a driver on your team that all the others want to get with? Having a kitten as fine as that in your crew *always* breeds bad blood.'

Jericho shrugged, conceding the point. He swung his beams on to Tanner.

'I'm a "yes", Bowman says "no". You've got the casting vote, Tanner. She'll be on your team when we go on the raid tomorrow, your responsibility. Do you want her in?'

'Doesn't anyone care what I think?' Quentin blurted. Jericho and Bowman both turned very slowly to stare at him. 'Never mind,' the kid muttered.

Tanner tried to compose his thoughts. How had it come to this? An undercover police officer wasn't meant to direct the subjects of an operation. That way led to entrapment and mistrial, and the whole house of cards tumbling down. Yet here he was being asked to decide a young woman's future on a storm-swept dock with a crew of villains and only his own severely dented moral compass to guide him. He glanced off across the water. A shining rill of light was creeping along the horizon. It would be dawn soon, a whole new day.

Tanner blew out a tired breath and made his choice.

* * *

Tanner wandered over to the waiting candidates, maintaining a carefully neutral expression as he closed the distance. They all straightened in front of their cars and unconsciously arranged themselves into poses resembling the poster for a bad action movie. A fresh clean wind stirred their hair, but already you could sense the muggy Louisiana heat recharging. It was like a muttered threat: don't get too comfortable, the hatred of nature never tires.

'Guys, Jericho wants a word,' Tanner told the Haitian and Canadian Killer Eyes. 'He'll give you your instructions. Well done. Those are some fine skills you got.'

Navarro's lips tightened. Her jaw went hard and her gaze became glassy with furious insolence. The other drivers exchanged speculative looks, glanced curiously at Navarro, and then mutely trooped off towards the hut. Navarro stood very still, radiating resentment. Tanner tried to draw her aside, but she resisted his tug.

'You can tell me whatever you have to out here where everyone can see,' she announced coldly. 'I don't want any special treatment. I'm as good a driver as any man.'

'OK,' said Tanner with a heavy sigh. What the hell was he doing with his life? It was cold and he was wet through. He'd only had a handful of hours' sleep in the last few nights and, frankly, he was really struggling to tell the smart choices from the dumb ones these days. When you were young, everything seemed so simple. This is good, this is bad, this is right, this is wrong. Black, white, job done. It was as if all your decisions came with flashing neon subtitles. You get to your thirties and you realize you as might as well just throw dice for all the good it does you. He passed Navarro a blurry map print-out.

'Go to this crossroads tomorrow at midnight. That's where we'll be mustering for the assignment. Drive the S2000 and bring something to hide your face,' he told her in a matter-of-fact tone. 'You're in.'

Tanner didn't know what reaction he'd been expecting, but, given how much fire she'd put into defending her right to compete, Navarro surprised him by simply nodding.

'Don't bring heat,' Tanner continued. 'We'll be given pistols, probably, but the idea is to never have to use them. We're drivers, not muscle. Understand?'

Navarro nodded again. There was something in her face, some mix of intense feelings churning deep down, which he couldn't quite identify.

'Aren't you going to shake my hand and welcome me to the firm, then?' she asked in a sardonic husk of a voice, her face drawn and pale in the harsh electric glow.

Tanner glanced over his shoulder at Jericho, who was deep in conversation with Bowman and the other drivers. Grainy light glinted off the barrels of his shotguns, peeking out of their holsters round his hips. Jericho sensed the weight of Tanner's attention and looked over. His eyes were like black empty holes cut in the mask of his face.

'Not tonight,' said Tanner softly, and then shivered involuntarily.

A gull cried plaintively in the distance, searching for somewhere safe to land.

After the try-outs Tanner went back to his NOPD-supplied studio apartment and knocked back a few shots of Jack Daniel's while strumming his battered steel-string bass guitar (which he never seemed to get any better at, probably because he only ever practised while drinking). The department had rented Jones a spindly three-storey house in the genteel Garden quarter – a verdant oasis of gothic plantation style mansions and wide cypress-lined boulevards – but Tanner needed to be slap bang at the heart of the action in the French Quarter.

He listened to the couple arguing next door and tried to come to terms with the choices he'd made. He watched the morning steal its way into the room, touching all the bland objects with lemon fingertips. The apartment was a sterile attic conversion decorated with all the homely warmth of an android choosing furniture out of an Ikea catalogue. The place was little more than the abstract sum of varnished floorboards, insipid black and white wall prints and orthopaedic chairs designed by sadists. Dispiritingly anonymous, it felt more like a bar in a movie than a space anyone actually lived in, especially on nights like these when any sense of human connection was already hard to come by.

Tanner mostly sat on the bed, which was appealingly retro and therefore the only comfortable piece of furniture in the apartment, rather than the malevolent chairs, or dangled his feet off on the little balcony to watch the neighbourhood ebb and flow below. There was an attractively seedy bar on the ground floor that played live music until three in the morning and as far as his informal observations could gather catered exclusively to women in tight-fitting dresses with skin the colour of mocha coffee and men wearing iridescent shirts and suit jackets who moved with the agile twitch of flamenco dancers.

After a while – or at least after a few more shots – Tanner started to relax into his decisions, and even came to see the positive potential in what he'd done. Half a bottle later, when he probably wouldn't have still been able to spell the word 'rationalization', he had become actively optimistic about how the night's events had turned out. He reasoned it this way: now he would actually be with Navarro whenever she was in danger. They were both in the gang, and driving together, so he could keep an eye out for her and, quite legitimately, bail her out of any rough spots. He would be her Tobias Jones, her guardian angel.

All right, it was true he would have to record any crimes she committed during the course of his undercover operations, but a crucial component of building a watertight case against the Indian was to find witnesses willing to testify against him. Who better to try and flip than Navarro? He was sure he could persuade Powell into offering her immunity for what would be her, comparatively, minor infractions in return for handing him the Indian on a plate.

To Tanner's inebriated mind this seemed like a eureka moment. A line of reasoning that – far from the shores of sobriety, where he currently bobbed – actually seemed pretty sturdy. In all honesty though, the hard drinking and deep thinking was a way of avoiding his bed. Tanner found rest rarely came easy at the best of times. His mind was always buzzing with plots and schemes and feints, always five moves ahead of the enemy. As such he didn't hold out much hope for sleep on such a turbulent night as this. Still, he'd give it a shot. He leaned the bass against the wall, drained the last of the whiskey, kicked off his boots and dropped face first on to the quilt. Within seconds he was snoring away like a fat kid in an empty larder. For once, Detective John Tanner allowed himself to sleep the sleep of the just.

The next night Tanner made his way back to the fateful lock-up in the French Quarter. This was to be the first raid they'd run with Navarro on the team. He actually parked the Challenger out on the street and took a quick stroll around the block to clear his head and compose his strategy for the evening's activity. It would also allow him to check that the wire strapped to his chest was transmitting properly to Jones in the van.

The streets were almost spookily deserted, as if someone had run ahead ringing a plague bell. He passed a couple of jocks trying to persuade some students from the University of Texas that 'beads were for ALL year round, not just for Mardi Gras'. He gave a beat cop chatting to a group of teenage girls outside a cinema a very wide berth. He thought about tonight's criminal mission.

It was bizarre to think of brutal gang lords in economic terms, but tonight's raid was all about liquidity. The Indian needed cash, lots of it, and fast. He employed a vast network of soldiers, drivers, dealers, spotters, smugglers, enforcers, as well as paying out sizeable monthly bungs to various corrupt public officials. All these 'employees' were like chicks constantly cheeping in the nest, greedy beaks forever open, never satisfied. He might not have to worry about a violent assassination ending his reign – his quasi-mystical reputation saw to that – but his organization could very well implode just from simple financial mismanagement. He'd expanded so rapidly and remained this faceless legend. That was fine for constructing a bloodcurdling notoriety, but meant that he'd never claimed a social security number and only dealt with banks through proxies. It all just piled layers of unnecessary complexity on top of an already violent and fractious criminal empire.

In this context, the botched van heist was actually more of a setback than it might have initially appeared. There had been a steadily growing tide of mutters among the rank and file since the fiasco. The loss of faith was almost as serious as the loss of revenue. That was what doing the rounds of the top dealers with Jericho had been about. It was also why this new raid tonight was so important.

They were targeting the Indian's nearest rival and until a few years ago the most feared mob in all of New Orleans: La Lame Rouge, the Red Blade gang, often just called the LLR. Jean-Baptiste Lavache, the boss of the LLR, was a towering bony scarecrow of a man with blue-black skin, fake tribal cheek markings and dyed scarlet sideburns. Lavache had always been a violent and unpredictable chieftain, but with the inexorable rise of the Indian his natural instability had descended into near-psychosis. Rumour had it that he now employed homeless kids from South America as food tasters, slept with a samurai sword under his pillow (a literal red blade), and had taken to wearing a cloak woven of human hair, animal bones and 'cursed' shards of melted glass sourced from house fires. In a risible and puzzling echo of the Indian's own mythology Lavache referred to this garment as his 'voodoo coat of many colours'. As unhinged as his behaviour had become, however, the LLR remained a force to be reckoned with. Lavache still controlled a sizeable chunk of the New Orleans drugs trade, and was said to be a crack shot with his antique ivory-handled Colt .45.

The next best thing to stealing from the police was to steal from other criminals. They couldn't report the theft, couldn't call for official back-up, and they tended to have huge untraceable pots of cash just sitting around as a consequence of their day-to-day activities. If successful not only would the Indian refill his depleted coffers, but he'd deal Lavache a humiliating blow in the never-ending war of gangland propaganda.

Information had leaked out of the LLR that they were scheduled to take delivery of a vast shipment of high-grade coke with a street value of several hundred thousand dollars. The exchange was to be made tonight at an isolated location way out in the bayou at the head of a tributary leading directly to the Gulf Coast. This was how the LLR's Colombian connection was able to access the mainland and smuggle its product into the country. This was the ideal opportunity for a sneak attack: one bulk stash of drugs *and* cash all kindly gathered in one place at an isolated site far from any reinforcements.

Tonight their crew would be the four drivers – Tanner, Jericho, Bowman and now Navarro – with three other tooled-up rough nuts along as muscle, plus Quentin in case they encountered any locks which needed his very special 'open sesame' treatment.

Tanner's cell phone chirruped as it received a text message, ruining his concentration. The message also worked its way into the cracks of his hard-won composure. Jones had written: 'When u goin to xplain how letting Navarro join = a good idea?'

Tanner scowled at the text. He wasn't always wired

to record as he was tonight – not all interactions with the gang were deemed likely to generate high-value intelligence or prosecutable felonies – and it was extremely rare that he wore an earpiece to converse with Jones. There was too great a risk of accidental discovery. They had to be a bit more creative and engineer clever workarounds to communicate with each other.

Now, Tanner sent his own coded response back to his friend by flicking the microphone on his chest as hard as he could.

'Fuck you, Jones,' he muttered, needled by his colleague's scepticism. He grinned in cruel satisfaction at the image of his cool handler roaring with anger as he ripped his headphones off after the screech of feedback. 'I know what I'm doing,' Tanner asserted, before strolling down a narrow lane almost entirely choked by ivy that led to the courtyard housing the gang's lock-up.

Game time, he thought grimly as he prepared himself for the night ahead.

The illumination in the lock-up was just as dingy as before, its walls encrusted with ancient cobwebs, clods of impacted filth and dry rot. Two-thirds of the muscle were already here, a leathery fortyish biker sporting iron-hard jail-yard abs, and a Mexican kid with a scar running through the tip of his mouth so that he looked as if he was perpetually sneering. They stood impassively listening to Quentin spin outrageous stories about his imaginary romantic conquests (he was currently working through a list of beauty queens on a state-by-state basis). The third tough nut, a newly recruited guy from out of town, was yet to arrive.

Once the men were assembled they'd be setting off for the rendezvous with Navarro on the outskirts of the city. This was Bowman's suggestion, allegedly to defuse any friction her presence might cause amongst the new team. Tanner wondered if Bowman's paranoia about Navarro's disrupting the crew was just projection, and masked a wild attraction of his own. He'd always considered the hulking Creole to be one of the most level-headed members of the Indian's gang, but, really, who knew? He resolved to keep a closer eye on him in future when Navarro was around.

Keen not to let the 'pre-match' tension in the garage disrupt his focus, Tanner drifted over to the work-bench where he examined the collection of weapons Jericho had assembled for the raid. They peeped through the yawning wound of an unzipped sports bag, glistening like viscera. Tanner selected a M4 Super 90 combat shotgun and worked its well-oiled action appreciatively.

'Do we know what sort of hardware they're going to be packing?' he asked Jericho over his shoulder. 'This is a good-sized team we've got, but that shipment is crucial to the LLR. We all know how paranoid Lavache is. I don't like surprises. We expecting Uzis? IEDs? Rocket launchers?'

'We've got all the firepower we need here,' Jericho

responded with robotic calm. 'It's in, out. Smash and grab. The money and the shit goes in the bags, we go out the door. Ten minutes tops. Our final guy just sent a message to say he's walking up now.'

While they talked, Quentin was playing his court jester role, attempting to explain why his pistol was such a cheap potential death trap.

'See, look, I know my gun's a total piece of shit. When I've earned my place in this crew, then I'll get a better gun. Until then I'm just a Jedi Apprentice. Darth Vader wouldn't give an apprentice no light sabres straight off the bat, would he?'

He peered expectantly round his audience for approval. Jericho, Bowman, the Mexican kid and the biker all stared at him for a long interval without a reaction. None of them blinked, so Quentin appealed elsewhere for support. 'You know what I'm talking 'bout, don't ya, Tanner? I'm like a Jedi Apprentice, aren't I?'

'I don't have a single clue what you're talking about, Quentin, no,' Tanner told him laconically. Quentin groaned and shook his head in exaggerated disbelief. In spite of himself Tanner snorted with amusement.

He had begun to relax a little. This was more like a standard operation for him. He could work with this. He was proving his worth to Jericho, cementing his trust, getting closer and closer to meeting the Indian. Also, he was gathering concrete evidence that could be used to charge gang members or flip them later on. There were no more ex-best friend's half-sisters to pop out of the woodwork, nor idiotic political double crosses from his own side to deal with. His mission was tuned up, fully serviced, and running smooth as a freshly churned butter . . .

. . . or so he thought, until the third enforcer, the new guy in town, arrived. Sean Shields, a truly ferocious thug from Frisco's notorious Tenderloin district, swaggered into the room and stared straight at Detective John Tanner.

The man who'd put him behind bars five years ago.

Chapter Ten

Six years earlier, when Tanner had first met Sean 'Black Pepper' Shields, the brutal Irish-American bruiser had been an enforcer for the O'Leary family in their crime-ridden little patch of San Francisco's Tenderloin district, located on the southern slope of Nob Hill. The O'Learys operated out of a strip joint called Bang! Bang! and Shields had been brought in to help defend them against a vicious challenge from the Filipino Bahala Na gang. Rumour had it that he'd been the button man for a series of audacious but horrifying broad daylight shootings on Bahala Na senior leadership. After the war burned itself out like an over-extended forest fire, however, Shields became a trusted figure to the O'Learys. He doled out punishment beatings to debt defaulters, uppity mom-and-pop store owners who refused to cough up their protection money, or over-ambitious street soldiers. His favourite technique – and how he got his street name – was to walk nonchalantly past his victim on the street, then at the last moment pepper spray them in the face before delightedly setting about them with a ball-peen hammer.

That was bad enough, but it was Shields's recreationally vile behaviour which had really rung Tanner's bat phone. The Bang! Bang! was a deeply unsavoury joint, the cover for a prostitution ring and heavy drug-dealing. Shields was nominally in charge of all discipline within the gang's operations and took it upon himself to 'educate' a number of the dancers in spectacularly brutal and depraved ways for a host of spurious transgressions. Tanner vowed to put him behind bars for the rest of his cowardly, moronic life. He half succeeded.

Tanner pursued Shields relentlessly. Whenever the thug turned around to drop a candy wrapper, Tanner was there cold-eyeing him, grinning like the devil on execution day. This quickly drove Shields into a constant state of macho paranoia, snapping at everything, posturing and resorting to unreasoning violence at the slightest provocation, which was when he got sloppy and made the mistake that brought Tanner to his doorstep at three a.m., bearing a blood-stained swatch of fabric and a DNA sampling kit. Shields hadn't wanted to accompany Tanner and his friends from the homicide unit at first, and he definitely hadn't wanted to provide a DNA sample, but that just meant Tanner got to experience the grim satisfaction of grinding his cheek into the sidewalk in front of all his gaping neighbours.

It was a darkly sweet moment, but it didn't last too

long. When the brutal enforcer came to trial his defence dug up irregularities in how physical evidence on the case had been stored. Tanner strongly suspected that a thick vein of O'Leary corruption ran through the department and someone had been paid to mishandle evidence. Their case was in danger of collapsing completely and the prosecution was forced to offer Shields a deal. He got eight years, served six. Disgust at that outcome had been one of the major factors that had driven Tanner into undercover work. He had wanted to make bringing those thugs down a very personal experience. He wanted to look them square in the eyes as he beat them. From that point on Tanner had to have complete control over his cases, or he wouldn't even take them on.

Back in the present, Tanner saw Shields. Shields saw him. His mouth fell open as he stared in disbelief.

Shields *recognized* him.

'HEY!' Shields roared, his face contorting with hatred. It was all he managed to get out before Tanner smashed his jaw with all his might.

'Fucking snitch!' Tanner screamed.

Shields reeled from the haymaker, leaking a bloody cascade from his shattered mouth. The thug staggered and almost fell. He spat a loosened tooth out on to the filthy concrete and his eyes filled with a bestial rage. He let out an unthinking bellow and launched himself at the undercover cop without another coherent word. It was exactly as Tanner had planned.

'You fucking rat!' the cop yelled at Shields. 'You

fucking sold me out in the Little Saigon heist, you fuck! The cops flipped you and you led them straight to our Skid Row hide-out! You sold us ALL out—'

Whuff.

Shields tackled Tanner and his bulk and momentum drove them to the hard floor, knocking the wind out of the cop. Still, he was nimble enough to swing his attacker's weight around so he didn't end up trapped beneath the burly thug.

The fight that followed was a clumsy, ill-disciplined ruck as so much spontaneous violence is apt to become. They spun together on the garage floor, kicking up plumes of dust, each man holding the other in torturous body locks to prevent the other from delivering any knock-out blows. They just traded a succession of gut jabs, rabbit punches and muddy flails, though that was certainly enough to cause a host of minor injuries, cuts, contusions and serious bruises.

Crucially, though, neither man was able to gather enough breath to issue any further accusations, much to Tanner's satisfaction. During the combat, the rest of the gang members just stood around staring in bafflement at the unexplained fury unfolding on the floor. Finally Jericho bellowed for a halt, and the Mexican lad and the biker pulled the combatants apart. A wide demilitarized zone was dragged out between the bellowing men.

'Duhn't lissthen tuh him,' Shields tried to say the moment they were divided, gurgling incoherently through his cracked jaw and broken teeth, both of which Tanner had specifically targeted so he'd end up sounding exactly like this

'He'th a copth! He'th a futhing copth!' Shields half shouted, but just ended up squirting a mist of spittle and blood and dribbling pink mucus on to his T-shirt collar. Some of the flecks drifted on to Jericho's boot cap.

The hitman didn't respond for a moment, then he slowly swivelled to stare blankly at Tanner, who had levered himself back on to his feet to gain a height advantage on Shields, who still rolled around in the dirt like a snorting hog. Tanner's chest heaved as he tried to catch his breath, observing the hitman closely. Jericho still had Quentin's 9 mill in his grip. Tanner's muscles coiled, preparing to leap aside if the need arose.

'That man is a cop?' said Jericho to Shields. 'That man saved my life.'

He shot Shields in the stomach.

The thug let loose a sound like a cross between a roar and an air canister bursting. He was kicked on to his back by the force of the blast. His gut had been drilled with a wet red pit, his shirt and skin torn so badly that it was difficult to tell which was which at a cursory glance. Wine-dark blood gushed out in waves, soaking his khaki pants as the pool spread out from him with alarming speed. After his initial cry Shields fell silent with shock. Now, as the pain really began to bite, he started to hiss and kick his legs in a blurring frenzy like a half-dead steer run over by a pick-up truck. His face, deformed by Tanner's previous beating, wrenched into an agonized knot.

Quentin stared on in frozen horror.

'T-that was my gun. Y-you used *my* gun!' he finally stammered once his tongue had thawed out.

'He's a snitch.' Jericho shrugged indifferently. 'Bullets from that shitty peashooter are all he deserves. It'd be an insult to my shotguns to kill him with them.'

Tanner stared across at Jericho. This was a crucial moment. There must still be a tiny worm of suspicion crawling at the back of his mind after Shields's accusation. How Tanner reacted next would be critical in determining whether that worm began to grow, or shrivelled away to nothing.

'Thanks,' said Tanner with a bloody grin, teeth reddened from a busted lip.

Jericho nodded his acknowledgement before chambering another round into the 9 mill and aiming it nonchalantly at Shields's head. Tanner started to chuckle. Jericho shot him a puzzled look. Tanner shook his head, making a big play of trying to suppress his laughter. It wasn't so easy, as Shields was wheezing pitiably, like a wounded animal, or a crying child – a sound that burrowed right down to your core.

'Let's leave him,' said Tanner with a thoughtful grin, as if he was just working out this extra horror right there and then. 'Do you know how painful a shot to the gut is? The stomach is filled with hydrochloric acid. As the blood begins to mix with the acid, it causes fatal toxaemia, and agonizing, screaming torture. It's the only death a snitch deserves. This place is sound-proofed. We chain it up, leave him to bleed out. We can send in some clean-up guys later to dispose of the body, or even give it to the Indian to feed to his dogs.'

Quentin stared, eyes huge, aghast. Jericho, however, nodded his approval.

'This is why I like you, Tanner. Like I said before—you're savage when it counts the most. These here are the sort of deeds the Indian built his reputation upon. I think he may actually want to meet you some day soon.'

Tanner didn't react. He didn't know how to react to being likened in a complimentary fashion to a psychopath like the Indian. He wondered, briefly, what it would be like to meet Shields's mother and say, 'I was just doing my job.'

Jericho proffered the pistol back to Quentin, who stared at it as if it was a live scorpion. He swallowed. His fear of Jericho eventually overcame his disgust, and he gingerly accepted the firearm.

'Dump it in the swamp,' Jericho told him, raising his voice slightly over Shields's wet moans. 'And spend the extra money next time to get yourself a grown-up's gun. You're in the major leagues now.'

Quentin nodded numbly, his face grey. He looked as sick as Tanner felt. The cop didn't betray his stress, though. He was used to hiding his trauma in plain sight.

'We need to get rolling, brothers,' Bowman said softly from his station in the shadows by the workbenches. 'We need to meet our kitten at the rendezvous.' His teeth gems caught the light weirdly, so that for an instant it looked as if Bowman was metal on the inside. Quentin didn't need any more persuading. He was already at the door, desperate to escape the terrible room. He wouldn't even glance at Shields trembling in the grime as he passed by.

The Mexican kid and the biker exited next, followed by Jericho, who might as well have been cleaning his nails for all emotion he showed after having just shot another human being in the gut. Tanner risked one last look at the leaking sack that was Sean Shields. He was curled up into an anguished comma, barely clinging on to life.

As Tanner turned to follow the others out of the building his heart was racing and a metallic taste coated the back of his throat. He instinctively touched his collarbone, where the wire was attached.

'Goddamnit, Jones, please be on the ball tonight,' he whispered to himself.

Then he snapped off the light on the dying man.

'Man, that was cold,' Quentin mumbled in the car, shaking in the passenger seat beside Tanner. 'D-did ya hear how that poor bastard was screeching? That didn't have to go down that way . . . I mean, did it?'

125

The Challenger brought up the rear after Bowman's Cadillac and Jericho's Dodge, racing quietly through the outskirts of the city. Neighbourhoods gradually spread out, frayed, before finally fading raggedly into proper countryside. The radio was on, but way down low, fading in and out of some southern Baptist preacher who had such a surfeit of godly fervour in him that he felt he had to keep beaming his fire and brimstone out into the airwaves no matter what time of night or day. The darkness outside the window was so deep in places that it seemed to stick to the windscreen like spats of ink.

Tanner was preoccupied. He chewed his lip. Shields was his own minor breed of demon, but he'd certainly been innocent of the crimes Jericho had punished him for. Crimes Tanner had invented. If Tanner hadn't done it, then Jericho would have shot him instead. But this was escalation, Tanner couldn't deny it. First Tycho, now Shields. It was the price he was paying for making friends with a psychopath. Clearly he needed to accelerate this mission. Worm his way into the Indian's inner circle, and put both Sepion and Jericho behind bars.

He just had to keep pushing on, even though he felt he was hip-deep in blood already. Ultimately, he'd be saving far more people if he brought the Indian down.

Quentin was whining from the passenger seat. 'Shit, fuck, fuck, fuck, I got some of that guy's vein water on my shoes. Aw shit, there's blood on my boots, dawg! What're we doing? I . . . I don't think I can go through with this, chief. Can you just drop me off here and I'll walk back to town?'

'You can't bail now,' Tanner told the kid gravely. 'Jericho will slaughter you without a second's hesitation if you leave.'

Quentin looked very small and frightened. 'Aw, shit, *shit*. Aw, see, I . . . really don't know if this is the life for me after all, Tan-man.'

'Not everyone has the stones for it, and there ain't no shame in that,' Tanner replied. 'Being good at coping with what you saw back there, it isn't something to be admired. If it didn't tear you up, kid, then you'd be turning into something less than a person.'

He glanced at the ratty little redneck and suddenly took pity on him, as if he was a mouse he'd found struggling in a trap meant for rats. He sighed for what he was about to say next.

'Look, you suck it up for tonight, keep your head down and then vanish. Go visit your country cousins. Take a plane to Europe, whatever. How you disappear, that part's up to you. But I'll cover your back if they start asking questions, OK? Only, if you ever – ever – call me Tan-man again, I'll twist your arms off myself. Geddit?'

Quentin nodded, and then stared blankly at his busted-up, bloody knock-off Timberland work boots for the rest of the drive.

Eventually they arrived at the rendezvous point, a ghostly deserted set of crossroads in a dense copse of cypress and oak. A black hump lurked in a shadow-

127

strewn lay-by: Navarro's Honda S2000 abruptly purred to life. She flashed her highbeams at them as a coded greeting.

'What kept you?' her hushed smooth tones crackled into Tanner's headset. She sounded tense already.

'Nothing you need to worry about,' Jericho growled over the common band before Tanner could answer. 'There were team-management issues that had to be worked out ... and they were. Stay there. I have something for you.'

Tanner frowned with concern. Jericho stalked across the road; his dark silhouette interrupted the glare from Narravo's headlights momentarily, like someone standing up in the cinema, and leaned into her window. Tanner caught the brief motion of his hands, and then Jericho returned to the Dodge.

'W-what was that about?' Quentin wanted to know, his fingers dancing nervously in his lap.

'He gave her a gun the cops can't trace,' Tanner answered with a grim sense of foreboding. The S2000, Dodge and Cadillac pulled away. Tanner bumped the Challenger into gear and followed smoothly, quickly picking up speed to match the others.

Together they rushed out into the looming hot night of the Louisiana bayou.

Chapter Eleven

It was like barrelling down an underground tunnel.

The limbs of the southern live oaks lining the dirt track arched over to form an oppressive canopy strung with fronds of Spanish moss lolling down from the branches like lacy pennants. The only illumination was the cones of their headlights, thrown ahead and jolting as their cars negotiated the rut-ridden pathway. They were racing through a subterranean world of gnarled wooden claws and drooping green cloaks, a mysterious alien territory half fever-dream, half B-movie sci-fi set.

Shortly, a swift shower began to filter through the branches, misting their convoy with spray; after that fallen leaves plastered the Challenger's windscreen in a haphazardly beautiful black mosaic. A moment later, the car's momentum had snatched them away, leaving only ghostly trails etched across the glass.

At one point the tree cover to their right broke and they realized they had been travelling alongside a brackish body of water coated by sluggish patches of marsh mist.

Throughout the journey Quentin was uncommonly quiet. Even though the violent jouncing of the car frequently barked his elbows or knees painfully against the upholstery, he never made a complaint, but instead stared blankly out of the side window. He chewed incessantly on a thumbnail, and once Tanner caught a bright speck of scarlet out of the corner of his eye.

The open windows blasted speed-cooled air around the Challenger's interior, but Tanner knew the moment they came to a stop the clammy fist of bayou heat would close over them again. Faces would gleam, shirts would stick to the smalls of backs: discomforts that would only magnify the tension of their mission. For himself, Tanner had actually come to think of the heat as a blessing; its oppressive pressure was a constant reminder that he could never, ever afford to relax.

His earphone buzzed: 'Now,' Jericho commanded.

Tanner flicked off his headlights. At the same instant, so did all the other cars, leaving the road in almost total blackness. Quentin made a fearful noise, even though he'd been fully briefed on the plan. Tanner paid him no heed. Every scrap of his concentration was sucked into following Bowman, the tail of his car just visible swerving up ahead. It was a dangerous trick, but the LLR men would be sure to be on the look-out for the approach of any suspicious headlights.

As agreed, all four cars soon peeled off the dirt track in a snaking chain. After a short, hair-raising plunge through the undergrowth they pulled up inside a roughly circular clearing, which Bowman had reconnoitred a few days earlier. The ragged limits of the glade were defined by a palisade of ferns, swamp dogwoods and chestnut oaks, which formed an almost impenetrable screen to the surrounding swamp. Sound was muffled; light veiled. It was the perfect staging ground for them to assault the LLR, and prevent them from calling for back-up. The plan was to leave the cars parked here while an advance strike team closed on foot through the undergrowth and slipped inside the venue to 'pacify' the enemy. Once the LLR and the Colombians were subdued, the cars could return to the road and drive up to the jetty where the cash and the product would be loaded. It should only take a few minutes to complete the shake-down, then they would melt back into the bayou and vanish like ghosts.

There was a flurry of dim motion in the crawling dark beyond the windscreen: the other members of the gang were getting into position. Tanner rummaged underneath his seat. He produced a cheap plastic wolf-man mask, which he briskly donned, then cracked the driver's side door—

'W-whoa! W-where you going?' Quentin blurted, suddenly jerking back to life. 'You're just a wheelman. You don't get out. You don't get involved.'

His eyes were glazed with barely suppressed panic. He now saw Tanner as his life-line and wanted to hang on to him with both hands.

'Tonight, I do,' Tanner told him. 'Without Shields we're a man down. I'm just going along to make sure the situation doesn't get out of hand.'

Quentin's jaw slackened. He was visibly appalled.

'Relax,' Tanner told the kid. 'Remember what Jericho said: I'm savage. But only when it counts. I won't let this turn into another bloodbath.'

This was a slight revision to Jericho's meaning, but Quentin swallowed it. He was scared and in the dark. He just wanted some sort of reassurance. The kid went back to staring at his lap, like a computer gone into sleep mode. Tanner noticed he was gripping the edge of his seat so tightly his knuckles gleamed white in the meagre light. Tanner exited the Challenger.

Don't start feeling sorry for Quentin, he told himself. He's a safe-cracker, a career criminal, dumber than shit on a biscuit and meaner than a scrapyard dog . . . even if that's because he doesn't know any better. An overdose of empathy was the last thing he needed right now. He had enough to worry about without adding this idiot to his list.

Tanner bumped the car door closed with his hip and padded softly across to the huddle of masked figures. Jericho gave him a calculating glance from behind his Halloween vampire mask and then nodded in terse agreement. He communicated their plans to the team – Tanner, Bowman, the Mexican kid and the biker – with a collection of sharp hand motions and curt whispers.

As they moved off, Tanner caught sight of Navarro's

face through the side window. Her eyes were questioning. Why was he getting involved in the raid and intentionally putting himself in danger? her look demanded. Wasn't he the one who'd told her that they were 'drivers, not muscle', and the whole point of the exercise was never to have to use a pistol? Tanner didn't return her gaze. He dissolved into the trees after the others. If he stuck close to Jericho, then there was a chance he might be able to put a check on the hitman's propensity for spontaneous violence. That was his real mission tonight: damage limitation. Keep Navarro and now – goddamnit! – Quentin out of the line of fire. Keep Jericho and his thugs from hurting too many people.

Tanner's hands tightened on the grip of the Super 90 combat shotgun he'd liberated from the lock-up stash. His palms were already slick with perspiration.

They fanned out through the rustling undergrowth, keeping low, moving in organized waves from one bush to the next, never hurrying, always advancing with deliberate, measured steps. The marsh around them swarmed with nocturnal life: the constant chirrup of frogs, trilling bird calls, small rodents – racoons, bobcats, armadillos – snuffling through the bushes at their ankles. A barred owl suddenly took wing from a branch overhead, startling Bowman. The bird alighted just above their heads in a laurel oak and regarded them quizzically with its head cricked on one side. Its beady eyes were like a widow's buttons.

Bowman raised a palm over his shoulder to indicate that everything was fine. A mosquito buzzed so close to Tanner's ear that it sounded like a jet engine taking off, but he suppressed the urge to slap it away.

They pressed on, yard by sneaking yard. The brush was definitely thinning out now. A buttery electric glow from up ahead had begun to cast its highlights across some of the glossier leaves. Soon, they heard the low steady whirr of an outboard motor; it was clearly approaching. Creeping forward they arrived at the tree break, and crouched motionless in the shadows to observe their target.

The venue for the drug deal was a slightly dilapidated fishing lodge on the banks of a mist-clogged creek. The lodge was a sagging, weathered-wood building about three times the size of conventional rural Louisiana cabins. It had been constructed in a rustic style and topped by a quaint tiled roof. Since the land here was so prone to flooding during heavy rains the ingenious first settlers had hit upon the scheme of lifting their dwellings up on poles, and this lodge was upraised a good foot and a half above the swampy mulch below.

A lichen-scarred jetty projected out over the flat, stagnant waters of the creek. As they watched a beam of light haloed the edge of the lodge. Within moments a small manoeuvrable freshwater jon boat nosed into view, its aluminium sidings glistening with a mosaic of sword-shaped green leaves broken off immature cattail stalks along the riverbank.

Two burly men in sleeveless denim, one white, one black, stood at the edge of the pier to receive the incoming vessel. They were joined by a thinner man in a cheap white suit who continually patted his forehead dry using a scarlet handkerchief. As its starboard wales nudged the jetty, the black and white denim 'twins' rushed to tie up the jon boat. Inside its low hull, jammed between the parallel struts of the seats, sat a pyramid of tubular-shaped packages covered by a tarpaulin. There were three Colombians on board, so similar they could have been brothers, all dressed in iridescent silk shirts – one blue, one red, one green – all armed. The two younger men – blue and red – began to unload the stacked narcotics on to a pallet jack the LLR soldiers had prepared on the lip of the pier, while the green-shirted Colombian who had been operating the outboard motor watched on impassively with an AK-47 across his knees.

While the LLR and Colombians were preoccupied with the unloading, Bowman slid out of the trees and crouch-ran up to the side of the building. He quickly moved along all of the windows, snatching glimpses into the lemon-glowing rooms within. He hunkered down against the wall and displayed his hand to them, thumb bent over the palm: four more soldiers inside.

Over on the jetty the white-suited man had selected one of the packets at random and split its corner with a bowie knife. He sniffed, licked, then he nodded towards the green-shirted guy, satisfied. He ambled back along the decking towards the lodge and disappeared inside.

That was when the Indian's team struck.

Speed and surprise will overwhelm almost any enemy, and the masked, black-clothed gang members kicked through the lodge like a storm in combat boots. It was a total rout. The soldiers in the house were barged to the ground, shotguns in their mouths, then hog-tied with law-enforcement-grade zipper bands. In the back corridor leading to the jetty they fell upon the denim twins, breaking the white man's jaw, then slamming his black counterpart into the wall. They caught the red- and blue-shirted Colombians trying to unholster their ridiculously over-sized hand cannons in the cramped back porch doorway. Jericho grappled their screaming white-suited leader into a neck lock while the last Colombian – Green Shirt – was still calling out from the end of the pier.

Jericho marched fearlessly along the jetty towards the jon boat, propelling white-suit guy irresistibly ahead of him as a human shield, his Double Eagle revolver grinding into the man's temple. The guy was babbling hysterically in Spanish and Creole.

'*Dé lo para arriba o I' el ll lo mata!*' Jericho barked.

Green Shirt didn't seem to be much bothered that Jericho was threatening white-suit man, however. He instantly jerked out an arc of AK bullets towards them, stitching the LLR lieutenant's immaculate jacket with spreading red lilies. As white-suit man choked and expired, Jericho returned fire. The Colt Double Eagle coughed once, almost languidly it seemed to Tanner, and across the jetty the Colombian rocked back in his seat. He ended up with his head right back, staring blankly up at the branches, a dime-shaped hole between his eyes. The bloody mush of his brains drooled out the back of his splintered skull and pinkly clouded the stagnant water.

Fuck, thought Tanner. He shook his head, glancing down at his hands. His fingers betrayed the slightest of tremors, but when he clenched both hands into fists the shakes immediately fled.

In truth, he was impressed by Jericho's marksmanship. That was a championship head shot, bull's-eye at 10 yards in low-to-little light while someone filled the air with lead all around you. The hitman's rep wasn't all just flim-flam and heat lightning then, he really was a formidable opponent. A detail to keep in mind if they ever ended up going *mano a mano* somewhere down the line.

Jericho disdainfully shrugged the dead white-suited dealer off the jetty into the bog. The body vanished with a slow sucking plop. The hitman strode to the end of the deck, unslung his sawn-offs and blasted two ragged holes at the jon boat's centre. Within moments the narrow vessel had begun to glug beneath the treacly olive bogwater. It would take many gooey minutes for the boat to fully submerge, but it certainly wouldn't be offering anyone an escape route in the meanwhile. The hull quickly began to fill. The dead Colombian's chinos ballooned, his nerveless fingertips paddling in the beige water.

Jericho wandered back along the jetty casually wiping blood on to his black combat pants. He glanced around at the other gang members. He was still wearing his vampire mask and his eyes through the holes glinted like chips of ice.

'Come on. If we don't get a move on, some wetback sheriff will happen along next, and I'll have to do him ... then his deputy ... and all the other fucks they send after that. GO!'

Tanner felt a little unwell, but he choked it down. The other gang members shook themselves out of the death fugue the killings had brought on, and swiftly went to work. Even for career hard nuts such as these the sight of a man's brains casually slopping into the drink like a scoop of melted strawberry ice-cream was stomach-churning.

Firstly, they locked the manacled prisoners in a storeroom without windows and shoved a crowbar through the door handle. Then Tanner, Jericho and Bowman returned to the original clearing in a flinty silence while the others worked on unloading the drugs. As they trudged back towards the cars Tanner noticed that the bushes were alive with the restless scurrying of small creatures agitated by the general commotion. Tanner felt a lot of sympathy for their panic.

Along with Navarro's Honda they drove all the cars up to the lodge's gravel parking bays, where the Mexican and the biker had already rolled the pallet jack laden with coke and heroin parcels. They started to laboriously divide up the packets and load them into the trunks and back seats of the waiting vehicles.

'Can I stay in the car?' Quentin asked in a small voice as Tanner was getting out. He'd heard the gunshots and drawn his own conclusions from the wheelman's reticence.

'Sure. I'll just go tell Jericho you've decided to sit this one out, thanks.'

Quentin nodded and almost tripped over himself in his speed to sprint to help with the grunt work.

Tanner closed with Jericho, who was overseeing the work, arms folded across his massive chest. He was still wearing his mask, which made him seem even more intimidating. A towering statue of a serial killer in the gloom.

'Make a sweep round the back,' Jericho told him. 'Make sure there's nothing we've missed.'

'Why do we care if the LLR know who we are?' Tanner asked, staring at Jericho's mask. 'I thought the whole idea was to humiliate them as we rob them?'

'Masks don't only hide identities,' Jericho replied, his voice carrying a slight buzz through the plastic. 'We wear them to fill our enemies' hearts with fear and make them piss their shorts at the very sight of us. Plus, it's better for team morale if they can't target individuals for reprisals. Oh, Lavache will know who stole his pride and wrecked his livelihood tonight.'

'Won't any sheriff's investigation lead back to them, not us anyway?'

'Never hurts to do your due diligence. Kick any-thing which might hold our DNA into the bog. The water's acidic enough to eat that shit clean away.'

Tanner nodded. He returned to the riverside, brooding on the enigma that was Jericho: an utterly brutal psychopath with impressive middle-management skills.

The jetty was scrawled with black trails of gore like a butcher's graffiti, and it made Tanner pause in dark reflection. He couldn't see anything that really counted as evidence by Jericho's standards. Lavache would know who had bent him over and reamed him, but Tanner's own law-enforcement colleagues wouldn't glean any hard forensics to link the Indian's men to the scene. Well, if you didn't count Jones recording every single word through the wire strapped to Tanner's chest. The undercover cop smiled without humour. It was some small comfort to think that there were enough charges here to put all the black hats in orange boiler suits for several con-secutive lifetimes.

The darkened creek was like an illustration from a *Lord of the Rings* coffee table book. Islands of emerald algae floated like scum over depthless tea-coloured waters. The looming press of diagonal boughs made you feel you were standing in the maw of a sleeping dragon. The odour was something like grass clippings in a compost pit mixed with the tang of freshly dug earth, not foul but musky. In spite of the occasional rustle of wildlife, or the soft pop of a bowfin breaking the surface to gulp for air to fill his swim bladder, the creek had an over-riding air of stillness that made the hairs on the back of Tanner's neck prickle with anticipation. Hidden out in the undergrowth one bird's call cut through the scene like the *peep-peep-peep* of a deep-space probe's signal, transmitting in from the furthest reaches of the solar system.

An a/c unit was thrumming deep inside the house. No, that wasn't in the house. Tanner turned around on the spot, trying to locate the source of the hum, but the acoustics of the swamp defeated him. Were those car engines approaching? Too loud to be a boat, but not high enough to be another 'copter.

Tanner ran back round to the front of the lodge. The biker and the Mexican had just finished loading the last of the packages into the Dodge. Bowman already had his engine revving. Jericho emerged from the building bearing two cheap 'wood effect' brief-cases. The money.

'Roughly half a mill.' Jericho's tone affirmed that this was an 'acceptable' haul.

'Can you hear cars?' Tanner asked, unsure of his own senses. 'There's a humming, or a droning.'

The harsh flat glare of the lamps out on the porch made their faces look like cheap plastic. The lights themselves were humming like a hornet's hive. Jericho cocked his head. He nonchalantly swept out an arm and blew out both bulbs with a puff of exploding glass. He listened intently for a second or two in the gaping silence which followed. The only illumination was the nasty false glare oozing out of the lodge windows. It turned the shadows into spindly knives.

'No, that's not on the road,' Jericho concluded with an arrogant certainty. 'It's behind and to the west. Probably the interstate or trucks headed to Bayou Teche or St Martinville to park up for the night.'

Tanner grudgingly surrendered the point, but then he realized that all the cars were rumbling, ready to roar, except the Honda, which sat cold, dark and empty.

'Where's Navarro?' Tanner demanded, suspicious. Jericho shrugged.

'Said she needed to piss. First job can take people that way. Went to use the bathroom in the lodge.'

Tanner was gobsmacked, though he just about managed to hide his apprehension. 'And you let her?'

Jericho was stone-faced. 'The mission's a complete success, and you remember what I said? If you want to control people, you don't always use blunt tools. Lenience can be a tool too. If the Indian ever makes you a lieutenant, you'd do well to remember that. Don't sweat, she's coming. That girl's a definite asset to me.' He paused, and then corrected himself. 'To the Indian. You go. We'll rendezvous back at the crossroad as agreed.'

Tanner hesitated for a beat – eyes locked with Jericho's – then, satisfied the hitman was sincere, he jumped into the Challenger. He could still hear the motors, very faintly, but Jericho was right. They weren't cars and they weren't nearby. He twisted his key in the ignition, bumped the car into gear.

'Finally,' whined Quentin. 'Thought I wuz gunna die of old age back here.'

An image leapt unbidden into Tanner's mind: the jon boat slowly sinking below the creek's surface, a smut of his own liquefied brain matter gleaming on the Colombian's green collar.

'Make that your wish,' he told Quentin in a low voice. The kid couldn't look him in the eye.

Tanner led the way back the way they'd come, bouncing along the rutted 'main road'. Thirty seconds later he wrenched on his wheel and pulled off the dirt track not far from their original staging clearing. The Dodge and Bowman's Cadillac both flashed past. Jericho's ghost white face scowled momentarily through his side window in a freeze frame, then they were gone. Still no Navarro. Tanner checked his watch.

'C'mon,' he muttered under his breath.

'What we waiting for?' Quentin pleaded querulously.

Tanner grimaced. 'Something isn't right.'

He cracked his door and stood half in, half out of the Challenger. He closed his eyes and just concentrated on the spaces of the night piled all around him.

The drone was definitely still growing louder, he was sure of that. It was drawing nearer, but how? If cars were approaching by road then surely he'd be able to see their headlights by now?

Then it struck him. They weren't approaching by road because the engine noise didn't belong to cars.

Those were airboat motors.

The LLR reinforcements were arriving by river!

Julia.

'Get out,' he told Quentin. The redneck began to purse his lips to form an objection but caught Tanner's expression and instantly thought better of it. He tumbled out of the side door as if there was an invisible boot up his ass.

'Phone Bowman, get him to come back for you,' Tanner instructed. 'Start running now, you'll be fine.'

'W-what about you, dawg?' Quentin stammered.

Tanner chambered a round into the Super 90. 'I may be a moment or two.'

He plunged into undergrowth as if he was diving beneath the surface of a fast-moving stream. Quentin stared after him, swallowed loudly, and then dashed in the other direction while scrabbling to drag his cell phone out of his hip pocket.

Chapter Twelve

Seconds later, Tanner was peering through the tangled mess of branches that surrounded the lodge and desperately fighting the urge to launch himself out of the bushes, guns blazing, in a suicidal frenzy. Lavache's LLR thugs had Navarro's car surrounded, as many as ten of them, broad backs and tattooed shoulders blocking off his view. They all lifted up their weapons as one, a motley assortment of sawn-offs, pistols, hunting rifles—

Tanner's breath caught.

They opened fire. The scene around the building seemed to transform into a stop-motion movie as their muzzles spat flame, jerking into frozen frames. They honeycombed the Honda with violent perforations, riddling the doors, the bodywork, webbing the windshield with buckshot and bullets. The noise was like a nail bomb exploding in a junk yard.

Tanner's hands on the combat shotgun gripped so tightly they immediately cramped, but he wouldn't relax even as fiery daggers seemed to be raking up and down his calcified tendons. It took all the self-control he possessed not to break cover.

After thirty seconds the relentless detonations ceased. Silence yawned over the scene, only interrupted by the sporadic tinkle of glass splinters, which rained on to the gravel beneath the shattered Honda. Muttering incoherently under his breath – maybe a running commentary, maybe a voodoo curse – Lavache shoved his way through his crowd of henchmen to the demolished vehicle. He tugged on the passenger door, which creaked aside. The compartment was empty.

Tanner's heart leapt.

Lavache suddenly threw back his head, his neck stretching out like a slinky caught on a doorknob, and let out a piercing scream towards the boughs above. The sound was pure bestial rage, inchoate and unthinking. A number of his soldiers flinched. They all wore distinctly uneasy expressions. Lavache started to tremble, a millipede ripple of quivers starting at his feet and then spreading up the whole length of his body, as if he was being possessed by the voodoo spirits he supposedly now worshipped.

'I'm not scared of the Indian!' he shrieked as the tremors reached his throat. 'He ain't a man! He don' come down here an' face me! He a filthy scrap o' spectre! I ain't scared of no GHOST!'

His antique ivory-handled Colt .45 appeared in his vibrating claw and belched fire at the night. Tanner flattened himself against the moist earth as the bullets whisked overhead. It seemed to Tanner that this reckless gunfire was like a bellow of shrill defiance. Lavache came from a gang culture of towering machismo, yet he'd become a cornered beast, outclassed, overwhelmed, and driven to dressing up as he *thought* his rival did in some misguided attempt to retain the fear and respect of his men. The disgusting cloak of hair, bones and glittering trinkets rattled around his gaunt shoulders like a reeking animal pelt. He couldn't admit he was afraid, or one of his lieutenants would slit his throat in the night. He couldn't back down and he couldn't win, so he kept on screaming and firing, but it was just a furious wind howling through an empty cave. His desperation was as pitiful as it was dangerous. Tanner covered his head to protect himself from the rain of chaff. Lavache continued to pump out shots until the revolver clicked empty.

His brow fell forward and coils of unkempt dreadlocks unfurled like black caterpillars over his face. Even from his distance, Tanner could hear his strange drawn-out moan. Lavache was clearly on the verge of losing it completely, his grip on sanity as slippery as his authority over his followers. His men flinched and swapped uncertain glances.

'Search the forest!' Lavache suddenly yelled. 'Go on. GO! Kill anything that moves!' he screamed at his men.

Galvanized by Lavache's raving his hoods began to spread out from the lodge. Tanner drew back silently into the shadows. This was actually good. Lavache was unhinged, verging on a full breakdown by the looks of it. It might make him unpredictable, and thus highly dangerous, but it also meant his tactical thinking was all to shit. He'd have his men chasing their own tails for ever in the bog, and any bobcat he thought might be the Indian tiptoeing up behind them would be filled with enough lead to shred an elephant. They weren't even searching the lodge itself yet. It might be possible for Tanner to spirit Julia away right under his nose and for them to both escape without a scratch.

Back bent low, Tanner started to creep around the perimeter of trees, carefully flanking the LLR so he could approach the creek.

Attempting to cause as few ripples as possible, while simultaneously trying not to think too hard about alligators, Tanner waded across to one of the windows on the far side of the lodge. Luck was with him: it was hanging half open. He levered himself up on to the sill, stuck his head inside the frame and shouldered his way inside. He found himself in the kitchen extension, a long galley-type affair designed to serve large fishing parties; once a stainless-steel vision, it was now all rust-wrecked and decrepit.

The bathroom was on the other side of the building (assuming Navarro was even still in there). Tanner padded silently to the inner door and waited for a moment, listening for reports of anyone moving around inside the building. Voices were milling around on the porch, but nothing inside – yet. Tanner slipped into main building and ghosted through the warren of damp mouldy-smelling lounges, bedrooms and corridors. Clearly one of the soldiers had managed to radio Lavache before Jericho's team overran them.

Moving along an outside wall Tanner suddenly heard a heavy foot tread on the jetty less than a yard from his head. He froze. There was a 2-inch barrier between him and the LLR thug. Tanner had been caught hunkered down beneath a window overlooking the creek. If the goon turned even slightly he would catch sight of the wheelman. The cop held his breath, and debated whether it would cause less uproar if he smashed the window pane and tried to punch the goon out, or just shot him. Neither seemed exactly ninja-like in their spectre-ish stealth. A few seconds hobbled painfully past then Tanner heard the man sigh and a stream of liquid splash into the creek. *Thank the Lord for the call of nature*, thought Tanner, though, of course, if it hadn't been for someone's call of nature he wouldn't have been stuck in this situation in the first place.

He edged into the store area and used the interconnecting space to dash through to the front of the building. It was extremely fortuitous they'd decided to tie and gag their prisoners in the box room. If they'd been free, they would have already been hammering and bellowing fit to raise the dead right now. He moved quickly through the foyer and breathed a heavy sigh of relief. Success! The short linoleum-carpeted corridor leading to the bathroom was crossed in a heartbeat and he crouched in low, shoulder braced against the door. He couldn't make out any noise from within. Soft as he could, he rapped on the balsa wood panel.

A .22 slug blew a ragged hole through the door about three inches above his skull. He stifled a yell of surprise. Navarro's scared and apologetic face appeared along the edge of the door, the stubby barrel of the pistol Jericho had given her poking out.

'Jesus, I'm sorry!' she gasped, but already they heard shouting through the walls. Hollers echoing round the creek. Doors slamming open. Tanner grabbed Navarro's wrist and yanked her back towards the kitchen. As they entered the foyer an LLR thug with a starburst facial tattoo was running in from the lounge. Tanner's shotgun roared once and the edge of an occasional table was transformed into flaming matchwood. The thug dived for cover.

'Fuckfuckfuck!' Tanner muttered, retreating clumsily, colliding with Navarro, who was following too closely. They almost fell, but managed to stay upright. Wobbling awkwardly, they spun around – just as the starburst thug risked popping his head up again. Before he had the chance to squeeze off a round Tanner clenched on his trigger again. The blast of the Super 90 was stupefying. All they could hear afterwards were their eardrums singing. Navarro tugged insistently on his shoulder.

'In here,' she mouthed and they dived through the doorway she'd indicated, before hauling shut the massive stainless-steel door. It locked with a meaty thunk. They were trapped in a defunct walk-in freezer.

'OK, we're trapped, but this is the sturdiest room in the place. That door will hold them up for a few minutes.'

'We're not trapped,' said Tanner simply. 'Stand back.'

Navarro's eyes widened as she intuited what the wheelman had planned. She danced back to a safe distance as Tanner aimed at the floorboards and emptied a succession of shots into the floor. The boards buckled, cracked, dissolved into clouds of wood chippings expanding through the air.

Tanner and Navarro lost their balance and tumbled into the pit below.

Surprisingly, the total floor collapse made far less noise than the repeated shotgun blasts: with luck the LLR wouldn't have realized what had happened. Tanner and Navarro were on their bellies, lying flat in the gap between house and bog, wallowing in sucking filth. Tanner spat out a mouthful of dirt. There was a terrific rumble on the floorboards overhead – like someone rolling a hundred bowling balls down a ramp – as the LLR stormed into the building.

'You couldn't have just held it in? Or taken a leak in the bushes?' Tanner hissed.

'Not all of us are hardened career criminals who deal with this on a regular basis. When I get really,

really nervous for my life, I need to pee, and I drive better on an empty bladder and I didn't want any of you lowlifes trying to peek at my ass through the bushes! I didn't expect Jean-Baptiste fucking Lavache and half the psychopaths in New Orleans to come piling on to the jetty, did I?' She glared back at Tanner, eyes hot. 'Also, I thought my so-called crew were meant to be looking out for me!'

Tanner rolled his eyes. 'OK, look, shhhh. Your car's Swiss cheese, we can't use it. The Challenger's on the dirt track back over to the west where we originally parked. Jericho blew the lights outside on the porch so we can use the dark as cover to get into the trees. After that, it'll be an easy run through the bushes with tons of cover. We might as well be invisible by that point.'

'What you mean is it'll be a deadly game of cat and mouse with a gang of highly motivated coked-up maniacs in Yoda's freaking forest?'

'Yes, that too. Now shut up and follow my lead.'

There was a great deal of commotion up above as the LLR thugs rushed through the thin-panelled spaces, shouting out as they checked each room. Tanner thought he could detect Lavache's wailing imprecations in amongst the din. There was a sudden clamour of excitement as they located the prisoners and began to untie them. That was Tanner's cue.

'Now,' he urged, and they both speed-crawled through the slime, rising just beyond the front porch, caked stiff with wet earth. They made a break for the bushes while Lavache and his thugs were engrossed inside the lodge. Their mud-sodden boots flew over the gravel. Only a few feet left—

'There!' someone shouted.

Other calls instantly started to converge on their location, the febrile beams of torches scissoring drunkenly towards them. Tanner cursed under his breath, risked a lightning glance over his shoulder and saw Lavache's Colt .45 licking out a 2-foot tongue of flame.

A bough inches from Tanner's head disintegrated in a cloud of sawdust, speckling his cheek with stinging needles. One moment later, though, and Tanner and Navarro threw themselves into the dense under-growth beyond. They dodged and weaved, swerving desperately round trees to prevent their pursuers from drawing a bead. Tanner's neck itched as he imagined the hot pinprick of a sniper's sight burning into his back . . . but no shot came.

The forest was inky black and they were constantly being lashed by razor-tipped branches, which they couldn't see or take the time to avoid if they wanted to stay ahead of their pursuers. The ground was cracked and uneven, so perilous that it was like running on crazy paving made out of wet foam. Every step Tanner was sure he'd catch his toe on a root and go flying. Suddenly they were engulfed in a wispy drape of webs, filmy strands that clogged their eyes and mouths, tickling their cheeks. Navarro spat and flailed, her wrists tangled up in the ghostly impediment.

'We should have sticks for this to dislodge the spi—'

A huge spider landed on her shoulder. To Navarro's credit she only let out a strangled gasp, but it was clear from her face she was petrified. She brushed it away with a disgusted shiver. Yells barked out to their rear and they plunged on as fast as they could. The light-less flight seemed to stretch on endlessly, as if they were trying to run in a nightmare, but then Tanner's eyes made out what lay ahead.

'The road!' he hissed excitedly to Navarro.

Just then, Tanner's toe snagged on a snaking root and he went into an impromptu dive, smashing into the forest floor like a dropped sack of coal. His leg below the knee screamed, but Navarro grabbed him. She ducked her head under his shoulder and heaved him upright in an impressive show of strength for her slender frame. Only yards to go, but by now Lavache and his men were so close they could almost be giving Tanner and Navarro back rubs.

With Navarro desperately supporting the hobbled Tanner they burst out on to the dirt track. Tanner had never been happier to see the shameless yellow hull of the Challenger in his life. He hauled on the driver's door and heaved himself inside, his ankle protesting with stabs of agony; Julia leapt into the other side. But the most fleet-footed LLR thugs were already explod-ing through the tree-line.

Someone opened fire. The car's right tailgate in-dicator blew out with a crack.

The Challenger's engine turned over first time. It thundered into life. A few of the straggling LLR thugs tried to take pot shots as well, but by then it was over. The wheels squealed like a banshee, kicking up spumes of pebbles, dirt and smoke in an impromptu burnout. Then they were gone.

Behind them, Lavache half tumbled, half capered out on to the road, his insane scarecrow's cloak whipping round him like a death shroud. He raised his Colt, but the gap was already too wide for a guaranteed shot. All he could do was watch them blaze away.

Navarro twisted to peer back along the narrow, sinuous track unspooling out from their bumper. Her breath was racing, clearly hot with excitement. Her laughter made Tanner go cold all the way down to his heels. He was pretty sure she'd actually enjoyed much of that. In a civilian, that wasn't a particularly good sign, especially considering how tangled up she was in the fate of this mission.

As they raced away they heard Lavache screeching, a tiny figure impotently shaking his tiny fist as he receded in the rear-view.

Chapter Thirteen

When Tanner arrived back at his rental studio at one in the morning he instinctively paused. Something was wrong. His eyes fell to the stripe of illumination sketched out along the foot of the frame: someone was inside.

Tanner drew his back-up .38 from its ankle holster and kicked through his front door in a blur, the barrel already panning, locking on to—

Jones, who was sitting on the bed looking exhausted and pissed off. He raised his hands in an ironic surrender. 'Don't shoot. Your chairs were all designed by the Spanish Inquisition, and the bed's the only soft place to sit. Don't get any funny ideas.'

Tanner grunted without much humour, and toe-punted the door closed behind him. There was a tight pause in which both men regarded each other with weary resignation.

'How is he?' Tanner cracked the silence.

Jones sucked his teeth, stared off through the window for a beat before returning his tired gaze to the room. 'He'll live,' he finally admitted. 'I broke my own rule. Hightailed it out the van to look after the bastard myself. Even went with him in the ambulance. Drew the line at holding his hand, though.' He paused, shrugged. 'He might not ever strut his stuff on a clothing optional beach again but he's out of the woods.'

Tanner absorbed this expressionlessly. After a moment he crossed to the sideboard and disinterred his bottle of Jack. Didn't bother with ice, splashed himself out a mega measure and tipped it to his lips.

'It's not your fault,' Jones said quietly.

Tanner froze, one hand braced against the wall. He swallowed the amber liquid down, relishing the smoky burn along the back of his throat.

'Sean Shields is not worthy of the description "human being"' he said finally. 'Sean Shields is a woman-beating lowdown pervert bully, and would-be murderer. Sean Shields is the film of scum from the devil's own outhouse, but he shouldn't have been shot through the gut tonight and I'm responsible.'

'Bad things happen to bad people all the time,' Jones murmured. 'He chose his life just like we chose ours. Grown-up cops and robbers is a dangerous game.' He sighed as if he was a million years old. 'What are you going to do about his vanishing "corpse"?'

Tanner pulled a face. 'Told Jericho I'd deal with it myself. He congratulated me on my ambitious, go-getting attitude. Only that fucking ice monster could see disposing of a body as an entrepreneurial career move.'

They were both quiet for a moment, alone with their murky thoughts.

'You wanna eat?' Jones eventually asked. 'I can make something, assuming you got some ingredients in your fridge that ain't Coors or Corona.'

Tanner flapped a fatigued hand to get his friend to stand down. 'I don't even know how to turn on the cooker in this freaking style mag limbo. Normally I go down the stall on the corner and get crawfish gumbo or red beans 'n' rice to go. But it's too late and I'm not hungry. Not now.'

Jones watched Tanner's face cloud over. The silence curdled between them.

'I tell ya, this mission is just fucked down to the marrow,' Jones muttered in a dark tone. 'It's poison and we need to admit that and start doing something about it. We oughta never come to this viper's nest in the first place.'

But Tanner was already shaking his head vigorously. 'No, no, it's all good. We just need to feather the brakes a bit. I'm not going to let the Indian get away with the things he's made me do. I swear, Jones, I *will* take him down.'

There was a manic gleam in his eye, and Jones regarded him with sceptical unease. 'Don't you go all Captain Ahab on my ass, Tanner.'

The mania sluiced out of Tanner as quickly as it arrived. 'Fuck it,' he said, scrubbing his face to slap some life back into it. He looked around for his glass, realized he was already holding it and took another glug. He grimaced, stamped into the kitchenette and tossed the dregs down the sink. 'It's evenings like this really make you think about all the wrongs you've done in your life, all the people you don't see,' he coughed in a husk of a voice, leaning over the taps.

He looked down at himself, staring numbly at his mud-caked clothes for a second, then his face flinched with disgust as if only seeing himself for the first time. 'I gotta shower, man.'

With that, shambling like the living dead, he headed off towards the bathroom. Soon Jones heard the shower hiss. He ambled over to the hulking over-priced tomb of a fridge and selected a couple of eggs.

When Tanner emerged from the bathroom washed, shaved, in clean clothes and feeling almost human again he found Jones had been busy. There was a frying pan brimming with delicious-looking Spanish omelette on the hob.

Tanner grinned, but then he got a good look at Jones under the harsh kitchen lamplight and he saw how bone-tired, drawn and grey his friend appeared.

'How about you? You look like shit.'

'Don't worry none 'bout me. I'm a careful man. I take precautions.' He took out a small bottle and rattled it, grinning. 'Multivitamins.'

Tanner joined Jones in the kitchenette. He shovelled himself out a portion of omelette and leaned against the breakfast bar to eat it. Suddenly he was famished after all, and wolfed down the food with ravenous enthusiasm.

'So, how's Powell taking it all?' he enquired airily between mouthfuls. The omelette was good. If Jones had been a woman, Tanner would certainly have considered marrying him years ago.

'Oh, Powell's happy as a clam who's just found out he's not goin' in the chowder,' Jones replied. 'The Indian loves you, Powell loves you. *All* your bosses are havin' a party.'

Tanner flashed his friend a weary shrug. 'But you're not so chipper?'

Jones snorted and broke eye contact. He went to fix himself a glass of juice. 'Ah shit, I don't know.' He sipped the orange, swilling it thoughtfully around his mouth before swallowing.

'In the end it was a successful mission, Jones,' Tanner said gently.

'Who for?' was the flinty response.

'They got half a mill. We got evidence that could put them all in the big house.'

'Including your little pal, who I never heard anything about before the other night, I might add.'

'She . . . she shoulda never got involved in this life. But it's cool. It'll all work out. I'll sort it. They're all minor charges and I'll flip her. She'll turn state's evidence, we'll give her a new life, far, far over the rainbow. Job done.'

'Yeah, and denial is just a big river in Egypt.'

'Look, what do you want me to say? What other freaking options did I have? If I tried to stop Julia auditioning for Jericho, then I risked exposing myself. Trying to exploit this friendship with Jericho is already like riding a tiger bareback! Tonight's fucking horror show proves that.'

Jones began to pace restlessly. 'I don't know, man, there's something about this girl that troubles me.'

'She's OK. Shit, she's just a good kid who took a couple of wrong turns. Who of us can't say that?'

'It's not just that. I know how much she means to you, but . . . she's reckless, John. She's dangerous. That girl's not a loose cannon, she's a loose Apache attack 'copter. There's something she's not telling you, something underneath, I'm sure of it.'

'You don't know her like I do. She's not a black hat. She's good people. I'm certain.'

'John, you're a circus plate-spinner right now, not a cop. You've got too many things you're trying to fix: Navarro, Jericho, the Indian – Jesus, even Quentin now! You're spreading yourself too thin. The only one way that ends up is with broken eggshell all over the damn floor.'

'You're mixing your metaphors,' Tanner told his friend quietly.

'Yeah? Well, I don't claim to be a literary man. What was the last thing you read where the last line wasn't "80 per cent proof"?'

Tanner shot him a dirty look.

'I thought so.'

In defiance Tanner returned to the sideboard and pointedly sloshed himself out another measure of spirits. Jones relented.

'OK, I'm sorry, that was uncalled for. But, dude, this is some deep dark Serpico shit right here. I'm just worried about you, man. Not just as a cop, but as a friend.'

Tanner wasn't looking at Jones; his eyes were averted, bottle of JD drooping gently from his spongy tired fingers.

'The operation is fine,' he said softly, dodging Jones's real point. 'It'll be fine and it'll all work out . . . fine. We'll get there. The Indian goes down. Don't worry. I know what I'm doing. You just gotta trust me—'

There was a loud tap at the window. They were three storeys up.

The two men exchanged alarmed glances: if Jones was discovered in Tanner's flat, it could be disastrous. Jones scurried to hide under the bed.

Tanner moved warily towards the balcony, though he was convinced he knew whom he would find out there. Sure enough, Julia Navarro was crouched outside like a sexy imp amongst his sprays of inherited potted periwinkles and Mandevilla creepers.

'Come on, let me in, you big doofus,' she snapped, her voice muffled by the glass. 'It's more slippery out here than jello night at a fetish club!'

Jones shot him a warning look from under the bed, but Tanner ignored his partner and nonchalantly unlatched the balcony door. Jones scooted back under cover with an exasperated growl. Tanner grinned at his friend's aggravation. Navarro tumbled inside, rubbing her hands. She pulled a face while pumping her hands to restore some feeling to the fingertips.

Her hair was damp and she was wearing fresh clothes, a man's black and turquoise T-shirt, more sprayed-on jeans, this time in fire-engine red, and a flaky-soft biker's jacket the colour of old rust. She smelled of coconut-oil soap, expensive skin cream and a perfume with a citrusy tang that Tanner couldn't quite place.

Navarro looked at Tanner. Tanner looked at Navarro. Suddenly the events of the evening caught up with them and an awkwardness descended upon the room. They both glanced off, searching for something to spark up a conversation, not knowing how to address the strangeness of the situation. Finally, Navarro plunged into a confession.

'Hey, I know this is odd, me turning up here out the blue. But, well, we haven't seen each other for fifteen years and . . . I just wanted to say, y'know . . . I think we kinda bonded again out there in the swamp. You came back for me, Tanner . . . John. With all those pop-guns going off and the dark – and, man, the freakin' spider – I thought I was done for. But you had my back and . . . and that means a lot . . .'

Navarro stepped in and rather formally offered her palm to him. After a beat Tanner took it and they shook hands, grinning like idiots. Tanner frowned.

'Soooo . . .' He trailed off.

'Well, OK, this is awkward and now I feel stupid for crawling up on to your balcony . . .' Navarro filled the dead air. 'I came over . . . basically . . . 'cause I couldn't sleep.' She chewed her lip. 'You get that?'

'Only all the time.'

She grinned, and hooked her thumbs into her belt like a gawky teen not really knowing how to pose herself. 'I know, right?' she exclaimed unselfconsciously. 'Man! The adrenalin . . . The ideas and plans and shit running round and round your head . . . What you're going to do with the money . . . How you're going to trick out your ride . . . All the mad things that happened, the close shaves, the triumphs . . .'

Tanner shrugged in sheepish agreement. He realized with a shock how fond of Navarro he was, and how, in spite of how beautiful and competent she'd become, she was still basically the same cute, eager, over-excitable and slightly annoying kid to him. She glanced down at her Converse All-Stars, abruptly bashful as she built up to some proposal.

'What?' Tanner prodded, suspicious.

'Let's go for a drive,' she suggested impishly from under her fringe.

'You don't have a ride any more,' Tanner pointed out.

Navarro grinned cheekily over her shoulder, already heading out of the door. 'Thought we'd take your car, big bro.'

Tanner sighed and grabbed for his jacket. 'Clearly I

have to come along. You need someone to keep you safe from yourself.'

On the threshold he threw an apologetic glance back at the bed. Jones was glaring hotly at him from under the metal frame. Tanner gave a helpless shrug before slamming the door over his partner's accusing face.

Chapter Fourteen

Navarro drove the Challenger like a demon with a grudge against asphalt. From the moment she jumped behind the steering wheel Tanner knew she was planning to play games. She kicked off by performing a crazy doughnut outside the downstairs bar. Whether she was merely showing off her skills to prove how far she'd come in the intervening years, or, as Jones thought, she really was just a loose cannon, he couldn't tell yet.

Still, there was just something playful about Navarro's most reckless behaviour. The doughnut she pulled caused the college dickheads and flamboyant queens who'd given her a hard time on the balcony to scream and leap back in fright. She flicked through a crisp J-turn, reversing directly towards the customers outside the bar and causing them to scatter, before swinging round a deft one-eighty to accelerate smoothly away.

'Dude, I do still live here,' Tanner chided his companion. She just giggled and floored it. Tanner shook his head and sighed as they roared off.

* * *

They powered out of the city and into the dark, wet countryside beyond. Navarro took a long loop along the shore of Lake Pontchartrain down Mandeville way. A briny draught blew through the open car windows, deliciously fresh across their cheeks and brows. It was the same wind that pushed a chain of short, sharp storms ahead of them. The storm clouds were bleak scribbles of smoke towering away in the distance. Heat lightning moved over that way, too, like a giant with electric fingers tapping restlessly along the horizon. The waters of the Pontchartrain were choppy and grey, the tiny red eye of a buoy winking back at them from the vast dark bowl of the lake, its bell tolling faintly and ominously.

It was an exhilarating night for a drive, but Tanner felt uncomfortable in the passenger's seat. It wasn't because he was some chauvinist asshole who didn't think women could be truly great drivers, or even because it was Navarro behind the wheel. Tanner just hated not having complete control when he was in a car, and especially not in his own car. There was a perpetual queasy itch at the back of his mind warning him that if the vehicle did hit difficulties he wouldn't be able to do anything to save them. Tanner could be thoughtful and compassionate – given the right run-up – but basically he was an action man and not what you'd call a natural passenger.

Still, this did free him up to ruminate. For someone who often spent a lot of time by himself, John Tanner was not a man given much to introspection and he wondered sometimes in his darker moments whether that made him difficult to get close to. Jones was his only real friend and he'd chosen a job where, by necessity, he was surrounded by people he had to lie to 24/7 and potentially betray at the drop of a hat. Shit, maybe he was just getting too old for this paranoid double-life shit? He wasn't Superman and he didn't have a spandex-wearing alternate persona to change into whenever he needed to solve crime.

He thought a little bit about Navarro and Slater, and their past together.

'Do you know what you're going to do with your wage from the raid?' Tanner asked Navarro, trying to distract himself from further brooding.

Navarro slid down a gear to glide across a tight bend, smooth as ice along glass, and made a non-committal noise. Tanner waited for something more, but when no other details were forthcoming he rolled his eyes and glared out at the dark waters speeding past. Great, two emotionally incommunicative adrenalin junkies trapped in a hunk of speeding metal together. Weren't girls meant to be good at this sort of thing? His cell phone abruptly buzzed against his thigh, as he received a text in silent mode.

Tobias had written: 'Whatevr else u do, don't tell her yr a cop. Rem shes still a crook.'

Tanner turned off his phone and casually dumped it in the glove box on top of the tangled mass of spark plugs, oil rags, cans of WD-40 and balled-up copies of

Gearhead magazine that clogged the space like a block of cavity wall insulation.

They were flashing through a tiny picture-postcard white-picket town, barrelling along a main street so deserted it might as well have been the back drop for the opening shots of a zombie movie. Navarro leaned on the steering wheel and drifted gracefully on to the cross street leading out of town. Tanner had never even caught the name of the place, and already he was leaving it.

The Challenger pulled up at a set of traffic lights slung on wires high above the road. It was a slight shock to find another car drawing up beside them: a purple Jeep, full of raging dickwads.

'Hey, look at the man letting the chick drive his crusty old banger, so later he'll get to bang . . . her!' bawled the dude behind the wheel. He guffawed and high-fived his bros crammed around him as if he was the Gen-X Oscar Wilde. They were all sloppy post-college running-to-seed fratboys in sports jerseys with beer-bong bug eyes.

Navarro looked across the dash at Tanner, her expression begging for permission. Tanner nodded. It had to be done: you just didn't stand for that level of disrespect. Not from dickheads in a freaking modern Mustang.

'Scalp 'em,' he instructed.

'Aye aye, cap'n.' Navarro grinned, her eyes lit up. The Challenger's wheels screamed out smoke, whirling on the spot as Navarro performed a tasty little burnout – then the vehicle leapt away like a bullet from a gun. She tore ahead of the jumped-up muscle car, the Challenger's proud yellow colours describing two lightning streaks all the way along the parade of shop window storefronts on either side.

Just outside of town, the college boys managed to score some points with local knowledge and sneaked ahead of Navarro around a blind and unexpected bend. On the straight flat road which unfurled after, Navarro gunned the Challenger, pulling level with the Jeep, and they raced along the two-lane highway neck to neck, neither able to nose ahead. Navarro flicked a look over at the other driver. The Challenger was the one in the oncoming lane, but Navarro was relaxed, while the college boy was red-faced and shining with sweat. Now there were lights up ahead, an eighteen-wheeler heading towards them, its blazing headlights like the flaming cauldrons of hell.

Racing side by side with the Jeep, neither willing to back down, the truck roared directly towards the Challenger.

'You don't need to do this to impress me, Julia,' Tanner said calmly. Being calm was a tool like anything else. You could learn it, teach it, and use it to get what you wanted. Right now Tanner was using it to try and talk sense into Navarro because he knew exactly the limitations of the Challenger. If she didn't ease up or back down there was, he calculated, a good 80/20 chance they'd be dead in the next five seconds, but it wasn't in his nature to panic about that.

Navarro didn't ease up *or* slow down. She kicked on the gas and laughed like a suicidal skipper tacking into a perfect storm.

Tanner drew in on one sharp breath—

The dude driving the Jeep bottled it.

He stamped on the brake and wrenched to the right to try and avoid the smash he was certain must be coming. Tanner saw all the fat jocks scream in fear, throwing palms across their faces to protect themselves, their mouths four identical stiff hoops of terror.

Navarro whooped as they slotted through the gap between Jeep and truck with microseconds to spare—

She was still cackling like a hyena on ecstasy when 40 tons of metal, rubber, glass and a freight load of commercial office furniture buffeted past with the force of the space shuttle coming in to land. It almost blasted the Challenger clean off the road, but Navarro deftly managed to control their tail wag.

'Losers!' Navarro screamed back at the college flame-outs choking on her exhaust fumes as the Jeep jolted to a halt in a water-logged ditch. 'That was fun!' she cackled triumphantly.

Tanner turned right round in his seat to pierce her with a withering look. 'I think we need to have a long, hard conversation about your risk addiction,' he observed in a tone as dry as sand-blasted beef jerky.

Navarro cursed. They screeched off the road into an overgrown lay-by and Tanner snapped hard against his seat belt as they came to a dead stop. His pectorals stung with old bruises.

Tanner turned to Navarro. She was staring straight ahead, shaking with barely controlled rage that seemed to have emerged from nowhere.

He stared at her. 'So come on, Navarro. Why are you really getting caught up in all of this?'

There was a long pause. Without looking at him, Navarro half whispered, 'It's because of my dad.'

Tanner frowned. He hadn't seen much of Navarro's family since Slater's accident, especially after he became a cop. Ernesto had been a proud fearless bulldog, grizzled and tank-chested. It was difficult to think of anything that could have bowed his iron-haired head. A fierce union man, tireless battler against bosses and bullies, he'd worked in the automotive industry in one form or another for most of his life. It was how he'd managed to forge a genuine, if occasionally scrappy, relationship with his car-nut stepson, Jason, and clearly those passions had shaped Julia's future as well.

'I always liked your old man,' Tanner said.

'Do you want to go see him?' she asked.

Tanner was stumped. He could tell from Navarro's face that she was totally serious.

'OK, if you think he'll still be up,' he answered slowly, 'I've not seen him in a long time. It'll be good to catch up.'

Navarro's expression was unreadable in the frail dashboard light. Tanner couldn't really see her eyes at all, just the shaggy bronzed tips of her fringe that hooded her gaze. She sat very still; the only motion around her was the heart cross pendant at her neck, which trembled and danced with the last of the car's discharging momentum. She very slowly closed her palm around the pendant to make it still.

'Yeah,' she said very softly, with a slight catch in her voice. 'Be damn good to catch up.'

Chapter Fifteen

Ever since the founding of the city during the seventeenth century, burial in New Orleans has been a complicated affair. The extremely high water table in the region makes traditional entombment very challenging, as the original settlers quickly discovered – to their dismay. Since the city lies below sea level and was constructed on reclaimed swampland, normal graves quickly became waterlogged before the grave-diggers had finished. In heavy rains graves would fill with water, the airtight caskets floating up through the sandy soil and gliding down the flooded streets.

Eventually the inhabitants began building vaults above ground. And so were born the Cities of the Dead: rows and rows of ornate crypts of all different sizes with narrow, dark paths between the tombs.

It was to one of these Cities of the Dead that Navarro took Tanner. The sky was overcast, the colour of a deep-sea crevasse, but the cemetery's shadowy maze was grazed here and there by starry highlights, twinkling grave-lights that lent the aisles a haunting ambience. There was a doleful beauty to the rusted iron scrollwork, the cracked marble slabs, white-washed brick, looming crucifixes and muddle of mismatched shadows that fell from a thicket of statues, crosses and effigies sprouting from the tops of so many tombs.

The two visitors stood before a modest white brick crypt, their faces lit by the trembling glow from the candle that Navarro held cupped in her hands. Some time passed when there was only the rustling of leaves and the chirrup of insects and the vast stillness of the night surrounding them. Navarro bent and placed her candle in a protective metal cowl on the stone lip of Ernesto's tomb. She fastidiously arranged the yellow lilies that were already resting there, along with a framed photo of Ernesto as a young man, smiling.

'I didn't know, Julia,' said Tanner in a hushed voice. 'I'm so sorry. He was . . . Shit, Ernesto was one of the best . . .' He trailed off awkwardly, unsure how to continue. These were real emotions, not another role to play, and totally unexpected. It was a broken tree limb of his own past jutting dangerously into the present. After all his months and years of professional fakery among people he secretly despised, he was at a loss as to how to react when those two worlds collided.

Navarro's gaze was stapled to the burial plaque, eyes brimming. She didn't look at Tanner. If they weren't looking at each other they could pretend that she wasn't really crying. Tanner knew she needed to be seen as strong enough to play – and fight – with the big boys. Tanner had affection for her both as the girl he once knew and the grown woman he was trying to get to know today. The moments passed by like icebergs, cold and slow and silent.

'C'mon,' she finally whispered in a thick voice. 'I want you to come see where he . . . w-where they . . .' But she couldn't finish, the words draining off into dregs of hurt and frustration.

'Where he died?' Tanner coaxed gently.

'Where they slaughtered him,' Navarro spat.

It was an alley exactly like every other in the Quarter.

The walls were grey brick with crumbling mortar, graffitied half-heartedly in gang colours near the mouth, and it was overhung by wooden balconies, leaving only a cramped slot of open sky visible above. The paving stones were worn with a sag to the centre, probably by the passage of feet over many decades. Two men could just stand shoulder to shoulder in its width.

'Whenever I come back I always expect to see the stains,' Navarro whispered as she tracked along, peering at the pitted imperfections of the wall's surface. To Tanner's eyes the cruddy lane did look pretty stained – by the overflow from a clogged drain and the discharge around the rim of a black municipal bin – but he knew better. Those weren't the stains Julia meant.

She pointed at the chipped, rotting mortar. 'All this damage is new, the brickwork going, and that's only –

what? Shit, three years. That's water deterioration. It's always water in this city. It's in the foundations, the roots, the walls. The whole place is constantly on the verge of drowning.'

She reached towards the wall, but didn't fully connect. Her fingertips darted back and self-consciously grazed the star-shaped scar at her temple instead.

'How did you get the scar, Julia?' Tanner asked.

Navarro didn't reply. She stepped back and peered up at the summit of the nearside building instead.

'You can't get up to the roofs of these ones so easily, which is a shame. There're all these balconies, but it doesn't really feel the same if you're allowed to go up, if you're meant to be there. When I was little, Dad and I would go sit up on our garage roof. We'd be working in there all afternoon. He'd be tinkering on his car or motorbike. He always had some project on the go, had to keep his hands busy. I got that from him. I'd be drawing, or doing my homework. Afterwards, we'd clamber on to the flat roof – him giving me a boost up, then dragging himself up after. He'd sit in an old deck chair with a beer, while I'd perch on the edge with my sandals off. We'd watch the sunset together.

'I remember gushing to him once about how I wanted to be a science teacher when I grew up. I don't think he said anything at the time. He knew a little bit 'bout chemistry, but after that he learnt all the rest he needed to know, just so he could help me out. We worked on a massive presentation for the science fair together.'

Navarro fished out her heart cross necklace and held it in the palm of her hand. It glinted in the grainy half-light from the streetlamps beyond the mouth of the alley.

'He gave me this necklace for winning first prize. Really, he was the one who did most of the work. He wasn't a guy who could talk about what he felt. His love was all wrapped up in the things he made and the things he did, how hard he worked. His love was solid like that.

'Once we moved to Nawlins, after Jason's crash well, a lot of things changed. I drifted back into cars, partly because I'd seen how cars had kept him and Jason close. I was worried I was losing him.

'Dad never really took to this place. It was the climate mostly, but he didn't really understand the relaxed vibe of the place either. Then there were all the set-backs. The failed start-ups were like body blows – the restaurant, the coffee shop, the TV-repair business, the engine tuning – and he threw himself into every one. There were never any half-measures with Dad. He was endlessly beating his heart against a wall, and it couldn't help but affect his health.

'But the cars were good for both of us. We'd always have an old banger we were rebuilding over in a lock-up Dad rented nearby . . . well, until he couldn't afford it any more. We were trying to recapture those garage-roof days. I found work in auto-repair shops, driving jobs, and helped Dad out. I dunno, maybe that's part of why the necklace means so much to me, because it represents a vanished time, a long-gone moment.'

She moved across and indicated the building on the left, which now seemed to house some aromatherapy outfit.

'This is the place we were renting at the end,' she clarified. 'We had a little 7-Eleven, if you can imagine it. Dad serving microwavable rice packs and jars of pickles in brown paper bags!' She smiled fondly and shook her head. 'He wasn't good at it, but, dude, if you could have seen how much effort he put in. "If a man doesn't put in all his effort every day, then he is not a man!" he always chanted whenever I asked him to slow down.

'Of course it was his pride that did for him, or, well, I suppose his sense of equality really. We weren't making much money and it was touch and go whether the store would go under, but he'd worked damned hard for what we had. Maybe if he'd worked less hard he wouldn't have bumped heads with Sepion's meat-heads. He might have been able to let the whole thing go, but he simply wasn't wired that way. He was just that sort of guy. I'd have liked to have seen his face when they came round to shake him down that first time. "What? I have to pay *you* what I've earned from my sweat and tears just because you threaten me? But you've done nothing for this money!" It was exactly the same as when he was a union foreman. Bosses, gangsters, it made no difference. He chased those first two wetbacks outta the store with a baseball bat. God, suddenly I'm craving a smoke telling this story. Four years without and all of a sudden it's like ants crawling under my skin. You got one I can bum off you?'

Tanner showed her a crooked smile. 'Sorry. It's the one vice I don't own. Shame, because otherwise I'd have had the whole set and could claim my free ring binder.'

Navarro smiled back a little wanly, but appreciative of his attempt to lighten the mood. She started walking again and pointed to the store's side door.

'He was putting the trash out when they came back, locking up, pulling down the shutters. I heard their voices from upstairs – we were living directly above the shop, then. At first it sounded like friends chatting, then came raised voices, and the sound of fighting. I came barrelling down into the kitchen swinging a golfing umbrella Dad had won in a raffle the previous year – it was the nearest thing to hand. My head was down and I was seriously booking it, man, steaming in to help my dad. Then it all went a bit Keystone Cops. I think one of them must have heard me coming because *bam* he opened the door straight in my face as I was coming out. I went wheeling back and hit my head on the edge of a stainless-steel sink. You can tick off how I got my scar now, if you're keeping score.

'Well, I was seeing stars, with blood all over my face. I heard the . . . the . . . noises from outside. There used to be a panel of frosted glass in the door, but it was in pieces on the floor. The thugs never got to see what I looked like but through the door I saw framed a huge silhouette. I saw his eyes glint when he half turned, and I knew it was the Indian. Eventually, after about five minutes of lying there, I heard the fuckers leave and eventually I managed to drag my sorry hide outside.'

At this point Navarro paused and began scanning the wall with much greater concentration. She hunkered down to get a closer look. 'Ah, there ... There it is. That's where I found him.'

Now she reached out and put a palm to the wall, patted the spot she'd identified. She stared at it for a long lingering moment.

'They beat him with wrenches and tyre irons, put out his eye, cracked his skull in a whole bunch of places and smashed bones almost everywhere else on his body. He was so strong, though, my dad, he didn't die. He was trying to talk to me in the ambulance, though I couldn't make out what he was saying. In the hospital he slipped into a coma – all those blows to the head, you see. His brain was swelling and he had blood clots ... Well, he was like that for days. I slept there; I fell apart ... It took weeks before I worked up the courage to have the machines turned—'

She choked off for a moment. Tanner started towards her to offer comfort, but she warned him back with a fierce look before continuing.

'Whenever I think of him now he's standing above me,' she whispered. 'Tall like he would have seemed when I was a little girl. I'm looking up at him and the sun's in my eyes but I can see his shoulders high and proud, his back like a mast, straight and true. The old

181

black guys who used to sit on the porch across the street drinking bourbon all day used to call him the colonel. Not because he'd ever been in the army, but because he always stood so straight. I was so proud of that, like I can't even tell you. I had a dad who everyone knew for being a real man.'

She shivered, looked directly at Tanner.

'Dad stood up for himself, John. He always faced down the bullies, and that's what the Indian is. When you strip out all the hoodoo fairytales, and the rumours about his dogs, his acid hallucination torture, and all that other contrived phantom bullshit, he's just another bully. So let's not call him "the Indian"; that's more card-trick nonsense. He's André Sepion and he's the big kid picking on the whole of New Orleans, stealing its lunch money. I am going to bloody that bully's nose and put the fucker back on his ass . . .' She paused, breathing heavily. 'And I want you to help me.'

This was a huge confession and a desperate risk for her. For all their past together and these new bonds they were making, as far as she knew Tanner was the trusted confidant of Jericho, the Indian's right-hand man. She was as much a shoot-from-the-hip, go-with-your-gut adrenalin junkie as he was. No wonder they got on so well. She knew Tanner was the one to help her; she just didn't know why.

'You want justice for Ernesto?' said Tanner slowly, as if struggling to come to terms with this revelation.

'And all the others like him.'

'You want to put Sepion behind bars?'

A beat. Navarro's eyes were gleaming with tears.

'This is why I really came out to see you tonight. I wanted to ask you to help me. I don't know what journeys you've been on since Jason's crash to get you from there to here, John. You have your reasons for working with these ... people. I won't judge you if you say no, but ... Shit, I know this isn't you! The John Tanner you were fifteen years ago wouldn't have stood for this sort of injustice, and I'm betting, after seeing you these last few days, that you're still that same guy inside.' She paused and pierced him with her grave-black eyes. 'Help me to bring down the Indian, John. Please.'

Tanner could barely stop himself from laughing at the irony. He ached for her loss and for the life of Ernesto, who was truly and sincerely one of the most honourable men he'd ever met in his life. On the other hand, it felt as if a great weight had been lifted from his shoulders. This explained everything: her sadness, her erratic and reckless behaviour, her desperate obsession to prove herself. It made him elated that Jones had been so dead wrong about her.

Navarro wasn't a villain, she was an avenger, and that he could relate to. John Tanner had sworn to uphold the law, but in his heart of hearts he was far closer to the vigilante end of the spectrum than Jones ever would be. Tanner lived with criminals for months at a time. He came to know how unforgivable some of their crimes really were. He knew what it meant to feel hate for bullies and abusers and every day he yearned to strike back. That was what drove him.

Tanner didn't say anything straight away. He was still trying to process this piece of good luck and how best to utilize Navarro's obsession to both help the mission and provide her with justice. As she waited for her answer the skies above them unzipped and started to cascade down warm, glittering sheets of rain. Within seconds water was leaping up and down on the gleaming black street.

'Come on, let's get inside,' Tanner called through the hammering downpour, but Navarro wouldn't budge. She just stood there glaring at him, her jaw tight, her eyes shining with the intensity of her emotions. Her jacket was steaming and her sodden fringe clung to her forehead.

'Will you help me?' she shouted over the hotplate hiss of the rain against the sidewalk. There was a beat when all the world was reduced to rain and rush and waiting, then . . .

'Yes!' Tanner shouted back, raising his voice to be heard.

They grinned at each other and ran for the car. Back in the driving seat, Tanner felt better than he had in weeks.

It took a bit of a drive, but eventually they found a place to just sit in a booth, have a coffee and cool their emotions off. It was a tiny truck stop on 1-55 out Laplace way, little more than a workman's hut with ideas above its station, a chipboard and Formica kind of place with Willie Nelson and Waylon Jennings in a never-ending loop on the jukebox. The café was empty apart from a waitress in pink gingham with dark circles under her eyes, and a trio of overweight truckers who were passing round a porno mag and snorting over it like fourteen-year-old boys. Navarro and Tanner slid into a booth as far away from them as possible.

'Of course, no one gets in to see the Indian,' Navarro started glumly, stirring creamer into her coffee. 'Not unless he asks to see you first.'

Tanner stared ahead, thinking, then he said, 'We need a guaranteed hook. A way of impressing him so spectacularly that he has to want to meet us.'

Tanner upturned the sugar shaker, but only a couple of grains trickled out. The only other dispenser was on the fat truckers' table. Tanner blew out a weary sigh then sauntered over to them. 'You're not using it, so can I just grab that sugar off you fellas?' he asked with exaggerated courtesy, hoping not to spark up any situation he really couldn't be bothered to deal with.

The largest trucker grinned a buck-toothed smile and reached politely over for the shaker. 'Course you can, buddy,' he simpered, and then very deliberately knocked the plastic cone off the table, spilling a dirty grey-white pile over Tanner's feet. 'Ooops,' he squeaked, affecting a camp little wriggle. 'Look at me, butter fingers.' The other truckers snickered like all good moronic sidekicks should.

'Hey!' the waitress called out in indignation. 'You cut that all out, y'hear?'

The truckers ignored her. They kept their eyes on Tanner, watching for his next move.

Tanner gazed down at the mess of sugar, grit and dust bunnies on the filthy linoleum flooring, chewing his inner lip. He looked back up and smiled equitably at the truckers. 'Not to worry. I'll just take it black and bitter like normal.'

'No one asked 'bout yer boyfriend!' roared one of the lesser truckers before high-fiving his nearest buddy.

'Hey, pretty boy, what kind of a jacket is that for a grown-assed man?' demanded the leader. 'You look like one of them Lego men with those yellow stripes down your arms. Are those Bart Simpson's skid-marks?' The other goons guffawed once more.

Tanner had had these guys pegged the moment he set eyes on them. They had a rhythm they had to adhere to. This was the only way these morons could relax after driving all day: get loaded, get fed, get some violence, get some shut-eye. From their point of view, it was a happy accident that Tanner had walked in, otherwise they'd have had to stagger off to find a late bar and waste time antagonizing some locals.

'OK, well, you have a swell rest of the night, y'all. I'm going back to rejoin my friend,' he told them evenly, turning to go.

'Er, no, senator. You owe us a crisp twenty-dollar note.'

Tanner swung back. Eyed him dangerously. 'Do I?' he asked with deceptive mildness.

'Oh yeah . . . For spilling cruddy sugar all over my nice new cowboy loafers.'

Tanner looked down. The trucker was wearing the most cracked, ugly, ancient, shit-stained ass-boots he'd ever seen. There wasn't a single grain of sugar on either of them.

For half a second Tanner was tempted to get into it with the fat truckers, but he realized he was tired right down to the marrow. He was a professional and he had a serious job he needed to get up and attend to in the morning. It had already been one of the longest nights of his working life.

Then he caught sight of something beautiful beyond the diner's smeary plate-glass window. It was just sitting there, utterly perfect beneath the gleaming magic beams of the security lamps. An idea struck him . . .

'Sir, may I ask, is that your rig out there on the fore-court?' Tanner enquired of the lead trucker in a distant tone.

'Why yes, dear faggot, that there beaut' is my gal and if you don't cough up the cash by the time I count to five me and my associates are gonna beat you so hard yer own momma wouldn't know you on the brightest day of the year.'

To everyone's surprise Tanner took out his wallet, peeled off a fresh twenty note and slapped it on to the greasy table-top. With a puzzled, dissatisfied look the lead trucker made to pick it up, but before he could Tanner seized his wrist in a vice-like grip. Eye to eye he grinned at the alarmed trucker.

'Make sure you get some change when you pay. I'm sure you fellas don't have cell phones and you're gonna need a quarter for the pay phone real soon.'

Then he turned on a heel and strolled back to his booth grinning. Navarro eyed him with wary reserve.

'What would you say if I told you I'd just found us the perfect way to catch the Indian's attention?' he asked with a mischievous twinkle in his eye, before adding: 'As well as scoring you a sweet new ride into the bargain?'

Navarro just looked back at him as if he was insane, which only made Tanner's grin even wider.

Chapter Sixteen

Ghost Beard was all muscle and don't-fuck-with-me attitude, but he didn't have much of a chin to speak of and that had always made him self-conscious. When he started earning some serious scratch after joining the LLR, he'd eagerly experimented with gold chains and studded bracelets and other gang bling to distract the eye, but none of it had really needed. After that he'd tried to grow a goatee but all he could manage was a patchy strip of irregular dark specks that barely covered his non-existent chin. Basically, it was a 'ghost beard', as some wise-ass pointed out in the second week after he started growing it and, damn that bastard, the name had stuck. Ever since, that's how he'd been known.

It made him so mad. Sometimes being in a gang was like being back at high school. It was the same mess of stupid cliques and petty gossip. Just because of a dumb nickname no one took him seriously any more. He was the butt of everyone's jokes and it wasn't fair. Ghost was bright. He noticed things most of these other dumb meatheads would walk straight past; he could follow orders but also improvise; and he could shoot straight. Well, his astigmatism didn't cause him too many problems, and, anyway, with those boxy little Mini-Uzis they'd given them you just had to spray and pray, right? Did any of this matter to his career advancement in the LLR? Did it fuck.

Just take tonight. Here he was stuck out at the LLR's stronghold, an out-of-town lakefront villa southwest of New Orleans. The building was a hangover from the plantation style, a Greek Revival mansion, all ice-cream pillars and 10-foot-tall spindly windows. Out back there were stables constructed around a vine-wreathed courtyard, which was attached to the main building. These stables had been converted into rows of individual garages to house Lavache's fleet of classic sports cars. The cars were his pride and joy, maintained with scientific precision by a pair of German engineers who lived on the first floor of the villa itself – yet Ghost Beard and his crew weren't even allowed into the big house.

They had to hang out in a suite of guard rooms adjacent to the back gate. Sure, they were nice offices all right, fitted with sweet-ass plasma TVs and videogame consoles, DVD players and all that crap, but it wasn't the same. That made Ghost Beard mad as all hell. Every day these last few months he'd been telling himself he was going to get out of this bullshit life and this chicken shit gang. That said, in spite of all the slights and numerous humiliations, he wasn't quite ready to give up the small measure of power being in the LLR granted him. He was not ready to be little people again. At least the LLR had given him an Uzi.

Tonight, though, they'd all been called in like dogs by their master to supply extra security for Lavache, who was insanely fixated on the spectre of the Indian. He was terrified of assassination attempts, especially on a night when there was so much at stake. Ghost Beard and the boys got themselves tooled up and hung out in the guard block, but then the panicked call had come through: the Indian's strike team had appeared out of nowhere like voodoo spirits at the abandoned fishing lodge. Come immediately!

After the call Lavache had run around screaming wildly for his 'A-Team', then all those fools had piled down to the river together, armed to the teeth, and dived into their fleet of airboats. Within seconds they were just a subdued hum in the distance, heading away deep into the bayou. Neither Ghost Beard, nor any of the crew he was with – Raylon 'Toe Taps', Chester, Lester, Gabriel Grass and Fat Raimond – had been asked to come along, or even told precisely what was going on, not even as an afterthought. They were just 'the help', left to cool their boots out back until 'massah' came home.

This was mainly how it had been in the LLR during this last year since the Indian had really begun to rise: panic and disaster in steadily accelerating cycles. The moment one calamity had settled down, another flared up like a rash no ointment could ever cure. There had been a steady stream of deserters to the other side, street soldiers being mown down in ambushes, dealers and corner men just giving up on the Life completely. The Indian's operation was better funded, better organized and simply more ruthless. They never stopped expanding. They aggressively nibbled at the edges of a rival's territories for a few weeks before unexpectedly taking a huge bite.

The LLR was being trampled into the history books right across the greater New Orleans metropolitan area. Some of their neighbourhoods were still holding out: North Rampart, Marais and spots of the Seventh Ward in particular; but precious few of those bastions remained. The Red Blade gang was going out of business, and it was only a matter of time before the receivers were called in and they were told to shut up shop for good and everybody left alive got a bullet through the brain. No wonder Lavache had devolved into such a schizophrenic loon these last few months.

So, while all those supposedly top-division guys had hightailed it out into the swamp to deal with this latest catastrophe, Ghost Beard and the other Z-graders were left behind to hold down the fort. Not that any of the others shared Ghost's seething indignation. In fact, they just fired up the flatscreen, knocked on a games console and sparked up some fat ones. The reefers started circulating the room like holy smoking artefacts, reverentially passed from hand to hand while they played Rainbow Six multiplayer.

Without Lavache in residence, no one realistically expected an attack tonight, so why bother patrolling when you could just as easily kick back and share pizza and beer? Still, something, either dumb habit or the need to prove to everyone that he could do this moronic job despite his reputation for incompetence, kept Ghost Beard from just slacking off like all the others.

'I'll just do the rounds then, check the perimeter . . . and shit,' he announced to the room in general. No one looked up from the screen. Ghost Beard scowled and exited. He made a half-hearted tour of the ground-floor guard block, which overlooked the courtyard. Most of the windows were barred for security, but everything appeared normal when he glanced through the gaps. He twisted back towards the games room—

Which was when he caught something whipping past in the periphery of his vision.

Or he thought he saw something. It could have just been the after-effects of the hash they'd been toking. It always made him a bit tweaky and paranoid. There was nothing there when he swung round to check. He took a quick second look around, nosed behind curtains, peeked through the windows. Nothing. Slightly unnerved, he returned to the rowdy games room. Inside, the top-of-the-range 5.1 stereo surround system was chopping out such fat beats that the walls themselves were shaking and it was difficult to hear what anyone was saying inside the room, let alone anything outside in the courtyard.

'Did any of you guys hear something just now? See anything?' he asked the group crowded round the TV.

'You wanna shot, Ghostie?' Fat Raimond proffered him a joypad, ignoring his question.

'Shit, man, don't give it to Ghostie, he can't shoot straight in real life, let alone in the pixel zone!' mocked Chester.

Normally Ghost Beard wouldn't rise to the bait. He hated his nickname but he knew it would only make matters worse if he started flaming out whenever anyone used it. It made him fume with impotent frustration, but if he showed even the slightest hint that the name-calling got to him, then the other gang members would rip into him every moment of every day. Right now, though, he was actually thinking of their proper duties and he was damned if he was going to let them undermine his work ethic.

'Fuck you,' he shouted. 'This isn't about none of that, ya bunch of kids. Am I the only one here who cares if we do our jobs right? There's something going down.'

He stamped back out into the long corridor that ran the length of the block adjacent to the courtyard. He walked all the way along, pausing, listening intently. Mainly he could only hear the bass boom issuing from the games room. He opened a window shutter. The night looked still. He turned—

Something blue tickled the edge of his vision. He twisted back, scowling. Couldn't see anything out of the window, but his suspicions remained, a lingering acid

194

reflux of unease. He ran back to the games room again.

'Hey, hey, turn that fuckin' noise down!' he barked, trying to keep the stress from infecting his growl. The others ignored him. This was the last straw. Ghost Beard jumped over to the television and shut it off in the middle of the game. The thugs howled with indignation.

'SHUT UP!' Ghost roared. 'There's something happening, seriously. Noise in the courtyard, and . . .' He raised one finger up as if he was testing the wind. 'There's a breeze coming in. A window's open somewhere.'

'Whoa,' said Toe Taps, staring fixedly over Ghost Beard's shoulder out the kitchenette window they'd all ignored. 'How long has that fucking gate been open?'

The instant the words were out of Raylon's mouth the thugs all leapt up in horror. Pizza, bottles and joypads got stamped into the carpet under their desperate rush to get to the control kiosk. Ghost Beard's breeze was coming through a window that someone had stealthily jemmied to let them into the little cabin, where they had plainly operated the gate controls. Now the LLR soldiers were able to view the CCTV feed every man's skin went cold and his testicles contracted in fear. They could now see what Ghost Beard hadn't been able to from the sight lines of the long corridor: all the garage doors were open. Lavache's silver 1960 Chevrolet Corvette screeched out of its bay and flashed through the open gates before any of them could react and think to hit the close button. The driver was a caramel-skinned fox who flipped the CCTV's lens a contemptuous bird as she passed by. Ghost Beard's stomach fell through a trapdoor.

'This way!' he yelled, leading the way towards the front of the building. The thugs fought and elbowed each other as they piled into the maze of narrow wood-panelled corridors. They crashed out into the long hallway on the front side of the building which looked out on to the riverfront vantage. They skidded over to the security-barred windows and stared through in disbelief.

A gleaming car-transporter truck was sitting outside on the esplanade. Even as they watched the insanely hot Latina chick drove the Corvette up the ramp into the back, slotting the final car into the jigsaw. She jumped out and secured the car's tyres with wheel chocks. You couldn't hear it through these windows, but it was clear from her face that she was laughing as she worked. Ghost Beard and the other LLR soldiers simply gaped at this unfolding scene as if this was some elaborate *Candid Camera* sting, Then it struck home like a kick to the balls.

All of Lavache's precious cars were being stolen!

There was no way of breaking through these fortified windows, all of which were fitted with bullet-proof glass. Ghost Beard and the others raced back through to the main courtyard door. It was locked.

Chester leaned round the side window and saw that

one of their own maintenance vans had been backed up against the door to jam it from the outside.

With the music off they could now clearly hear the revs of the transporter truck's engine starting up.

'Break the windows! Break the fucking windows!' Ghost Beard screamed.

Toe Tips drew his Mini-Uzi and opened up on the window panes, but the reinforced glass held tight.

At this point they all heard the truck's air horn sounding off cheekily as the vehicle rolled away into the night.

'They got away!' bellowed Toe Taps, beating on the door. Then he slowly revolved to look at Ghost Beard. 'This is all your fault, dude.'

Ghost Beard's mouth fell open in astonishment. They weren't really going to try and pin this one on him, were they?

'Yeah, Ghostie, you're gonna be in so much shit over this. Why the fuck weren't you taking your guard duties more seriously?' Fat Raimond sneered.

As one Chester, Lester and Gabriel Grass turned to stare accusingly at Ghost Beard.

Handling the car transporter felt like driving an aircraft carrier balanced on roller skates, Tanner thought as they rumbled their way through the outskirts of the city. Fully loaded with Lavache's whole fleet of classic cars – a Porsche 365, Jaguar E-Type; Mercedes 300SL Gullwing, the Chevrolet Corvette and multiple other muscle cars – the weight distribution was quite unlike anything Tanner had ever driven before. As he swung out round a bend at speed there was a teetering moment of sheer terror as he felt the whole rig tip, and he couldn't help but imagine the whole edifice keeling over and surfing away on a skirt of 6-yard-high sparks.

Right now, they were lumbering through a deserted retail park, low flat rows of boxy hanger-shaped buildings smearing past, long lanes of shop units stripped with gaudy multi-coloured logos, all marooned in a concrete ocean of parking bays stretching out as far as the eye could see. The car transporter might not be fast but it sure built up an impressive sense of momentum. There was a feeling of sheer scale and unstoppable might that you simply didn't get in even the largest cars, and, although it might be a guilty pleasure, Tanner couldn't have denied he was enjoying himself. If it hadn't been for their obvious need not to draw attention to themselves he would have joyfully sounded the air horn again.

'You know, I'm actually having fun,' Navarro observed airily over the thundering reverb of the motor. 'I suppose it's always nicer when your plans go off without a hitch, though.'

'Some people keep that sort of shit stowed until they're actually tucked up safely in bed at the end of the mission.'

Sure enough, as if on cue, Tanner spotted a couple of black Cadillac Escalades and a metallic-green Chrysler 300C slew into view in his monstrous side mirror. 'And there's the hitch,' he quietly observed.

The cars approached swiftly, swallowing up the road within seconds.

Navarro craned round to get a better look back at their pursuers and sucked on her teeth in apprehension. 'We haven't got a hope in hell of outrunning them, John.'

'They might hold off on shooting for fear of damaging their boss's beloved car collection, though.'

At that moment a stray bullet whizzed past the cab and deflected off the trailer frame, causing them both to flinch.

'OK, or maybe not. Right, we need another plan.'

AK-47s and Mini-Uzis began to sputter out in nervous quick bursts behind them. Tanner briefly wondered how long it would take a fully loaded car transporter being chased past a parade of outlet stores by a gang of machine-gun wielding maniacs before someone thought to contact the police. On Cochrane's watch, he reflected, perhaps it would still take some time yet.

The Chrysler made an adventurous bid to overtake them, but Tanner gave the transporter a jolt. The truck gave a lazy flick which waggled out behind them. Alarmed by these seemingly suicidal tricks the Chrysler dropped back to the following pack.

Tanner knew it wouldn't take long before the drivers regained their confidence. The next time their pursuers wouldn't be so easy to block. If any of the LLR cars managed to pull level they would just hose the cabin with bullets and it would all be over. In his mind Tanner scrabbled at the biggest, most reckless ideas he could see floating by.

Go big or go home, he told himself.

'Here, you drive. I'm going out back to give our friends something else to think about.'

Even as he was saying it Tanner had already started to swap places with Navarro, sliding behind and bodily bundling her over into the driver's seat. He guided her hands to find the correct angle on the colossal steering wheel.

'OK,' she said with a slight wobble in her voice. 'You are aware that I've never even driven a minivan before, let alone something the size of a whale?'

'You'll do fine,' Tanner told her with more confidence than he felt. He hauled open the passenger's side door and the night air rushed inside. The speeding wind tore at his clothes.

'Be QUICK!' Navarro bellowed over the roar of the road. Tanner didn't bother responding, just swung himself out to where he could cling on to the side of the cab.

He shimmied precariously along the side of the cabin, grunting as he hopped along to the back of the trailer. The speed buffeted him all the way, constantly threatening to blast him off the side of the truck and dash his body against the tarmac. He lunged out and grabbed hold of a steel brace to haul himself into the rattling framework where the cars had all been snugly slotted. Luckily the metal structure afforded a certain amount of cover from gunfire, as well as some protection from the elements. Tanner continued on towards the rear of the transporter. With painstaking care he picked his way along the treacherous slopes and ramps of the trailer, bullets continually flying past. Some ricocheted in amongst the steel supports with a piercing metallic whine, but Tanner grimly kept his nerve. As much as possible he used the chassis of the stolen cars as a shield whilst worming his way around their slippery shells. Finally he reached the rearmost car, the Chevrolet Corvette, where he was perilously exposed.

He hunkered down and began to unlock the chains and remove the chocks. Every second he expected a bullet to explode his life into eternal darkness. His fumbling fingers were slick with sweat and numbed by nerves.

Suddenly he heard Navarro yelling something out of the cab window but a rush of the wind snatched her words away. She tried again but he simply couldn't catch the sense of it over the din. A moment later the whole world lurched and swung away from him. Tanner clutched on desperately for dear life as he belatedly worked out that Navarro had been shouting: 'CORNER!'

Luckily the floor righted itself within a matter of seconds, allowing Tanner to regain his equilibrium and quickly return to the task at hand.

The moment the Corvette was unlatched it dropped back on to the flashing black tarmac and threw up a leaping sheet of sparks. The back end veered out alarmingly, and then the momentum dug in and flicked it like a toy. A ton of precision sports car was now tumbling laterally across both lanes towards the pursuing LLR cars.

'Oops,' murmured Tanner to himself. 'Now that I did not expect.'

Behind him brakes screamed in panic and tyres screeched.

Moments later Tanner yanked himself back into the trailer cabin and settled into the moulded passenger's seat with a satisfied sigh.

'So, that's the last we'll see of them,' he confirmed with a certain amount of relaxed cockiness. Navarro didn't break her gaze from the road ahead.

'Jesus. Driving this thing feels like you're bringing a space shuttle in to land – underwater!' she exclaimed. 'No wonder those truckers were such assholes. You would be too if you had to ride this bitch for eleven hours at a stretch.' She stole a glance his way and frowned. 'Well, what you waiting for, Indiana Jones? You've completed your feats of derring-do, now bring us home already. Phone Jericho.'

Tanner smiled back, very pleased with their work. He began dialling his cell. All in all, this once never-ending night of disaster had worked out rather well.

Could this be the beginning of a beautiful partnership?

Jericho, Bowman, the biker and the Mexican kid – named Cole and, bizarrely, Love Money respectively

– were waiting for them on the docks. The sky overhead was charcoal but with a growing luminescence beginning to shine through. In the shadow of the gigantic cargo shed Tanner carefully reversed the truck. He took his time so as not to scratch against the stack of shipping containers and botch their perfect entrance. After a stunt this daring the one thing you didn't want to do was ruin the effect with a sloppy finish.

Bowman whistled his appreciation as he peered up at the transporter.

'This sure is one sweet haul,' he observed. 'We pretty much gutted the LLR tonight and hung Lavache up by his toes.'

Jericho stood with his arms folded. He resembled a man-sized rock cairn, his face a mosaic of slab-like shadows. Tanner jumped down from the truck, while Navarro stayed in the cab with her feet up on the dash. She lit up a cigar she'd conjured up from somewhere and began smoking blissfully while Tanner strode over to Jericho. He squared up to the expressionless hitman.

'I want to meet the Indian,' Tanner told him bluntly. 'I think I've earned it. It's a simple question of respect now. You tell him that.'

Jericho stared back at Tanner, not blinking for a long time. Finally he nodded. 'OK. One way or another you'll get your answer soon enough.'

He spoke with his customary lack of inflection, so it wasn't even clear whether this was simply a statement of fact or a veiled threat. Was their partnership fraying as Tanner started to push at Jericho's authority? Tanner didn't care, though. He matched Jericho's unrelenting gaze and he wouldn't back down.

Chapter Seventeen

A few nights later the gang held an impromptu celebration in a seedy, biker-tinged live-music joint near the edge of the French Quarter. A Cajun band rocked out onstage, the drinks were flowing all night, and there were strippers and blow in the back rooms screened off by crushed velvet curtains. The room was a low-ceilinged dripping dive decorated with bronze painted trimmings and classic seventies detective movie posters on the walls in scratched gleaming frames.

After their own contribution to the gang's victory Tanner and Navarro were the belles of the ball. They couldn't go ten steps without some tattooed fuck-knuckle wanting to pat their back, high five, or in Navarro's case grab a kiss, hug or a grope, all of which she deftly rebuffed. The place was a heaving jumble of black leather and body art, rammed with buffed-up bodies and shaken by loud music and a hundred shouted conversations. The club was suffused with the throbbing atmosphere of too much testosterone and it gave the party the constant air of incipient violence. There had been three fights already, and one attempted broken-bottle stabbing. *This is what a party in one of the less fashionable circles of hell must look like*, Tanner thought to himself.

Everywhere he peered through the smoky space he saw familiar faces he knew from the gang. One well-placed bomb would have destroyed the Indian's entire army, but the Indian's men were the undisputed rulers of this city now and no one would dare to try and crash *this* party. These were aggressive men who wanted to toast their utter domination and for the whole world to see it. Jericho himself sat alone on a high bar stool near the entrance, back against the wall, observing the roughhouse fun with his sawn-off shotguns across his lap, like the Devil's own doorman. Tanner nodded to him as he arrived, but they didn't talk. Tanner's ultimatum was crackling in the air between them and it still wasn't clear which direction that might go.

As he waded through the crowds Tanner spotted Bowman leaning against the bar and headed over to join him. The big Creole was twirling an alcoholic popsicle round his mouth as he eyed the room with a lidded lizard's gaze.

'Been talking to your girl,' Bowman rumbled while Tanner was getting served a Jack Daniel's in a dirty glass.

'Navarro?'

'Ahhh yeah,' Bowman agreed, nodding with slow

molasses relish. 'Sweet Julia Jaybird. That's what you'all used to call her when she was a shorty, yeah?'

Tanner stiffened imperceptibly. He shrugged a disinterested confirmation.

'Strange that you'd both end up in the Indian's posse and you knew each other way back when down San Francisco way, yeah? Weird coincidence that.' Bowman stroked one long brown finger along his upper lip. 'Did you hear that Quentin's vanished? No one's seen hide not hair of him since the bayou raid. Doesn't that seem a shade ... suspicious? You know anything 'bout that, senator?' he asked with a long drawn-out glance at Tanner, sucking his popsicle speculatively. 'Ah mean, he was in your car with you most of the evening ...'

Tanner snorted. 'That little shitbird probably just got spooked by his own shadow on his way home, and he's been hiding under his bed ever since. But seriously ... who cares?'

Bowman sucked his lolly, shark-smiling. A dark illumination simmered deep within his eyes, some unholy mixture of narcotics, desire and sin.

'Do you know what a Donkey Punch is?' he suddenly asked, his reptilian gaze never leaving Tanner's face.

'Can't say that I do, nor care to learn,' Tanner replied quietly, his face very still. Bowman ignored his words and carried on obliviously.

'Donkey Punch is punching some bitch and making her buck like a donkey, making her scream. And there's nothing in life better than making a fine bitch scream. Julia Jaybird is all sorts of a fine-ass bitch, ain't she? You ever knocked boots with that fine piece of ass, Master John Tanner?'

The air between them boiled with Tanner's distaste. His expression was flat and cold as a glacier, though, his eyes like chips of ice.

'Can't say that I have,' Tanner replied in a dangerous tone. 'Like you said, I knew her when she was young so I feel a lingering bond of affection. And protection. That's a friendly warning there, by the way. It could get a lot less friendly real quick if you push this any further. Get my meaning?'

There was a simmering pause, then Bowman's trademark bass chuckle rolled out and his gaze broke off, ending the confrontation. 'Yeah,' he drawled. 'But I'm just fucking wid ya, pilgrim. I would never hurt that fine honey nor anyone of the soft and female persuasion. Cross my heart and hope—'

'To die?'

'Oh, not tonight, my friend.' Bowman grinned indulgently back. His teeth gleamed yet his eyes were hard black marbles under the red and rose lighting.

He flicked his lolly stick into Tanner's half-empty shot glass on the bar with a musical *tink*, then he headed off to join a group of his Creole buddies who'd colonized a booth overlooking the milling dance floor. Tanner watched him go with a churning sense of foreboding. He'd always considered Bowman the least of his worries. Guess it was time to edit that playbook once again.

Ten minutes later and Tanner was still at the bar. He'd been scanning the room for Navarro and throwing back the JD, but for the life of him he couldn't locate her. No matter how much he drank he couldn't relax after his confrontation with Bowman. Tanner sucked his teeth in frustration and turned to order another drink.

The barman was a shivering empty-eyed stoner in a skinny-fit T-shirt and punk black eyeliner who'd smashed four glasses already and took three strikes to get Tanner's single order right. Once he'd finally collected the glass Tanner returned to scanning the room. Eventually the scrum of bodies on the dance floor loosened enough to reveal Navarro dancing in the far corner. Tanner made a bee-line for her.

'TANNER!' shrieked Navarro and leapt towards him, coiling her arms drunkenly around his neck. He winced with unease at her touch and kept her back with the flats of his palms.

'You and me, the dream team!' she slobbered too loudly into his ear.

The thugs who were stomping the boards around her gave a little cheer. Navarro giggled, and pirouetted away from Tanner to dance at the centre of a semi-circle of hungry-eyed violent men. She spun her body with sensuous abandon, arching her back to pop out her chest with a showgirls flick, lashing the air with her sweat-damp hair. Tanner watched the thugs restlessly. The heat of their collective gaze looked as if it could strip paint. They licked their lips like wolves, their movements slow and heavy.

To Tanner's expert eye Navarro wasn't actually drunk, though she was doing a very creditable impression of a bombed-out party slut. Though that did beg the question of what the hell did she think she was playing at?

He barged a couple of the meatheads out of the way, and snagged her wrist. 'What are you doing?' he hissed as she danced provocatively against him.

'Having fun. Enjoying our victory!'

'No, I don't think you are.'

Navarro turned her back and shimmied her ass against his side. The unwelcome brush of her buttocks reminded him of how she'd innocently shined her ass off Slater's Eclipse fifteen years ago. Julia Navarro was definitely not that girl any more, and this was not a welcome change.

'Don't push it,' he warned. 'And whatever you do, don't talk to Bowman again. Believe me, he seems like a straight shooter but underneath he's a fiend, and he's had his eye on you since you first showed up. Steer clear.'

'OK,' she told him, nodding exaggeratedly, eyes wide . . . then broke free and instantly headed towards the booth where Bowman and his leather-vested cohorts lounged. Bowman's gaze met Tanner's over Julia's head and the contact sizzled with animosity. The Creole grinned silver. That one look told Tanner that this was now much more than a standard dick-swinging contest. Bowman saw this as an issue of gladiatorial pride between two bad men. The fact that Tanner had warned him off chasing Navarro now meant he had to have her. Tanner silently cursed. Why hadn't he read Bowman's instability before now? His judgement was getting seriously glitchy. He left the dance floor and went directly outside to the Challenger to fetch his Hi-Point .45. He returned to the pulsating club with it jammed uncomfortably down the back of his jeans.

For the next hour, the club gradually drained. Tanner sat at a table overlooking the dance floor and watched Navarro and Bowman slow dance. Before long they were the last couple there, all the other meatheads either having paired off with party girls, or drunk themselves into such a stupor that they had to be hauled off the floor.

Tanner's gaze never left Navarro and Bowman, though. Bowman leaned over Navarro and his dreads slithered over her shoulders like amorous snakes. Her cheek rested in the hollow of his mahogany chest. Bowman didn't look up at Tanner, but he knew the wheelman was watching him and he continue to toy with the cop, stroking his hand down Navarro's spine towards her ass. Every time he repeated the psych-out, Tanner touched the butt of the Hi-Point now resting in his lap.

OK, reasoned Tanner, he needed an exit strategy. Don't get cute or clever, make it simple and overwhelming. Walk over, clock Bowman with the butt of the .45, throw Navarro over his shoulder and hightail it out of here. He'd deal with the fall-out tomorrow. He could invent some perfectly legitimate beef with Bowman over jealousy regarding Navarro – which was halfway the truth anyway – and hope that Jericho backed his play as he had up until now. So, not great, but workable.

Unfortunately, Tanner had been drinking steadily since he'd sat down and while he might not be wasted – his tolerance was way higher than that – his bladder was painfully tight. First things first, quickly see to the immediate physical obstruction, then get Navarro out of here. He'd only be out of the room for a few seconds. Still, best to keep all the bases covered. On his way out to the bathrooms Tanner swung by the bar and button-holed the zoned-out barman. He pointed to Bowman and Navarro.

'Whatever you do, don't let those two leave. He owes me money.'

'Uh, OK, boss.'

Tanner exited. A moment later, when he returned from the john, he froze. There was no sign of Navarro or Bowman. Tanner bore down on the bar like the wrath of God. The barman was half-heartedly mopping up beer dregs with a bar towel and singing Nine Inch Nails hits to himself woefully off key.

'Where did they go?' Tanner demanded, trying to keep the alarm out of his voice.

'Where did who go, maestro?' the junkie drawled without looking up.

'The big Creole with the teeth jewels and the girl. We just talked about them thirty seconds ago. Hey, look at me, up here, fucktard.'

The barman beamed back a blank brain-donor stare at Tanner. He was completely roasted. 'Girl?' he mumbled. 'What girl, dude?'

Tanner had to restrain himself from leaping over the bar and bashing his teeth in against the hard wood surround of the beer pump.

'The fox in the biker's leather with the punky hair,' he grated out with enormous self-control.

The stoner blinked and then frowned, as if he was trying to figure out high-level calculus in his head. 'Aw, naw dude,' he finally mumbled. 'She left with the other guy, the cat with the beard.'

Tanner was baffled for a second. Who? Guy with the beard? What the fuck—

Jericho.

Even though, after adrenalin, alcohol was Tanner's drug of choice, he didn't much like bars. Or, rather, he didn't like the experience of trawling them, shuttling from one ill-lit noisy space to the next, never settling, constantly wheeling woozily from A to B to C across the whole smear of a night. Tanner was the sort of drinker to camp out on a bar stool and quietly get hammered while swapping the occasional friendly word with the serving staff and toasting himself ironically in the mirror behind the spirits optics. He might have a game of pool with a stranger if the mood took him, then stagger home as dawn touched the sky.

Having to sprint into more bars than he could comfortably count as he frantically searched for Navarro was something like a drug-induced nightmare. All the rooms looked alike: the same hot sweaty faces, the same shouts and shrieks and spinning lights, like a hideous never-ending party where all the people looked identical but you never saw a face you knew. He didn't see any sign of Navarro and with every minute that passed his concern for his friend grew and grew. Bowman might be an abusive sadist, but at least his perversions were a known quantity. Tanner didn't have the faintest clue what Jericho was capable of doing to a woman like Navarro, and he desperately didn't want to have to find out.

As he jogged from street to street and corner to corner, sticking his head into bars, peering down sinister alleys, he kept hitting speed dial on his cell phone. Once, twice, three times, monotonous as a robot. Every time he just triggered the same curt voicemail message in his ear.

He wondered if he should start phoning emergency rooms, or even risk his cover by getting Jones to issue an APB on Jericho. He dashed along Basin Street, Canal and Bourbon, his frustration swelling into a violent torrent, at Jericho, at Bowman, at the world, but mostly at himself for putting Navarro in this peril. He started to lash out as he ran, shouting as if he was suffering from Tourette's, denting metal signs with random blows. Of course he was drunk as well, which just twisted the dial on his emotions to the maximum.

He almost got into a fight with a couple of over-zealous doormen who wouldn't let him take a peek into their sports bar if he wasn't going to pay the cover charge. Tanner saw the red mist draw down and felt his hands clenching into fists. The instant before he threw the first haymaker, however, his cell phone abruptly began to sound out of his top pocket. It was a camp little ringing bell that seemed faintly ridiculous in the high tension of the moment. He turned away from the bouncers to eagerly check the caller ID. It was Navarro. He scrambled to answer.

'You been looking for me,' she suggested, her voice husky. Tanner bit the inside of his mouth to try and keep calm. He tasted the coppery tones on his tongue.

'Where are you, Julia?' he asked very evenly. 'I've been calling and calling. I was . . . concerned. I mean, with all the villains at that bar, and you just vanishing like a Jesus freak on Judgement Day . . . I was a mite worri—'

'Yeah, I'm on the shore of Lake Pontchartrain,' she cut him off. 'Not far from where we smoked off those homeboys. Come meet me and we can discuss why the fuck you think you've replaced my daddy now.'

She snapped off the connection before he could reply.

When he found her she was standing beside a sheltered inlet surrounded by ragged palm trees shooting bottles off a tree stump with a meaty Ruger .45 ACP. The long-fanged leaves of the trees whispered together as the breeze passed by. The Ruger growled like a pitbull on a leash. Another bottle exploded with a dull whoosh. The surface of the Pontchartrain was choppy in the darkness, a cauldron of molten lead boiling all the way out to the black horizon.

Tanner parked up a short way along the road and ambled slowly back towards the inlet, trying his best to to compose his thoughts.

'What happened to the twenty-two Jericho gave you?' he asked in a carefully neutral voice, maintaining a respectful distance behind the shooter. Navarro didn't look back. Narrowed her eyes and squeezed off another round. A cloudy brown bottle vanished into a cloud of sparkling shards. Bull's-eye. Silver Glaser Safety Slugs. Showstopper rounds. Navarro wasn't fucking around. He'd been worried about her safety in the company of killers like Jericho and Bowman, now he wasn't so sure. Perhaps he should have been concerned for them?

'That little BB gun won't get the job done,' she murmured in a preoccupied tone.

'What job?' Tanner asked, enunciating with great care and precision. He wanted to impress upon her how serious this was and get her to consider how reckless her behaviour had become. Julia didn't reply.

'Where'd you get it?' he asked.

'Friends in low places.' She smiled coldly to herself, turning so she shared only her profile with him. She was outlined with moonlight.

'Why did you go with Jericho?' Tanner demanded.

'You're a big boy, you figure it out.'

Tanner grabbed her elbow and spun her around like a doll. 'This isn't a game of Catch Me Quick, you know. Trying to manipulate the likes of Bowman and Jericho is like dousing yourself in petrol and running through an exploding firework factory.'

'You have your way of getting close to the Indian, I've got mine,' she told him fiercely.

Tanner stared at her, not knowing how to deal with this. This was definitely not the Julia Jaybird he once knew and it was all his own fault for stupidly assuming he could manage her vengeful obsession. How had he been deluded into thinking this wouldn't complicate the mission further? By agreeing to help Navarro he'd basically thrown napalm on the situation. But meeting her again and being reminded of his past had brought into sharp focus all of the things he was forced to do in this sewer of a job, all the compromises he had to make. Of course, he knew why undercover work was necessary and he'd gone into the profession with his eyes open, but you stand under a drain long enough you're bound to start smelling eventually, and this particular stink didn't rub off so easily. He'd hoped that if he helped Julia achieve some measure of justice then it would absolve him of his own dark taint. Now, though, he wondered if his decision hadn't simply made everything a hundred times worse.

Navarro cut away from Tanner to continue her

target practice, filling the night with thunder again. The shots cracked across the water and rebounded like a leather whip off a boulder.

'You're not my brother, John,' she spat, jerking another bullet into the bottles. 'You're not even my half-brother.'

BAM.

'You don't need to look out for me.'

BAM.

'I don't want you to.'

BAM BAM BAM.

'You're nothing but a friend, and this is just a partnership. We're working together to serve a greater purpose, so don't overstep your boundaries, understand? I live my own life my own way.' She paused to reload, twisting at the hip to glance back at him. 'What's caused this over-protectiveness anyway?'

'This isn't about me,' Tanner muttered darkly

'Oh, I think it is. I think it's mostly about you.'

'I'm not the one shooting bottles off a tree stump like a crazed sniper preparing to climb up into a clock tower come the morning. Tit-for-tat killing isn't the answer. If we just murder the Indian, then we're no better than he is.'

Navarro's eyes flashed in the shadows. 'Maybe we aren't better than he is? Did you ever consider that? See, I've been talking to your buddy Bowman – and Jericho.' Tanner couldn't prevent a twitch pulling at his cheek when Jericho's name was spoken, but in the dark, luckily, Navarro didn't notice. 'They say all sorts of pretty fucking unsavoury things about your behaviour, John.'

'Don't believe everything you hear from villains,' Tanner grated.

'Villains like you, you mean?'

There was no answer to that, so Tanner just said nothing and they stared at each other in a flinty mistrustful silence. Abruptly his cell phone chimed and he dug it out gratefully to crack the tension of the moment.

He stepped away from Navarro to speak. His expression grew steadily more sober as the conversation with the unnamed caller progressed. He muttered a few terse words into the cell, nodded and then cut the connection with a curt snap. His face was unreadable as he returned to Navarro, who'd been watching him intensely throughout the whole exchange.

'Who was that?' she asked in a charged, trembling voice.

Tanner didn't answer straight away, just tapped his cell phone thoughtfully against his lip as he peered off across the seething steel-coloured lake.

'Jericho,' he eventually replied. 'I've been invited for an audience with the Indian.' He paused. 'Only me, not you.'

Navarro's face was a pale stiff mask hanging in the gloom.

'I'm going alone,' Tanner quietly concluded.

Chapter Eighteen

Later, it was the barking that Tanner would remember most vividly.

The Indian's bull mastiffs were so aggressive, so quick to anger at any tiny shift in their environment that they seemed to keep up a constant barrage of blood-curdling noise. It was a demonic sound, a broadcast of unthinking, unreasoning violence from an animal bred with one goal in mind: to hurt other creatures, as bloodily and painfully as possible. This was a sound with fangs and hot staring eyes and slavering jaws and it never gave up.

Tanner hadn't been allowed to drive to the Indian's current abode himself. The gang leader had a whole host of boltholes, which he cycled through at random to maintain the mystery of his voodoo legend and guarantee his personal security.

Thankfully, the men who picked him up didn't insist on blindfolding him or trying to shove him in the trunk, though they did follow a circuitous route, which left him slightly at a loss as to their exact destination. He was able to work out that they were heading deep into the Central Business District, which was strange. Still, it was as good a place to hide as any, he reasoned. Mythical voodoo drug lords rarely rubbed shoulders with day traders and merchant bankers, so it was pretty unlikely that anyone would try and look for them there. Tanner had made Navarro swear that she wouldn't try and follow him to the meeting and, to his relief, he didn't detect any vehicles trailing them down the broad open boulevards.

The thugs remained tight-lipped throughout the whole drive. Tanner had never seen any of them before and wondered whether they were some kind of élite 'honour guard' of specially trusted flunkies, who'd been indentured to Sepion as repayment for some dark misdeed.

The house, when they arrived, was remarkably unremarkable. It was big, certainly, a bloated four-storey American townhouse with a red stucco façade and a second-floor balcony, but all its windows were closed off by peeling storm shutters and it had the air of a vacant business property. Inside it was stripped bare, no furniture, no carpets, just naked walls and boards, which meant that every tiny sound was reflected all throughout the building, rebounding round and round like moaning spectres trapped in a bottle. Tanner heard the dogs the moment he stepped through the door and shivered. He couldn't help but visualize those grisly photos from Powell's office.

Before the trip Tanner had agreed with Jones, who'd run it up the wire to Powell, that this was to be just a quick drive-by, a sweep to get the lie of the land. It was the first time the NOPD had managed to get an operative into the same house as the Indian, and the last thing they wanted to do was to spook the target. Today's meet was strictly a fact-finding mission. He would speak when spoken to, tug his forelock and accept any assignments he was issued without a word of complaint, even if he was told to clean out the toilets.

Consequently, Tanner wasn't wearing a wire or any other recording device and he'd gone in unarmed, a decision that Jones had vociferously argued against. Tanner had insisted he could look after himself even bare-handed, and could definitely talk his way out of any tight corners. Jones reluctantly conceded, and it turned out to have been absolutely the correct decision as the Indian's honour guard thoroughly searched him in the creaking empty entrance hall. There was no way anyone was getting guns into this place unless they tied them to a brick and threw them through the window.

He was escorted up to the third floor and made to sit in a high-backed chair in a sizeable bedroom. The room contained the only furniture he'd seen so far, three more chairs and a low table, each covered with dust cloths. It was a mothballed house, standing empty waiting for new tenants who would never arrive. The perfect bolthole. There were probably even buyers listed somewhere: a fictional young professional couple perhaps? Tanner heard heavy movement in the room next door, muffled voices droning through the thin walls, and the dogs barking. Always the dogs. Two of the hoods entered and took up stations against the wall; one had cornrows, the other had a Jheri curl tickling his ears. They stared straight ahead, neither glancing at Tanner.

Tanner began to wonder idly if this house was so empty because it was easier to clean blood off that way, and whether, in fact, it was a place Sepion brought his victims to feed to the demon dogs. Tanner flexed his hands in his lap and then held them a few inches above his knees. They didn't tremble. He was ready for this. 'Look the devil in the eye and tell him you think his horns look just swell,' he whispered to himself.

Far away downstairs he heard the front door swing open again and rattling bootsteps enter. This was followed by men talking. Then a woman's voice echoed up the winding stairway, and Tanner's heart fell.

He prayed that he was wrong as the voices approached, rising up through the house in a buzz of motion and conversation, but he knew he wasn't. Navarro walked into the room with Jericho's arm slung over her shoulder. She hadn't followed Tanner; she'd found her own ride. As she'd come in with Jericho they hadn't patted her down for weapons,

Tanner knew that instantly. He remembered the Ruger .45 ACP roaring in the night, the bottles vaporizing into a thousand glinting shards. He thought of her empty promises.

Whenever Navarro's hand brushed her hip, or reached inside her jacket for a stick of gum or a tissue, Tanner cringed. He wondered how many people she could shoot before he grabbed one of the thug's guns and put her down – and if it came to that, whether he'd be able to pull the trigger, or even if he should.

She never looked at him directly, preferring instead to drape herself over Jericho, her lithe body pressed against his rocky frame. He rested a hand on her hip as if she was a piece of expensive designer luggage he didn't want to let out of his sight. Once he drew her in to a functional, passionless kiss, more an act of territorial marking than sensuality. When they parted Navarro's lipstick wasn't even smudged. The image of Jericho pawing Julia Jaybird was deeply offensive to Tanner, but in the end it was basically the same tactic he'd used himself. Both he and Navarro had made unwise partnerships with a sociopath to further their goals, only hers was more effective, if considerably more perilous.

'When are we going in? Is the Indian actually even here?' he asked, trying to move things along.

'He's here,' rumbled Jericho. 'But I need to discuss some matters with him first. Wait here and work on that impatient streak of yours,' he instructed, then he stepped out of the room.

The guards didn't move, just continued to stare into space, and Navarro wouldn't sit. She paced out languorous steps in front of the shuttered window, a studied performance of sexy boredom. But what was really scaring Tanner were the minute cues her body gave away that only he could see, because only he knew why she was really here. She radiated a host of twitches and tells that screamed: Dead woman walking.

She took out her make-up bag and began to refresh her lipstick, but a slight tremor caused her to fumble the cylinder and it tumbled to the bare boards with a sharp clatter. She covered very well – kneeling gracefully to retrieve it – and then shrugged to the room.

'I'm just a little nervous at meeting the king of New Orleans,' she confessed with an embarrassed smile

But her fingers were still shaking as she returned the lipstick to her bag, and she didn't repeat the attempt to fix her make-up. Tanner stood to cross the room towards his friend, but the guards instantly snapped their collective gaze on to him, their expressions suspicious.

'Settle down, boys. I'm just stretching my legs,' he told them gruffly.

He took a quick turn around the room, but saw it would be virtually impossible to talk to Navarro covertly. He retreated to his seat, and waited there strumming with tension. This situation had become a runaway train and Tanner knew all too well the final terminal they were roaring towards, yet he was powerless to avert disaster. He'd never felt more impotent. He wasn't armed, he couldn't pull Navarro aside to try and bark some sense into her (not that he'd had much luck with that so far). All he could do was look on helplessly as the end of the track raced towards them.

He racked his brains for some way out, some clever scheme or plot, but his concentration was shattered by the endless barking. Sweat dampened his armpits, pooled down the back of his jeans. The very walls seemed to vibrate with the cacophony of the dogs. The sounds were so much louder now the beasts were just next door. Occasionally there was a strange pause, and a sort grizzled moist noise which Tanner could only assume was . . . chewing.

The dogs were spooking Navarro as well. She flinched every time they let rip a fresh salvo and she finally went over to one of the other chairs where she sat on her shaking hands. Still she wouldn't look in his direction so he couldn't even signal to her with his eyes. Then Jericho abruptly returned, making them both jump a little.

'Those fucking dogs, eh?' Tanner weakly tried to lighten the mood.

'You get used to it,' Jericho replied robotically. 'Come on. He'll see us now.'

The blood drained right out of Navarro's face. The

moment she'd been preparing herself for was finally here. Her lips compressed into a thin white line. Her breath came in tiny tight shivering volleys.

Jericho led the way back out on to the landing and they followed him as a snaking chain as he continued on into the Indian's lair next door. As they swung into the room they saw that this was the only properly furnished room in the house, with luxurious rugs on the floor and expensive art on the walls.

But Tanner only had eyes for the figure looming behind a vintage oak writing table not unlike the one in Anton Powell's office. Tanner frowned in puzzlement.

The Indian was fat. He hadn't expected that.

In fact he was more than just fat, he was positively corpulent. His distended belly was beaded with perspiration like a Coke bottle straight out of the freezer box. He was naked from the waist up, dressed incongruously in satin pyjama bottoms, an emerald velvet smoking jacket lashed around his hips. He was tall, certainly, six four or five, but stooped with the soft rounded shoulders of a man long absent from any regular exercise regime; powerful, but massively unhealthy. It was true that you could see the Cherokee blood in his face: the noble hawkish nose, the wide proud lips and dark mane. But those features were swamped by the puffy marshmallow folds of his cheeks and his hair was greasy and unwashed, lying flat against his back. Someone had tied a few bright decorative feathers into his locks, presumably as a concession to his moniker, though in his current state it did look more like he'd blundered drunkenly through a bird sanctuary one night. He sniffed constantly, and even at this range Tanner could see his septum was half dissolved, leaving ghastly ragged holes where his nostrils should be.

The room was long – possibly it had once been a formal dining hall in centuries past – but had been filled in a totally ad hoc manner with a random collection of luxury items. There appeared to be individual pieces from three different furniture sets, none of which matched, a punch-bag, and a jetski, which was being used as an impromptu clothes horse. Along one wall a 52-inch hi-def television was propped like a discarded art print. The screen was surrounded by an X-Box, Playstation, Wii, various DVD and Blu-ray players, none of which were plugged in. Piles of DVD and CD cases formed an ungainly ring fence of precarious towers all around. There were golf clubs, beanbags, hunting rifles in a rack, Persian rugs, and what looked like a solid gold footstool. There was even an eleven-thousand-dollar stainless-steel wrap Northland refrigerator humming obediently in the far corner. The room was a glittering Tutankhamun's tomb of impulse buys.

Behind Sepion's desk was a beautiful chaise lounge, on which lolled a skinny party girl in a crumpled white sheath dress. She was making tiny noises of delight as she slowly stroked her own arms with the sensuous fascination of the chemically enlivened.

Three truly colossal black bull mastiffs were chained to the wall about halfway down the room, ropes of slaver falling around their snarling fangs, their eyes rolling. Beside the dogs sat a steel cage bolted to the floor. Its bars were filthy and worryingly flecked with scarlet. In the corner, curled up in the foetal position, was a naked man. His exposed flesh was filthy and spangled with a constellation of cuts and scabs. If he had been able to sit up the cramped space would have barely been sufficient for him to crouch with comfort, but he simply didn't move.

Ahead of Tanner Navarro was trembling. He could sense tension spilling out of every pore of her being and he instinctively knew why. He'd known from the moment she stepped into the bedroom on Jericho's arm. For her this was the lair of her father's killer, and it was as clear as day to Tanner that she was about to draw her .45 and put a bullet between his eyes. Tanner was bringing up the rear of this strange procession of supplicants, and everyone's attention was locked on the Indian himself, up ahead . . .

Which enabled Tanner to suddenly kick the nearest bull mastiff as hard as he possibly could.

The ferocious brute exploded into motion, surging out to the choke point of its chain in an eye blink. The noise coming out of the creature was like being beaten on the eardrums by hammers. Its mouthful of fangs looked wide enough to swallow your head up to the neck. Tanner almost expected to see its saliva eating through the floorboards like acid. Julia leapt back in fear and shock. Tipped off balance she collided heavily with Tanner who was trailing closely behind. He was ready for her, and bore her weight easily, as his free hand dipped beneath her jacket and briskly liberated the Ruger .45 from its holster. Navarro's face whipped round in alarm, her eyes flashing, but it was too late. Tanner stepped back swiftly so that she couldn't attempt any foolish grab back, and stowed the piece surreptitiously under his belt, with an apologetic look. Tanner had covered the encounter so smoothly that no one else had the slightest idea what had passed between them.

But now they realized they were in the presence of the enemy, and both Tanner and Navarro turned as one. The Indian regarded them from under heavy brows.

'Like my dogs?' he asked Navarro with vile relish. His accent was thick as swamp water, a drawling gumbo of French, African, Latin, all stewed in back-woods southern, soft around the syllables, lazy and musical, but sinister emerging from those corpulent lips. 'They sure seem to like you,' he whispered.

Julia didn't react. She seemed numb with the gravity of this meeting with her nemesis, but the Indian didn't notice. On his desk sat a chaotic mess of food cartons and plates bearing meals of many varieties: noodles, torn scraps of greasy half-eaten fried chicken, boxes of beignets and icing-topped doughnuts, a melting tub of Ben and Jerry's cookie dough ice-cream, random quadrants of pizza, bowls of chips and peanuts.

'When I catch that slimy, sister-fucking little rodent Lavache, I'm going to stick him in a cage with my beauties, Cheveyo and Honovi and Otaktay, and let them get to know him real well. Oh, they'll like the taste of his tenderloin!'

As the Indian talked he walked around the desk and ate from the bizarre smorgasbord, seemingly at random, so his words always issued out of a pit of masticating mulch, and his chin constantly shone with grease.

'They'll tear him into barbecue strips fresh for roasting! But he's like a cockroach, wherever you spray, he always comes back. You smash off his legs and he keeps on coming, but he won't win! I'm the big man here, in the swamps, in the city. I'm the hunter! What is he? He's nothing, a turd, a speck. Fuck Lavache! And fuck the stinking police always sniffing around my empire! All my enemies! I'll eat them all. I'll swallow them down without even chewing . . .'

While he ranted Sepion stuck a fist into the chicken and to punctuate his sentences he intermittently flung out handfuls of meat across the room towards the dogs, who leapt up against their chains, howling to claim his greasy beneficence. Occasionally the scraps would land equidistant between two of the mastiffs and this would spark off a snarling tug of war that made Tanner and Julia wince at its savagery.

Sepion scuttled back and forth, head down,

spouting into his chest. He would suddenly stop dead for no reason, then skew off in another arbitrary direction and shout at the windows, moving with the spasmodic energy of a remote-controlled toy car whose batteries were fading.

What was odd to Tanner, though, was that he was fixating on Lavache. Surely the whole reason he and Navarro were here in the first place was precisely because Lavache and the LLR were now a spent force? Yet here Sepion was babbling away as if he barely knew what was going on in the world outside. What's more, just as his movements were apt to suddenly veer off in a totally new direction, so were his thoughts. Halfway through a vivid description of how he'd like to rip open Lavache's stomach and feed his intestines to the dogs like a rope of sausages, he suddenly glanced up in astonishment at finding Tanner and Navarro standing there in front of him.

'So, you're the two crazies who stole Lavache's entire fleet of cars from under his nose?' he asked with a glazed look. His eyeballs were bloodshot, an eggy chequerwork of blown blood vessels laid across two orbs like peeled lychees.

'Yeah, that was us,' Tanner replied, going quickly with the slaloming of what you could only laughingly call a conversation. He was used to this sort of free-associating junkie logic, though it still surprised him to find it gushing out of their ultimate foe's mouth. 'We're both outta San Francisco originally, but joined your crew a few months back. We're drivers, so it made sense to steal all our enemy's sweetest rides, right?'

However, Sepion's concentration had already skidded off again, and he was now only paying attention to Navarro. He stalked in close to her, until he was only inches from her face. Tanner saw her toes retreat minutely, her spine go hard.

'Now you sure are sweet fresh meat, *chèrie*,' the Indian crooned with a crooked leer. He brought a pudgy hand up to her cheek and gently grazed it. Even a few feet away Tanner could smell the over-ripe stench of the drug baron, and shuddered at what it must be like for Navarro to have his hot breath upon her, with all the baggage she'd brought with her. A tiny quiver chased through her shoulders and the moment seemed to hang like half-molten candle wax, extending on and on.

'She's delish, ain't she?' the party girl called out. 'Can we have her come live with us, sweetie? Can we?'

The girl came to lean against Sepion's corrugated back and gazed at Navarro with narcotic-fuelled craving. She picked up a soggy-looking croissant from the desk and nibbled its horn. Navarro's eyes widened slightly in frightened revulsion.

'She's with me,' grated Jericho from the corner. It was a statement of fact, not a request. That was interesting. If there was even a hairline crack between their target and his chief lieutenant then it was definitely something they should try and lever apart.

But Sepion merely glanced over his shoulder at

Jericho and something darted deep within his gaze. 'Naw, girl,' he admonished softly, and pushed his paramour back towards the chaise lounge. 'This girl's got skills. I need my road girl out on the streets where she belongs . . .'

He returned to his bizarre roaming across the floor.

'But when we're finally done here, when we've trampled over all our rivals and I have my boot upon the city's neck, then I'll need strong lieutenants. Jericho vouches for you, so you will be my chosen ones. For now, though, I must keep moving. Never stay in one place or they'll catch up, my enemies, the cops and the feds – those fucking cops, sending their spies, and all their treacherous never-ending schemes—'

He flashed towards Navarro with an unexpected burst of speed, clutching hold of her bicep like a cobra striking. However, just as swiftly the mania deserted him again and he became lethargic once more.

'I have such plans for this city,' he mumbled, absently scratching his balls, his other hand still holding on to Navarro's arm with a bird's claw grip. For Navarro to be so close to her father's killer and yet unable to take her planned revenge was clearly taking its toll on her emotionally. Her face was grey, her eyes dull as old rubber.

'But will you be a hero for the city?' she croaked. 'Will you be a Robin Hood for the little people? Or are you just being ridden by the Loa or the will of the Great Spirit? Are you a man or a holy puppet?'

Tanner tensed. He had a gun now. He put his hand beneath his jacket.

Don't antagonize him any more, Julia, Tanner thought desperately. But the Indian wasn't paying attention. His eyes rolled away, skittering off over the ceiling. Spasms twitched through his flesh like electric jolts and he started to hum distractedly.

'Are you OK, boss?' Tanner asked in an even tone. 'Get you a glass of water?' It truly was baffling to find this supposedly ruthless general in an almost schizophrenic fugue.

'I . . . I can't deal with this straight, all these questions,' Sepion mumbled. 'I need a fix, drop some snow on the mountain tops.'

'Here, baby, have some of mine,' simpered the party girl, advancing with a small leather pouch containing her stash.

'NO!' The Indian roared so loudly that a bubble of bloody snot inflated out of his ruined left nostril. The party girl leapt back in terror and the room took in a collective breath. Even the mastiffs seemed to sense the change in the mood and restricted themselves to an underlying low snarl.

'I only trust the shit Jericho brings me,' Sepion spat.

With that he beckoned feverishly to Jericho, who stalked across the room like a court physician, his steel-tipped boots heavy as tomb lids closing. He opened a small metal box and disinterred a hand mirror, an engraved platinum snorting tube, and a pristine bag of high-grade cocaine.

'Come on, come on . . .' Sepion muttered feverishly as Jericho laid out the drug kit before him, not caring who witnessed his feeble addiction. His bleary eyes became saucer huge as they beheld the beautiful powder.

This is the Indian? thought Tanner. This sybaritic, bloated wreck was the spectre who had terrorized all New Orleans? Sure, there was brutality here, and a savage insatiable appetite. The Indian obviously still inspired fear in his troops, but he had no self-control, no discipline, and seemed utterly detached from reality. He was as unstable as a child hurling toys around in a petulant fit. This was a leader making decisions based on whim and crippling paranoia.

Ultimately, how was he any better than Lavache, who so desperately tried to emulate him? They were both gibbering, whimpering shells of men, the only difference being that somehow the Indian had stumbled into power. In Sepion's whining, wheedling tone Tanner caught an echo of an earlier voice: Tycho, the pathetic, broken drug dealer whom Jericho had so effortlessly controlled.

Tanner was frozen to the spot as an icy understanding swept over him and the whole dark puzzle clicked into place. Jericho handed Sepion a small hand mirror marked with four immaculate lanes of fresh snow-white powder. The Indian snuffled up the coke like a pig in the trough, utterly without moderation or restraint.

Tanner stared at Jericho, his gaze burning holes in

the other man's cheek, but the hitman didn't even look up. All his concentration was focused on the Indian. The dogs began to roar again but this time nobody reacted. A muscle in Tanner's cheek began to jump. Sepion slumped back in his throne chair, bare chest dusted with coke like sugar frosting, his expression empty. He grabbed the party girl and pulled her greedily on to his lap.

'We're done now,' he absently told the room, groping the girl's tit as if it was a foam stress ball. He dismissed his audience with a palm flick while his other hand began to dig aggressively between her thighs.

Jericho urged them all to clear the room. He toe-punted the cage as he passed by it, but the naked man inside made no reaction. Perhaps he was already dead? On the threshold they all heard the Indian groan, with ecstasy or pain, who knew? But the door slammed on the scene before they were afflicted with any more unwelcome knowledge of the supposed king of New Orleans.

Out on the landing again, the thugs all spilled off downstairs but Jericho stood in the open study doorway.

'Tanner, Bowman, through here,' he instructed.

Already poised at the top of the stairs, Navarro raised a suspicious eyebrow. Clearly she hadn't been expecting this. Wasn't Jericho keeping her in the loop?

'Can I sit in?' she began. 'Tanner and I are as good as partners now—'

'No,' Jericho cut her dead without looking. 'Go wait for me downstairs.'

Navarro's face went hard and white like moulded plastic.

Tanner wanted to say to her, 'Don't worry. This is good. The more we can keep you out of this, the better.' But he said nothing and cut his gaze away so she couldn't appeal to him. He headed into the disused office. There were a few crates covered in dusty cloths where Bowman had already taken up a pew.

'There's a mole in the gang,' Jericho announced flatly the moment the door slid home.

Tanner was still in the process of easing himself down on to the crate and it took all his presence of mind not to freeze in shock. He settled himself down next to Bowman, skin crawling for all sorts of reasons. Was this it? Was he exposed and Bowman was here to act as witness and executioner?

'Or that's what the Indian believes,' Jericho went on. 'I'm still not convinced. We have the source from the NOPD who sold us the compromised inform-ation about the money truck raid. You saw him next door.'

The man in the cage thought Tanner, unnerved.

'With a little persuasion from the Indian and his pets, he confessed to everything.'

Except I know he wasn't responsible for alerting Cochrane, I was, Tanner reflected grimly, *and the only reason that man confessed was because he was being tortured.*

238

The informant had been passing on police operational details which undoubtedly compromised countless missions and led directly to many officers being hurt, yet Tanner found it difficult to stomach the thought that he might be responsible for this nameless man's torture. *Bury it*, he told himself. *The ends justify the means.* It should be the undercover cop's motto.

'Anyway, the Indian still thinks there are leaks in the crew and he's the boss, so we investigate.'

Just beneath the surface of Jericho's smooth composure Tanner detected a seething layer of irritation, which revealed that he believed this was a waste of time and the Indian was a paranoid fool. It wouldn't necessarily be clear to someone who hadn't spent ten years honing their psychological skills on low-life scum, but Tanner could see Jericho was just going through the motions. That was a relief, as the last thing he needed now was to pretend to investigate the gang for himself.

'You two are the sharpest knives in my toolkit right now, so I want you to go and do a little casual digging. It's not a sure thing so don't make it a high priority, but keep your ears to the walls and your eyes to the keyholes. Report back with anything that doesn't smell right.'

Bowman and Tanner nodded as if they were joined at the jaw by wire. Being in synch with Bowman over anything was not a pleasant sensation.

'OK, make tyre tracks, Bowman. I got another

errand for Tanner,' Jericho rumbled. Bowman exited out on to the landing without apparent curiosity. A different sort of tension pooled in to fill the gaps. Tanner decided to poke the elephant in the room, just to see if it would stampede.

'I'm real pleased you came to me with this. I was beginning to worry I wasn't on your Christmas list any more. I thought after I saved your hide we were going to be tight for life, blood. Don't you trust me any more?'

'You're doing well, Tanner. The Indian is always impressed with an entrepreneurial spirit.'

'That's great, but—'

'Only there's a command structure to this organization, that's what he'd tell you if he were here, and I agree. Everyone got a little bit carried away over the stunt you pulled with Navarro.' She had been all over him like moisturiser and yet he didn't even use her first name. Classy. 'So as an exercise in humility the Indian wants you to play delivery boy. You're to go to the lock-up in the Quarter where you'll find a pristine BMW 550i with a full tank of gas. Drive it over to Baton Rouge and deliver it to a specific address within an allotted time period.'

Tanner didn't get it. What the hell was the angle here?

'That it?' he asked, nonplussed.

'Should there be anything else?'

'I dunno. Guess not. Am I at least allowed to know what this is for?'

'The car's "payment in kind" for a sympathetic zoning officer, who has been very useful to us recently.'

Ah, kick-backs. Yet still something wasn't quite adding up here. Why Tanner, and why now when the war with the LLR was at such a decisive moment? But he couldn't puzzle it out, his mind was still reeling after the sight of Jericho feeding Sepion his coke. He couldn't leave without prodding those suspicions. *Go big or go home*, he silently told himself. He leaned in confidentially to Jericho.

'Level with me,' he asked. 'The Indian can't operate without you, can he? You're the real power here.'

Jericho watched him impassively for a long while, saying nothing. The only sound in the room was the quiet inrush of their breath. However, Tanner had become accustomed to his intimidating silences and knew how to decode them.

This one said, *Yes, I am in control. I'm the one.*

Shit, thought Tanner, I need to get out of here.

He realized now how badly he had misjudged this whole operation. He needed to get by himself to work through all the appalling ramifications with a clear head. He needed to talk to Jones and to run these revelations up the chain of command to Powell. Tanner was very badly shaken.

He stood and moved to leave. He had to get out, now.

'I'll call once the car is delivered. I won't let you down.'

As he moved, Jericho suddenly said quietly without looking up, 'Drive carefully.'

Tanner hesitated for a beat with his shoulder propping the door open. He glanced back at the hitman and sucked his lip. He couldn't think of a suitably anodyne quip to offer so just nodded awkwardly and left.

When he got back downstairs Navarro was gone.

Chapter Nineteen

The reptile house was just as greenly lit as before, but it reeked far worse. Something was rotting in the display cases, either flesh or leaf mulch. One thing hadn't changed, though: there were still no cold-blooded inhabitants visible and this time Tanner and Jones were the only human visitors as well. The whole room had a haunted, otherworldly atmosphere. The air was so hot and close that it pushed against their faces like a second skin.

'I've been with the Indian this whole time and didn't even know it,' Tanner spat. He was still very shaken. He'd never misjudged a mission quite as badly as this. Jones frowned at him, not quite following.

'OK, now hang on, bro, maybe Sepion isn't what we imagined he was but that doesn't mean that he isn't as serious a threat—'

'No. Powell's wrong. I was wrong. We all under-estimated Jericho.'

'But the Indian conquered New Orleans by himself. His rise to power began long before Jericho ever arrived on the scene.'

Tanner nodded, struggling to see the full shape of the story in his head as he stared into the shadowy depths of the unkempt vegetation behind the glass.

'I'm certain the Indian did it all himself in the first place and clearly he still has some power today, but with power comes complacency. He's become fat and weak and obsessed with clinging on to his little empire. It's likely he was the one who weaved his boo-gieman persona and used it to terrorize the city, but these days Jericho is the one influencing him from behind the curtain. He's the brains. The Indian is just his front. All these aggressive incursions into other districts, gobbling up all the competition, *that* has Jericho written all over it. The thing about Jericho is he's all about control. He's gradually manipulated Sepion deeper and deeper into addiction as a way to influence his actions. He's used the Indian's instability as his means to control him.'

Jones didn't look at all convinced. 'I think you're getting carried away. You've not got any proof of this, John. All you have is a "gut feeling", most of which is based on vague similarities between how Jericho dealt with some scabby no-name dealer from the Melpomene Projects and how he supposedly controls the most powerful criminal figure within a hundred-mile radius!'

'I know what I saw,' Tanner insisted fiercely, though deep down he knew how fanciful and unconvincing his assertions sounded.

'I'm sure you believe that, and I do trust you – you

know that – but you've been under incredible strain for months now.'

'No. Jericho has been four steps ahead of us the whole way.'

'But there's no evidence for that.'

'You reviewed all of the recordings. Is there anything conclusive on Jericho in any of them? Even during the bayou raid. Bowman, the Mexican kid, sure, all the rest we've got dead to rights, but never Jericho. It's like he knows just what to say, or exactly when to stay silent. I'm starting to wonder if he doesn't even know he's being recorded somehow!'

'Seriously, John, listen to yourself. You're sounding as paranoid as the Indian. You've spent too long with those animals without coming up for air.'

'It's precisely because I've been in so deep that I'm able to see these connections . . .'

'Thing is, John, I don't see how any of this changes our next step. We want to bring down the Indian's organization, Jericho is part of that organization, ergo, we're already in the process of bringing down Jericho.'

'We're not,' Tanner ground out stubbornly. 'If we don't refocus all of our attention on him, he'll slip by us like poison gas.'

Jones shook his head. He didn't put much credence in Tanner's claims, but their friendship was too important to just dismiss them out of hand. Tanner had picked up on his reticence, though.

'OK, I get it: you don't believe me. But at the end of the day, you're not the one I need to convince. Powell has to be told what's going on. We need to shift our energies away from the Indian and on to Jericho and he needs to get on board with the new plan to release new resources.'

'Powell will never go for that, and you know it. He's fixated on the Indian as his key to City Hall. Outside of you, me and some true crime bean counters in the records department no one else has ever heard of Jericho. There's no PR bump to bringing Jericho in, no headline grab in hoisting up a nameless hitman on a pike for the media to ooh and ahh over. All Powell can see is the Indian.'

'Then we have to make him see otherwise.'

Tanner glared at Jones, drilling his conviction into him. Jones squirmed on the skewer of Tanner's gaze for a few heartbeats, before eventually capitulating with an explosion of exasperated breath.

'All right! I'll talk to Powell. I'll get him to look at the case files and put your argument forward. That's as much as I can do.'

'I want to come in and see him, too. I need to prove this to his face.'

'OK! Jesus, John, when you get the bit between your teeth you don't ever let go, do you?'

The two friends regarded each other resentfully in the alien light. A sour silence curdled between them.

Julia Navarro was waiting outside as they came out of the reptile house. They were so clearly together they might as well have been holding hands. Tanner felt

Jones go rigid with shock behind him, but his own undercover reflexes kicked in like a jolt of nitrous oxide to a dragster's engine.

'Didn't expect to see you here,' he said smoothly. 'Well, you've caught us. Julia, this is my buddy, T. He's going to help us with our . . . little situation.'

Whenever you are compromised, always seize back the initiative as swiftly and with as much conviction as possible.

'What the hell are you talking about?' Navarro countered hotly, not letting him defuse her ambush so easily. 'Who the hell is this, and what gives you the right to interfere in my life? I should grab that gun right now and shoot you in the gut for what you did back at the house. It's my father who was murdered, Tanner! I swear, if you try and get between me and that vile beast again, I won't be responsible for my actions! This is justice for me, and for Dad, and you do not get to dictate the terms of my retribution . . .'

Tanner let Navarro vent off the initial heat of her rage before calmly stepping in to douse the fire.

'This is my fix-it guy, he's the one who's going to make it possible for you to have justice without having to commit murder before dying in a hail of bullets.'

'What are you talking about?'

'If you just calm down a little I'll tell you—'

'Stop treating me like I'm still ten years old and tell me now!'

'OK. OK! Tobias used to be a cop in San Francisco,'

Tanner started. 'He worked in vice and he busted me for some petty misdemeanour. He was a techie guy, good with soldering irons, great in the surveillance van. Well, that is until he got himself kicked off the force for taking tasty kick-backs. Hey, everybody else was doing it and he had relatives to support. After that, though, suddenly we weren't so different any more and we've been partnering up on all sorts of "grey market" projects ever since. I'm the Can-Do Dude, he's the Backroom Back-up Guy.'

First rule of dishonesty: always fly as close to the actual truth as possible, and you'll save yourself an awful lot of sleepless nights down the line.

'You've been working with a cop!' Navarro hissed. 'Why don't you just go the whole hog and tie a webcam to your head when we do our next job for the Indian!'

'An ex-cop. Everybody's life has a second act, Julia. They change and move on. You of all people should know that. That's why you've got to get over your trust issues.'

Navarro didn't answer, just regarded him sullenly from behind a wall of suspicion. Tanner pressed on in a more conciliatory tone.

'Look, I've acted out of line, Julia. I've been over-bearing and overprotective. I'm not your brother, I know that. I fucked up . . . But I genuinely do care for you as a friend and I want to see Ernesto's death avenged.

'Now, I've got this one errand to run for Jericho. It's

248

just a bullshit delivery-boy duty as a slap on the wrist for the stunt with the car transporter. After that I'm going straight back to the Indian and I will get him on tape confessing to your father's murder. That's a promise.'

Navarro stared at him without any reaction, her arms banded across her body tight as steel braces. It was as if her whole body was a protective shell to contain the emotional fire at her core, and she feared that if there were even the tiniest breech she would lose control and be utterly consumed from within.

'So, do we have an agreement that you won't try and kill the Indian again?' Tanner prodded softly.

After a long hesitation Navarro nodded. Just a tiny terse bob of the forehead. It was the only reaction she could safely let slip without risking an explosion. Tanner believed her, though.

'And you trust me?' he asked her.

He was already talking to her back, however.

Navarro turned on a heel and stalked away along the leafy pathway, quickly vanishing beyond the green curve. Tanner turned back to Jones, radiating a confidence he didn't fully feel

'We're good,' he said. 'She won't do anything stupid now. I'm certain she bought the story about you being an ex-cop. Of course, she'll be mad as hell when she eventually finds out once we ask her to testify, but we'll jump off that bridge when we come to it.' He drew in a breath. 'You'll check back with Powell then? I *have* to see him, Jones. Seriously. It's imperative.'

Jones shrugged his agreement, though his expression remained unconvinced and he glanced warily in the direction Julia had gone.

'I will, but don't hold your breath. You know Powell has a hard-on for the Indian the size of the Space Needle. It won't be easy to change his mind . . . And, honestly, John, I'm not sure it needs changing. I'll back your play because you're my boy, but just because you're my partner doesn't mean I automatically agree with you. I think you're getting too close to this.' Jones's handsome face was very sober as he went on: 'Navarro has made it personal for you like never before. You got all this shared history, and when I see you both together my alarms bells go off. I know you want to protect her because, deep down, you think it might help relieve some of your guilt for what happened to her brother, but, shit, that girl's the game-breaker, John. I've said it all along. No matter how much you think you've convinced her to be a team player I'm still worried she's eventually going to blow her lid and bring a whole world of hurt down on all of us.' He pursed his lips with disquiet. 'You be careful, John, y'hear?'

Tanner assured him that he had everything under control and the two men fist-bumped solemnly before going their separate ways.

Jones exited the zoo by a side gate, lost in thought. There was an ice-cream van parked beside the gate, which was in the process of being mobbed by sugar-addicted pre-schoolers. A host of brightly coloured balloons bobbled in the air like the severed heads of excitable cartoon characters. Jones navigated his way through the press of lunchtime crowds towards the car park.

'Hey!' someone called out behind him, and without thinking he turned.

It was Navarro.

She came up to him quickly and announced very directly, 'You're not just John's fix-it man, are you? You're his friend. I can tell.'

Her eyes locked on to his, searching for the tiniest clues in his expression. A frantic explosion of lies, stories and diversionary tactics sleeted through Jones's head.

'Yes.' His reply was simple but careful, devoid of any inflection or incidental information. If he looked away it was as good as screaming, 'I'm a liar! I'm hiding something!' So he kept his cool gaze upon her.

'You care about him, what happens to him?'

Jones nodded. Navarro glanced away herself now, chewing on her lip.

'He's not a killer, is he? He *is* a good man . . . ?'

Jones considered his answer for what seemed like an eternity, but in actuality it was probably less than four seconds.

'I think so,' he finally confirmed. 'He's tough when he needs to be, he cuts corners, sure, but however much he hides it, he's on the side of the angels. He knows right from wrong and I'd trust him with my life.'

Julia nodded, her eyes hooded. 'That's good,' she murmured quietly, before doubt again clouded her expression.

Without another word she twisted away and merged back into the stream of the crowd, her perfect shoulders hunched with hidden tension. Deeply worried, Jones watched her go . . .

As did the person across the street, the one who'd been taking photographs of both of them with a digital camera. The person who now started up their own engine the moment Jones got into his Chevy Camaro. The watcher trailed the police detective as the Chevy crawled out of the parking lot and headed off towards the Garden District.

About an hour later Quentin phoned Tanner in a panic.

He was trapped in what he insisted upon referring to as his 'safe house' – an ex-girlfriend's brother's rat-infested box room in the subdistrict of Tremé – and when he said 'trapped', he meant that whenever he planned to leave town he got halfway to the bus terminal before spotting someone he thought he recognized, or sometimes just someone who seemed to be watching him too closely, and then fled back to his rock to hide under it again.

Tanner listened to the kid's verbal diarrhoea with a stony face for some time before sighing heavily. At the end of the day, if the only way to get rid of Quentin was to actually drive him away in person, then it was probably a price worth paying.

'Be ready at seven,' he grumbled. 'I've got to run over to Baton Rouge. I'll take you myself, and you can make your own arrangements from there.'

This concession caused Quentin to become incredibly excited. 'Aw, I knew you'd come through, chief! I'll go in the trunk. I gotta hide my features, man, or they'll shoot me with snipers and shit. Put me in the trunk, Tanner. I'll go in the trunk!' he babbled in a wearying fizz of words.

'The hell you will. You'll sit up front and keep quiet or I'll punch your teeth out through the top of your head. Understand?'

He did.

Tanner picked up the keys from Bowman at a bar on St Philip Street not far from Lafitte's Blacksmith Shop; luckily the pass-over was very light touch, so he didn't have to make small talk with his reviled counterpart. Afterwards, he wandered down narrow alleys to the lock-up, turning over the past few days in his mind.

It felt like aeons since he'd last been to the lock-up but in reality he could have comfortably measured the interval in hours. Undercover time, hyped up on paranoia and adrenalin, was a wholly different beast to normal life. It was compressed, too bright, hyperreal. Days could feel like weeks. Sometimes

Tanner wondered if this was what he was addicted to, the feeling that the time he spent undercover was somehow better, shinier, more important than anything else. Did the life he had outside of his mission feel anaemic in comparison, greyed-out and faded? When he was doing his job he was always pretending to be someone else. Did that mean he could only enjoy himself properly when he was being another person? He tried to put this unsettling line of thought out of mind as he arrived at the lock-up.

The BMW turned out to be a beautiful ride, and it purred its way to the crooked crack neighbourhood where Quentin was staying. The car was riding a little low to the road, bit sluggish on the corners; it clearly needed some work on the suspension.

Perhaps this would be the first uneventful mission of his stay in the Crescent City? Past experience said probably not, but, hey, it was nice to want things. Something continued to niggle him about this set-up, but he couldn't quite put his finger on it. It was just a bog-standard delivery run, so what was his subconscious trying to tell him?

He picked up Quentin, who threw himself lengthwise into the passenger seat as if he thought they were under heavy fire in a hostile war zone. The kid was wearing a weird black hooded top on to which he stuck a multitude of tiny scarlet dots, scraps of fluorescent masking tape which he'd cut out with craft scissors. When he sat up Tanner swivelled to stare at him.

'To fool snipers,' Quentin told him knowledgeably. 'They won't know which dot is their laser sight, so they'll all get confused which'll give me time to dive for cover!'

Tanner stared at him for a long moment, and then nodded sagely. He started up the engine. Some people are so stupid they needed those warning stickers on steam irons that said, 'Warning: Do not use while clothes on body.' Quentin was one of those people. Soon, though, he would be out of Tanner's hair for good and only a danger to himself. Not that he'd get any thanks for that from Quentin himself, probably.

It was a ghostly night out on the interstate. The address for the delivery was a club in Baton Rouge, and Bowman had provided a blurry, barely readable map print-out for the final stage. He'd probably used a low-ink setting, cheap bastard. Quentin had the attention span of a gnat and quickly got bored; he plucked up the paper off the dash as the only object of interest which wasn't nailed down. His brow creased as he read the directions, then his whole face lit up.

'Aw, hey, I know that joint . . .'

Tanner frowned. His spidey sense started to tickle. 'You do?' he asked sceptically. 'You go clubbing in Baton Rouge?'

'Naw, never, unless you count the time me and all my cousins went to see the freakshow in

Prairieville . . .' Quentin started bouncing up and down in the passenger seat like a hyperactive toddler as he strained to recall the details. 'Why do I know that joint? No, don't say a word. It'll come to me in a sec . . .'

Tanner clicked his tongue uneasily against his teeth. He saw a gas station up ahead and impulsively pulled on the wheel. He parked away from the pumps. The BMW's tank was practically full, but he needed a moment to think and make a quick phone call. Preoccupied, he got out without speaking to Quentin.

'Aren't ya going to ask me if I want anything from the store?' the kid piped up.

Tanner glowered back: 'Do you?'

'Hell yeah! If they've got some beef jerky and – oh! – grits meals in a tub an—'

Tanner slammed the door in his face.

He phoned Jones the moment he'd shoulder-bumped his way into the gas station: 'Pal, I need you to run an address for me, see who owns it,' he told his friend, and then wandered idly along the aisles as he waited for an answer, peering at labels and the looming grey clouds of fog that rolled on to the plate window like breakers against the beach. After a few minutes Jones rang back.

Tanner listened to his friend's urgent words without expression. Then he closed up his cell one-handed and left the store without buying a thing.

* * *

Quentin was extremely agitated as the wheelman dropped heavily back into the driver's seat. His eyes gleamed with alarm. 'Chief, we cannot go to dat address. I just worked out who owns it—'

Tanner cut him off: 'Jean-Baptiste Lavache.'

He bumped the car into gear and pulled out of the gas station, rolling the conundrum around his head. How would the Indian – or even Jericho – benefit from sending him straight into Lavache's arms? If the Indian wanted him dead there were far easier, less expensive – and guaranteed – methods. Nothing added up here.

They powered away down the interstate. The Beemer's handling was lethargic and the acceleration still felt a little sluggish. Tanner gritted his teeth and jammed his boot impatiently on the gas to compensate for the car's weight.

Suddenly an unpleasant thought occurred to the wheelman.

He drove on for about half a mile before pulling off into a lay-by. The fog above was an eerie amber colour infected with light pollution from the nearby conurbations.

'Stay there,' Tanner warned Quentin in a decisive tone before stepping out into the curdled semi-dark.

He walked around to the trunk of the car, his unease growing as the mist curled ominously around his ankles. With the trunk open he couldn't see anything untoward, but then he started to feel around the recessed edge of the moulded foam and polyurethane panel that formed the bed of the trunk. He eventually located a raised lip to get his fingernails underneath and gingerly lifted the board up to reveal the secret cavity beneath.

And the bomb that nestled inside.

Chapter Twenty

Tanner took a picture of the device with his camera phone and messaged it to Jones. A few seconds later he got an alarmed reply via text. It read: 'Don't use phone. Cud be remote detonation by cell. Find landline.'

Tanner closed the trunk as gently as he could. As he walked slowly back to the driver's side of the Beemer he thought that he should probably warn Quentin that he was driving around with 220 pounds of razor-sharp shrapnel and gel-based explosives not 3 feet from his back.

Then he decided that he really shouldn't tell Quentin anything. Ever.

He got back into the car, hesitated for half a second and then restarted the engine with a rush of confidence he didn't really feel. The car woke with a silky purr. Thank the Lord for German precision engineering, he thought.

Quentin pointed his rodenty face in Tanner's direction. His features were pinched and worried in the pale interior light.

'What that all about?' he wheedled. 'We hit a raccoon?'

'Don't ask,' Tanner told him gruffly.

Quentin didn't and Tanner pulled away from the kerb very, very carefully.

'We're trying to get a bomb-disposal team out to you, but they're on a job with a suspicious package at Louis Armstrong airport.'

'Damn. That's no good, Jones,' Tanner hissed into the chipped receiver, his breath crackling with suppressed anxiety. 'I've got an iron-clad deadline on delivery for the car. Jericho was weirdly specific about that – and now we know why.'

He was sheltering under the moisture-spangled yellow hood of a pay phone on the side of I-10, not far out of Gonzales. A light shower had come on minutes earlier, which had chased away most of the mist. Its feathery drizzle softened the edges of everything outside of a few yards. The trees on the far side of the road were black. The illumination inside the car, however, highlighted Quentin with his boots up on the dashboard. The kid was banging out a tune with his heels. Tanner gripped the handset tighter. If the BMW erupted in a cataract of flame right now at least one of his problems would be solved, he thought sourly.

'Now, I'm no expert on these types of devices so I can't tell if it's on a timer, or whether they've got some way of triggering it wirelessly. If it's the latter then they might have someone with a cell-phone trigger shadowing us, or someone waiting by the club in Baton Rouge. There's no way of knowing, so we can't take any more chances. Just the fact that we're talking now is an appalling risk.'

'Well, there's no other choice then. We have to evacuate the club.'

'Jones, we can't. If that club gets emptied by the police – even if you dress it up as a fire scare – my cover is blown. Jericho and the Indian will instantly know it was me and the whole operation is toast. That bomb has to go up and it has to go up in the vicinity of that club.'

'We can't let a club full of people be blown to pieces just to preserve our op, man – even Powell would see that!'

'Of course not, but there has to be another way round this,' Tanner muttered.

Slowly the answer came to him, but he grimaced as he saw how it bordered on the suicidal. He took a moment to consider if there was any other way, but there wasn't so he finally said: 'I've got an idea, but you're not going to like it. This one's going to be real seat-of-the-pants stuff. You just have to trust me, Jones. I want you to wait fifteen minutes after we hang up. Then I want you to put in an anonymous call to Jean-Baptiste Lavache.'

This was a potentially lethal hand he was playing, Tanner reflected as they coasted into the thinly populated Baton Rouge suburbs, but he couldn't think of any other way to satisfy both of his masters.

They might still get away with it, and keep both their skins intact, but only if they were able to adhere to a swift schedule. With the countdown to the car's delivery rushing towards them like a freight train, there simply wasn't any time left to spare. Speed was of the essence, but with a potentially volatile explosive device rocking around in the trunk that wasn't such an easy proposition. Even Quentin realized something was up.

'Why we driving so slow, chief?' he asked, puzzled, as Tanner arced the BMW softly round an already very forgiving corner. 'I thought for a second you were going to get out and carry the car round that one.'

'I'm in a laid-back mood.'

'Aw, OK. But I don't think those cops you just crawled past are gonna swallow that.'

Just as the kid said it the red and blue stars began to cycle in Tanner's rear-view mirror. It was testament to how wrapped up in driving like a eighty-year-old Mormon grandma he'd been that he'd totally failed to spot the speed trap. A siren hooted out behind them. 'Pull over,' blared the police car's PA system.

With an exasperated growl Tanner downshifted gears and sailed in to the kerb. He flicked open the glove compartment and retrieved his (false) driver's licence and papers.

'Stay here and don't say or do anything and DON'T get out of the car no matter what happens,' he warned Quentin. 'In fact, why not close your eyes and hum for a few minutes.'

He exited the car with a heavy heart. This really wasn't what they needed right now. Strictly speaking he should have remained in the BMW so as not to risk antagonizing the cops, but he really needed to move things along. Anyway, he knew how to appear non-threatening and they'd only make a fuss about that if they were the worst sort of obstructive jobsworth dicks.

The cops from the patrol car were both in their twenties. The first was a wiry, weaselly-faced guy with a bow-legged gunslinger's walk; his partner by contrast was an overdeveloped muscle mountain with a lazy eye and a trim goatee. He was trying to radiate command presence as if he was a three-bar heater. He presumably thought that the expression he wore was coldly dis-passionate, but as someone who'd regularly been on the receiving end of truly chilling lack of emotion Tanner felt the cop just looked faintly constipated.

'Hey, officers, was I doing something wrong? Did I run a stop sign? I'm new round here,' Tanner called out amiably, with just the slightest trace of simulated nervous vulnerability.

'Well, no one asked you to get out of the car, for a start,' droned Command Cop. Tanner groaned inwardly, though he maintained a co-operative, puzzled mien as the men moved up close to him. Command Cop crowded Tanner closely, but the wheelman wasn't one to intimidate easily and kept his cool.

'Licence and registration please, sir,' asked the

Weasel. He was behaving marginally more professionally than his colleague, who was now stalking round the BMW as if he thought he was fucking Batman. He shone his fancy multi-beam torch into the passenger seat and dazzled Quentin who was – thankfully – remaining docile.

Tanner handed over his impeccably falsified documents provided by the NOPD, and suppressed the urge to tap his toe or visualize a huge countdown clock on the top of the bomb. Weasel took his sweet time reviewing the pages.

'These seem to be in order, sir, but I am going to ask you to take a Field Sobriety Test in a moment, which, I should warn you, will involve various physical and mental multi-tasking exercises as well as the use of a portable breath tester. If you *have* imbibed any alcohol tonight, then now would be the time to speak up.'

Tanner's optimism for a swift exit shrunk like a pricked balloon.

'Really, officer? Are you sure? Of course, I'd be more than happy to comply, but I haven't had a drop – surely you can't smell anything on my breath?'

'Would you like to explain why you were driving so erratically, then?'

Well, slow is not the same as 'erratic', thought Tanner, but now didn't seem quite the time to quibble. He tossed an anxious glance over his shoulder at Quentin, who was staring moonishly through the wideshield.

'Look, it's my cousin there. I'm doing my sister a favour, he's . . . he's a good kid, but he's real simple.

Y'know, learning difficulties. The age and size he is now he's a real handful. Fully grown teen with the mind of a five-year-old. She never gets a break, so I offered to take him off her hands for a few days. We rode out to the gravel pit so I could give him a go behind the wheel, but he got all scared and shouty. I just wanted to keep him calm on the way back, so that's why I was driving this carefully. I know I was pushing it, safety-wise, but I've learned my lesson. If you could just let me off with a warning then I'd really be super grateful and I'm sure my sister would be too. I could take your badge number, I'm sure she'd send you a little thank-you message or even a present . . .'

Tanner smiled encouragingly, praying just to get this farce over with as quickly as possible. Of course, he could just reveal he was a cop, but with these two ass-holes and Quentin in the car that might just be squirting gasoline on the flames. Within minutes the whole house could burn down. The deadline on the bomb was eating away second by second so they didn't have time to waste with bad decisions. Maintaining his cover was the path of least resistance, and hopefully the quickest way out, too. Weasel peered over at Quentin, who helpfully gawped like a guppy fish. The cop chewed his dilemma over for a long time, before finally nodding.

'OK, well, just this once. But be a little more circum-spect in future. Next time you might not run into law-enforcement officers as reasonable as we are.'

Weasel made this seem like the biggest concession

this side of nuclear disarmament. Maybe he wasn't such a bad guy after all, though Tanner was already nodding with exaggerated gratitude – when Command Cop's voice suddenly rang out.

'Can you open the trunk please, sir?' he intoned.

Tanner closed his eyes for a moment and breathed very evenly to keep his cool. *So it's going to be like that then, is it? Well, OK . . .*

When he opened his eyes Weasel was actually chiding his own partner. 'Aw, c'mon, man. No, Steve. Let's just let these idiots – no offence – on their way. We'll take a break, go have a coffee and fries at Mack's Place. Whaddaya say? My shout?'

Command Cop ignored Weasel. In fact, if anything, his attitude intensified. Tanner saw his jaw visibly tighten. To Tanner he growled: 'The trunk – now! I won't ask a third time, punk.'

Punk? Seriously. And was he doing a gravelly Batman voice now, too?

Weasel pointedly turned his back on the scene and stood petulantly with his arms crossed, staring into the undergrowth.

Tanner walked slowly towards the back of the car, flexing his fingers by his sides. He smiled at Command Cop in a comforting way, then he lifted the trunk wide.

It took a microsecond for Command Cop to rear back in shock from the bomb, and in that instant Tanner struck. Using the slight imbalance in Command Cop's stance, Tanner flicked the policeman's feet from under him and shoved his shoulders over the lip of the trunk. He then jammed the door on top of him, thus rendering him immobile. He unholstered Command Cop's Glock in a flash and aimed it at Weasel, whose own pistol was barely half drawn. Realizing that Tanner had got the drop on both of them Weasel swiftly raised his hands in trembling surrender.

Quentin was thrashing about inside the car in a state of hyperventilating panic. He busted his door open a crack.

'STAY!' Tanner barked with *real* command presence and the Beemer's door instantly slammed shut. He dragged Command Cop out of the trunk and booted him to the ground. Once there he retrieved the blustering cop's handcuffs, all the while keeping Weasel covered. Once Command Cop was cuffed, Tanner jerked him to his feet and frog-marched both of the policemen back to their patrol car. He made sure he was out of earshot of the BMW, before he started speaking.

'OK, here's the deal, fellas. I'm a San Francisco undercover cop on a mission for the NOPD which absolutely cannot be delayed or people will die. So, as you can imagine, you delaying me for stupid-ass purposes *really* is not what we needed tonight.' He nonchalantly showed them his badge. 'Now, I haven't got the time or the inclination to hang around while you dumb hicks confirm who I am, and what I'm doing, and why it's OK for you to let me keep doing it. By then, we'd probably all be dead.

'So, instead, we have this not entirely satisfactory compromise. But when you call it in ask to talk to a Detective Tobias Jones and your Deputy Chief from the Bureau of Investigations. They'll set you straight on the whole deal. Make sure I don't see either of you chuckleheads – or any of your buddies – for the rest of the evening. This plan is going to be difficult enough to pull off without you dimwits sticking your oars in. Oh, and when you speak to Deputy Cochrane, tell him Detective John Tanner sends his love. He'll appreciate that.'

He got them to sit on the tarmac while he cuffed them to the car. He threw their guns into the under-growth along with their car keys, but left the radio handset dangling on the front seat. It was far enough away so that they could reach it with a certain amount of craning, stretching and teamwork, but it would take time. Tanner saw it as providing them with an impromptu trust-building exercise, which they sorely needed.

'Tip for the future, Steve,' he said as he turned to leave. 'Listen to your partner in future and, brother, seriously, chill the fuck out.'

He leant into Command Cop, who flinched, afraid, but Tanner just unclipped his high-powered torch from his belt.

'I bet on the advert they say this thing has "one million candle power", right?' Command just looked sullen, which proved Tanner was right. He chuckled. 'OK, I'm commandeering this for my assignment. I'll courier it back to you when I'm done with it. I've got your badge numbers.'

Then he moseyed on back to the Beemer. Quentin's face in the window was almost worth all the dangerous inconvenience, and Tanner had to fight not to smirk, but he soon returned to seriousness.

Right about now Jones should be making his call to the LLR. They were severely behind schedule.

Since the fateful night at the villa Ghost Beard had lived his life in fear. Everyone present had been shouted at by Lavache's lieutenant, Poppa Leon. Their pay was slashed and all privileges – free drugs, food from restaurants who paid them protection, nights with LLR street girls – were curtailed. No one had come after him – yet – and he'd been allowed to carry on with his gang life – so far – but he could sense an atmosphere curdling round him, like the stench of death. More than ever he just wanted to leave, but he was being watched too closely for that. There was no way of him absconding safely while the heat was this high.

Ghost Beard felt like a dead man walking. He knew it was only a matter of time before he suffered some sort of retribution. The leadership would want to make an example of someone after such an abject humiliation, especially now that his companions had conspired to make him the only scapegoat. Other street soldiers wouldn't work corners with him any more, or drive on jobs together unless they were forced to. Every time a breeze bumped his window shutter at night Ghost would jolt awake and grab for the 9 mill under his pillow. It was the waiting which was unbearable.

Now, though, he had a chance to redeem himself.

As punishment for their failure Ghost, Toe Taps, Chester, Lester, Gabriel Grass and Fat Raimond had all been cast out to the cold borders of the LLR empire: they were running door security at Lavache's Goth metal bar, Torque, in Baton Rouge. They were tasked with enforcing the peace, stamping down on any non-LLR dealing or whoring in the club, but that was about it. They even had to pay for their own drinks. It was the lowest of the low, as far removed from the golden days when the LLR were the undisputed ghetto kings of the Crescent City as it was possible to be.

However, then the call had come in. The fool responsible for all their misery – the driver who'd stolen Lavache's cars, the cocky son-of-a-fuck who'd actually driven the transporter – was here. He was in Baton Rouge tonight, right now; what's more, he was heading towards Torque! So it turned out that this dead-end posting was the most fortuitous assignment Ghost Beard had ever had.

The instant they got the news the entire Torque security staff dropped everything – to the bafflement of clubbers and bar staff alike – and threw themselves down the narrow back corridors and out into the club car park. Men with biker tats and piercings clumsily rolled over the hoods of cars in a ridiculous jostling panic, cramming six men into vehicles meant for four or even two. It might have looked laughable if it wasn't for the array of guns they were all cradling. Engines began to roar; wheels spun in a cacophonous storm of burnout squeals. Smoke billowed from protesting tyres.

The information on the Indian's driver had come in from an anonymous tip, which wasn't so unusual. There was always someone in the underworld community looking to make a fast buck.

Ghost had tumbled into the back seat of the metallic-green Chrysler 300C. Already inside were Fat Raimond and his infamously unclean brother, Thin Patrice, who wasn't even an LLR member, but just along for the thrill of it. Up front, Chester had the wheel while Toe Taps rode shotgun. The other cars in the posse were all identical Cadillac Escalades, blacks and blues. The whole car park courtyard vibrated with the pent-up power of the cars.

Ghost Beard grinned to himself as they squealed away down the side alley on to the main drag. He was on the job, and no one could stop him now. This was his last chance to redeem himself.

He caught a fleeting glance which passed between Raimond and Patrice, both of whom then darted their eyes conspiratorially towards Ghost himself. His heart began to hammer. This was why Patrice had suddenly turned up. The leadership had contracted out his killing to the brothers. Once he stepped out of the car he was dead, but maybe if he showed how invaluable he was then he could persuade the brothers to spare him?

He just had to kill the Indian's driver, and all would be well. Probably.

Ghost Beard purposefully worked the slide on his Mini-Uzi as the convoy of cars flashed down into the adjoining warehouse district. They didn't have to go very far to catch sight of their quarry. The BMW 550i they'd been warned about was just idling on a deserted corner. The bastard even winked his lights. Ghost Beard's blood boiled. The driver was laughing at them. He was rubbing their faces in their failure, as if they were naughty pups who'd made a mess on the kitchen floor. The LLR had to put that motherfucker in his place once and for all.

The whole posse raced towards the BMW like an oncoming storm front. It was time for a little payback. Unfortunately, the BMW just reversed down a cross street and was gone. He wasn't even hurrying, that was the thing that stung. When they reached the corner – the Chrysler was leading the posse – the LLR saw that the road where the BMW had disappeared led to a warren of narrow lanes behind a complex of interlinked warehouses. It was a puzzle of blocked access roads, dead ends, loading cul-de-sac, and constricted turning circles. There was no sight of the rogue car. It had already vanished into the maze.

The chase was on.

* * *

Tanner's solution to their dilemma was pretty straight-forward.

If they arranged for the club to be evacuated the Indian would know that Tanner was a mole, but they obviously couldn't let it be bombed. However, if they were intercepted by LLR drivers on the way and prevented from delivering the device then no one would be any the wiser. Even if the Indian had sent a trigger man to trail them and detonate the bomb remotely then he wouldn't suspect Tanner's loyalty, especially if the wheelman was engaged in a deadly cat-and-mouse chase through the commercial district, a pursuit made even more perilous because he didn't dare push the car's performance since there was a pile of volatile explosives in the trunk. Tanner thought back to the phone call with Jones.

'Drive as carefully as you can, John, and for chrissakes don't get into any unnecessary scrapes. One bump and the whole thing could go up.'

'Nah. I think it'll take a couple of bumps,' he'd quipped at the time, but it felt a lot less amusing now when they were being harried by machine-gun wielding maniacs.

The BMW edged out across a tight cross alley, only to be confronted by an LLR Cadillac facing them two warehouses down the row. The LLR thugs instantly opened fire, a hail of slugs buzzing around Tanner and Quentin. The rear driver's side window shattered, showering glass into the interior. Quentin cried out, and Tanner slammed the car into reverse, praying that the bomb didn't have some sort of tilt-switch. He performed a smooth yet terrifying J-turn and, with bullets still pranging off its once pristine surface, the BMW darted away down a cut between two back-office Portakabins.

In this tangle of alleys the LLR drivers were at a clear advantage. There were more of them, they were communicating, plus they were armed to the teeth. Surely it wouldn't be long before the wolves had them boxed in? Still, while it was true that one dog pitted against an entire pack of wolves could never hope to triumph, one man versus a pack of wolves didn't have to rely on his teeth to win the day. His intelligence could still save them.

Quentin was whining in fear as normal. 'Why did we have to go to the club if we knew the LLR controlled it?' he wailed. 'You said everything would be OK!'

'You've known me for long enough now. Do you really think I would lead us into the kill zone without an escape plan?'

Quentin was sweating against the passenger seat, but this did at least seem to pacify him. Right then something caught Tanner's eye and he finally thought of a plan. He sent the Beemer through a silky smooth drift into a nearby underground car park, smashing through the barrier with a yelp from Quentin.

Once inside he began to systematically shoot out all of the strip lights.

* * *

The Ford GT flashed into the echoing box of the car park and Chester immediately slammed on the brakes. The space was pitch black. The only illumination came from the streetlamps filtering through the entrance-way behind them.

'No! Keep on going! Don't stop!' Ghost Beard yelled in horror.

'Who you orderin' around, ya great black fucksicle?' Chester bellowed at the back seat. He then jerked forward in his seat as the following Cadillac ploughed straight into their bumper. Chester wasn't wearing a seat belt and his head smacked into the steering wheel nose-first. The force from the Cadillac wasn't enough to cause any terminal damage but when Chester reared back from the wheel blood sprayed the dashboard from his broken nose, and he moaned woozily.

The other cars screeched into the garage and only just managed to veer aside at the last moment to avoid the fate of the first Cadillac. Neither that Cadillac nor the Chrysler were write-offs, but neither one was very pretty any more.

All the LLR cars had come to a stop in a shallow semi-circle peering into the depths of the car park. Their headlights sliced the darkness into a weird jungle of angular-shaped shadows. The pillars obscured the full extent of the room, and reduced their sight lines, but they could tell something was moving out there. Ghost Beard lifted up his Uzi, flicking off the safety—

Pfft, pfft, pfft, their headlights started to pop out one

by one in puffs of burst glass. The driver was shooting out their only illumination! Complete darkness fell like a coffin lid. Ghost was abruptly struck by how vile the inside of the Chrysler smelled: body odour, leather, cheap aftershave, motor oil, fast food. A blazing beam of light suddenly dazzled them, causing Toe Taps, Raimond and Patrice to yell out in panic. A bullet shattered their side window and whirred through the car; more shouts. The beam snapped off. Seconds later it bathed them in blindness from another angle. Another shot rang out, and a window on one of the other Cadillacs exploded.

Instantly the street soldiers opened fire, blindly raking the dark with machine-gun fire. The next few seconds were a horrifying tumult of sparks, bullets, ricochets and screaming. In their haste the LLR soldiers had forgotten that they were arranged in a semi-circle and as they wildly sprayed the blackness for the enemy they were shooting at each other.

'Stop! Stop shooting! He's gone!' Ghost Beard desperately tried to be heard above the bedlam.

After he'd screamed it a few more times, the shooting finally did halt. The silence that followed was almost painful. Into its centre trickled the faint distant screech of a car heading away up a faraway ramp.

'Hear that? There must be another exit somewhere. He's gone,' Ghost Beard growled.

'We lost him! He ain't here no more. Back up. Back up!' Chester shouted at the others. His crushed nose made him sound as if he had a heavy cold and Ghost

Beard couldn't stop himself smirking. They all got out and reviewed the gang's injuries. It turned out no one had been badly hurt in the shoot-out. A few flesh wounds, some near misses, and the car's bodywork was pretty badly shot up.

'Back to the club!' Toe Tips shouted. 'We'll circle round and search the quarter street by street. That fucker ain't escaping the Red Blades again!'

The LLR soldiers cheered over the combined noise of their cars as they headed back outside. Ghost Beard didn't join in with their war cry. He was beginning to suspect that the enemy driver had planned all of this and that the whole scenario was unfolding to some secret plan of his, or the Indian's.

His escape also had worrying implications for Ghost Beard's own future. As they emerged back into the sodium night brightness he saw Thin Patrice was watching him very closely and his hand was resting casually inside his jacket pocket . . .

Tanner had doubled back to the club. His plan wasn't quite done yet. The Indian wanted a devastating spectacle, and Tanner was determined to give him one. The BMW surged out of a side alley four or five blocks down from the LLR pack. Their cars had all pulled up in a baffled circle outside of the Torque. With this distance between them, even at their safety-conscious top speed, it would be child's play for Tanner to get himself and Quentin to safety. The LLR drivers hadn't even spotted the BMW yet.

Tanner performed a brisk three-point turn and then carefully manoeuvred the car until it was aligned dead centre to the street . . . pointing directly at the LLR cars.

'Wuh-wuh-what are you doing?' stammered Quentin in terror.

Tanner revved his engine.

'OK, Quentin, I'm going to tell you something in a moment,' Tanner began conversationally. 'And if you panic I'm going to beat you so hard the stupid juice will come squirting out of every pore on your body. Clear?'

The boy nodded mutely. A number of the LLR drivers had noticed them now, and they began to shout and leap back into their vehicles.

'Right, in the trunk of this car there's a huge bomb on a timer or possibly activated by cell-phone signals. In a second I'm going to drive as fast as I can towards those LLR gunmen and when I say "now" – and not a moment before – we're going to leap out of the moving vehicle. Did you follow that?'

Quentin whimpered but nodded.

'OK. Then off we go,' said Tanner brightly and hit that gas one more time.

The LLR cars streaked towards them, bolts of green and black and gold under the yellow streetlights, Mini-Uzis coughing out of their side windows. A few rounds raked the BMW's hood with a sound like an industrial nailgun shooting tin cans in a corrugated iron shed.

Despite all the warnings Quentin couldn't prevent

himself from screaming at the top of his voice, but Tanner decided to indulge him.

Ghost Beard stared with increasing alarm at the sleek black shape racing towards them.

'Uh, Chester. I . . . I don't think he's going to stop!'

'Fuck that. He'll pussy out and we'll tear right through him, or my boy Toe Taps here will fill him full of lead. Either way we're turning that motherfucker into strawberry jam. That boy will blink first.'

'No, no, seriously, Chester, he won't!'

'SHUT UP, GHOSTIE!' Toe Taps bellowed back from the front passenger seat. He stuck his Mini-Uzi out of the window in anticipation.

'End of the road,' hissed Thin Patrice and pulled out a stub-nosed pistol which he waved at Ghost Beard. 'Get ready for the rest of you to become a ghost as well!'

Fat Raimond snickered. This close the BMW looked to be the size of an ocean liner bearing down on them.

'Why does no one ever listen to me?' Ghost Beard shrieked, then hit his side door handle with as much force as he could muster and tumbled out on to the speeding tarmac.

The street ahead of the BMW was basically a wall of steel battering rams speeding unstoppably towards them. This whole night had turned into a succession of death-defying face-offs and Tanner was loving every minute.

With the seconds until impact shredding away like confetti on the wind, Tanner leaned under the dash to wedge the accelerator down with Command Cop's fancy torch. It looked as if he wasn't going to return it to the policeman after all.

Tanner straightened. The LLR cars filled his view; some dark bulk spun away from the lead car, a green metallic Chrysler, and struck the kerb, but he couldn't see what the object was and there was no time left. 'Ready?' he called to Quentin.

'No,' the kid whimpered.

'Great. On three. One . . . two . . . GO!'

Tanner roared and shouldered out into the black fast air beyond; Quentin screamed and followed suit. The impact was excruciating, a smash like being beaten with a metal bat on every part of his body all at once. There was tumbling and spinning and no sense of up or down or sideways and then, after an even greater jolt as he hit a wall, mercifully, there was stillness.

A heartbeat later the whole world turned red and yellow and flame all over as the bomb went off.

Ghost Beard was lying in a gutter in agony, his clothes soaked by the pooled mulch of rubbish and rainwater, the fabric of his jeans ripped by the friction of his tumble from the car. His left arm was flung behind him like the broken spoke of an umbrella. He rolled over the moment he heard the explosion, but let out a strangled curse as the pain lanced through him. He watched a pillar of flame, metal and smoke launch into the air not 50 yards down the street. He could feel the terrific waves of heat that beat against his skin even at this distance and saw the asphalt beneath the blasted shells of the devastated vehicles bubble and spit. The perimeter of the explosion had been vast. The fact that it had been so destructive, and yet managed to cause so little collateral damage, made it seem as if this had been the plan all along. The façade of Club Torque wasn't even touched. Clubbers were even now sprinting out on to the street to investigate, grinding to a halt when they saw the flaming devastation on their doorstep.

Through the twisting ghostly veils of soot and heat, Ghost Beard could make out the cars that had been following the leader: the Cadillac Escalades that had pulled up closer to the fire. The BMW and their own lead car – the Chrysler he'd been riding in – had been utterly consumed. Silhouetted figures transformed into stickmen by the glare of the flames stood around beside the Cadillacs staring dumbly into the burning wreckage. Every now and then one of them would make a weak foray to get closer but they were always beaten back by the heat.

He levered himself painfully to his feet, then hobbled as swiftly as he could down the nearest darkened alley.

Chapter Twenty-one

Tanner had to ride back to New Orleans by bus.

The journey was humid, crowded, and his seat was weirdly pungent with some smell that was part spicy foodstuff, part animal excreta, but he had far greater problems to preoccupy him, specifically whether Jericho or the Indian had deliberately tried to blow him into a hundred thousand flaming scraps of skin and bone.

They drove south from the LSU campus along Highway 30 through the grim wasteland of Louisiana's 'Cancer Alley', an industrial corridor of petrochemical facilities, power plants and multiple refineries squatting on one grizzled strip bordering the Mississippi. The sepia-tinged landscape with its skeletal superstructures crouched on the river's edge was a fitting backdrop for Tanner's mood. He stared out at the acidic scrawls of smog scribbling away into the sky as he considered the previous night's events.

After they'd managed to evade the emergency services around the site of the explosion, Tanner and

Quentin took a circuitous route to the Greyhound station to put the kid on his way.

They stood on a blank concrete concourse beside a row of stuttering halogen streetlamps to make their goodbyes.

'Go away, go far. Don't let me see you again,' Tanner told Quentin wearily. 'Stop cracking safes. Put on a tie. Get a real job.'

He regarded the ratty kid wearily. The boy was chewing Bubble Yum and there was dirt from their dive out of the car on his earlobe. His chin and cheek were scraped a Barbie doll pink but otherwise he'd escaped unmarked. Being fond of Quentin would be like getting misty-eyed over a mouse he'd found living in his cellar but didn't have the heart to kill. Even so Tanner still made sure he got on the Greyhound and watched until the coach pulled away just to make sure he didn't somehow get into trouble again before finally quitting the city.

Whenever this operation ended and whatever else happened down the line, at least he could say he saved one person.

When Tanner's bus eventually pulled up at the Union Passenger Terminal on Loyola Avenue, Jones was there to meet him.

'Get me in to see Powell,' Tanner rasped to his friend the moment his foot hit the pavement.

'I've tried,' Jones protested, hands shoved deep in his jacket pockets. 'He still won't meet you and he won't pull you out of the field. But even if you did get in to see him, John, he won't listen. He's utterly convinced that the Indian is the greater threat.'

'Greater boost to his election campaign, you mean? He wants to use Sepion's downfall to launch a senate bid. I saw it in his lizard eyes the moment we first met.'

'Look, I *have* tried, John, tried 'til I'm blue in the face – and for a proud black man like myself that is a serious concession.'

'Try again. Try harder,' Tanner retorted without smiling.

Jones nodded with a sigh to indicate his capitulation.

'So,' he began a few moments later. 'What's our next move? Where do you go from here?'

Tanner's face was a rough-hewn carving in the morning shadows, dark hollows etched beneath his iron-grey eyes. 'Well, either Jericho or the Indian tried to blow me up last night. So I'm going over to their place to ask them why,' he said simply.

It was a different house, but the dogs were the same.

The Indian's paranoia must be at an all-time high if he was shuttling from bolthole to bolthole every other day. Tanner's mood was understandably a little antsy.

The house was double-width camelback in the Bywater district, downriver from the French Quarter and very close to the Industrial Canal, a shotgun house with a partial upper floor over the rear of the building. Back in the day such dwellings were a tax dodge since most cities categorized them as single-storey houses, not that the Indian cared about counting the pennies. More importantly from his point of view, it was situated in a laid-back yet fairly rambunctious neighbourhood. The area was full of sound pollution at all hours and live music or noise from the canal would easily drown out the din of the dogs. Right now Tanner could hear someone playing a mournful horn solo down the street, a sad clean thin thread of melody that cut up through the thick hot morning air like a knife before drifting away across the roofs.

The house was built across two lots rather than one, and was much larger as a result. Unlike the Indian's previous abode, however, it didn't just exude an air of abandonment. This house was in an open state of dis-repair. The wooden planks of the porch were warped underfoot and the white paint on the exterior was peeling away from grubby rotten timber beneath. Overgrown ivy hung like witches' hair around the porch apron, whilst rust encrusted the metal brackets that supported the canopy.

Interestingly, rather than being escorted in some cloak-and-dagger operation to a secret location, Tanner had been given the address by Jericho personally and the wheelman drove himself there. Given how paranoid the Indian had become, was this a further hint of division? Still, at the front door Sepion's praetorian guard checked him thoroughly for concealed weapons and for the wire he still didn't dare wear, before they ushered him into the long, poorly lit hallway of a main room. Beyond the kitchen out back there were stairs leading up to the upper half-storey. Tanner went up by himself and sat on a bare stool against the wall on the grim landing. Over the row of the bull mastiffs he could hear voices through the chipboard-thin walls. Two speakers, the Indian and Jericho. There was an odd staccato rhythm to their muffled exchanges.

Tanner's gaze swept across the interconnecting wall. His eyes snagged on a spot near the outer frame where damp wood had bowed out into a maze of fissures and gaps. He crept across the bare boards, testing each step to minimize any creaks that might give away his movements. When he reached the cracked area, as he suspected, he was able to hear the bulk of the conversation unfolding next door.

'. . . could have been more targeted,' Jericho was saying. It was still difficult to make out more than a few words at a time. 'You should have told me what you had planned.'

'I don't have to tell you what . . .' the Indian boomed and then presumably turned his back on the wall, which masked the rest of his bluster. Whatever the actual detail of the conversation, they were clearly in disagreement and Tanner had arrived just as the antagonism spiked.

'. . . more efficient if there's a chain of command . . .' Jericho responded. His tone was very calm, but having spent time with him Tanner could tell he was suppressing a rising frustration.

'. . . deny the results! Running like vermin . . . This is my city, my . . .' Sepion roared, his voice fading in and out like a poorly tuned radio station. Tanner imagined him pacing as he ranted, gesticulating and pointing, his eyes popping.

'Yes, a major victory . . . so why not relax? You've achieved a lot . . . almost there . . . kill them all . . . Do you want some . . . to help you unwind . . . any product you want . . .' Jericho's timbre was smoothly persuasive, but now Tanner heard the Indian moving swiftly and drawing in closer to his lieutenant. Luckily they were both near the wall.

'How do I know you haven't turned on me? . . . paid to poison my drugs?'

'Why would I defect to a losing team? You were just telling me how effective your schemes have been . . .' Jericho countered convincingly. The Indian could be heard to grunt in reluctant acceptance and his bulk shifted away, the floorboards protesting.

'. . . not going to touch that shit again . . . no downers, no relaxation . . . not 'til they're all dead . . . drag them in here, feed their faces to the dogs . . .'

The tenor of Sepion's voice suggested this was going to spiral into another one of his tirades, with little more useful intelligence to be sifted free. Safer to cut his losses and digest what he'd already heard. The implications were clear, though. The Indian and Jericho arguing. The Indian was losing his temper even with his most-trusted lieutenant. Was Tanner hearing a struggle for power?

Tanner had previously speculated that Jericho guided the Indian's decisions in precisely the direction that most served his own goals, but perhaps it wasn't as simple as that? Like so many mad scientists before him, had Jericho created a monster he ultimately couldn't control? Clearly his hold over the demon of New Orleans wasn't anything like as secure as Tanner had assumed. He didn't have everything his own way in the gang, which was a point of irritation, but neither was he prepared – or able – to seize control on his own behalf.

Tanner was beginning to shift his opinion. It seemed clear now that the Indian had gone way off the reservation. His paranoia had become so volatile, so toxic, that it had pushed him beyond any limitations of good judgement. The bomb showed that, and the fact that he hadn't even told Jericho backed it up. Jericho seemed to be doing his best to rein him in, but failing. The Indian was like one of his own dogs driven rabid, straining at a leash Jericho could no longer hold on to. The Indian was feral and couldn't be reasoned with or manipulated by his puppet-master. It didn't seem there was much to be gained by exploiting the rift between them any more. Tanner was forced to agree with Powell: the Indian had become the clear and present danger. They would risk more bloodshed if he wasn't brought down as soon as possible. Jericho might be a thug, but he was predictable, rational and could ultimately be contained until they were able to secure watertight evidence against him.

Tanner returned to his seat and waited to be called. After another minute the door opened and Jericho beckoned to him sternly. If he felt any lingering irritation after the dressing down from Sepion even Tanner couldn't detect it. The one thing you had to admire about Jericho was his iron self-control.

The meagre 'office' within had none of the luxury trappings of the Indian's previous hide-out; what's more the dogs were being kennelled in one of the other rooms. There was a chipboard table with a PC and a lamp, and a curling map of New Orleans was pasted up on one wall. Tanner instinctively imagined that this might have been the Indian's first base when he originally arrived in the city. It had the look of a dismal hole where a ruthless and hungry future crime lord might have planned his rise. Along the wall by the window were a succession of slashed and battered tailor's dummies, beside which a rack of medieval weapons reposed in a rack: samurai swords, a cudgel, brass knuckles; evidence of how the Indian would exorcise his excess energy when the drugs didn't work.

'You tried to kill me,' Tanner told the Indian bluntly.

Sepion leered up at Tanner, his eyes glittering deviously, and chuckled back at the wheelman's insolence. He licked his lips and let the seconds draw out uncomfortably before finally replying.

'If I had done, do you think I would admit to it?'

'You tell me,' Tanner intoned, unamused by his coyness.

'But why would I kill my new top lieutenant?' Sepion giggled like a loon. Jericho blinked slowly, but otherwise didn't react to that dig. 'I mean, nothing shocks you, Tanner, eh? You open your trunk and find a concealed bomb, you don't bat no eyelid. You just carry on with the delivery ... and when those LLR SCUM come after you, bullets zinging all around, you just lead them on a merry little dance, THEN turn around and JAM that mother so far up their asses that the whole world sees the firework show for miles around! It's the stuff of legends, *mon frère*.'

'What can I say? I'm a resourceful guy. But why the fuck was I driving a car crammed full of explosives in the first place?'

The Indian's eyes sparkled with madness, his fat cheeks running with sweat. 'Terror!' he declaimed like the devil's own preacher, jigging and dancing on the spot. 'Why do terrorists use explosives? To spread fear and uncertainty among their enemies. Exactly as we have done, and it's worked. And the reason I know it has struck terror into the pygmy hearts of our enemies? Because the weakest rats have already begun leaping off the ship.'

Puzzled, Tanner cast a questioning look over towards Jericho.

'The bosses of the smaller gangs are suing for peace. They want to make a non-aggression pact and join forces with us. They came to me.' This was a distinction Jericho underlined crisply. 'We're having the first talks tonight and I want you along as my back-up. It'll just be you and me.'

'Is this another attempt to get me killed?' Tanner asked drily.

'You tell me.'

The hitman and the wheelman stared at each other. Neither blinked.

Jericho hadn't been responsible for the bomb after all, and he seemed to working towards an orderly transition of power. This peace treaty with the smaller gangs was an encouraging sign. Anyway, it was in Jericho's interest to try and eliminate turmoil in the local drugs market. It was all about the dollar. They could still deal with him and – however much it made him baulk inside – Tanner could continue to work as his 'partner' for the sake of the greater good.

'When do we leave?' he enquired mildly.

Armand 'Blue' Bergeron and Rex Vidrine were strictly minor league players on the New Orleans gang scene. Bergeron's Water Tigers controlled a few corners in the lower Ninth, though their power fluctuated madly as inveterate infighting continually thinned out their membership. The more stable Black Skull Partisans were Vidrine's crew and still a force of sorts in Tremé. Both had independent supply lines into the city, but they only dealt in vanishingly small quantities of product when compared to the LLR or the Indian's crew. The Indian's footsoldiers had danced a few tussles with both gangs, but never really even bothered to expand into their modest areas. They were simply too small fish to bother with at this stage. Both gangs had been content to trundle along, doing their little business and trying not to think about the day when the Indian would eventually gobble everyone up. However, the car bomb had changed all that. As the Indian had intended, it had been a chilling wake-up call.

The venue for the peace talks was a randomly chosen room in the imaginatively named Red Maple Lodge, a Bates Motel wannabe near the airport. All day and night planes overhead shook the windows and yawning commercial travellers sat in the anony-mous rooms trying to sleep or watch TV, or just staring at the patterned curtains.

The men met in the gravel car park. Both Bergeron and Vidrine had followed instructions to come alone, though the unspoken contract was that all four of them were armed. They trooped up the steps to the second-floor walkway together. Jericho unlocked the door into a room that was cheap and cramped: one single bed, one table, one TV, a bathroom and a Gideon's Bible. They shuffled inside and stood awkwardly around on the shiny linoleum under the fly-spotted lightshade trying not to look like men who were fingering guns in their pockets.

Bergeron's tongue flashed out and licked the centre of his upper lip like a lizard, a nervous little tick he couldn't control, all his fear darting out in the tiniest tell. Tanner saw that he was blinking far more rapidly than normal. Bergeron was smooth and puffy, pouch-cheeked, while Vidrine, by contrast, was one of the hairiest men Tanner had ever seen, more wolf than human, with a soft Cajun accent, shark lips, pock-marks and beady suspicious eyes. The seconds stretched as they all regarded each other like gun-slingers at twenty paces.

'Come on,' Bergeron said. 'Are we going to do this thing or stand about like spare dicks?'

Tanner chose a seat. The others grudgingly joined in. Shortly, hesitantly, they began to talk.

Bizarrely it was Quentin that Tanner had to thank for saving the lives of the other gang leaders. As they sat around the chipped plastic-topped table while Jericho began setting out their agenda Tanner found himself focusing idly on Bergeron's shirt. The man dressed like a cartoon pimp in a hip-hop video. Even though he was whiter than Quentin he had a wide-brimmed Mac Daddy hat, black crocodile-skin boots, shimmering dark jeans, a rhinestone cowboy jacket and a seventies-style wide-collared ruby satin shirt. There was a lighter spot of red under the collar, which Tanner hadn't noticed when they came into the room. It looked like the dis-coloured dot a splash of bleach might make. The spot jiggled. He thought of Quentin—

'SNIPER! DOWN!' Tanner bellowed and hurled himself across the table, charging the two men to the floor with his arms outstretched. Multiple muted cracks followed in rapid succession as window splintered. The frightening whirr of displaced air followed as bullets tore through the room, embedding themselves in the wall, mattress, bedside table.

Rolling around on the floor, Tanner's mind raced. How could there be snipers out there? Who could possibly know they were there? Did the Indian's crew have another mole? Or could it have been the Water Tigers or the Partisans who'd snitched to the LLR? All four men were on the floor and now rowed backwards until they were beyond the killing range of the window where they levered themselves to their feet. Tanner gingerly flicked the blind across the shattered pane to shroud the room from any further sharpshooting.

A second later Bergeron, Vidrine, Jericho and Tanner were all pointing guns at each other. Bergeron was a picture of goggle-eyed terror, while Vidrine kept twitching like a cobra about to strike, his 9 mill's barrel jerking agitatedly between potential targets. Jericho was a block of stone. He was probably thinking: Two targets, two sawn-offs: worth playing the odds. Apparently it was down to Tanner to take on the mantle of diplomat.

'Put your guns down,' he urged quietly. 'This doesn't have to get out of hand if we can all just trust each other.'

'Fuck you. You put *your* guns down, you j-just tried to kill us!' Bergeron stuttered. 'F-fucking peace talks, my fat dripping schlong!'

'No, we didn't try to kill you and I've got no more idea than you who fired those shots.'

'Why should we believe you?' hissed Vidrine.

'Because I'm the one who saved your lives,' Tanner replied simply.

Bergeron threw a tormented glance at Vidrine. 'He's right. We'd both be dead if it wasn't for him.'

Vidrine wasn't having any of it, though. His knuckle whitened worryingly behind the 9 mill's trigger guard. 'I don't trust any of this shit. It stinks to hell.'

'OK, look, here. Watch me. I'm putting my gun down.' Tanner knelt to deposit his Hi-Point .45 on the lino. Vidrine's expression remained unconvinced. Tanner straightened, his palms open by his shoulders.

'Look, I will personally assure your safety,' he said, locking eyes with Vidrine, radiating waves of sincerity. 'No harm will come to you, I promise. Come on. If we all start shooting, who knows how many hats end up on the floor? Seriously, this is all just a misunderstanding. You've come here to make a deal because you're small players. We don't care about you. In the wider scheme of things, you're meaningless. The LLR is all we care about and I'm sure they're the ones responsible for this attack. We make a peace deal with you and move on to bigger fish. Look into my eyes, I'm telling the truth. You can see that.'

Bergeron looked as if he might cry. Sweat was raining off him, soaking his ruby shirt purple. One huge drip dangled at the end of his bulbous nose. It bobbled and trembled and shivered.

Bergeron made a little noise at the back of his throat and relinquished his revolver to the floor. To Tanner's astonishment Jericho was the next to drop his weapons, though he was smiling faintly as he did so. With an enraged grunt of frustration Vidrine also surrendered his gun on to the ground.

And that was when five of the Indian's footsoldiers charged into the room from the walkway, and Jericho's smile widened. They seized Bergeron and Vidrine, beating them into submission with vicious blows. Tanner was appalled; this had been Jericho's plan all along, and he had inadvertently helped him to disarm the other men. Bergeron was sobbing now, wailing with terrified rage.

'You said to trust you, you son of a whore! You treacherous lying fuck! You said "TRUST ME"!' he screamed, struggling on the sweat-slippery lino, but Jericho's thugs lashed a rag round his mouth to silence his cries. Vidrine was stubbornly silent even before they gagged him, but his accusing gaze never left Tanner's face. Body strumming with emotion, Tanner tugged Jericho to one side.

'Why didn't you tell me it was going down like this?' he demanded. 'You should have warned me if you were planning an ambush. I thought we were partners.'

'Oh, we are. But sometimes it's useful to have someone on your team who believes the lies they have to tell. Sincerity, like mercy, can be an invaluable tool. Consider that another lesson.'

Fuck. He'd been played. Jericho had manipulated him just like he'd twisted the Indian and Tycho and who knew how many other gullible fools before them. Anger throbbed through Tanner's body, burning deep in his tissues like sunstroke. He stepped stiffly back towards the captured bosses kneeling on the floor, their faces shining with sweat and fright.

'What are you going to do with them?' he asked Jericho in a low voice.

Jericho took off his jacket before replying, dropped it on to the table and flexed his biceps as if he was warming up. He didn't answer Tanner straight away.

'Let's get them into the bathroom,' he told his henchmen. 'I've always been keen to try out waterboarding.'

The thugs hauled the gang leaders up and thrust them roughly into the bathroom.

'Don't worry,' Jericho murmured without looking round. 'Once we get their bank details, and location of all their secret stashes, we'll strip 'em and dump 'em on the side of the road as a lesson to all their men. Their own folk might kill them for the humiliation, but I won't. After we've got all their money, what use are they?'

He moved towards the bathroom, but paused on the threshold.

'I know how much you enjoy these refined interrogation techniques, but there's not enough room in there for fans in the gallery. The men will enjoy it and I like to award them a "bonus" occasionally. Soldiers stay committed if they're given a little reward every now and then. Basic management psychology. You hang out here 'til we're done.'

Tanner didn't trust himself to reply, so merely nodded his assent. He knew just as well as Jericho that 'refined interrogation techniques' was a euphemism the Gestapo used for torture. The bathroom door slammed closed. Behind the flimsy barrier he heard taps begin to run, water splashing ominously into the bath tub . . .

Tanner stood very still near the cracked window. He could see, round the edge of the blind, the darkened walkway, the blunt diagonal of its handrail slicing across his viewpoint. However much he might wish to step outside the room and on to that walkway it would be a cop-out. Tanner peered beyond the railing as he listened to the awful noises creeping under the bathroom door. He saw the sad oblong of the motel swimming pool, its surface littered with fallen palm leaves. He watched the jutting tower of the motel's neon sign glowing out its welcome into the sweltering night. Tanner forced himself to endure it all, made himself stand there and listen just in case he ever felt tempted to dismiss Jericho as the lesser evil again. The motel sign was faulty and flickered with a migraine-inducing pulse, like the flutter of a dozen trapped moths inside the luminescent tubes.

Suddenly Jericho's jacket began to vibrate to a counter-rhythm. Surreptitiously Tanner dug out the hitman's phone; it read: 'Caller I.D. withheld'. He considered his options for a moment, then curiosity took over and he answered, hoping it would be Navarro.

'Yeah?' he growled into the handset, his eyes never leaving the bathroom door. He could hear a panicked scuffling inside, the slosh of water over the edge of the bath then splattering on to cheap cracked tiles. He imagined feet in croc-skin boots slipping, trying desperately to find a purchase against the wet floor.

'Tanner?' It was Bowman's heavy drawl.'Why you on Jericho's line? Put him on. I got some real sweet news for him.'

There was a hum behind his words, a background rush. He was calling from a car on the move. Tanner clicked his tongue, debating for a moment, then said: 'He's all tied up right now. Tell me. I'll pass it along.'

'OK, but don't let it linger, this is classic gold. The rat in the gang is that bitch, Navarro. She's gone to ground, but I've found her contact. Trailed her and saw them together outside fucking Audubon Zoo, if you can believe it. Followed the contact afterwards and found out he's a cop from San Francisco. His name's Tobias Jones. He's living in a rented safe house in the Garden Quarter, and I'm on my way to smoke him right now.'

Chapter Twenty-two

Tanner had his hand on the motel door handle when Jericho exited the bathroom drying his hands. His shirt was soaked. His bare arms gleamed. He raised an eyebrow at Tanner.

'You leaving?'

'I'm just an extra wheel round here, you can take care of it. Buddy of mine tends bar at the Robber's Mask. Thought I'd go down there and pump him for news on Quentin. I'm still kind of burned that people think I had something to do with his disappearance,' Tanner lied as smoothly as he could under the circumstances.

Jericho put his head quizzically on one side. 'No, that never occurred to me and I've never heard anyone say it.'

Tanner had literally no idea whether Jericho was being ironic or not.

'But it's a good idea. So, go,' the hitman concluded.

He turned back to the bathroom winding the hand towel into a rope between his two fists, and leaving

Tanner with awful speculations about how even a simple towel might be used as an instrument of torture.

Tanner couldn't stop himself from blurting: 'I thought you said you weren't going to kill them.'

'*I'm* not,' Jericho murmured over his shoulder before vanishing back into the bathroom.

But even that wasn't important right now. Tanner hit the room door at a run. Every lost second was precious – or potentially lethal.

Tobias swore as he accidentally knocked his cell phone into the half-full washing basin.

Wearing half a ridiculous shaving-foam beard he unleashed a volley of epithets as he chased the slippery black lozenge around the opaque water. The precious device came out dripping wet and Jones cursed even louder.

This was all Tanner's fault. Tobias had wanted the phone close by to ensure he didn't miss a call from Powell's office. Tanner had insisted his partner contact him the instant he heard whether Powell was going to grant him a meeting, and since he hadn't been allowed any private contact details for the Superintendent he had to keep the phone with him even in the bathroom. That said, he wasn't about to skimp on his personal grooming just because of Tanner's increasingly suspect obsession with Jericho.

Tobias had discovered that his cousin was in town at

a small businesses conference (she ran her own catering company), so he was taking her out for a meal at a Cajun seafood restaurant tonight. Tobias's man code said that if he accompanied a beautiful woman out on the town – even if she was a relative – he simply had to look the part.

Reviewing the drowned phone, he judged that the damage might – *might* – not be as catastrophic as he'd first feared. They built tech like this pretty hard-wearing these days. Even so, better not to take any chances. He carefully removed the battery and SIM card, and left the handset to dry out on the window sill.

You know what, screw Tanner, thought Jones with a sudden spray of irritation. He was off the clock and deserved an evening without having to worry about the wheelman's issues with authority. The Indian's own paranoia seemed to be leeching off into Tanner, and it was driving Tobias crazy. Tanner should know that Powell wouldn't play ball whatever he said. Anyway, the wheelman was supposedly at gang 'peace talks' with the leaders of the smallest, most in-effectual gangs tonight. That should keep him out of trouble. If Tanner wanted to get a hold of him, for once he would just have to whistle . . .

'Damn, damn, damn,' Tanner hissed as he desperately thumbed his phone between gearshifts. 'Pick up, Jones!'

Every time he rang Jones's cell phone he was repeatedly kicked to answerphone. This really wasn't like his meticulous handler, and that turned Tanner's gut to icewater.

'Hey there, friend. Can't take your message right now, but . . .' Tobias's message purred in his ear, yet again.

Tanner spat more curses and hurled the phone on to the passenger seat to concentrate on a perilous over-steer across a tricky crossroads. He clipped the sidewalk and narrowly missed an intricately decorated iron fence. He was blazing through the polite uptown avenues of the picturesque Garden Quarter. The Challenger sped past chocolate con-fectioners, barbers, cafés, private schools and a parade of other extraordinary historic buildings. Everywhere were the splendid grounds that gave the Quarter its name: immaculate green velvet lawns, beautifully manicured trees, award-worthy rose gardens and constellations of blossoms in every hue. The neighbourhood had the genuine feel of the Old South, with its palpable history, conspicuous wealth and refined, easy-going tempo.

All of which was being besmirched by Tanner's desperate rampage through their streets.

Tanner had never driven this recklessly on an operation before – or perhaps in his whole life. Sure, he'd often taken risks that would make a normal driver blanch, but those were carefully regulated gambles, the calculated risks of a virtuoso. John Tanner had never driven like this before, because John Tanner had never driven this scared. His best friend was in mortal danger. He might already be dead. The awful anticipation was like a bolus of mercury deep in Tanner's gut, which pulsed with poisonous weight as he skated through every skid and booming leap.

'C'mon, c'mon, C'MON!' he muttered. There was a clumsy knot of three pick-ups and a Nissan Sentra at the upcoming crossroads. The vehicles were all jostling for precedence and had managed to block the whole street with their pig-headedness. Tanner didn't even slow, he just cut across a lawn on the nearest corner, slashing two raw brown scars through its jade perfection. He tore off along the next street at close to fifty.

A flash of purple four blocks ahead pricked at his recollection. Not purple, more plum-coloured . . .

Like a plum-red Cadillac CTS-V.

Bowman only had a few blocks lead on him! He wasn't too late. Tanner's focus shrank down to a claustrophobic grey tunnel. The Challenger roared like a thing possessed and screamed after the Cadillac. Within minutes, however, Tanner realized his folly. Despite risking life and limb – using clutch kicks, popping up two wheels on the kerb to break rear traction for insane jump drifts – Bowman stayed stubbornly ahead. Tanner hammered at the steering wheel in frustration. Their vehicles were too finely matched, and the lead Bowman had already accrued negated any benefits Tanner might have gained from his greater skills. At this rate the assassin would easily have time to arrive at Jones's safe house and make his attack before Tanner caught up. Tanner's breathing tightened. The Creole wasn't quite Jericho, perhaps, but he remained a seriously talented marksman with a supernaturally cool head and nerves of steel.

Swearing like a docker in a downpour Tanner scrabbled up the cell from the passenger seat. He dialled for an ambulance with a heavy heart. No one else could be quick enough to help now. No deus ex machina was going to swoop out of the clouds and save the day. Out here at the limits you had to make your own luck. It was time to start taking drastic action.

Tanner glanced along a sharp angle to the side road that the Cadillac had just disappeared down. He drew an invisible line to calculate the trajectory of his quarry, projecting out its path along the parallel street. If he couldn't beat the Cadillac in a straight race, he would have to take a more direct route . . . Tanner yanked on his steering wheel, rode up on to the sidewalk and rammed through the nearest mansion's gate. Once inside the drive he pulled a brisk handbrake turn so as not to collide with a brace of matching Bentleys. Then he cut diagonally across the beautiful lawns, dodging around the larger water features, but ploughing through any trellises, garden furniture or more flimsy impediments which blocked his way. It occurred to Tanner that someone really should pay compliments to the head gardener here: this was a silky-smooth surface to glide across. Hopefully he'd been well compensated for his services. He'd certainly have his work cut out to fix the damage Tanner was now causing. In spite of the appalling tension there was still a tiny anarchic part of Tanner's heart that rejoiced in such wilful wrecking of a wealthy playground.

As he flashed past the vast gleaming conservatory tacked on to the side of the mansion Tanner caught a glimpse of a middle-aged woman in a silk dressing gown with her palms pressed up against the glass, her mouth a frozen rictus of outrage. Bill the city, lady, thought Tanner. This is an emergency. If his on-the-fly calculations were correct he'd emerge through the manicured hedges at the back of the property actually *in front* of the Cadillac.

He emerged from the shadow of the west wing and was suddenly confronted with something that would never have been an issue in a million years if he'd decided to cut through the yards of any other neighbourhood in the city. Dead ahead of Tanner was the looming block of a Swedish-style sweat lodge.

Tanner roared in alarm; milliseconds to react. Tyres veered, the weight of the back end pulling, pulling and then the Challenger spun like a top. Tanner wrestled for control, managed to evade the sweat house, but skidded halfway across the unblemished lawn, tearing out two horrifying black trenches before coming to a halt mired in a turmoil of ripped turf. Seconds later he heard the Cadillac blast past along the road behind the garden fence. His plan would have worked ... But now his wheels spun impotently in the wet earth, spraying jets of rich brown slurry. More precious seconds burned out like flaring matches as Tanner fought to free the Challenger. He roared with frustration. Jones's house was about two blocks away. Right now, though, it might as well have been on the far side of the moon.

His daredevil risk could have cost his partner his life.

Precisely on schedule for his dinner date Jones left the absurdly extravagant three-storey safe house where the NOPD had inexplicably billeted him.

His eye was immediately drawn to a strangely familiar plum-red Cadillac parked at a strange angle out on the street. It almost looked as if it had been prepped for a quick getaway. Jones suddenly caught motion blurring in the corner of his eye, and ducked by instinct. Something blew past him like a supersonic wasp and the window exploded with an ear-shattering crash.

Jones ran out on to the lawn, dragging frantically at his concealed service piece. A towering straight-backed figure wearing a beautiful velveteen coat strode across the lawn towards him. The figure wore a Frankenstein mask, a lurid glow-in-the-dark spectre looming like a fuzzy photographic after-image behind the all-too-real S&W tactical Glock 35 pistol.

Tobias already had his gun drawn and was raising it to the firing position when the masked figure pumped five rounds into him. The policeman hurtled backwards as if he'd been kicked by a shire horse.

Using his car mats for traction Tanner had managed to free the Challenger in under a minute, which was amazing but still felt like slow motion when your best friend's life hung in the balance. Now, as he zoomed along Jones's street, Tanner watched everything in glacial clarity. He saw the waiting Cadillac, saw Bowman with his arm outstretched, saw Jones—

Saw him drop.

Tanner's heart clenched. His foot jammed on the brake and he swung the car into a lethal swerve across the bend. The wheels locked and fanned out a perfect arc of burning rubber along the blacktop. The Challenger hit the kerb with a jarring snap and rose up in a black and yellow blur like a tiger leaping on its prey. Tanner had managed to control the vehicle's momentum perfectly and it didn't tip or shudder even a fraction as it came to a halt in the middle of the lawn. He was already moving, though, without bothering to kill the engine. Every microsecond counted.

Tanner threw open the side door; the window dissolved into a mist of jewelled fragments. He tucked in his neck and went into a forward roll behind the cover of the door. The metal screamed with the impacts of Bowman's second and third shots. Tanner twisted as he cleared the door. His shoulder hit the grass, side on, his arms outstretched, the ACP in his grip. Already he was firing.

Bowman managed to crack off one more round, but it shrieked wide. Tanner's three slugs, however, took him all centre mass, dead-aim. The force of the bullets made the massive Creole stagger. His knee buckled and he toppled like a mighty oak. Tanner jerked to his feet. He skidded round the side of the car and came out across the sparkling dewy grass in a rush.

Tanner dashed past Bowman. Blood glinted around the slot-like mouth cut into the Frankenstein mask. The elastic band had snapped, so that the mask was slightly askew, which made it look unsettlingly as if his face had come unscrewed. Tanner punted the assassin's long-barrelled Glock 35 deep into the rose bushes with the tip of his boot. Not that Bowman was going to be rooting through the thorns to find it again anytime soon – he was wheezing like a cracked stove – but Tanner didn't spare him a second glance. He flew to his fallen partner and hugged his unresponsive friend.

'Come on, Jones! Fuck, fuck, hang on. I've phoned an ambulance, they'll be here in a minute . . . if . . . if you can just hang on. Talk to me, Tobias. Say something—'

'God, get off! You're crushing me!'

Tanner gasped in delight. Overjoyed, he cautiously helped his friend to sit up. Tobias winced. He loosened his shirt to reveal the deformed cinder-coloured plates of the Dragon Skin ballistic vest he wore underneath.

'Also, you gotta stop underestimating me,' he chided. 'Told you enough times before, I'm a careful man. I always take the necessary precautions when I go out.'

He was breathing raggedly, which probably meant he had either bruised or cracked ribs. He didn't seem in any further distress, however. One bullet had grazed his shoulder, but was only leaking a little, a flesh wound. Tanner nodded with ironic remorse.

'Your shirt,' Tanner pointed out sardonically to Jones to mask his concern. Jones checked his torn sleeve and scowled.

'Shit damn, but I only bought this yesterday. Fresh on, hundred and eighty dollars. Jesus.' His gaze flicked resentfully over to the dark hump lying on the pathway. 'Who's the shooter?'

'Bowman.'

'Fuck. He still in the game?'

'Not sure. Three in the chest. I was kinda focused on you, bro. Didn't really think I had time to check.'

'Go on, I'm fine. He might still be a threat, go.'

Jones was right. It was lousy procedure. Tanner's concern for his partner could have left them both wide open to reprisals. It seemed as if this whole operation was one long string of compromised decisions on Tanner's part. He cursed silently, thankful at least that Jones was safe.

Tanner pushed himself to his feet and stalked over to the downed Creole, pistol held at attention by his shoulder. When he arrived, though, he saw that his

310

foe was in no fit state to offer any resistance. The assassin's mask had come off fully now and he was holding his smartphone in one shivering claw. He was in a bad way. His breath came in tight, agonized gasps as his dying fingers fumbled over the virtual keypad. However, his blood was smeared across the touch sensitive screen, and the device kept giving him error messages. Relieved that Bowman hadn't been able to blow his cover to anyone else, Tanner kicked the cell out of the Creole's hand and stood on his wrist. The phone shattered into five very non-functional pieces, much to Tanner's satisfaction. He'd really never been much of a technology fan, and cell phones in particular had always offended his independent spirit.

Bowman chuckled; it was no longer the same trademark bass boom now his lungs were filling up with blood. 'You,' he managed to wheeze wetly.

Tanner nodded.

Bowman attempted to laugh again, but his gallows humour dissolved into a volley of racking coughs that wrung his body like a dishcloth. It took him a moment to recover and when his lips peeled open again his teeth were stained scarlet. 'Cop?'

Tanner shrugged out a confirmation. Bowman nodded as if this too was merely an amusing piece of after-dinner trivia. Already the approach of ambulance sirens could be heard over the roofs.

'Don't try and speak,' Tanner told the Creole without much compassion. 'The ambulance will be here soon.'

But the light was already fading in Bowman's eyes and he couldn't move. He was making an appalling waterlogged choking at the back of his throat and his neck shook in distress. In spite of himself, Tanner leaned in to see if he could ease the Creole's suffering, which was when Bowman spat out the mouthful of blood he'd been collecting. Tanner jerked back in surprise, but the assassin hadn't been strong enough to project his final gory insult and it just bubbled weakly out on to his chin and silk collar. When Tanner returned back to hover cautiously over Bowman again he saw that the man was dead.

Lost in thought, Tanner returned to Jones and sat down on the ripped-up grass beside him, ignoring the torn-out clods of fresh earth that ruined the green bay.

'This is a bit of a turnaround, ain't it?' Jones said in a pained voice.

'How so?'

'Well, you told me I couldn't ever understand what you went through because I was never in danger. I was just the dude in the van with his headphones on while you were out running with the wolves.'

Tanner grunted, looked a little sheepish. Glanced at his shoes. 'Uh, yeah, I may have said something a bit like that.'

The two friends looked at each other for a few moments and then started to chuckle.

'So, we might not be exactly equal on the "life in peril" index, but you gotta admit this changes our . . . Owww, shit—'

Jones had started to wobble, then sway. Alarmed, Tanner propped his friend up and checked him again for injuries, which was when he made the awful discovery. It was true that none of Bowman's bullets had penetrated his partner's chest armour, but what neither of them had initially noticed – Tanner because he was still full of adrenalin from the shooting and Jones because shock had prevented him from properly feeling his injuries – was that he'd been struck in the thigh.

'I feel kinda dizzy . . .' Jones mumbled, his eyes rolling like a drunk's at a beer festival. Tanner examined his partner's trouser leg. It was sodden with blood and the ground beneath his body was drenched with red.

Jones lost consciousness after a few minutes inside the ambulance, but Tanner kept talking to him throughout the jangling bumpy journey. There were no windows to see out of the back of the vehicle, but from the ride he imagined they must be tumbling freely end over end down a mountain. Tanner didn't mind holding his friend's hand, but Jones's flesh was clammy, tepid, corpse-like.

'If you die, I swear I'm going to kick your ass so hard. Don't give up, Jones.'

At the hospital Jones was whipped away on a gurney by the receiving trauma team and sucked into the efficient vortex of emergency medical care. Tanner was left to pace the waiting room for anxious hours. He drank more cups of coffee than he could easily count. His fingers didn't start to shake but the world gained a faraway metallic sheen and his headache became like a steel spike gradually being hammered in above one eyebrow. Eventually the surgeon came to find Tanner.

The wheelman listened, grim-faced, as she explained that Jones had lost a lot of blood – she repeated that for emphasis, a lot of blood, which chilled Tanner to his core – and there had been complications. His major wound had been treated successfully, but afterwards he'd slipped into a coma. He might wake up in five minutes, five hours, weeks, decades or never. All they could do now was watch and wait. Tanner thanked her and sat down for the first time in hours. He stared at his hands for a long while but didn't really see them.

The next morning the bodies of Bergeron and Vidrine were washed up some way down river near Carlisle: the corpses were both missing fingers and toes, and had a total of three eyes between them, along with sundry other cuts, slices and burns. Bergeron's stomach had been sliced open and his lower intestines attacked with a soldering iron. None of the wounds were *post mortem*. Both men had been kept alive while the injuries were inflicted.

They had quite literally been tortured to death – on Tanner's watch.

The gold-finish door handle buried itself about two inches into Police Superintendent Anton Powell's office wall. The door had gained its velocity from Detective John Tanner's boot against its exterior and Tanner swiftly followed the handle inside.

'Don't stand. I won't be here that long,' he told Powell, who looked up from his almond croissant and Americano with startled rage flashing in his eyes.

'I'm so sorry, Superintendent,' Powell's PA gushed, wringing her hands with distress as she appeared behind Tanner. 'I couldn't stop him . . .'

'What the hell is wrong with you, Powell? Are you some kind of moron?' Tanner spat.

Powell's eyes went flat, unnerved by the prospect that he might be humiliated in front of his subordinates.

'Ah, Fiona, that's fine. The detective and I have some matters to discuss, if you wouldn't mind giving us a moment's privacy, thank you.'

Once Fiona was gone and the damaged door closed as best it could be, Powell leaned back in his luxury leather chair to regard Tanner. His shrewd pale gaze was no longer perturbed. He was back in control. For the first time Tanner noticed the Superintendent's resemblance to Jericho and the hitman's carefully moulded persona. They were both creatures who craved power and little else. The two policemen regarded each other, the fan above barely cutting through the antagonism thickening between them.

'Why have you been stonewalling me?' Tanner demanded.

'I haven't.'

'I've been requesting a meeting for days.'

'We haven't found a gap in my schedule. I'm a busy man and to my knowledge the operation was proceeding exactly as planned. You'd infiltrated the Indian's inner circle. Impressed him with your loyalty and daring. The next stage was to secure incriminating evidence on tape.'

'Haven't you been paying attention to my reports? Didn't Detective Jones make this crystal clear? The Indian isn't the dangerous one, Jericho is.'

'Respectfully, I disagree. Furthermore, your own reports don't support your borderline hysterical assertions. Who is this Jericho? Where's he sprung from? He's barely featured on any of our threat assessments to date and with good reason. He's a button man, a nonentity.'

'He's never featured on your assessments because Cochrane's surveillance team is worse than incompetent. By your own admission you've never had anyone this close before. Jericho is clever, subtle, he doesn't make any waves.'

'Detective, did you not understand when I said that the Indian was the devil himself in human form? When I showed you photos that would have given Jeffrey Dahmer nightmares?'

'The Indian is the front. Jericho's the real power behind the throne. You're obsessed and it's blinded you to what's really going on.'

'No, I think it's clear it's you who's lost perspective,

detective. You've gotten far too close to this case.'

'I'm the one on the ground – that's the whole reason you brought me in. When I took this case on you told me I'd have the authority to run it exactly the way I saw fit, without interference.'

'That's when I thought I was seconding one of the most effective undercover officers in the country. But even your own partner has serious misgivings about your objectivity on this case. He mentioned it only yesterday when we were trying to arrange this meeting. Neither one of us suggested "when Detective Tanner feels like kicking your office door in" as a potential date for an appointment. Though I understand Detective Jones was seriously wounded last night. My sincerest condolences—'

'No. Your stubborn pursuit of the Indian has put . . . many of my mission-critical assets in danger.' In his anger he almost blurted out Navarro's name, which would have been disastrous for his argument; he had to keep her out of the picture until she was locked in as his key witness. 'It's your obsession, Powell, that's led directly to Jones being shot.'

Powell fixed him with his reptilian glare: 'Do you want to be removed from this operation, Detective Tanner?'

'You can't. You need me,' Tanner toughed it out, calling his bluff.

Powell weighed the situation up with an ironic little hand juggle, 'Maybe yes, maybe no. It would be a blow, I'll admit, but I think we've already got enough evidence here to take this one to court and try our chances. I'd far rather that than have one rogue officer hold my whole department to ransom. I won't let you derail my investigation, detective.'

'Your political ambitions, you mean?'

'What was that?' Powell snapped dangerously.

'You heard me.' Tanner matched him with menace. Powell straightened in his chair, neck stiff with barely controlled anger.

'Detective Tanner, if you do not return your full efforts to the named target of this investigation, André Sepion, then I will pull you off this case and have you on the short bus back to 'Frisco so fast it will make your ears bleed. That was your last warning.'

Dismissal delivered, Powell returned to his fancy coffee and copy of the *National Journal* marked with a silver maple-leaf bookmark. Tanner's jaw tightened. He knew he'd been out-manoeuvred. There was no way he could let Powell bounce him off the case, not when so many lives depended on him. He'd thought Powell was the smart one, the consummate politician, and Cochrane the bumbling oaf who couldn't see the bigger picture. Now it turned out Powell was the most short-sighted fool of them all.

Tanner sketched out a mocking ironic salute. 'Hope I didn't damage your door,' he muttered, but Powell didn't even look up as he left.

Tanner stamped out into the hallway and paced back and forth, seething like a boiling pan. Normally, when he reached this point and he was beating his head against the idiocy of authority, he'd talk it out with Jones and together, somehow, they'd figure out an answer. He thought of his friend lying in his bed in the hospital, needles in his arms, tubes down his throat. Tanner grimaced.

'Hoo, hoo, hoooo,' an unwelcome voice sniggered over his shoulder. Tanner spun around. 'Someone looks like Daddy just gave 'im a spanking,' Cochrane observed.

He was leaning in the doorway of his office slobbering over a shrimp and oyster po' boy takeout sandwich. Tanner wasn't surprised to see that the Deputy Chief ate with the grace of a hog snuffling through a trough. Gravy, mustard and spats of grease marked his crumpled shirt, adding to the pre-existing gallery of sweat stains. He winked at Tanner with an open-mouth grin.

'When I told you I'd be keeping an eye on you I didn't expect you'd end up shitting the bed so badly that you got your own partner shot!' he chuckled.

'Unless you want to continue this conversation looking back at me through the wall I've just pounded you into, *sir*, then you better show a little more respect to my partner, Tobias Jones,' Tanner told Cochrane in a very low voice, his gaze utterly still.

'Aw, that's just you all over, ain't it? Mouthy insubordination and a hollow threat you wouldn't dare follow up on: classic Tanner. All the while your poor little bum buddy is wrapped up in hospital with a boo-boo because you couldn't do your job properly.'

Tanner took a single purposeful step towards Cochrane, who danced backwards in fluttering alarm. He recovered quickly, though.

'Want to know the really interesting thing about you, Tanner? You are a tiny little shit speck . . . Oh yeah, you're the smallest floating whiff of animal crap I know. You're not an NOPD officer. You barely appear on any paperwork in this office. You're only in New Orleans on some vague bullshit informal basis. You . . . don't . . . exist. If Jones dies, then Powell 'n' me get hit by a truck, and you got shot while "undercover", it could take weeks, months – hell, *years* until anyone even found out you weren't the common pond scum I know you to be!' Cochrane's mouth pinched into a mean little beak.

The unsettling thing was that he was right. Tanner had never been this exposed on a mission before.

It didn't take much to stare down the likes of Cochrane, however. A couple of seconds of Tanner's full high beams and the fat man was sweating it behind his bluster. The Deputy Chief knew what Tanner was capable of and his bravado wrinkled away like a deflating balloon. He turned hastily into his office with a mocking grunt, but not before Tanner caught his dry gulp of fear.

Tanner had known this assignment was poison from the moment Powell tossed the viper into his lap. Why hadn't he trusted his instincts and told him to stick it where the sun don't shine? Was he a risk addict? An adrenalin junkie unable to curb his desires for ever more self-destructive thrills, all of which he cloaked in the convenient fiction of defending the peace?

He knew one thing for sure. He had to get Jericho off the streets, by any means necessary.

Chapter Twenty-three

The plan was pretty straightforward, if not especially creative, but Tanner didn't have time to work up anything in more detail. He needed Jericho behind bars before he caused any more harm. They could work out how to keep him there on a more permanent basis once he'd been yanked off the chess board.

Tanner knew that Jericho always kept a supply of back-up armaments in the Dodge with him, ready for any violent contingency. He knew for a fact that the hitman didn't have permits for his infamous shotguns, and was willing to bet the same applied to the rest of his arsenal. It was a simple task to tip off a couple of patrol cops and arrange for them to swoop in with a random stop and search at a suitable juncture. He even arranged for both himself and Navarro to be in the car at the time. It wouldn't be a pleasant journey, but there would be a double pay-off. Tanner would be able to ensure his nemesis arrived at the right spot at the right time, and

Navarro would be arrested as well and this would deflect suspicion if Jericho ever came to suspect he'd been set up.

Well, not foolproof by any means, especially if Jericho decided to try and shoot his way out of the ambush, but it was the best Tanner could manage at such short notice. The fact that he wouldn't be armed himself was a concern and he wasn't thrilled to be involving Navarro in the sting as well. She was another wild card variable. Still, at the end of the day sometimes you just gotta throw them dice.

They were travelling to see the Indian to discuss his plans for the future of the city, post-Lavache. When the Indian was undisputed crime lord of New Orleans he'd assign each of his top lieutenants their own fiefdom. Navarro was already in the passenger seat when Jericho picked Tanner up outside his apartment.

Tanner winced as he jumped into the back of the Dodge, niggled by injuries he'd sustained over the course of the operation. Navarro turned round to greet him and her eyes widened.

'Rough night,' he lied a shade uncomfortably. He really wanted to talk to her alone, as they'd not had a chance to touch base since the charged encounter at the zoo, but there was no chance with her boyfriend in such proximity.

They drove in silence, with just the drone of the air conditioning drilling into Tanner's composure. His constant need to be in control of the driving was intensified by being in the back seat, but he crushed that sensation down with ice. Fifteen minutes into the drive it was time for him to make his move. He motioned to a likely-looking convenience store.

'Hey, can we just pull up there for a sec? I'm out of nicotine patches. Don't want to be crawling the walls when we meet the boss, eh?' Because that's the boss's job, he felt moved to add, but restrained himself.

Jericho parked up without any fuss, but as Tanner's hand stole to the door he suddenly growled, 'No.' Tanner tensed. 'Let Julia go. I want a quick word with you regarding that subject we talked about after you first met the Indian.'

Uh oh, thought Tanner. The search for the mole and, presumably, now Bowman's disappearance. It wasn't quite what he'd planned, but nothing he couldn't improv around. He relaxed a little. Navarro shrugged and jumped out.

'Hey,' Jericho snapped at her. 'Little sugar.'

It was a command not a request. He put his head on one side, dark eyes piercing. Tanner could sense how reluctant she was, but the girl covered it like a pro. She leaned back into the car and put her face to Jericho's. They kissed for a long time. Tanner couldn't stand to see Jericho's filthy hands on Navarro's skin, their lips touching. He looked away and stared out of the window until they were done.

'This is going to be an important meeting,' Jericho told her as they parted. 'This is for our future. You look good. Go. Buy yourself a smoothie while you're there. Fruit is good for the skin.'

He patted her hip to dismiss her, and Navarro sashayed airily off into the store. Tanner thought she looked cocky, clearly feeling she'd fooled her mark. The instant she was out of sight, however, Jericho drew out his sawn-off and chambered a round with a chilling snap of the wrist. The crisp clack of the weapon was very loud in the narrow confines of the Dodge.

'Whoa! Jericho! Chill out. What's going on?'

'We're not going to see the Indian. I called ahead and cancelled. We've got something else to take care of.'

'I don't get this. I told you I really don't appreciate you playing me for a fool—'

'We're making another trip instead.'

'Have you lost your mind? This is insane, it's broad daylight . . .'

Jericho's inky gaze swept across him. 'I know who the snitch is, the one who's been working with the police all along, feeding them information on our every move.'

Jericho's gaze was colder than the lightless reaches of the solar system. Tanner's whole body clenched.

'And I think you know too,' the hitman continued.

'I've no idea what you're on about—'

'Yes you do, but that's OK. I know why you didn't tell me. Got a picture message from Bowman the other night, just before he vanished. No text, just one image.

325

I didn't understand at first, but then it slotted into place like a magic puzzle.'

Jericho showed Tanner the image on his cell phone. Tanner felt that his whole body had suddenly transformed into a hollow statue, and he might shatter into a million shards at the slightest jolt.

The photo showed Jones and Julia outside Audubon Zoo. So, the dying Bowman had been able to use his cell phone after all. Fuck.

'I know you've been protecting her and I can understand that,' Jericho rasped. 'Loyalty is an important trait – but that stops right now. We're going into the swamp together, all three of us, and you *are* going to play along. We're going to do what needs to be done, and that will make an end of it. Do. You. Understand?'

Tanner stared long and hard into the gaping shotgun barrels. There was only one way this scenario could end now, Tanner knew.

'PUT DOWN THE MOTHERFUCKING SHOTGUN NOW, JERICHO, OR WE WILL TURN YOU INTO SWISS CHEESE!' thundered the voice of the police car's PA system not 10 feet away.

Right on time, thought Tanner.

He turned his head slightly and saw a second cop in a perfect squared-off shooting stance, wrist-locked, his Glock trained unwaveringly through the driver's side window and on Jericho's right temple.

A few minutes later events still seemed to be unfolding at slightly less than full speed for Tanner. Tanner had been dragged from the car and restrained, but it felt almost as if he was floating. He gazed over at a female police officer who was dipping a cuffed and shell-shocked Navarro under the door frame of the police car's back seat.

With enormous satisfaction he stared back at the Dodge as the two patrol cops slammed Jericho's cheek down on to its gleaming black hood to cuff him. The hitman's face was as impassive as ever and his body language utterly relaxed, but one thought filled Tanner's mind. He'd won. He'd done what everyone was too blind to see *had* to be done. He'd captured the true enemy, and just in time to save Navarro's life as well. If only he'd known all along it was going to be this simple he might have saved them all a lot of grief.

Jericho was going to jail.

Tanner stared into the blindingly white interrogation room through the one-way mirror. In his customary all-black garb Jericho seemed to suck all the light from the space into him. He waited as a robot waits, a machine on standby, preserving power. The only sign that he was still alive was a minute tap of his right index finger against the table-top. It wasn't a nervous tick, more like a metronome keeping time.

Powell entered the observation room behind Tanner. His eyes were cold steel. 'A concealed weapon rap? Is that *it*?' he spat.

'It wouldn't have been my choice either, but some anonymous tipster called it in. We've got him here now, though. In fact, we got him off the streets just in time. He had photos of Julia Navarro and Jones together and he was convinced she was the mole. He was going to kill her.'

'That's what you claim. So the girl picked up with you is her? Julia Navarro, small-time crook and violent gang member,' Powell remarked with a sneer.

'The crimes she's committed are infinitesimal in comparison to the monsters in Sepion's gang.'

'Really? You didn't think to dig out her past rap sheet, then? If you had, you'd have found a string of charges for auto theft. It's only by the skin of her teeth and the poor eyesight of witnesses that she's not done time before.'

Tanner shifted a little uncomfortably. It was true: he had been so wrapped up in *his* history with Julia that he'd not taken the time to trawl through her more recent past.

'That changes nothing,' he continued as confidently as he could. 'She's going to be my key witness and I refuse to have her placed in any more danger than she needs to be. When we take down Jericho, when we mop up the Indian, she'll be the one up there in the witness box. She's our ace in the pocket. I give you my personal guarantee on that.'

'Absolutely not, detective,' Powell countered. 'She's judicial poison. Any defence attorney worth his salt will use her stink to douse the jury like a skunk. They'll not believe a single word of the prosecution case for the rest of the trial. I'm not about to hang one of the most important operations of my career on the tainted testimony of a woman who is at best a un-repentant career criminal and at worst a borderline vigilante!'

'That's bullshit,' Tanner growled. 'She's just a good kid who's made some bad decisions—'

'I know about her father, detective, and her hunger for vengeance. Did you think I wouldn't find out?'

'That's all under control,' Tanner replied firmly in a lower voice. 'It just motivates her even more to want justice for Ernesto.'

'Is it "under control" like the fact that you knew her as a kid? You neglected to tell anyone about that conflict of interest!'

'Look, we can get into all of that down the line. Right now, I know we can make this weapon charge stick. It's enough to keep Jericho behind bars until we bring down the Indian and then we'll get all the hard evidence we need for some proper charges. But in the meantime, though, he *has* to stay here.'

Powell had picked up the sheaf of arrest notes and was skimming through them, no longer properly paying attention.

'Powell, he has to stay inside, understand? Navarro's life depends on it.'

'Hmmm, yes,' Powell agreed absently.

'Then look me in the eye and say it!'

Powell's gaze snapped up, eyes blazing. 'You really are in no position to lecture me, detective. Your little thief friend is hardly the highest thing on my agenda and I don't intend putting her welfare above my

329

pledge to keep all of the genuinely innocent people of New Orleans safe. I'll see Jericho kept inside, but not for you or her. Because it's the right thing to do. I know my job.'

He stepped to the door, then turned back for an instant.

'Oh, and if I manage to prove it was you who tipped off those uniforms, I'll have your badge. No one manipulates my investigation.'

He stalked out. A minute later he and Cochrane entered the interrogation room behind the glass. Jericho barely reacted. The only indication he gave that he was no longer alone was that the frequency of his tapping fingertip increased slightly. Powell sat opposite Jericho, Cochrane stood at his shoulder in his customary post.

'Good morning, Mister ah—' Powell checked the paperwork and frowned. 'I see we still don't have your full birth name yet. That'll have to be seen to, unless you'd prefer to clear that up with us now?'

Jericho ignored him.

'Hey there, fucko!' Cochrane shouted. 'You were asked a question.'

Behind the mirror Tanner rolled his eyes. *Fucko?* Powell and Cochrane's interrogation technique was as subtle as a brick though a church window. Jericho seemed to think so, too. He watched them go through their stagy little routine with a faint smile.

'If you don't start singing in the next five fucking seconds I am going to hurt you in so many ways. No bruises, nothing obvious, but ALL pain,' bellowed Cochrane, beetroot-faced. 'Five . . . four . . . three . . . two . . .'

'I've often played Good Cop, Bad Cop when I've been running my own . . . interviews,' Jericho said to no one in particular. 'I never thought to go Asshole Cop and Stick-up-his-Ass cop. Thanks for the inspiration.'

Cochrane surged forward, face darkening. 'Why, you sonofabitch—'

Powell warningly touched Cochrane's shoulder and he retreated. While his attack pup paced at the back of the room, Powell tried another tack, his voice honeyed.

'You're in a very serious situation, Jericho, but we want to help you. We know you just follow orders. You're not a leader, Jericho. You're more . . . logistical support.'

'You don't have the brains or the balls for real power is what he's trying to say,' Cochrane sneered. Powell acknowledged this uncomfortably.

'Quite . . . Well, here are the facts. We have the unregistered guns from your vehicle and no paperwork has been forthcoming. Also, those guns were not carried openly. Now, these are all actionable offences, Class One misdemeanours carrying potential jail time and large fines.'

Jericho barked out a contemptuous laugh. 'Concealed weapons, is that all you've got? Don't make me laugh. My lawyer'll be kicking through those charges like he's knocking down sandcastles. I'll be back on the street in a couple of days.'

Powell edged his chair round so he was closer to the impassive hitman. At that moment, a young admin assistant stuck his head round the door.

'Uh, Detective Tanner, Superintendent Powell needs you to sign some insurance forms.'

'Now?' Tanner sighed, exasperated. 'I don't think so.' Events behind the glass were just getting going.

'He was very insistent. This is paperwork relating to your recent, uh, journey through the Garden District when Detective Jones was shot. If it isn't done immediately he said there would be serious reper-cussions. He said it was insubordination, which could lead to suspension.'

So Powell was going to use all the damage he'd caused saving his partner to boot him off the case. Tanner weighed up his options. This would only take a moment and clearly Jericho's grilling could run to hours. It was worth it to duck out and keep Powell's machinations at bay. He nodded to the aide, and they left together. Fifteen minutes later he stepped back into the observation room and instantly froze.

The gleaming space beyond the mirror was empty. Tanner ran back outside. 'Powell!' he bellowed.

A few curious faces down the corridor looked round, but there was no sign of the Superintendent. Tanner ran to his plush office. The door was locked and there was still no sign of the Superintendent. Cochrane wasn't in his office, either. Tanner grabbed a smirking civilian aide and slammed him against the wall.

'Where's Cochrane?' he snarled.

The man quailed. 'Uh, the can, I think . . .'

Tanner kicked his way into the men's bathroom. Only one cubicle was occupied. He heard the rustle of clothes, the clink of a belt buckle against the flooring tiles, a heavy body shifting. He hammered on the door and its inhabitant jumped in panic.

'Where the fuck is Jericho, Cochrane?' he shouted.

Cochrane's sneering laughter lofted out from inside the cubicle and bounced around off the glossy reflective surfaces.

'Released without charge. See, Powell's playing the long game. He doesn't want the Indian to hear that his right-hand man's in jail. He might get all spooked and burrow back underground. So Powell made a deal with your public enemy number one. The concealed weapon charges go away on the condition that he gives up the Indian to us on a plate. Jericho rolled over like a puppy and let Powell scratch his belly. He went for that deal so quick I thought we should have thrown it for him like a bone. Real hardened warlord that one, Tanner. If he'd stayed overnight in the cells I'm sure he'd have pissed himself in fear.'

Rage and terror in equal measures chased through Tanner's body. 'What about Navarro?' he managed to grate out. 'Powell knew Jericho had threatened her. He'll be sure that she sold him out. I told Powell her life would be in danger if he let Jericho go, yet he did it anyway! What was he thinking?'

'Hmm, let me see. I think our esteemed leader's exact words were: "Let that dumb poke swing in the wind, after all you can't make an omelette without breaking some legs." Putting her in jeopardy is an acceptable risk if it brings down the Indian. I expect Jericho's long gone by now, though maybe if you run you'll catch him in reception.'

Tanner's mouth compressed into a jagged line. He ran to the door, paused, then ran back and took the janitor's mop from its station. He jammed it through the cubicle's handle, trapping Cochrane inside. The Deputy Chief realized something was amiss and leapt to his feet to shout, trousers still around his ankles. Tanner ducked out, smiling grimly as Cochrane's cries of outrage echoed in his ears.

He sprinted down the dim echoing hallway leading out of the police HQ, his boot steps booming like thunderclaps, and he smashed through the double doors into the car park. Outside, he blinked in the dazzling mid-morning blaze. The heat struck him like a dumbbell to the head after so long in the climate-controlled womb of the police department. Tanner desperately scanned the sidewalks and pathways for the black-clad figure of the hitman. There were civilian clothes everywhere and the powder-blue shirts of NOPD officers in abundance, but no Jericho.

He'd vanished into the chaos of the city and now he was on his way to kill Navarro.

Chapter Twenty-four

Tanner listened to the dialling impatiently. There was a soft clunk.

'Hey,' murmured Navarro from the handset. 'What's up?'

'It's me,' he replied.

'Wow. You slipped out quick. You weren't carrying, I take it?'

'No. But that's not why they let me go. I need to see you. Now.'

He could hear the frown in her voice: 'What's going on, John? What's wrong?'

'I can't talk over the phone. Can I come over? It has to be now.'

He'd never been to her place before and his urgency was spooking her but after a moment she reluctantly gave him the address.

Navarro lived on an impoverished block in the lower Ninth Ward, the sort of neighbourhood so devastated by the attrition of petty crime, vandalism and under-investment that it looked like a post-apocalyptic nightmare future. She rented a little apartment in a poorly maintained wood-fronted three-floor walk-up. As Tanner stood outside her door he jiggled his palms agitatedly against his sides as he desperately tried to work out how to play this. He had his speech, of course, his justifications and explanations, the hows and whys and wherefores, but when it came down to it and he was actually staring into Navarro's eyes all he said was: 'I'm an undercover cop.'

He saw from her face that she believed him instantly and hated him for it.

'I need to come in, please. You're in danger.'

She stepped back robotically to let him past.

She kept on nodding, her head bobbing away like a toy dog on the dashboard, as if she understood and agreed with every point he was making, yet one hand was clamped across her mouth and her eyes above her fingers were wide and bright and accusing.

'The best thing is if you go into hiding.'

'Have the police authorized a safe house for me?' she asked in a husk of a whisper.

Tanner hesitated, uncomfortable. 'No . . . They don't know I'm here yet. It's a bit of a rush job, so I'm sorting it out myself, but . . . You trust me, don't you?'

A pause. She nodded.

'Look, it's not safe here any more. Let's talk about it on the way.'

She nodded.

'Throw some things in a bag as quickly as possible while I keep a look-out.'

She nodded and then walked into the bedroom without speaking. Tanner drew his pistol and crept to the window to keep an eye on the street below: all he could see were some kids shooting hoops, but he stayed there, motionless, behind the curtain, his gaze trained on all the access points and potential sniper spots.

Ten minutes later Julia re-emerged wearing her rust-coloured biker's jacket with a sports bag hanging limply, mostly empty, over one shoulder.

'Right,' said Tanner firmly. 'Let's go.'

Julia pulled a face, embarrassed. 'I have to—' She indicated the bathroom weakly. Tanner was already shaking his head.

'No, Julia, no. They could already be on their way. You're not a child, you'll just have to hold it—'

Out of nowhere, Navarro exploded. 'Fuck you, John! You've lied to me, used me, betrayed me, taken me for granted and put me in danger time and again without sparing me barely a word of truth since we met on the docks. You've humiliated me and utterly abused my trust. Those aren't the actions of a friend. The very fucking least you can do is to let me empty my fucking bladder!'

Chastened, after a beat Tanner nodded tightly.

'Make it quick,' he rasped.

'Fuck you, John. Fuck you very much.'

The bathroom door almost shook off its hinges Julia slammed it so hard. Tanner waited a respectful distance away by the front door. The street was still clear, but for how much longer? A minute passed, then another, three, four. By five Tanner's guilt had receded and his suspicions were swelling. He ran to the bathroom door, put his knuckles to the wood.

'Julia? Are you OK in there?' Nothing. 'We have to get going.' Silence. 'I'm not messing around any more, Julia. Get out here now . . .' Total silence.

Tanner's stomach suddenly lurched. He hadn't checked if there was a window large enough for someone to escape through in the bathroom. Idiot! He stepped back to brace himself and then kicked through the lock. The flimsy wood splintered and the door folded in. Tanner surged forward. The room was empty and the window high up on the far wall gaped, its curtains fluttering wispily in the breeze. Cursing, he stepped forward on the off-chance she'd left any clues as to where she'd gone.

The instant he was fully inside the room Navarro stepped out from behind the shower curtain and touched her taser to his neck. She pressed the stud. Tanner saw the world transform into an electric spasm of stars and blue fizzing outlines for a second, then darkness took him.

As he passed out all he could think of was the expression of betrayal etched on to her face.

* * *

When Tanner came to, the room had darkened considerably. From the slice of sky he could see from his vantage point on the floor, he judged it was late afternoon and he'd been unconscious for some time. Julia was long gone. He was lying half in, half out of Navarro's bathroom.

He sat up, feeling creaky and little nauseous. Shook his head to try and shift the high-pitched ringing the taser had left in his left ear. That didn't shift it. How old was too old to be in a job where you risked getting electrocuted in your daily work? He gingerly rose and wobbled over to Navarro's busted old sofa. He slumped there for a moment trying to recover, his head between his knees. He didn't groan. That wasn't his style and, seriously, what good would it have done?

He checked his cell phone. There was one voicemail message. It was from her. Tanner hesitated for a moment, then he thumbed the key. Navarro's voice echoed tinnily in his ear. In the background he could hear the boom and rush of trucks blasting by. She'd phoned from somewhere on the side of an interstate, probably I-10, but not definitely.

'I'm sorry, John, I didn't want to hurt you . . .' Julia whispered, her voice cracked with emotion. 'But I just can't trust anyone now. I've gone away and I won't tell you where. You lied to me, John.'

The message ran out into the menu and Tanner cut the connection. There was something else amiss, a familiar weight that he only now felt the absence of.

With an awful sinking feeling his hand crept to his ankle holster. Empty. He was too weary to even curse. He sat stiffly on the sofa considering how badly he'd fucked everything up since he'd arrived in New Orleans.

Suddenly his phone began to trill again. Heart leaping he answered it in a panic: 'Julia!'

'Ah, no, Detective Tanner, this is Dr Freeman from Ochsner Baptist Medical Center. You asked for us to contact you if there was any change in your partner's condition. I'm pleased to say he's now awake.'

Tanner was already running out of the door.

'My mouth's gone dry again. Pass me some more of that juice, you crazy slacker.'

Jones was propped up against his pillow, looking haggard and weak, but the hand beckoning to his hospital side table was ramrod straight.

From his seat by the bed Tanner passed him the soft juice pack from his bedside cabinet and his friend greedily sucked at the straw.

'You think maybe because I've had three days just lying on my back I've actually added a few minutes to the end of my life?' Jones asked speculatively.

Tanner suppressed a smirk. He'd been sorely worried he might never have to endure his friend's random musings again.

'How do you feel?' he enquired.

'Like I could run a marathon.'

'Because from over here you look like crap.'

Jones pulled a face. 'Pfft, I'm fine. They're going to discharge me later.'

Tanner shot him back an impressed look, but Jones's expression suddenly turned shrewd. He pinned his friend with a sceptical gaze and Tanner braced himself for what was coming.

'So . . . you told her you were a cop?' Jones whistled and shook his head in disbelief.

Tanner had already related the sorry tale of what had transpired at Julia's apartment, along with the deaths of Vidrine and Bergeron.

'You really can't be left alone, can you? I fall into one little coma for less than seventy-two hours and this is how you behave!'

'It was the only foolproof way to get her out of the apartment without any argument,' Tanner countered defensively. 'Jericho was all set to kill her this morning. Bowman's picture convinced him she was the mole. What else could I do? Once the department let him go, I assumed he'd send murderers straight round to her place.'

'Powell is going to roast your guts and serve them to Internal Affairs as a finger buffet.'

Tanner shrugged. 'If he finds out, but I don't think Julia will tell anyone.' He hesitated. 'I trust her.'

'Like you trusted her not to taser you unconscious and steal your back-up gun?'

Tanner blew air through his lips and gazed off into the middle distance. 'Yeah, well, as we've established, my decision-making hasn't been quite tournament standard for some time now.' He looked back at his friend. 'Shit, I'm so sorry, Jones. Seems like I can't do right for doing wrong in this town . . .'

Jones shrugged back without rancour, and after a moment he smiled. 'Don't sweat it, brother. 'S all good,' he murmured. 'Jericho is the one we should be raging at.'

A silence fell around them then, punctuated by the hiss of a flash storm spitting against the window pane. Both men stared at nothing, preoccupied with their own thoughts, their recriminations and regrets. However, Tanner's doubts had begun to eat their way out of him, like a parasitic worm yearning to taste the air for the first time. His doubts couldn't be prevented from poking their heads out.

'Jones, do you think I only do this job for the thrills? That all the risks I take are because I'm addicted to the excitement and not because I want to protect people?' he asked hesitantly. Jones sighed.

'What I know is that all this moping and self-doubt isn't helping anyone,' he replied. 'Julia's gone. She doesn't want to be found. You fucked up; we all did. You just gotta get back in the saddle, partner. You'll do the most good if you're back undercover. We need to know what the Indian is planning, and what his endgame is. You need to do the job they pay you for.'

Tanner shot his bed-bound partner a grumpy look, but inside he knew Jones was right. He moved to leave, but at the door his partner called him back, and he turned.

'You're a helluva good cop, John. You take the risks for the right reasons and don't let anyone – even yourself – tell you otherwise.'

Ten minutes later Tanner was back in the Challenger, roaring through the New Orleans back streets once more.

Chapter Twenty-five

When Tanner arrived back at the gang's current hide-out – a warehouse in an industrial estate not far from the port – he was met with ominous news. A defector from the LLR sat on a stool in the starkly lit space being interrogated by the Indian, who was surprisingly controlled if you managed not to look into his electric, staring eyes. The defector was a big black guy with too many gold chains, a weak chin, and a chippy attitude. His left arm was bound up in a fresh linen sling.

'Lavache is insane,' ranted the defector. 'He's thrown every last cent he's got left into buying boom sticks. He's getting in a *massive* arms shipment. Not just iddy biddy fire-pipes, neither, serious metal: rocket launchers, grenades, mines, heavy machine-guns, M-249s, infrared combat specs, the fucking shit, man. Way more than anything you got round here. Lavache is out of his mind. It's an over-fucking-whelming shopping list he's drawn up with the one single goal of slaughtering as many fools as possible.

The guns are coming in tonight and the moment he's checked his inventory and got a till receipt, he's coming straight down here to kill the hell out of all of y'all, if you'll pardon my bluntness.'

A muscle in the Indian's cheek twitched like a plucked harp string. He leant in close to the defector, who recoiled slightly. 'How are we to know *you* aren't a trap sent to draw us into an ambush?'

'Nah,' sneered the defector. 'I'm done with y'all, and this life. After tonight I'm going down Maui way to sell sugar peanuts on the beach. You won't see me for dust.'

The Indian stroked his lips and cheeks thoughtfully. He actually seemed convinced by the defector's testimony.

'That's great, but why come drop this powder keg in our lap while you're busy speeding out of town?' Tanner called from the edge of the circle. 'Why not just melt away into the night and never look back? Let all us fools get eviscerated by Lavache?'

The defector's face creased with sudden rage. 'Because I *hate* those LLR fucks! All the times they laughed at me, called me names, shoved me around. They never listened to a word I had to say, even when I was trying to save their stinking hides. That Lavache was the worst of 'em all! Keep me in the outhouse, will ya? I'll show *you*! I want you to end those motherfuckers. I want them to die in a hail of molten retribution, then choke on lungs full of blood! Then, as they sputter out their last, you tell 'em Ghost Beard says "hi!" '

The rant was baffling, but no one could deny his spittle-flecked conviction. The Indian was so pleased that he actually let the man leave unmolested, and cut a fat block of cash out of his personal stash to see him on his way. So, there it was, the Indian had the time and place of a colossal arms delivery. The hide-out was suddenly abuzz with anxious activity as the Indian's soldiers prepared for the assault to come.

All-out war, thought Tanner.

He had to get the word out as quickly as possible, and have Powell mobilize an overwhelming strike force to arrest both the Indian's men *and* the LLR before the arms cache was ever cracked.

Almost as worrying for Tanner was the news that Jericho had vanished. No one had heard from him. There was no sign of him at any of his usual hang-outs, and he wasn't answering any of his phones. The general consensus was that he'd fled the city having somehow got advance warning of Lavache's attack. Tanner wasn't so sure, though. It wasn't in the man's nature to let the flow of events control him. Either way, following on so closely after Bowman's disappearance, this news undermined the Indian even further, stoking his paranoia to previously unscaled heights.

When he was informed that Jericho still couldn't be located, he'd launched into an astonishing five-minute screaming tirade. He lashed out at crates, kicked over loading equipment, stalked back and forth shrieking about betrayal until he was hoarse while his soldiers mooched about, shuffling their feet like embarrassed schoolboys. Clearly the Indian's state of mind was in shreds, which probably meant his strategic aptitude was blown to shit as well. Tanner was fearful of an upcoming bloodbath.

These fears were given even more credence when one of the thugs wasn't able to open the loading bay back door quickly enough and the Indian suddenly pulled a pistol on him. The thug started to step out of the way to let Sepion himself shift the stubborn door action, but he moved in the wrong direction and the two of them got tangled up. The Indian yelled in strangled frustration and shot the man straight through the thigh. Utter pandemonium erupted in the warehouse as the injured thug screamed, and the Indian screamed, and his élite lieutenants dashed around trying to find medical aid for the injured man while simultaneously attempting to calm down the situation in case the commotion drew police attention.

The Indian had, officially, lost it.

Tanner took this as his cue to slip out and phone Jones, who was now out of the hospital. His long-suffering handler would need as much of a heads up as possible if he was going to convince Cochrane and Powell to project the full NOPD might into the field. There was a lot riding on their swift and decisive action.

Three hours later Tanner found himself ferrying three tooled-up stone-cold killers through the snake's-pit warren of downtown alleys towards Jean-Baptiste

Lavache's arms deal. There wasn't space in the Challenger so the Indian had assigned him another ride, which turned out to be a Dodge Ram SRT10, the clone of Jericho's SUV. This one was olive green. They were just one car in a posse of forty or so guys spread across eighteen vehicles all rolling inexorably towards the same goal. Tanner was suddenly reminded of that fateful Bullit run in San Francisco so long ago. He thought briefly about Slater. He wondered what he was doing tonight. Was he playing cards with cellmates, or watching Nascar racing on a crappy jail television?

The defector had told them that the guns were being delivered to a disused commercial dairy, just outside the city limits and not far from the river. The whole crew mustered in a quiet copse of southern live oaks on a ridge overlooking the dairy. There was one central unit, a looming open-ended steel shed with a corrugated roof. Attached on the riverward side of the structure was a small complex of offices, staffrooms, and a mess hall. Under the shed the milking parlour was divided into individual pens. There was an unseen loading bay on the far side of the building, which served the road: that was where the guns were being delivered. The whole complex was in a reasonable state of repair – the firm had only gone out of business last year but no buyer had yet been found to develop the site – but Tanner could see odd gaps in the walls and roof where slats had rusted and come free. There were no lights burning in the shed itself, but torch beams swung back and forth around the grounds as the LLR patrolled their perimeter, and stray light from the office block showed that they were utilizing that space as well.

The trucks with the guns would be reversing up to the loading bay on the other side of the plot – perhaps they were already there – but the Indian's plan was to ambush the open-ended back of the building. The Indian's men crept down the slope, pistols and shot-guns at the ready. Tanner came in at the rear. He was keen to stay in the thick of things. The pressing question for him remained: What was Jericho up to? If he'd made a deal with Powell to give up the Indian then when would he make his move?

Forty hired killers slipped silently through the high reeds; frogs croaked in the dark around them. The dense clouds overhead were a black velvet masking moon and stars. They were seconds away from the ambush. Tanner was sweating, and not just from the savage humidity, which pressed against his cheeks like a veil. *Damnit*, he thought, *where the hell is Powell?* Blinding searchlights from a squad of helicopters and squad cars should have frozen them in their tracks long before now. So far . . . nothing. The first wave of the Indian's men reached the LLR boundary and chambered rounds.

Then a voice did ring out . . . but it came from inside the milking shed.

'It's them! I see them! Over there!'

Thirty or so LLR footsoldiers sprang up out of

hiding behind the half-walls of the individual milking pens. They opened fire. The night exploded, fire lancing out left, right, centre. The first row of the Indian's men went down immediately. Jean-Baptiste Lavache was at the head of the LLR attack, his grubby caterpillar dreads and stinking voodoo cloak flailing against the air as he snapped off shot after shot from his ivory-handled .45.

'Hear the spirits roar! Hear the spirits roar,' he was screaming. His palpable insanity didn't seem to be hampering his aim. The .45 gun coughed and Tanner saw Cole – the biker from the bayou raid – go down, his temple exploded into shattered bony turrets.

Belatedly, the Indian's men returned fire, but they were deprived of any meaningful cover and were swiftly driven back. The only vaguely encouraging sign was that, as far as Tanner could tell, the LLR were only using small arms, so presumably the new weapons hadn't been delivered yet. Clearly someone had tipped off the LLR that the Indian was coming, but hadn't given them enough time to rearrange the delivery or prepare a proper welcome. There was only one person who might want to add to the general chaos in such an elaborate way: Jericho.

Hunkered down at the back, Tanner searched the higher ground for police reinforcements. Saw nothing. 'Powell, I am going to rip your colon out between your teeth,' he muttered under his breath. He had to stop this becoming a rout of the Indian's forces. 'Here, follow me!' he hissed to the nearest soldiers and a couple of the other drivers. He led them back up the slope while the firefight raged behind them. At the top they encountered an apoplectic Sepion.

'What's going on? How can we be losing men?' he screamed.

'Someone tipped them off. We need a game-changer. I've got one.'

He looked at the waiting vans and then back at the Indian. There was a muffled barking coming from the van the Indian had arrived in. The Indian grinned, nodded.

Seconds later about 11 tons of speeding metal bellowed out of the shadows and down the incline. Five jeeps and vans – Tanner's Dodge leading the charge, footsoldiers firing from the windows – punched straight through the LLR's line. Lavache's men dropped like stones and he bawled with rage. The rear doors of the Indian's van flew open like dark wings, and four bull mastiffs launched themselves out into the middle of the battlefield.

Jaws pistoning, eyes rolling, the hounds bounded straight for Lavache, who screamed even louder and backpedalled desperately. His terror crippled his crack-shooting and his bullets ploughed wide. Eventually he winged one dog, drilled a second between the eyes, but then his heel caught on the uneven ground and he tumbled backwards with a yell. Before he could move the remaining beasts were upon him. A fanged maw clamped around his face to stifle his shrieks and suddenly the dogs were biting, and shaking their massive heads, and ripping, and shredding all around. Within a few heartbeats his ridiculous motley coat was drenched with gore. Dismayed, his nearby soldiers quickly riddled the remaining dogs with lead, but by then it was too late. The thing on the ground that had once been Lavache resembled a collection of butcher's garbage bags.

The Indian's forces rallied and swept unstoppably forward as despair at their leader's demise rippled through the LLR ranks. The Indian jumped out of the back of his van and stood, cackling, on the churned-up ground. He was wielding an AA-12 assault shotgun, blasting indiscriminately into the enemy, the walls, overhead. He roared with jubilation. He'd won, vanquished the spectre he'd focused all his demented attention upon. Lavache was dead. Now the Indian was the undisputed dark lord of New Orleans!

A brilliant column of light like the spotlight of an alien spacecraft surrounded him and the voice of God thundered: 'THIS IS THE NEW ORLEANS POLICE DEPARTMENT ... YOU ARE ALL UNDER ARREST ... CEASE FIRE ... PUT YOUR WEAPONS ON THE GROUND AND SURRENDER!'

Finally, Powell keeps a promise, Tanner silently exclaimed.

Unfortunately the gangsters didn't do as they were told. They stopped attacking each other and started emptying rounds at the helicopter instead. LLR and Indian soldiers began to drop as police snipers opened up from concealed spots in the trees. The high ridge behind them where the posse had mustered was suddenly fringed by red and blue circling lights and police officers opened fire on the exposed thugs below.

Tanner saw the Indian's face slacken with panic. He instantly abandoned his men to flee towards the dairy's back offices. Tanner cursed. He jumped out of the parked Dodge and began to chase after the gang lord. Even if Jericho was the real danger, and Powell was a fool, Tanner was a good cop and he couldn't let Sepion just run free.

Unfortunately, as he cleared the jeep and ventured on to the packed earth under the shed gunfire rang out and the ground at his feet ripped up in spurts. He was being shot at by the police. Tanner dived behind the nearest milking pen for shelter. They might be his own side but they had no idea who he was, and he had no way of telling them. Now he was pinned down.

Out of the corner of his eye he saw the Indian vanishing through the office door.

The Indian locked the office door behind him and blundered through the reception in a high state of agitation. He'd had it all – total triumph! But for a few seconds only and then the sky had fallen in. He'd been betrayed twice tonight by his closest allies. Who had it been? Jericho? Tanner? None of that mattered right now, though. He had to make good his escape while all attention was focused on the battle in the milking shed. He calmed himself and retreated through the dank, empty offices, entering the abandoned mess hall at the rear. Only the kitchen was between him and escape. It wouldn't be that difficult to slip out of a fire door round the back and high-tail it down the sheer grassy slope to the nearby road.

The Indian pushed backwards through the saloon-style doors into the kitchen, keeping the room behind him covered with his shotgun. Jericho and all those other whisperers might think his mind was soft as runny Camembert these days, but André Sepion was still clever and resourceful. He'd clawed his way to the top of the New Orleans underworld, and he could do it again, if need be. He could build himself back up. He didn't need Jericho. He didn't need Bowman or Tanner, or any of those snakes in the grass. A few months in hiding to get his head straight. A chance to clean out all of the brain-clouding poisons from his system might be just what he needed. André Sepion was a survivor.

He could hear the firefight was still raging out in the milking shed. Ricochets echoed off the steel shell like firecrackers in a tin can. The cops and the LLR would be way too preoccupied to notice his absence. Once he got to the road he could flag down a passing car and wave his shotgun in their faces until they gave up their vehicle and maybe some cash. The Indian grinned slyly. Everything was going to work out.

Then he heard a faint click and felt something cold and unyielding pressed to the nape of his neck.

'You killed my father, you fucking animal,' hissed Julia Navarro.

* * *

Machine-gun fire chattered all around Tanner. Sparks flew; men cried out in pain. The police marksmen were steadily picking off the remaining footsoldiers but a hardcore were stubbornly digging in and refused to give in to the inevitable. The confrontation was rapidly turning into the carnage he'd so desperately tried to avoid. Furthermore, he still had no idea how to get across to the offices and after the Indian. Probably he was already miles away by now. *Shit.*

A hand suddenly fell on his shoulder.

The wheelman twisted and almost blew the interloper away before he realized who it was: 'Jones, what the hell!' he hissed.

'Sorry, bro, didn't think you'd hear if I phoned your cell and wasn't about to shout across this chaos in case someone shot my head off!'

Tanner was hugely relieved to see Jones up and around again. His friend's face was a little haggard, but he didn't seem to be suffering unduly.

'I'm sure your surgeon would bust a blood vessel if she knew you'd gone straight from the ward to a gangland shoot-out.'

'I'm cool, but we got to put a cap on this insanity as soon as possible.'

'Agreed, but why the hell wasn't Powell here to stamp on it in the first place like we agreed?'

Jones's face darkened. 'Jericho's deal. He dropped a massive drug bust into Powell's lap a couple of hours ago. Said it would have everything we need to nail the

Indian. Powell didn't trust you any more and he's never really believed in this arms deal. Turns out Jericho was true to his word, suspiciously so, in fact. There *was* a huge shipment coming through the docks tonight exactly when and where he'd said it would be. We caught them red-handed. The Indian's fingerprints were all over it. The thugs we snatched all identified his photo. There're about a dozen ways we can connect it to Sepion. When we catch the bastard he's going down for a long stretch. Powell's happy as a sand boy. He's had reporters interviewing him on the scene, posing with the drugs, that's why we're here so late.'

Tanner was dumbfounded at Powell's short-sightedness.

Julia Navarro's whole body was trembling, her face contorted with emotion, yet the barrel of Tanner's back-up .38 never wavered from the Indian's corpulent chest. He reversed uneasily, palms raised, breath coming out as a fast jerking torrent.

'What are you doing, cherie? I'm on your side. I'm your mentor, your leader. I'm going to give you New Orleans to rule—'

'You killed him,' she hissed in a terrible voice, eyes glittering like the glint of knives.

'I don't know what you talk of, kitten! Truly, the Indian swears!'

'Your name is André Sepion; if you call yourself *that* once more I will drill you where you stand. My father.

356

Three years ago you beat him in an alley because he wouldn't submit to your tyranny. My proud father, Ernesto Navarro, a better man than you could ever dream to be!'

The Indian laughed then. Not the laughter of madness or false bravado, but a genuine bark of happy surprise. 'But I didn't do that,' he yelped with relief.

'Filthy liar! You don't even remember who he was, you wretched bag of guts! You'd say anything to save your fat hide!'

'No, no, but that's what's so funny. I do remember that night well. Clement Street, French Quarter . . . I remember it so vividly because it wasn't my idea!'

'You're LYING!' Navarro roared.

'It was Jericho's.'

'No,' she whispered, not wanting to believe but the instant the Indian spoke she realized it was the truth. Horror leapt up inside her chest. Jericho. The man who, in her pursuit of the Indian, she'd allowed to . . . her mind recoiled in disgust. In her memory she saw the huge shadow through the broken glass of the shop door on the night Ernesto died.

Jericho.

'He came to me,' the Indian continued. 'He said he wanted to make an example of some uppity . . . grocer, show him our might. He said he needed to do it himself, wield that power.'

Hate fountained back up into Navarro's throat like battery acid. 'Down! Down on your knees,' she screamed, driving Sepion's sloshing bulk to the floor. His bloated features wrinkled with fear, his flab visibly quaking.

'No! No! But it WASN'T me! I told you. It was Jericho! You CAN'T!' he blubbered, hot selfish tears splashing down his face.

'You didn't kill *my* father, but you've killed enough fathers in your time . . . And brothers and daughters and mothers and when you haven't actually killed them you've maimed or abused, or blighted lives in a hundred other ways. Innocent? Don't make me laugh!' she sneered. 'This is still justifiable homicide. This is still . . . justice. On your belly, snake.'

She ground him down as flat as his disgusting abundance would go amd put the gun back against his neck.

'Puh-puh-pleeeease! Have mercy! You're not like Jericho . . . or me! You can't just kill in cold blood!' Sepion begged, his words blurring into incoherence.

Julia glared down at this pathetic snivelling pile of a man. He was a diseased beast, a thing less than human, almost worthy of pity. She couldn't do this—

No, she *could*.

He deserved to die; a humane cull.

She jammed the .38 into the repulsive pillow of his cheek, pulled on the trigger—

The Indian screamed—

—and Julia relaxed the pressure as swiftly as she had tightened it. The hammer edged back into place, the gun's deadly payload still sleeping in its cylinder. The burning sickness for revenge left her all in a rush and once it was gone she felt utterly drained. It was all she could do just to keep her knees from buckling.

'No. You need to face true justice,' she said very quietly. She fished out her mobile and dialled one-handed, her attention never leaving Sepion's wobbling, tear-streaked visage. Tanner's voicemail clicked on in her ear.

'John, it's me, Julia. I have Sepion here in the office block,' she whispered into the cell. 'I'm not going to kill him. You . . . you were right. I see that now. I'll wait here for you. Come find us when you're mopping up. We'll be—'

Jericho struck her a massive blow to the back of the head, knocking her out cold, mid-sentence. Her phone and the .38 clattered to the steel floor, followed by Navarro herself, folding up into a silent heap. Jericho stooped to retrieve the gun. He was wearing leather gloves. He transformed the cell phone into a mess of crushed circuits with his boot heel, frowning faintly to himself. He stared down at Navarro's unconscious body, deep in thought.

'My lieutenant!' the Indian exclaimed with manic glee, throwing his arms out. His head went back and he boomed out a salvo of triumphant laughter. 'My right-hand man! My saviour!'

'Not any more,' said Jericho and shot him through his open mouth.

Outside the cops had finally got the firefight under control. Neither side had much left to fight for. They were all outgunned and outmanned and their leaders were dead or had fled. It might have been different had either side been able to claim Lavache's weapons cache, but that had never even materialized. Reluctantly, they surrendered and a wave of powder-blue-shirted figures flowed down the hill to claim them.

Powell arrived like visiting foreign royalty as the arrests were being made and clean-up crews and forensics had begun scrambling over the scene. He even had a small news crew in tow, though – thankfully – they weren't permitted to shoot any of the immediate aftermath of the shoot-out. Stony-faced, Tanner and Jones joined him near the news van. Powell, naturally, dismissed the guns' absence as proof that they'd all been a phantom in the first place. In his view the defector had just invented the whole story to pit the Indian and Lavache against each other. He didn't care; his deal with Jericho had given him all the evidence he needed to close out his case against the Indian. None of which prevented him from rubbing Tanner's nose in it.

'I hold you responsible for this, Tanner. Don't think you're going to get a favourable mention on any of the news reports.'

'I'm an undercover policeman, sir. I'll let that give you a clue as to whether I'm keen to get on the television or not,' he grated back. Jones flicked him a warning glance.

But Powell wasn't even listening. He'd already turned away to confer with the news team.

'How about we set up over here?' he asked. 'We'll need to find an angle that doesn't have any bodies in the background, though. There might be legal issues. Don't want any of their next of kin to sue, ha ha . . .'

They were all interrupted, however, by the approach of a forensics officer in full crackling CSI gear.

'Superintendent, we've found him, Sepion. Dead, sir,' the man announced. 'He was in the kitchen out back. No other bodies.'

Powell's lips pinched with irritation. The Indian was a far greater public relations coup alive than dead. A flashy show trial with Powell in a lead role as the towering enforcer who'd conquered the demon of New Orleans would have aided his cause immeasurably. To his credit, though, he sucked it down.

'Oh well, you can't make an omelette without breaking some legs, and I'm sure even his own backwoods clan won't mourn the loss of André Sepion. At least this makes it all neat and tidy.'

'One bullet, close range, up through the mouth but not execution style,' the forensics officer continued. 'Figure he must have known the shooter, or at least didn't consider them to be a threat. Used this . . .' He held up a sealed plastic evidence bag with a snub-nosed .38 special inside. Tanner's eyes widened.

'That's my back-up gun,' he admitted with an

abrupt sinking feeling. There was only one way that gun could have ended up beside Sepion's body.

'But you've already admitted you weren't able to pursue the Indian during the firefight,' Powell pointed out, puzzled. Tanner bit his lip.

'I gave my gun to Julia Navarro for her own protection after she'd been explicitly threatened by Jericho and was in immediate fear for her life,' he replied, tweaking the truth. Powell shot him a withering look.

'I guess we don't have to wait for the forensics report to work out whose fingerprints will be all over that gun then, do we, detective?' he sneered.

Tanner blinked and stepped away from the group as the conversation moved back to Powell's latest media spot. He checked his cell phone. One message. With a rising sense of disquiet he listened to it.

Seconds later he was barging back into Powell's circle, seized by a manic energy. Jones tried to hold him back, but he shrugged his friend off.

'She didn't do it! Navarro didn't kill Sepion.' He brandished his phone. 'She sent me a voicemail message during the firefight, saying she had him but she wasn't going to kill him. Halfway through someone knocked her out. Her attacker must have killed the Indian with my gun!'

He thrust the phone at the Superintendent and waited while he listened to the recording.

'I know who it was, and he also ambushed the guns en route here.'

'Let me guess: Jericho?'

'Don't you get it, Powell? He's played us all – played us against each other, and now he has Navarro and the arms cache. He's going to kill her!'

Powell shook his head, feigning mild fatherly disappointment for the benefit of the reporters, then he turned to Tanner and hissed, 'John, your obsession with this man has almost derailed our case time and again, but it's over now. The Indian is dead. All his men are in custody. Your job is over and the city of New Orleans thanks you for the small contribution you've made to this victory . . . Nothing in that message supports your fantasy. Jericho's voice isn't on the recording and what's more I already completed my deal with the man. He held up his end of the bargain. Why would he kill a man his evidence had already sent to jail, as opposed to a self-confessed vigilante who believed Sepion murdered her father?'

'She didn't kill him, and now she's in terrible danger.'

'Either way, like the rest of the raw sewage, I'm sure she'll bob up again somewhere down the outflow.'

Powell turned back to the huddle of reporters.

It wasn't a top ten punch, Tanner would have to admit. He was too crowded and didn't get enough of a wind-up, but it certainly rocked Powell back on his patent-leather loafers and a couple of the press guys had to catch him or he certainly would have fallen down. When you see red, you see red, and if anyone deserved a black eye it was that conniving soft-bellied serpent.

Jones grabbed his arms and forcibly wrestled him away from the scrum of bodies just in case he decided to follow up on the first attack.

'I'LL HAVE YOUR BADGE, DETECTIVE!' Powell screamed in shrill rage, his mask slipping for a moment – and, gratifyingly, Tanner caught a couple of the reporters exchanging alarmed glances – as Powell suffered his ultimate humiliation. 'YOU'LL NEVER WORK IN LAW ENFORCEMENT AGAIN, DO YOU HEAR ME? YOUR CAREER IS OVER! *OVER!'*

But Tanner wasn't listening. He sprinted as fast as he could towards the abandoned Dodge.

Jericho had kidnapped Julia Navarro and Tanner had to save her.

Chapter Twenty-six

Tanner knew instinctively where Jericho had taken Julia.

It couldn't really be anywhere else. Jericho didn't have a scintilla of humour in his body, but he understood irony and this would be the most ironic place of all. The house where his stooge, the Indian, had plotted his rise. The dilapidated insignificant shotgun home with a curling map of New Orleans pasted on the cracked office wall. The street where music played all night and no one asked questions or complained if dogs barked round the clock or phoned the police if they heard screams . . .

Tanner just prayed that he could get there in time. Who knew how long the hitman had already had Julia in his clutches and what he might have done to her?

Navarro stirred on the filthy bare floorboards. Opened her eyes, blinked, sat up . . . and instantly regretted it. Her skull felt as if it was two sizes too big for the skin that was holding it in. She put a palm to the back of her head and her fingers came back dusty with dried blood.

Somewhere nearby a dog barked angrily. Her eyes roved over the meagre wooden-slatted walls of her narrow prison. Jericho had her in his clutches and, according to Tanner, he already thought she was some kind of snitch. Fear gripped her.

She had to escape . . .

Tanner screeched into the Bywater street. Rammed a low wall, got out, didn't lock. He marched across the street with his Hi-Point .45 ACP openly drawn, stiffly braced in a two-handed grip up by his shoulder. There was no time for niceties.

A young couple came out of the next-door house but two, saw the gun and froze. Tanner gestured urgently for them to go back indoors. He crept on to the hide-out's porch to the side of the front door. As he looked, the door creaked open. A wide white face with a pierced eyebrow peered out to investigate, his machine pistol held by his cheek.

'Halt!' Tanner shouted, but man turned and raised his gun. Tanner's Hi-Point spoke, kicking the thug in the chest with a .45 slug. He smashed into the door frame and started to smear down the flat surface. Tanner was already past him and kicking his way into the house. Two more outlines loomed in the gloom; an Uzi sputtered. Tanner threw himself low and rolled, hit a wall, came up shooting. Suddenly one of the thugs was making wheezing sounds. He tumbled over, flailing and hissing in goggle-eyed panic, his chest cavity punctured. His distress drew his colleague's attention for a horrified instant, and that was all Tanner needed. He blasted the second man down before he could return fire. Upstairs the dogs were going crazy, their howls muffled.

Tanner didn't pause. He stalked on through to the back of the house without breaking his stride. Upstairs. She had to be upstairs where the dogs were. Jesus, no. Please.

His gun barrel led him on.

Julia began to panic.

She could hear dogs barking, along with some other sort of commotion. Raised voices, doors crashing . . . or was that gunfire? A car pulling up? Fuck, fuck.

The dogs kept barking and she became certain that Jericho was sending his men to feed her to them right now. He knew she'd used him, cheated him.

She *had* to escape.

Julia feverishly searched the wretched cell, her mind racing in a desperate search for inspiration. There was a sink, but the water was turned off. In the cabinet beneath she discovered various bottles of old cleaning products. Her nose wrinkled in distaste as a pungent reek distracted her. They'd left her a night-soil bucket to relieve herself if she needed to, but not even had the decency to slop it out. The air was rank with the stench of the last prisoner's piss. This sparked half an idea. She wondered if she might be able to evaporate the water out of the urine, and produce a concentration of ammonia. Ammonia plus bleach would produce powerful toxic fumes. But the toxic fumes would be just as likely to harm her as the guard, and she only had a small electric lamp as a heat source, so any evaporating was out of the question. As she stared at the plastic piss bucket, however, a dangerous plan occurred to her. It was nasty and much less cerebral, but it might work, and it was definitely worth the risk.

The noises were getting closer . . .

Up the stairs Tanner went, Hi-Point outstretched, swinging round the boxy corners.

He hit the landing where he'd eavesdropped on Jericho and the Indian. The dogs next door were furious. He smashed in one door, a storeroom. A second, and the fanged jaws of two bull mastiffs gnashed out at him. But the animals were firmly chained to the walls and looked far more sickly than the Indian's prize hounds. Tanner snarled back, but didn't shoot. One room left—

He smashed into the study. Instantly he saw the cage they'd erected and the slim figure rocking inside.

It was Quentin.

Shock jolted through Tanner's body. He'd got it wrong. Dead wrong. Jericho had out-foxed him again. He scrambled to free Quentin, had to blast off the lock to do it, and he saw that the kid was in a bad way. Various cuts and bruises from a major beating marked his skin, and his left foot had been comprehensively crushed by a heavy object. He was shivering and sobbing, but gulping with delight to see Tanner.

'S-s-sorry, chief. I-I fucked up. I phoned my ex-girlfriend's brother to tell him I was never coming back and t' sell my stuff. They beat it out of him then came and dragged me out of a hunting supply shop in Hattiesburg. They . . . they've had me in this cage ever since, b-bashing on me, threatening me w-with the hounds. They was saying it was an example to other traitors. They took pictures and filmed me. Th-they gave me pills. Made me see bugs crawling all over my skin, and AWFUL things. They went out tonight. Said that when Jericho came back they were gonna feed me to the dogs . . .'

The kid dissolved into bone-dry sobs, and Tanner patted him in sympathy.

'It's OK, kid. I got ya.'

'B-but this wasn't the Indian, Tanner. It's Jericho! He's taking over.'

'Quentin, I know. It's fine.'

'He's gonna kill the Indian. Th-the guards said, "The Indian's going to the big tepee in the sky, while Jericho's going to live in the big villa—" '

'What?' Tanner snapped and grabbed the kid. 'What did they say, *exactly*?'

'Th-that Jericho was taking over v-v-voodoo mansion, because after tonight no one's gonna be going back there.'

With his free hand, Tanner dialled Jones's cell as fast as he could.

'It's me. I know where Jericho's keeping Julia, his new HQ. It's the LLR villa just outside of town where we stole the muscle cars. We have to get there now. Can you rustle up some heavy-duty back-up? I've got Quentin with me. He needs medical attention. I'll give you the address. Oh, and you'd better contact animal control while you're at it.'

The prisoner was bashing on her cell door, screaming out for the guards.

Love Money was a trusted henchman now, after his faithful service on every assignment since the Bayou raid. Jericho trusted him and the kid took that faith very seriously. It was why he'd sent Keener and Claude packing. They'd pulled up noisily in the court-yard after getting back from the fake drug deal on the docks that Jericho had gone to a lot of trouble to set up. They'd come in high on that success and busted in with their dogs straining at the leash. They demanded to see the prisoner to spend some 'quality' time with her, insisted Jericho said it was cool. Which was utter bullshit and everyone knew it. Jericho had given specific instructions that only he was allowed to see the girl. Keener and Claude blustered and threatened but Love Money stood firm. Eventually they sloped off with a lot more barking and slamming of doors.

This was only a menial task, but Love Money was determined not to fuck it up. If he kept performing well at the small things, then soon enough he'd be given greater responsibility. Jericho was putting together his own élite crew right now and it always paid to be in on the ground floor.

'Help! I'm ill! My head's bleeding and I – I feel woozy ... I think I'm going to pass out!' the girl screamed from the cell. 'My skull's cracked, I'm sure ... M-m-my brain's swelling or I've got internal bleeding or something. Please! Help!'

Love Money sighed and shook his head: how stupid did this bitch think he was? He trudged warily down the narrow bare-brick corridor to the former wine cellar the LLR had converted into a cell. The one drawback was that there weren't any windows to check in on prisoners before you entered. He drew a bead on the door with his brand new gleaming 9-mill pistol and called out a warning.

'I'm coming in, girl. Got my piece right here. If you rush me, I'll plug you between the eyes. *Comprende?*'

'Uh, yes,' she called back uncertainly.

Love Money unlocked the door, cocked his gun and cautiously entered. His nose twisted as he detected the urine and saw the upended bucket on the floor nearby. What? Was this some sort of dirty protest? Love Money shivered with disgust. The girl was facing him, her back to the wall, and she looked white-faced with nerves. No, her back wasn't just *turned* to the wall, he realized. She was intentionally blocking something from his sight.

Snarling, Love Money took an aggressive step forward, brandishing his gun. His boot squelched on the rug and he instinctively glanced down in puzzlement.

He saw that the whole swathe of material was sodden with the piss from the bucket.

Love Money looked up in horror as he got it – but far too late – and saw Navarro step aside to reveal the lamp, and the glint of the bare wires she had stripped down and wedged into the rug where he was standing. His hand was even still resting on the handle of the metal door . . .

Navarro flicked the switch and in the micro-second before the shock hit him, and sparks started to flow like fireflies, Love Money realized the awful truth he'd always half suspected but never wanted to believe . . .

He really wasn't élite crew material at all.

Tanner, Jones and the SWAT team slipped into the LLR mansion's grounds like insubstantial shades. They moved lightly, keeping low and communicating by the subtlest of hand signals, so that they were as close to invisible as soldiers could hope to be. Jericho's sentries had dogs, but the strike force had come in downwind of the animals and their clothing was treated with game-hunters' scent eliminator. The SWAT snipers were armed with scoped tranquillizer dart rifles, and each member of the unit had been supplied with noise-suppression silencers for their sidearms.

The mansion was a towering silhouette that dominated the prospect, its dark bulk obscuring half the sky. One or two dim-burning oblongs were cut into its façade, but other than that the total absence of visible electric lighting made it look as if they'd somehow been transported back in time to the mansion's candlelit heyday. Of course, relocating to the LLR mansion made a lot of sense for Jericho, Tanner reflected. He knew when he'd set the LLR, the Indian and the NOPD on a collision course that Lavache wouldn't be coming home. This location was isolated enough for him to pretty much do what he wanted without interference, and he had masses of space for drugs, troops . . . the stolen weapons. Clearly he'd been planning to take over the LLR operations for months. The one thing he hadn't banked on was that his men might have loose lips, and that Quentin was so insignificant that, with all the night's other excitement, no one had even remembered to kill him.

Cloud cover dimmed the unkempt gardens into a treacherous maze of blackness, but every man in the unit wore IR goggles that transformed their view into a grainy, green-flaring tunnel of near-perfect tactical vision. The SWAT snipers crawled on their bellies the final distance, while Tanner, Jones and the rest of the team hung back beneath a set of topiary animal sculptures grown into nightmarish shapes with the garden's neglect. The snipers took aim . . . and two dogs crumpled. When their handlers stooped to check their animals, they too folded with barely a rustle.

The rest of the team poured forward as a silent wave and fell upon the remaining guards . . .

Navarro padded cautiously along the corridor back into the main house. The villa was only partially lit, looming and quiet. The dogs she had heard were out-side. It seemed as if Jericho had only posted patrols outside, which made sense since his one prisoner was supposedly firmly under lock and key and unarmed. She made her way stealthily to the front of the build-ing and found the high still space of the entry hall in double-quick time.

She didn't have any time to scour the place for side exits, so the main door was her best bet. The guards patrolling the gardens would only be expecting re-inforcements to come from the house, so they wouldn't even check on the door opening. She already knew quite a bit about the surrounding geography of the house and was pretty sure she could slip by any unwary footsoldiers and lose herself in the wild countryside. Come the morning she could find help. Decision made, she sped through the entrance hall like an apparition, but on the threshold something made her pause.

Jericho was upstairs.

The man who had incontrovertibly killed her father was holed up in one of the luxury bedrooms plotting the stages of his own ascendance to total dominance. He could be stopped for good here and now. She could stop him.

She stood with her foot hovering over the front step, staring back at the swooping staircase. No. She had to leave, now. It was a miracle she was still alive at all. Her sharp wits had allowed her to escape once, but there was no guarantee they'd save her again. She heard John's voice in her head telling her not to be a fool and live to take revenge another day. She put her foot down on the front step, resigned to her decision, the smart one—

Then she saw Jericho grabbing her and pulling her back into the Dodge like a possession, like baggage . . . like a whore. This man – this sociopath, this thing without common human feelings, without a soul – who had slaughtered her daddy. The beast who suggested it, ordered it, acted it out. This man, touching her, pawing her body, *licking* her skin . . .

She turned on the ball of her poised foot, a pirouette as graceful as a ballerina's, and hurried back through the house to where Love Money's body lay in the wine cellar. She feverishly ransacked his pockets and quickly located a tool for her dark scheme: a slim stiletto blade with an ebony handle, perfect for concealing inside a sleeve braced against your wrist. Ideal for assassinations in a crowd. Perfect for her plan.

She returned to the foot of the vast curving staircase and drew out her necklace. It sparkled in the dim lamplight glow. She briefly held her father's gift, the silver heart cross pendant.

Then she started to climb.

The same holes in the house security remained from when Tanner and Navarro had broken in to steal the muscle cars. Presumably discipline had deteriorated so far in the LLR that even such glaring malfunctions in their basic safety precautions had been ignored. The assault team managed to break into the vine-wreathed courtyard again and fanned out to take up defensive positions. They saw no more of Jericho's thugs and no one challenged them. It was as if the entire house was deserted.

Tanner, Jones and the SWAT captain conferred in a tense huddle.

'You're the one who's been here before: outhouses or main building for the first sweep?' the captain asked Tanner, who stroked his chin, debating feverishly with himself. If he made the wrong decision it could cost Navarro dear.

'The outhouses are like servants' quarters. Makes sense there would be somewhere small and secure to keep prisoners out here. Also, if Jericho thinks Julia is a traitor he'll want her as far away from him as possible and in the grimiest surroundings.' He hesitated, unsure for a second, then: 'Yes. Outhouses first.'

Within minutes they had found Love Money's body.

Relief bloomed in Tanner's chest. Julia had escaped. But where was she now? She couldn't have left the grounds of the mansion, otherwise the SWAT team would have caught her. Which left only one option. She must have headed inside the main house.

Which was also where Jericho was.

Navarro palmed open the door to the massive luxury bedroom, Lavache's, she presumed. Opposite the doorway Jericho sat at an antique writing table poring over documents, which were probably accounts, knowing his cold, orderly mind. Only Jericho would aspire to be a kingpin who kept his own financial records. The illumination was low and bronze, a couple of table lamps dialled down to their lowest settings.

Jericho glanced up. He was wearing reading glasses and they flashed, obscuring his eyes. Jericho wore reading glasses? Incredible. He wasn't armed, though. Navarro could see his trademark sawn-offs lying on the four-poster bed halfway across the room, his Double Eagle cannon tossed artlessly next to them, glinting dully.

'You got out. That was . . . resourceful,' he rumbled.

'You need a better standard of hired help. Your men are cretins.'

Jericho shrugged regretfully. 'Violence and intelligence don't go together as often as I might like.'

'You kidnapped me. Locked me in a cell,' she accused in a voice which wavered only a little. Jericho took his time before replying.

'I thought you were the rat, but now . . .'

'It was Tanner. He's been working against you all along,' Navarro said in a rush. She felt a sharp twinge of guilt at implicating John, but in a minute or so none of that would matter.

'Perhaps,' he murmured, his face very still.

'You knocked me out. You hit me.' Navarro frowned with careful disapproval.

'It was necessary. You were going to kill Sepion,' Jericho retorted evenly.

Navarro made a play of thinking this over, and then

nodded as if she understood. She crossed over to the hitman. Put her palms on his hulking shoulders as she stood over him. She could feel his heat through the rough cheesecloth of his black shirt. The sensation made her skin crawl, but you can endure almost anything if the emotions that drive you are strong enough – like love, parenthood, hatred, or revenge . . .

'I have to tell you something. I've wanted to kill your boss since I joined the gang. Sepion . . . he killed my father.'

Inside, this admission made Navarro very nervous. It was a calculated risk, predicated on Jericho believing that she still thought Sepion was Ernesto's murderer.

'I know. But you don't need to worry about him anymore.'

'He's dead?'

Jericho nodded. Navarro's eyes widened. She wasn't sure what to feel. That was for later though; here and now she was already committed to the deed. She eased herself into Jericho's lap. He didn't resist. His body was covered in packs of muscle; they felt like coiled steel traps. He could crush her with those hands if he wanted to, put his trowel-like palms around her neck and *squeeze* . . . No, put it out of your mind, she told herself.

Normally she knew when a man wanted her – and most did – but with Jericho she'd never been able to read his lusts. His emotions, if emotions he had, were caged somewhere in a tiny black cube deep, deep inside the centre of his being. His face was a mask that let no clues slip. Now, though, he stroked her ass idly, with speculative passion. Good. That's good, you repellent fucking monster, think of my ass. Don't worry. It won't be your last thought. I wouldn't want you to go out of this world with pleasant feelings . . .

She looped her arms around his neck, felt his cool breath across her collarbone, chilling the upper slopes of her breasts through the open gap in her unbuttoned shirt. She forced herself to stroke the back of his neck, even though she couldn't help but focus on the plastic-looking grooves of his vile slicked-back hair. Touching him now she imagined how it would be when his loathsome blood came gushing out of his punctured artery. It wasn't such a terrible image. Yes, she *could* do this.

Jericho began to undo her shirt from the bottom up, baring the strong smooth ripples of her stomach. He brushed her skin with his fingertips and she couldn't prevent herself from stiffening in loathing, though surely he would just read that as an involuntary spasm of arousal? Her perfect skin glimmered in the low light. She shifted her weight in preparation. The moment was coming. No more waiting. No hesitation—

'You know I could never turn on you, baby. You're my power line, my antihero . . .' she crooned as she let the stolen blade drop out of her sleeve into the hand behind his neck. She stared deep into the infinite chasms of her father's killer's eyes. Her muscles

379

tensed. She prepared to drive the blade into his un-protected jugular . . .

Which was when Jericho slipped a tiny .22 from his belt and blew a hole in the perfect smooth bowl of her stomach.

When they found her, she was surrounded by a pond of red, more blood than even Tanner had seen before. She was sitting on the floor, her back propped up against the edge of the four-poster bed and one hand clenched up against her chest. The blood had soaked through her jeans and shirt and seeped up into the bed's silken valance sheet. There was one perfectly preserved boot print in the sticky tide of gore. Jericho's accidental last signature on this tableau he'd created. But he was long gone.

Tanner fell on his knees in all that red and held Julia tight. Her once coffee-cream skin was ghostly white and she seemed so cold and slack in his arms whilst Jones was yammering something about paramedics and ambulances and then she murmured in his ear: 'It's not your fault.'

Her fist relaxed as the life whispered out of her and the cross pendant necklace was revealed sitting in her palm. But its silver surface only reflected yet more red: red all around, the red on the floor, the red on the bed and on the walls.

The red on Tanner's hands.

Chapter Twenty-seven

Powell was on TV again, grinning and posing with the drugs haul, the bright shiny buttons of his impeccable dress uniform shining with the cheap lustre of fake diamonds. He was on TV a lot these days. He'd used the double whammy of the drug bust and Sepion's death as a launch pad to announce both his resignation as Superintendent and his senate bid. With all the publicity he'd gained his numbers were already solid.

The only grim note of satisfaction Tanner took from the whole affair was that the shiner he'd given the ex-Superintendent was visible on every broadcast, even under heavy make-up. It wasn't much consolation, but it was something.

Tanner had organized Julia Navarro's funeral himself. She'd mostly lost contact with her former friends during the months of her tragic obsession, but Tanner tracked down as many as he could from her address book and, gratifyingly, there was a small gathering at the Basin Street cemetery for the interment. The day was bright and high and clean and a light shower just before they had arrived freshened the air so that they were liberated from the relentless fist of the Louisiana heat for an hour or two. The rain-speckled white tombs gleamed like lamps in the sun. Jones attended, tall and stoic in a beautifully tailored Brioni suit; also, surprisingly, Quentin. The kid wore scuffed black jeans and one boot, which he'd clearly cleaned as best as he could, along with his dirty cask on the other foot, and a grey-black jacket which looked as if it might have been used to carpet a chicken coop at some point in its life. Still, it was the thought that counted, and Tanner felt Navarro would have been touched to see him make the effort.

Tanner stood stiffly beside the rental tomb while the Catholic priest droned on, and everyone else wept or stared dolefully into the middle distance. Once the service was done Tanner slipped away down another crooked path and stood over Ernesto's modest white crypt. In six months or so Julia's remains would be transferred here, where she was truly meant to be. They'd be together again. Once he was sure no one else was around he carefully jemmied open the tomb and hid Julia's necklace where it wouldn't be found, but where it would be waiting for her when she eventually came home. Once the deed was done he stood for minute. He didn't linger long, however. The dead had earned their rest, and he'd proved that it was rarely peaceful for long around John Tanner. Afterwards he didn't talk to anyone from the funeral, he headed back to the less salubrious parts of town to continue his investigations.

In the days following Julia's death he'd mostly spent his time in his flat scanning the police radio frequency, or on the streets trawling dangerous bars, visiting crime scenes, and running his fingers repeatedly through the filthy waters of the New Orleans underworld. He was officially on leave – Powell ultimately hadn't had any real grounds to hurt his career – and had been told to go back home to San Francisco. But this was what he did now instead. Every day he obsessively carried on the search.

Figuratively, the city was in flames. As Powell basked in media glory – boasting how he'd cleaned up the streets and made the city a safe place to live in again – a new wave of violence had erupted. Jericho had assumed control of the Indian's operation and then cut a swath through what was left of the opposing gangs, eliminating any opponents, however trivial, with a series of brutal executions.

Of Jericho himself, of course, there was no sign. He'd taken all the lessons of the Indian's reign to heart and become the invisible man. But Tanner had sworn an oath that however long it took, and however hard he had to search, he would find Julia Navarro's killer.

He would avenge her.

It was an oppressive grey afternoon when Quentin phoned in a slightly hysterical panic. The kid was staying in police accommodation in the lead-up to his stint as the star witness in the gang trials. However, he still retained some tiny wriggling contacts to the underground through his ex-girlfriend's brother and felt he owed Tanner help with his quest. Finally he had news on Jericho, but it wasn't good.

'He's leaving. It's a freakin' convoy, boss. He's shipping Lavache's big guns out of town in an unmarked truck, with whole load of freelance wheel boys backing him up. He's the undisputed lord of Nawlins, and now he's franchising. He's got his lieutenants in place here and he's heading out!'

'Where?' Tanner hissed through gritted teeth.

'Out over the Causeway.'

'When?'

''Bout an hour.'

'Right.' Then something compelled him to add: 'You did good, Quentin. You're . . . OK. If I don't see you again, don't worry. You'll do fine at the trial. Tell it like you saw it and keep your wits about you and you'll be the one to put those bastards behind bars for good.'

'W-whaddaya mean, chief? You gotta be there at the trial as well. Yer not planning anything crazy, are ya? You can't take on that convoy by yerself, boss. It's suicide.'

'I know, Quentin. You stay safe.'

The line crackled softly with Quentin's breathing, as he debated what he wanted to say next.

But Tanner had already killed their connection.

The Lake Pontchartrain Causeway jutted out for 24

miles between the New Orleans suburb of Metairie, and Mandeville on the northern shore. A storm was threatening as Tanner sped on to the bridge through the Metairie toll booths. The sky was slowly cracking apart into vast dark fissures. Black clouds loured massively over the flimsy strips of the causeway.

As he drove, Tanner tried to come up with a single idea as to how he was going to stop Jericho's convoy. *But when all else fails*, he thought, *you improvise*. That was the creed of the undercover cop and the life of the speedster. Plus, he didn't know any other way, so why change the habit of a lifetime? His first job was to clog up access to the scene. He'd overtaken some innocent vehicles, business people in *putt-putt* Nissan city cars, sun-weathered guys in beaten-ass twenty-year-old pick-ups laden with hunting rifles. He didn't want any of these folks getting caught up in his revenge drama. So, time to kill two birds with one controlled accident.

Jericho's convoy was visible up ahead now. He'd arranged it as a classic sandwich: three outliers as rear-guards; the truck itself snug in the centre; a last car protecting the front of the cab; then, way out front taking point, Jericho himself leading the column.

Once he understood the formation Tanner nodded and stood on the gas. He drove one-handed and drew his trusty Hi-Point .45 ACP from its holster taped beneath the dash. The M4 Super 90 combat shotgun he'd retained from the Bayou raid bounced along gently in the dip of the passenger seat.

The first two cars trailing the pack were an Audi S5

– shame he was going to have to trash it – and a smooth purple Jaguar XFR. He'd hoped that the first wheelmen he encountered might not have been briefed on the Challenger's appearance, but as he closed the gap bullets began to zip around him like bugs speeding at the windshield. Luckily, their aim at this speed left a lot to be desired.

'OK, then,' Tanner breathed out. 'Let's do this.'

He roared past the Jaguar, feathering the brakes a little to spook the driver, who instantly fell back, though still close enough to take pot shots at Tanner's fender. And that was Tanner's cue to clip the Audi.

The Audi's driver wasn't ready for this and swerved into the barrier. He rebounded; the Challenger zoomed through the gap he had made, but the Jaguar didn't have time to brake and slammed straight into the back of his partner. In his rear-view mirror Tanner saw both cars spin and crash into each other again, then the Audi smashed through the barrier. It came to a halt with its bonnet hanging out precariously over the water. *Voilà*, one improvised road block. Tanner sped ahead towards the next sentry car.

Suddenly he frowned. Something was ringing, nearby, but not his cell. He palmed open the glove compartment. The wireless headset he'd used on the gang missions dropped out. He fixed the chirruping device over his ear and thumbed the stud.

'Yeah?' he drawled into the mic as if answering his

landline on a lazy Sunday afternoon, knowing already whom he'd hear.

'I suppose it was only logical,' said Jericho in a monotone.

'Yeah. How so?' asked Tanner as he swerved recklessly round the next car in the convoy, a sleek blue Range Rover Sport. The driver clearly wasn't expecting trouble, as Tanner shot out his back tyre with a clinical ease. The Range Rover spun out of control, struck the barrier and ground along until its engine stalled. Obviously Jericho hadn't had the time to hire any really talented wheelmen.

'I should have known that you'd betray me. That's the problem with having lieutenants who are brilliant and ruthless and ambitious – they'll always try and kill you in the end.'

'Well, you'd know. After all, you did just murder your old boss.'

'That wasn't murder. It was pest control. I was doing the city a favour by putting down a mad animal no one could manage any more.'

'Funny, that's exactly why I'm here today. I'm coming for you, Jericho.'

Grim-faced, Tanner powered on. The truck itself was next in the sequence, and he tucked in so tight to the goliath's side that its following wind buffeted him. It was definitely a test of nerves barrelling along such a narrow causeway and pulling such gnarly manoeuvres when one wrong twitch of the wheel could see you launched off into the water. He snorted at a 'Pass With Care' sign as it zipped past. Suddenly a bullet pranged off the Challenger's wing mirror, making him flinch. The trucker in the passenger seat was shooting at him. Tanner could see his pinched hostile expression of concentration in the cracked mirror.

'Shall we have a little chat about our poor dead Julia?' Jericho asked, his voice dripping with unaccustomed enjoyment.

Tanner ignored him. The car driving in front of the truck was a metallic orange Hummer H3, the last close guard for the shipment. The thug riding shotgun in the Neon actually had an Uzi and leaned round to pepper the Challenger. Tanner sent his car into a fishtailing wriggle and the thug's shots blew wide. The wheelman seized on the man's surprise to kick on the accelerator and pass his rival. As he did so he pumped four bullets through his side window into the Hummer's interior, shots intended to alarm not kill. The other driver shouted and his hands leapt off the steering wheel for a split second. Tanner pulled ahead and squeezed off one last shot – into the Hummer's farside front tyre.

The other driver panicked, slammed on the brakes – and the car flipped. The Hummer rolled four or five times before coming to rest diagonally teetering on its side, with space left to pass to the left of its high bumper.

Tanner smiled to himself. Sometimes improvisation really did work out.

'Would you like to know what we did together?' Jericho rasped into Tanner's ear.

Tanner said nothing.

'Would you like to hear what she tasted like?' Jericho crooned.

Tanner tuned him out and continued with his plan. He pulled up in the middle of the bridge and jumped out of the car, working the slide on the combat shotgun single-handed as he did so. In panic the truck driver had jammed on the brakes the moment he saw the Hummer flip and now, as Tanner strode out into the centre of the lane, the whole shrieking colossus finally squealed to a halt a yard from his chest.

'Or the sounds she made when I fucked her?' Jericho taunted openly.

Tanner's patience snapped. 'She strung you along to get what she wanted. No one could ever want you touching them, you deluded maniac . . . GET OUT!'

This last cry was bellowed at the truck drivers, whom Tanner was covering with the shotgun. They just gawped mutely down at him like goldfish in their bowl. He instantly blasted a shell though the windshield, which rained down in shards around their shoulders. Both men fell over each other to scramble out of the cab.

As the truck drivers sprinted back the way they'd come, the driver from the Hummer and his gunman – now minus his Uzi – limped past, streaming with blood. Tanner waved his gun at them and they limped a lot faster. He turned.

In the middle distance Jericho's Dodge described a crisp three-point turn. The jeep ended up facing back the way it had come, towards Tanner. He shrugged and jogged over to the Challenger, the shotgun tucked under one arm while he reloaded the Hi-Point .45. So be it. He slid into the Challenger's trusty leather embrace.

The headset crackled again. In the distance he could hear the Dodge revving its engine. The SUV's hull trembled like a racehorse's flanks on the starting line.

'You like to pretend that you looked after her like a brother, but really who are you trying to kid?' Jericho jeered through the ear-piece.

'Man, but I am going to enjoy the glass of Jack Daniel's I drink standing on your grave.' Tanner hissed before ripping off the headset and crushing it with his free hand.

The Challenger's wheels whirled out smoke clouds for a second, then Tanner let fly. The car screamed out towards his nemesis. Jericho kicked on his gas as well and the two cars scorched along this narrow channel towards each other: two bullets shot out of two barrels at exactly the same instant. Tanner calculated that the upturned Hummer marked the spot where they would meet, or crash into a million pieces. Well, it was nice to have something to aim for.

Head to head once again, thought Tanner. But Jericho wasn't a dumb fuck LLR yahoo. He wouldn't bottle it or twitch aside at the last moment. This was really on. This was what they'd been heading towards for weeks, since the very beginning. *I should have let that cop car crush you into bloody fucking oblivion*, Tanner thought with venom as his cold blue lasers locked on Jericho's tunnels of darkness. Their eyes never left each other as the distance between them shredded away, 40 yards, 30, 20, 10—

Jericho's Double Eagle revolver emerged from his driver's side window and roared, but Tanner had already made his play. A fraction of a second earlier he aimed the Hi-Point .45 at the exposed gas tank of the upturned Hummer. He timed it exactly right. Jericho's Dodge had just drawn level and was completely engulfed by the explosion—

But at the very same instant Jericho's bullets wrecked Tanner's windshield and punched into the Challenger's interior with a supersonic burst. Tanner grunted as one of the massive slugs tore out through his shoulder, the other finding his right bicep with a gory explosion. The final bullet cut a groove through his headrest and missed his head by less than an inch.

He saw that Jericho's Dodge and the Hummer had collided. Both were magnificently ablaze with an oily mane of acrid black smoke pouring off the conflagration.

Jericho really was a world-class marksman: three shots from a moving car at this distance and two solid hits, one near-miss. Then again, Tanner wasn't the one burning to death trapped in his car, so that's what you get for playing the macho sharpshooter card. Jericho had been a fool. Pain exploded through Tanner's body like white light. He passed out for a second. When he came to again the world was spinning and all he could think of was water and drowning and he grabbed the wheel. Even as it slid against his blood-slick palm, however, he retained the presence of mind to steer with the spin, not against it, and that saved his life. The Challenger hit the barrier but at an angle, so the car ground along the railing rather than crashing through it. The metal kicked up a shower of sparks and the car's momentum gradually dissolved until it finally ground to a dead stop.

The Challenger was massively damaged, but Tanner was safe. He twisted round to look at the bright torch of the Dodge – and yelled out loud at the agony from his wounded arms. That didn't matter, though. Jericho was dead. He'd done it.

Then the Dodge jerked. Its engine stalled, turned over, caught. The flames tightened their grip around the flaming shell as the fire intensified, incandescent snakes thrashed and constricted, gas dribbled out on to the causeway tarmac, sparks fell. Yet still the vehicle continued to roll. Slowly at first, then faster. Tanner glimpsed an indistinct man-shadow at the heart of the inferno, one arm flung over its face. The Dodge suddenly roared forward. The blazing jeep rammed the barrier and smashed out into space. Tanner was reminded of his own leap of faith off the bridge with Quentin, what felt like a thousand years ago now, but

You know you just about damn died on tha[t]
[le]dge?' Jones snapped back testily. 'If the EMTs ha[d]
[got] to you even a minute later, I'd have been getting
[my] black Brioni out of the closet again.'

[T]anner's face didn't move. 'We get knocked down,
[we] get back up again. That's the way it is with grown-
[up] cops and robbers,' he drawled distantly.

[J]ones sighed, still extremely worried by Tanner'[s]
[rem]ote manner. He'd never seen his friend quite this
[wa]y before. He was concerned that events might have
[alte]red him permanently in some fundamental way.
'[W]ell, at least Powell had to eat a bunch of craw. You
[got] to be a big hero after all, bringing in that huge gun
[mo]untain, dealing with New Orleans' newest crime
[bar]on all in one fell swoop. Shame they couldn't have
[nam]ed you on the news, might've been nice to take a
[bo]w for once.'

[T]anner said nothing and Jones's expression turned
[grav]e again.

'[Y]ou sure I can't persuade you to drive back
[tog]ether?' he asked. 'We can buddy up at truck stops,
[eat] all-day breakfasts, shoot the breeze. Maybe race a
[bit.] I'll even let you win once or twice . . . ?'

[T]anner didn't look up from the display case, and
[neit]her did he take the bait. 'I'm doing this run on my
[ow]n, Jones, and that's that. Got a lot to think about on
[the] way back.'

[J]ones regarded him closely for some time, sucking
[spec]ulatively at his lower lip. Finally he asked: 'Do I
[hav]e to worry about you arriving in SF, John?'

they hadn't fallen like this. The Dodge was nose-
diving, a burning fighter plane as it plummeted out of
a dogfight, stripped of any grace or control. This was a
dead thing shoved off a high ledge.

The vehicle hit the water with a terrific crash, spray
pluming out in every direction.

When the view cleared Tanner saw the wreckage on
the Causeway dripping and steaming, but any trace of
Jericho had been utterly expunged. No floating fragments, no bobbing corpse. He sighed with something
close to satisfaction. His arms were twin throbbing
balls of agony, heavier than dark matter. He fought to
keep his chin up, groaning. He could hear sirens,
nearby. That was good, he supposed. Time was flowing slower now. That was probably a bad sign.

Lake Pontchartrain below him was an inky vast
chasm and it jealously guarded its secrets. Tanner
stared into the water and it seemed to him that he
must be falling, but it was only the blood and the
strength seeping out of his body.

Dark depths claimed him.

Epilogue

In many ways – the gloom, the heat, the
the reptile enclosure at Audubon Zoo w
had ever been, but in one important asp
had changed.

'You know, don't take this the wrong
not sure you were worth the wait
Detective John Tanner told the bulbc
reptile calmly chomping leaves behind
nose-smeared glass. Puff the Boyd's Rai
was spiny, slow-moving, and utterly
the world beyond his glass home. *A lo
bosses I've known*, thought Tanner ruefu
truly ass-ugly sonofabitch,' he informe
malice.

While Tanner's attention was focuse
Jones leaned on the adjacent wall a
partner with concern.

'How's the damage now? You feelir

Tanner worked his shoulders up an
a little. 'Never better.'

'Oh, there's no fear of that. It's where Jericho's headed and I've gotta be there to welcome him back with both barrels.'

'The New Orleans PD are convinced he died in the fall from the Causeway.'

'He's not dead, Tobias.'

'Yeah, well, I still need you to be careful. You at least able to promise me that?'

Tanner finally turned back from the glass to face his friend full on. He smiled a little sadly with just a trace of irony, eyes gleaming in the jade light. 'I'll do my best, Tobias, but I can't make any promises. We both know I'm an adrenalin junkie, after all.'

Jones shook his head wearily and laughed.

'Later, big guy,' Tanner told the dragon as they left.

The two friends walked back to the car park together, not talking. They embraced at the gate, back-slapped, and Jones watched Tanner walk off towards his car like an old-time gunslinger. As the Challenger revved up Jones admired its wasp-coloured body, yellow and black in the high morning sun. The Challenger tore out of the car park and vanished into the mid-morning dazzle like a ghost.

'Damn,' said Tobias Jones very quietly to himself. Then for the first time in weeks he thought about going home.

About an hour into his journey to San Francisco, Tanner found himself at traffic lights on the mainly empty main street of a mainly forgettable white-picket town. A moment later a red Chevrolet Camaro full of college pricks bounced up next to him.

'Hey, Granddad,' sneered the acne-garlanded fuck-wit at the wheel. 'You and your tin can just time-warp in from the seventies? Wanna let us school you on how a *real* car rolls?'

His buddies all brayed like a paddock full of don-keys on laughing gas.

Tanner glanced over at his passenger seat. He imagined Navarro lounging there in her spray-on jeans, boots braced against the dash, collar up, cool as a winter breeze just come down from the mountain.

You can't stand for that sort of disrespect, she drawled in his memory, with a sassy smirk. *Scalp 'em*.

Before the lights had even turned, the dickheads in the Cobra leapt away.

Tanner floored it.

It didn't take long before the Mustang was just a tiny red dot in the rear-view. Kids these days, they just can't cut it. Can't drift, can't corner. Can't drive for shit.

Some time later Tanner was still sitting by the side of the road, just staring out at the cloud tops. A breeze rocked the car on its suspension. The sky hung like heavy dark drapes above him, but away on the horizon was a slim rind of eggshell, which promised that, even though a storm might be here now, clear sky – and perhaps hope – would eventually return. Tanner peered out along the stretch of highway ahead. There wasn't another car in sight for miles. Jericho waited beyond the horizon, along with danger and revenge and, perhaps, justice for a friend called Julia Navarro? 'You have to drive through the rain to get to the sun on the other side,' was something his mother used to say whenever life got tough. So strange to think of her here, now. A few spots began to patter across the windshield. He had a car and a full tank of gas and the open road ahead of him. He could do anything, go anywhere . . .

But, no. He had duties to fulfil and promises to keep and that wasn't such a terrible destiny after all. There was an unspent moment inside his chest, just hanging: a future waiting to be unlocked.

Tanner turned the key.

The roar of the engine rose up to meet him.